THE CURSED HEIR

BERKLEY WAMSLEY

1

For Elijah, who has never stopped believing in my dream (and has never stopped telling me to get my ass in gear and finally get this published). I love you.

And for Abbey, who has been my writing companion since we were just two kids on the internet writing fanfiction.

This book contains depictions of depression and anxiety; mentions of/allusions to suicidal thoughts; grief and loss of loved ones; mentions of and mildly graphic descriptions of death, corpses, blood, and violence; sexism/sexist language (in two chapters); slightly mature themes; vulgar language, and on a slightly less serious note, daddy issues. One chapter contains mentions and contains themes of homophobia, but nothing graphic.

a note to the reader

Dear Reader,

I want to thank you. If you are reading this, you must have taken the leap to acquire this book (or, at least, found it interesting enough in a bookstore to crack it open and get a sneak peek). *Thank you.* I am so humbled and blown away by the fact someone wants to read *my* writing. It's surreal.

I started out writing fanfiction on the internet, pulling all-nighters at fifteen just to finish reading or writing another chapter about my favorite characters. To this day, at nearly twenty-four years of age, I will still stay up into the wee hours of the morning to continue reading a really good book.

My hope for this book, and for you, is that it becomes one of those books. I hope it makes you *feel* something (hopefully nothing negative, but alas, that is a risk we authors take). I hope you enjoy it, that you love my characters and my words. This book has been my baby for the past 5+ years, and I cannot describe how terrifying it is for me to finally let it go out into the world and be seen by others.

Thank you, reader, for helping make my dreams come true.

Yours,

Berkley Wamsley.

CHAPTER ONE

THE TRACKS

KAI

*It was the same dream—the same **memory**—that she'd always had.*

It began as it always did: the car, flipped upside down with windows cracked and shattered, pieces of what used to be the windshield scattered amongst the overgrown grass of the hillside, leaving behind a messy trail of broken headlights and bits of twisted metal carved from the sides of the car by the jagged rocks they'd hit on the way down from the rain-soaked road above.

Her family hung suspended by their seatbelts around her like some sort of morbid marionette display; whether they were dead or merely unconscious, she could not tell, unable to hear anything over the sound of her own panicked breathing. A damp sniffle occasionally escaped her as she struggled not to sob outright, warm, wet tears streaming silently down her face and dampening the roots of her dark hair, which had been woven that morning into two neat braids.

She dared not call the names of her silent family members, dared not even whisper, afraid—terrified—of the answers that she might not receive. In the seat in front of her, her elder sister's shiny chestnut curls brushed the ceiling of the car alongside pastel blue-painted fingertips, pale and unmoving. Their brother's lanky frame was nowhere to be seen, and the fleeting memory of him unbuckling his seatbelt to reach for his dropped video game console had the small girl whimpering as she turned her gaze outside the window to search for him, unable to see anything through the thick veil of darkness that surrounded the overturned car. The headlights had long since ceased their half-hearted attempts to flicker back to life, and the switch to the car's interior lights was far beyond her reach.

Her parents were barely visible in the front seat, shrouded by the white airbags that had burst forth to shield them from the impact. Her dad looked as though he might simply be sleeping, his round glasses clinging crookedly to his long, weathered face, a jagged crack splitting the right lens. It was strange to see him so still, his features completely void of expression. She kept waiting for his scarred, crooked nose to twitch, for his graying eyebrows to push together as he dreamt, for any part of him to show some sign that he was indeed just resting, that he was still somehow, miraculously, alive.

She waited in vain.

Her mother...the girl could see little from her current position. Through the darkness, she could faintly make out the blood that stained her mother's golden-brown skin, crimson dripping down her mother's temple and onto the beige carpet of the ceiling, turning it a wet, ugly brown.

In the silence, the girl felt, perhaps for the first time in her young life, completely and utterly alone. She reached for her stuffed rabbit, chubby fingers straining to brush against the rough, tattered fur, nearly grasping it, almost—

Her heart stopped as she caught a glimpse of a reflection in the windows, breath catching in her throat as she saw the faint, dark outline of a person appear beside the front passenger seat. The figure crouched in the wet grass, barely visible in the dim light of the crescent moon, and a hand reached out, knuckles brushing gently against her mother's cheek, coming away smeared with blood.

The girl couldn't help the sharp gasp that escaped her lips as she watched the figure caress her mother's skin, and the fingers froze. A pair of dark eyes snapped toward her and, while she couldn't quite make out the rest of the mystery person's features, those eyes were forever seared into her memory, staring at her in something like bewilderment, brows furrowed in a silent question. What it was, she had never been able to figure out.

She heard someone call her name, and her own brows pushed together, an anxious sort of discomfort filling her chest. This wasn't supposed to happen—help hadn't come for hours, the wrecked car barely visible from the rarely-traveled back road above them. Faintly, she heard the call again, and twisting around in her locked seatbelt, she turned to look.

"KAI!" Blearily, she cracked her eyes open, uttering an unintelligible sound of confusion as she blinked hard several times in an attempt to clear her blurred vision. "Finally! I was beginning to think you'd slipped into a coma or something, jeez." With a wince, Kai swung her legs over the arm of the small sofa, sneaker-clad feet hitting the white tiled floor just a tad too hard for comfort. She rubbed her eyes with the palms of her hands, feeling weary.

"Sorry," she apologized in a voice thick and raspy with sleep. "I literally closed my eyes for like, half a second, and I must've just dozed..." she trailed off, her eyes widening. "*Shit,* how long have I been gone?"

"Ah, you're only like, a couple minutes late, don't worry about it." The blonde girl who had seated herself across from Kai waved her hand carelessly as she slouched deeper into her seat, kicking her feet up onto the small, wooden coffee table.

A slew of curses dropped from Kai's lips as she flew to her feet, yanking her tangled brunette waves into a ponytail and retying her white apron, the red, embroidered script on the chest reading *TANNER'S GROCERY.*

"Kai, calm down," said the blonde, whose name tag read *AVERY* in bold, purple letters. "You know my gramps adores you, and he completely understands if you're having a rough day. Hell, we all do." Her voice was soothing, but did little to calm the frantic brunette.

"Key word being *a* rough day, Aves," Kai countered, not unkindly, as she shoved her wired earbuds into her bag, tossing it carelessly back onto the hook by the door. "But I've fallen asleep on my break half a dozen times this month *alone*—I wouldn't blame him if he fired me." Avery sighed, shaking her head as she rose to her feet and put her hands on Kai's shoulders, forcing her to pause.

"Kai, you look like shit," she said bluntly, hazel eyes gazing unapologetically up into Kai's exhausted brown ones. "And I'm not the only one who's noticed."

"Gee, thanks," Kai interrupted wryly, lifting a brow at Avery's rarely displayed profanity. Avery's eyes narrowed.

"We're *concerned,* Kai. When's the last time you even *slept?*"

"I was sleeping just now!" Kai's voice pitched upward defensively, but Avery was unrelenting.

"Look, why don't you just go home early today? I'm *positive Gramps* will be fine with it—I'll be here to hold down the fort, and it's a slow day anyway, so just take the rest of the afternoon and get some *actual* sleep. Like, in a *bed.* For more than half an hour. *Please?*"

Despite the whiny tone and the puppy-dog eyes that the blonde was currently using to sway her, Kai had been friends with Avery long enough to realize that this wasn't a request, so, reluctantly, she nodded. As much as she hated to leave without finishing the rest of her shift, and as heavily as she doubted she would actually be able to get anything resembling *actual* sleep, she had to admit that she'd been having difficulty keeping her eyes open all day, her body heavy and sluggish with exhaustion.

"Thank you," she said gratefully, cheeks heating in embarrassment as she took off her apron and retrieved her mossy green bag from the hook, slipping the long, worn strap over her shoulder. Avery threw her arms around Kai, embracing her tightly.

"You know I love you, K." If Kai had had any tears left to cry, her eyes might have grown damp at the unfiltered affection in her friend's voice. As it was, she smiled awkwardly as they parted, managing a quick, jerky nod in return.

"Back atcha, Aves." Avery rolled her eyes, a fond smile curving her rosy-pink lips upward, cheeks dimpling. "I'll see you tomorrow."

It was warm out, but not unbearably so; while there wasn't a cloud to be seen, a light breeze was pleasantly countering the heat of the afternoon sun, and Kai paused for a moment to tilt her head back, basking in the warmth.

Not feeling up to faking smiles and forcing small talk with the acquaintances she would inevitably run into on the way home, she decided to take the scenic route, turning down the unnamed dirt road that would eventually take her to the rear of her apartment complex.

It was a pleasant walk, and though she still felt utterly exhausted, the fresh air did seem to be lifting her rather gloomy spirits. She had always loved autumn, harboring fond memories of jumping into mountains of red leaves and playing hide-and-seek in pumpkin patches with her siblings, and this was the peak of the season. The leaves scattered on the ground and clinging to the trees around her were painted every shade of red and yellow and orange, the colors making her feel warm inside, comforted. It made her crave a hot cup of tea, though it meant that she would have to wash one of the innumerable mugs currently cluttering her sink.

She hadn't walked this path in what felt like years, but just as she remembered, the road led her to a large, open field, bordered thickly on either side by a forest of tall trees. She had spent her childhood in those woods, camping with her dad and building forts with her siblings and their shared friends; somewhere amongst those trees, the little playhouse they'd scraped together with scraps of metal and bark might still stand, albeit rather run down.

And there, just as she remembered them, were the tracks.

Out of the woods to the left of the clearing, the train tracks ran across the entirety of the field before disappearing back into the woods on the right side. If she remembered correctly, the train would be coming along any minute now; she could wait a bit longer to go home and inevitably end up tossing and turning restlessly, Kai decided, letting her bag slip from her shoulder and fall to the ground, pulling the tie from her hair to let it tumble messily around her shoulders. Excitement began to bubble in her stomach as she remembered the *rush*, the adrenaline high of watching the train pass by so very closely, taking with it, even momentarily, every ounce of her misery.

And there it was, right on schedule.

Kai's ears filled with the familiar chugging and rattling of the wheels against the tracks, the roar of the engine growing louder with each passing second as the train neared, nostalgia pooling in her chest and tugging her ever-closer.

As if in a trance, Kai edged forward, not noticing when the toes of her worn, stained white sneakers brushed lightly against the tracks. Unconsciously, she began to lean forward, the anticipation making the dark hairs on her bare arms stand on end as she waited eagerly for the iron monster to race by. So focused, so eager to feel the impending adrenaline, Kai failed to realize that if she did not step back in the next three seconds, her life would be over.

Three. She didn't notice. She didn't move. The only thing that she could think about was how good it would feel to *not* feel, even for a couple of seconds. To let it all go, to just *be*—to merely exist for several blissful moments without fear or worry or exhaustion or *grief*.

Two. The train was nearly here now—she could practically *taste* the smoke rising in thick puffs from the engine, and her fingers curled, nails digging harshly into her palms. Her teeth sank into her lower lip, heart swelling with impatience.

One. It happened quickly—so quickly that later, she would have trouble wrapping her mind around it, replaying the moment over and over in her head as she struggled in vain to fall asleep, trying to make some sort of sense of it all.

The train was finally upon her when a set of long, slender fingers wrapped firmly around her bare upper arm and yanked her roughly away from the tracks, spinning her into a broad, solid chest. A strong arm curled just as tightly around her shoulders and held her firmly in place as the train rushed by. The train's horn, urgent and panicked and painfully loud, rang in Kai's ears as harshly as the wind whipping sharply through her hair, some of the strands finding their way into her eyes and mouth, her current position rendering her unable to brush them impatiently out of the way.

Even with her back to the train, the feeling that came over her was positively *euphoric,* rushing through her veins like wildfire and making her feel, for once, *alive.* It was even better than she remembered it; a wide smile spread across her face, pressing into the mystery person's chest, as the blood rushing through her veins sang in familiarity. She was trembling head to toe from the high, and if it weren't for the pair of arms holding her up, she was sure her knees would have buckled.

Before she had a chance to recover from the experience, to take a breath and fully appreciate everything that she was currently feeling, she was shoved abruptly away from the wall supporting her, the hands that had shifted upward to hold her shoulders in an almost painful grip shaking her roughly in agitation.

*"Are you out of your **mind**?"* A masculine voice demanded harshly, and, startled, as if only just remembering that she was not alone, Kai looked up, finally meeting the eyes of the stranger who had held her, and any breath that remained in her lungs abandoned her completely.

Towering above her was a boy—a young man, really, as he looked to be around her age—with a face that had surely been carved by angels. His honey-toned skin was flushed, thick eyebrows drawn low over narrowed, monolid eyes, so brown that they almost appeared black. Kai fought the urge to shrink back, intimidated by the force and intensity of his angered gaze. His lips, plump and slightly chapped with a prominent cupid's bow, parted again as he continued to shout at her over the dull roar of the retreating train.

Kai could scarcely pay attention to anything he was saying, mesmerized by the way that his hair—dark and wavy and pulled back into a half-ponytail, the ends just kissing the nape of his neck—seemed to gleam in the afternoon sunlight, looking soft as silk to touch. Wispy bangs framed his diamond-shaped face, and small ears decorated with silver hoops peeked out amongst the waves of black.

He was all sharp angles and high cheekbones, and dressed in all black as he was, he exuded mystery. Kai couldn't tell if the tingling sensation that washed over her was leftover adrenaline or anticipation of what this completely unexpected encounter might bring. She would think later how odd it was that she had not felt frightened—only a thrill of excitement and curiosity, and a need to know *more* about this stranger.

He shook her once more, brows rising in expectation and impatience. "*Well?* Are you going to answer me, or just stand there looking stupid? Which," he scoffed, "you *must* be—either that, or utterly suicidal." The spell broken, Kai bristled at his bluntness, yanking her arms sharply out of his iron grasp and stumbling back a step with the effort. She winced as the blood rushed back into her limbs, the imprints from the silver rings adorning his fingers white against her pale brown skin.

"*Excuse me?*" Even after putting some distance between them, she still had to tilt her head back to properly meet his eyes. He sighed deeply in exasperation, leaning forward and enunciating his words carefully.

"Are you *stupid*," he repeated himself, excruciatingly slow, making Kai's skin crawl with annoyance. "Or do you have a death wish?" Kai huffed, shoving her hands roughly against his chest in an attempt to gain some additional distance, fingertips brushing against cool skin where his shirt dipped into a deep *v.* He was like stone, unmoving, and profoundly unimpressed by her attempt, though he did her the courtesy of pulling away, his silhouette mercifully blocking out the glare of the sun. It gave him a celestial glow, a halo of gold circling his head, though, his words still ringing harshly in her ears, Kai did not let this distract her.

"I wasn't trying to kill myself," she said defensively as she glanced up at him, feeling rather chastened. He snorted, a short, sarcastic huff of air through his nostrils that made Kai's spine stiffen, her eyes narrowing.

"You could have fooled me."

"Okay, so yeah, the thought may have been *there,*" she admitted, continuing quickly as he lifted a skeptical brow. "But like, in the back of my head, like how you think that if you moved the knife over just a couple of centimeters while you're cutting vegetables that you might cut your pinky off—the thought is *there,* but I wouldn't actually *do* it." He said nothing, clearly not believing her. "Come *on,* you've never stood on the edge about to do something dangerous and wondered, just for a *second,* so fast that it barely even counts, what would happen if you took just one step forward?"

"No," he responded dryly, though something like recognition seemed to flash briefly in his eyes during the half-beat it took him to reply. "I can't say that I have."

"Yeah, well, then you're a weirdo. *And* a creep—what, were you just lying in wait for some poor, unsuspecting girl to come along and fall in front of a train so that you could play the hero and rescue her?" He looked away, his jaw clenching, and a tense silence followed. It was quiet in the clearing now, the birds not yet returned to their chatter.

After a moment, he turned back to her, looking idly curious.

"So if you aren't suicidal, and you aren't stupid—a claim that I notice you never denied" Kai's fists curled of their own accord "—then what *were* you doing?" Kai blinked in surprise, her lips parting softly, though for several seconds, no sound came out.

"I just..." she sighed, unable to find the right words to describe the confusing whirlwind of emotions knotting inside the crevices of her chest. She gestured vaguely before dropping her hands to her sides, at a loss. "Wanted to feel alive, I guess. Wanted to feel *something.*" Her cheeks heated in embarrassment, but a sort of understanding lit somewhere within those deep, dark eyes of his, and the judgmental expression on his face softened ever so slightly.

"There are safer ways of doing that, you know—bungee jumping and...skydiving," he finished lamely, the last word sounding unfamiliar on his tongue, and the smallest of smiles lifted the corners of Kai's mouth upward.

"Scared of heights," she said, and then, a note of bitterness in her tone, "Besides, do you see anything like that around here?" He was silent, and Kai shrugged. "That's what I thought. So...train." She gestured toward the tracks, and he snorted again.

"Whatever you say, sunshine." Kai rolled her eyes, allowing the smile to grow just a little, though she told herself it was against her will.

"Who are you, anyway? I don't think I've ever seen you around. Although," she added as an afterthought, "I'm not exactly the most observant, so I guess I could've just missed you." But she found it hard to imagine missing someone like him.

The stranger stiffened at her inquiry, his expression shuttering and his eyes going cold, and he smiled tensely, taking a couple of steps backward, hands shoved into the pockets of his ripped jeans.

"This has been fun and everything, but it's time for me to take my leave. Don't jump in front of any more trains, sunshine," he said with a wink, and before Kai could come up with a response, he disappeared.

Dissolved.

Vanished.

Dissipated.

All of the above.

Kai turned several times in a slow circle in an attempt to see where he could have gone, but it was no use: he had simply *evaporated,* gone invisible before her very eyes. Head spinning, it was several moments before Kai realized how late it was growing, and scraping her jaw off the floor, she snatched her bag up from the ground and swatted away the dust, glancing over her shoulder in search of the beautiful stranger once more before resuming her journey homeward.

CHAPTER TWO

COBWEBS AND REVELATIONS

THORNE

Traveling between worlds was a mundane activity, at this point; one moment he was standing in a clearing in the middle of nowhere, the wind in his hair and the sun on his back, and the next, his heavy black combat boots were brushing against dusty floorboards in a building that felt ancient.

He made his way silently through several long, empty hallways, the lights overhead dim and weakly flickering, eternally halfway between life and death, as was the case with everything in this place—this *In-Between*.

The floors he traveled were littered with old, wrinkled papers, the drawers of the filing cabinets lining the walls either hanging open or lying overturned on the ground. Every room that he passed was dark, utterly void of life; there weren't even rats here to dart out from the shadows and give him a start, no spiders hanging in the cobwebby corners of the ceiling to stare blankly at him with their dozens of odious eyes.

Turning a corner, he approached a set of heavy double doors and pushed through them easily, letting them swing shut behind him with a soft creak. His shoulders relaxed minutely as he entered the closest place he had to a home.

Desks were laid out in a random pattern across the spacious bullpen, documents strewn messily across their dusty surfaces and balls of paper left carelessly where they had been thrown on the gray carpet, piles of them surrounding half-full waste baskets. Broken-down desk chairs sat scattered haphazardly around the room like a game of musical chairs that had long since been abandoned, and jazz music played from a phonograph in some distant corner of the room, coming out crackly and muffled, like sound from a black-and-white film.

"Thorne!" The relative silence was interrupted by a tall, lanky youth by the name of Jai, who bounded across the room with the energy of a young puppy. He skidded to a stop in front of Thorne, who smiled wearily, a glimmer of fond familiarity in his eyes. "Back so soon?"

"*Soon?*" Minho, a long-legged man with a deep voice and brown hair pulled into a bun at the nape of his neck, arched a thick eyebrow from where he lounged on a small settee that used to be a bright yellow, but had long since faded to an off-color beige. A small book lay open in his lap, and a smile of amusement graced the corners of his full mouth. "It's been nearly two weeks."

"But one time he was gone for almost three *months*," Jai countered, to which Minho laughed in acquiescence.

"Ah, yes, the three long, tedious months of you whining about how much you missed him—how could I forget?" Thorne couldn't help but laugh along as the tips of Jai's ears reddened, head lowering slightly in embarrassment, strands of jet-black hair falling over his deep-set umber eyes.

Placing a hand briefly on Jai's shoulder, Thorne moved up the aisle and dropped heavily into a worn armchair, draping his legs over the side and letting his head loll against the headrest. Jai mumbled something to Minho about how he *really* needed to *let that go,* that he *hadn't **missed** Thorne, had just been curious about why he'd been gone so long,* and Minho laughed again, reaching out to pinch a flushed bronze cheek. Jai swatted his hand away.

"Enough," Thorne said, letting his eyes flutter shut. "You two are giving me a headache."

"You love us," Minho responded, waving a hand carelessly as if to brush him off. Nevertheless, he returned quietly to his novel.

"Whatever you say," Thorne returned in faux skepticism, cracking one eye back open when Jai hopped onto the desk adjacent the armchair, letting one of his long, knobby knees bump against Thorne's to catch his attention.

"What brings you back?" He prompted, and Thorne considered the question, unsure of whether or not he should reveal what had just occurred. He probably shouldn't—not yet, at least, not when he was still so very confused, himself, and especially since what he had done was so *very* against the rules. Then again, perhaps secondary opinions could be helpful.

The latter option won out, so, casually, as though it were a much more insignificant announcement than it actually was, he said,

"I saved someone." The silence was deafening. Even the music stopped playing for a beat, though this was pure coincidence, and half a second later it resumed, starting anew the same song that it had been playing since Thorne had entered the room.

Minho was the first to speak.

"You...saved someone," he repeated slowly. Thorne nodded, and Minho exchanged a glance with Jai, who said nothing. Minho looked back to Thorne, his liquid brown eyes narrowing. "I don't understand."

"It's really not that complicated." Though Thorne feigned nonchalance, his heart was pounding at the news that he had just revealed, at the recollection of how it had felt to hold a living being in his arms. "I simply grabbed her arm to pull her away—"

"You *touched* her?" Jai's eyes flew wide, his mouth falling open in shock. Again, Thorne nodded.

"I surprised myself, to be truthful. But—" he hesitated.

"But—?" Minho prompted, and Thorne gnawed at his lower lip, his gaze losing focus as he remembered the way that she had looked at him—*seen* him, *touched* him, as she had so vehemently attempted to push him away.

It was enough to tug at the strings of his frozen heart, wishing to go back in time and feel it all again. He hadn't experienced such things in so long, and to have it again for a moment—mere *seconds*—when he likely never would again...it was unfathomably cruel.

Minho and Jai were waiting, practically falling out of their seats with anticipation as they awaited his response with bated breath, so finally, Thorne said, very quietly, "She could *see* me." They were silent, Jai's eyes lowering as he pulled his lower lip between his teeth, his demeanor drastically changed from the happy-go-lucky young man he had been only moments before. He was the youngest one here, and the newest, still reluctantly adjusting to the job that he now had to do, and judging from the way that his fists spasmodically clenched at the news, Thorne knew that this must be hard for him to hear.

He continued quickly, pushing past the mild guilt tugging at his conscience.

"By the time I fully realized what had happened, realized that she could see me—really, truly *see* me...well, the damage had been done."

"What did you do, then?" Minho asked, and Thorne lifted a shoulder briefly.

"I left." Minho exhaled sharply, hands clasped between his widespread knees as he shook his head—in disapproval or disappointment, Thorne couldn't tell. Perhaps both—perhaps neither. Perhaps he simply didn't know what else to do.

"Thorne..." the brunette trailed off, gnawing at his lower lip anxiously. "Interacting with mortals beyond the scope of our job...it's *forbidden,* and for good reason. I really think that you're being too cavalier about this—you have no idea of the *consequences,* in your life *or* hers—"

"Yes, thank you, *mother,*" Thorne snipped sarcastically, rolling his eyes as he pushed himself abruptly to his feet, feeling profoundly irritated. "Look, I'm sure that everything will be *fine.* She gets to live another day, I get an interesting twist in an otherwise boring, miserable eternity. Everybody wins!" He threw his arms outward as he took several steps backward, before turning and pushing open the door to a small office in the rear of the room.

"You had just better hope that the Fates don't find out about this!" Minho called as Thorne stepped through the doorway, and Thorne paused.

"What are they going to do," he grinned, his tone and smile bitter, amusement glittering in his dark eyes. "Curse me?" Without waiting for a response, he shut the door, leaving Jai and Minho alone to quietly discuss the reckless actions of their friend.

Chapter Three
THE FATES

In a world far away, in a place dark and quiet and as old as time itself, a hooded figure swept hastily through a stone corridor, his sandal-clad feet making scarcely a sound on the cobblestone floors.

His dark, full cloak billowed behind him as he turned a corner, striding into a round room lit dimly by a cluster of candles sitting near a thickly frosted window, the landscape faintly visible beyond it a smear of blurred gray. Aside from this, the room was completely bare save for a single wall covered completely with mirrors; they were of all sizes and shapes and styles, and on each, thousands of images played at a speed that made the cloaked figure's head ache. The person standing in front of the mirrors, however, understood them all, and though his eyes did not stray from the images, he instantly sensed the presence of another.

"It is as you fear," he said, his voice deep and wise and terribly ancient. He shook his head and sighed deeply as he turned, hands the color of tumbled brown tourmaline clasped neatly behind his back. Whilst he, too, was cloaked, his hood was down; his hair, long, pin-straight, and silver as the moon, flowed over his shoulders and down to his waist, the top layer pulled back into a series of intricate braids. His eyes, too, were silver, though what most would find more startling about his appearance was the presence of his third eye, which was lodged directly in the center of his forehead, just above his brows. The newcomer, however, was used to this, and took little notice.

"I will admit, it comes as a surprise," continued the silver-haired man, looking thoughtful. "He is normally so predictable, despite his numerous attempts to appear otherwise." He sighed again, shaking his head in something like disappointment. "And while these actions were clearly a misguided mistake on his part, it is a mistake that must be rectified immediately—there is no time to waste." He turned fully to face the other figure at this, his expression solemn. "As you have an established relationship with the boy, I leave it to you to relay this message. There can be no room for interpretation here, Aristides—do you understand?"

"I understand," Aristides responded with a respectful tilt of his head, and the silver-haired man nodded his approval, turning back to his mirrors. As Aristides turned to leave, the man offered a final warning.

"We have all borne witness to what can happen when Fate is thrown off-balance, brother," he said, his three-eyed gaze fixed upon the rapidly moving images. "Be sure that history is not permitted to repeat itself in this instance."

"Yes, brother." Giving another brief nod, Aristides swept from the room, leaving the man alone with his mirrors once more.

CHAPTER FOUR

NIGHTMARES AND THE IN-BETWEEN

KAI

It had been yet another sleepless night for Kai, who had tossed and turned restlessly in her creaky iron-framed bed until the first rays of sunlight had begun to peek through the dusty blinds, signaling the start of a new day.

It was hard to convince her limbs, heavy with exhaustion, to push herself up and off of the bed, her very bones crying out for even an hour of uninterrupted sleep. Ignoring her body's protests, she forced herself up, knowing that any attempt to go back to sleep would be of no use; every time she had tried to close her eyes last night, images had played behind her eyelids like a movie in fast-forward: the train, the stranger, the accident, and a pair of eyes that had haunted her for the past thirteen years.

She had spent hours replaying the events of the afternoon in her mind, trying to make any sort of sense of it at all, but by the time she walked into the bathroom to wash her face in preparation for the day, she was more confused than ever.

People don't just disappear, she thought as she pulled on yesterday's jeans, pulling a second-hand plaid button-up over a fresh t-shirt. *A trick of the light,* she tried to convince herself, pouring a quick bowl of cereal

19

for herself and some chicken-flavored kibble for Mister Sylvester, her standoffish black-and-white rescue cat.

Or maybe, she reasoned as she triple-checked that her front door was locked before departing for her 9 A.M. shift, maybe she had simply *imagined* the entire thing—it wouldn't be the first time something like that had happened, if her childhood therapist was to be believed. He had been one among many who hadn't believed Kai about the figure that she had seen on the night of her family's accident. *"A stress-induced hallucination,"* he had said to her eight-year-old self in a manner meant to be comforting. *"A trick of the light, even,"* as he had patted her lightly on the shoulder when he ushered her into the lobby where her aunt was waiting to take her home.

This was the explanation she would choose to accept, she decided as she pushed through the doors to Tanner's Grocery. Whilst seeing imaginary persons would certainly seem an unappealing option to most, it was better than having no explanation at all—at least it was to Kai, who had spent most of her life without explanations for things that she felt deserved explaining.

And while having an explanation—or at least the semblance of one—comforted her enough to manage some idle chit-chat with a customer on the hunt for lavender-scented garbage bags, which was something that Kai never usually had the energy nor patience for, the lack of sleep began to take its toll about halfway through her shift, when Avery had to practically shake her awake as they stocked dry goods.

"Sorry," Kai apologized, hating the way it sounded; she'd had far too much to apologize for lately, and *sorry* was beginning to sound less and less like an actual word. "I...I didn't get very much sleep last night."

There it was again: that look of sympathetic concern. It was painted all over Avery's expression, and though she tried to hide it by swiftly averting her eyes back to the boxes of cereal that she was practically flinging onto the top shelf, it had been visible for long enough to make Kai's stomach turn in discomfort.

"You know," Avery began, then hesitated, biting down on her lower lip as though she had to physically stop herself from finishing her sentence. Kai waited, trying to resist the urge to cringe at the worry that she heard in Avery's tone. Internally, she chided herself, wishing she hadn't said anything—that she could have managed the simple task of not falling asleep on her feet at work so that Avery wouldn't have to worry about her at all. After a moment, Avery continued, though she seemed to be avoiding Kai's eyes as she spoke. "Maybe you should consider seeing someone again—at least to get some sort of prescription to help you sleep."

"I can't afford it," Kai responded instantly, almost robotically. They'd had this conversation before—several times—and every time, Kai had the same response at the ready: *I can't afford it.* "And besides," she added quickly, not wanting to give Avery the chance to offer her (generous, but too embarrassing for Kai to accept) financial assistance. "Even if I could, what good would it do? I was in therapy for *years,* and look where it got me: I still can't sleep, and I still have nightmares every single night. Therapy doesn't work—at least not for me."

The truth was, Kai had never really put much effort into her sessions, often staying silent or mumbling sullen half-responses until her biweekly hour was up, but she kept this to herself. Better to believe that it didn't work than to admit that she hadn't even *tried.* Why try when it seemed as though she had nothing to live for, and when no one believed anything that she had to say anyway?

"The nightmares are back?" *Damn it.* Kai squeezed her eyes shut, wishing that she hadn't let that particular bit of information slip. As far as Avery knew, Kai hadn't had a nightmare in nearly eight months—not since she had semi-excitedly informed Avery that she was officially two weeks nightmare-free. When the dreams had returned only a week later, Kai had felt too exhausted, hopeless, and *guilty* to bring it up, and then it had been too late—too much time had passed.

Since then, as far as Avery was concerned, Kai just had good old-fashioned insomnia—which wasn't a lie, but it wasn't as true as the fact that she had vivid recollections of the accident that killed her family every time that she closed her eyes for more than a few minutes.

"Yeah," Kai said slowly, brain scrambling to find a suitable excuse to soothe Avery's concern. "Only recently, though—I'm sorry I didn't tell you, I was holding out hope that they would just go away again." She felt another discomforting twinge of guilt for lying to her closest friend, but she told herself that it was for the best, shoving the feeling deep down in her chest, where it sat heavy as a stone just below her heart.

It wasn't that she didn't *trust* Avery, she just didn't want her to feel guilty about things that were out of her control. And above all, Kai was sick to death of telling people about the nightmares. First it had been the psychologists, and the guidance counselors, and her aunt, who had raised her after the accident until Kai was seventeen, when she had died from kidney failure—another name to add to the list of the people that Kai had lost.

And then it had been Avery, whose kind heart had felt so badly when she found out that she had slept over at Kai's apartment for three days in the hopes that the presence of another human being would keep Kai's demons at bay.

She was just so tired. *And maybe,* she'd thought when she had made the decision not to tell Avery that the nightmares had returned, *maybe if I don't talk about them, it will be like they don't exist.*

It hadn't worked, obviously, but that hadn't stopped Kai from pretending.

"*Really,*" Kai said reassuringly as she forced what she hoped was a convincing smile, one side of her mouth a little more willing to cooperate than the other, resulting in an awkward half-grin. She placed a hand softly on Avery's arm, waiting until her friend met her eyes to continue. "I'm *fine*—trust me, I've dealt with worse."

"Well, *that's* comforting," Avery mumbled, seeming unconvinced. When Kai frowned, Avery rolled her hazel eyes, sighing deeply. "*Fine,* I'll let it go," she agreed, albeit reluctantly. "But you have to promise me that you'll at *least* take some extra-strength melatonin tonight, okay?" Kai had tried that before, and Avery knew it, but nonetheless, Kai hooked her crooked pinky with Avery's significantly paler one.

"I promise."

Thorne huffed impatiently, running a hand through his messy bangs for the third time in as many minutes, shaking his head as he mumbled profanities under his breath, his boots kicking up gray dust and pebbles as he paced back and forth.

"Mysterious fucking asshole...honestly, is it too much to expect someone to show up for a meeting *they* arranged? Next time, I won't even come! That'll teach his oblivious ass a less—"

"My ass," someone interrupted in a cool, prim tone of voice, and Thorne spun on his heel, rolling his eyes slightly as he recognized the intruder. "Is *fantastic,* thank you very much."

"Aristides," Thorne greeted, irritation clear in his tone. He narrowed his eyes as Aristides drew closer. "Can we cool it with the creepy hoodie, please? *Honestly,* it's the twenty-first century—find some taste. *Ugh,*" he shivered, and Aristides chuckled, lowering his hood.

"For your information, it is a *cloak,*" he said delicately. Thorne snorted.

"Cloak, hoodie—same difference, really. Who cares?" Aristides sighed deeply and glanced upwards, looking as though he were praying to the heavens for patience. "You're late, by the way." Thorne moved to a beige settee that had not been present the moment before and sprawled himself semi-gracefully across it.

"When you have existed as long as I, you learn that time is an illusion, and 'late' merely a state of mind," Aristides said sagely, and Thorne stared blankly up at him, thoroughly unimpressed, and mildly befuddled.

Unsure of how to respond to that particular statement, he cleared his throat.

"Moving on from...that," he said, gesturing vaguely to Aristides' person. "Why did you summon me? I'm a very busy person, you know."

"Oh, I know," Aristides nodded in mock seriousness, seating himself in a dark purple wing chair that had appeared as suddenly as the settee. "I know all about the things that keep you so *busy,* Thorne: squatting in abandoned mortal apartments, eating—what is it?—*cup noodles,* shirking your responsibilities..." his gaze narrowed suddenly on Thorne as he added pointedly, "Rescuing mortals."

For the briefest of seconds, Thorne resembled a deer in headlights, caught off guard by Aristides' accusation. He recovered swiftly, however, smoothing his features into a mask of cool indifference.

"I don't know what you're talking about," he said lightly, and Aristides chuckled, though not in amusement. Thorne's stomach turned at the sudden change in the atmosphere, at the way that Aristides leaned slowly forward in his seat with elbows resting lightly on his knees, his demeanor changing from that of a friend to an interrogator.

"You should know better by now than to lie to me, Thorne; you forget, when you are in the mortal world, we can see *everything.*" The small, endless lines of foreign text that constantly circled his golden irises seemed to bolden briefly at that last statement, and Thorne resisted the urge to swallow, to show any sign that he was in the slightest bit uncomfortable.

"If you know something, Ris, stop beating around the bush—for *both* our sakes."

"Very well." Aristides straightened, rolling his broad shoulders back as his steady gaze held Thorne's in a chokehold. "You saved that girl—why?"

"Why not?" Thorne countered with a careless shrug. Aristides was unmoved.

"You know as well as I, Thorne—better, perhaps—that defying the laws of Fate is no small thing. That girl's Fate was to *die,* and you changed that; the consequences of your decision could be *catastrophic.*"

"*Catastrophic?*" Thorne's brows flew upward as he expelled a long, deep breath. "How very dramatic of you to say. Honestly," he continued as Aristides took a measured breath, the muscles in his chiseled jaw clenching minutely. "I didn't think that she was going to *die*. End up in the hospital? Absolutely. Fall into a coma from which she will never wake? A definite possibility. How bad can getting run over by a train *really* be? All *I* did was save her from some outlandishly expensive medical bills; the healthcare system in that country, *honestly—*"

"*Thorne.*"

"*Ris,*" Thorne mimicked, and his expression softened. He continued in a gentler tone. "It was a small thing. I was bored, and I wasn't thinking of the consequences; I saved her as...as a lark, that's all." It wasn't a *complete* lie, though it certainly wasn't the truth: that Thorne didn't *know* why he had done what he did. But he had no desire to confess that to Aristides—not here, not *now*.

Aristides sighed deeply again and shook his head, seemingly at a loss for words.

"This may seem like a small thing to *you*, Thorne, but it is a very serious thing to toy with Fate—I *know* that you know that." Thorne's lips pressed together, his eyes flashing slightly, and Aristides pushed quickly forward. "Whether or not you *intended* to save that girl, it was a mistake, and it needs to be fixed—*immediately*." Thorne scoffed.

"And what would you have me do, smother her in her sleep? That's not at all in my job description, Ris—nor yours, for that matter."

"No," Aristides agreed, looking thoughtful. His lips pursed slightly as he considered Thorne's words. "But Fate always finds a way to set things right; all that you have to do is stay out of the way and do your job. Nothing more, nothing less. Can you do that?"

"Yes, fine," Thorne snapped in annoyance, having grown quickly tired of this conversation. Aristides rolled his eyes.

"Good," he said. He softened as he looked at Thorne, and sighed lightly. "I do not like being this way with you, Thorne—angry and confrontational. I *understand* that you are dissatisfied with the way that things are, but it is not something that can be remedied, so you may as well accept it at some point." He paused, and when Thorne didn't respond, sullenly avoiding the taller man's gaze, Aristides rose to his feet, straightening the silver clasp on his cloak before pulling his hood back over his silken black hair. "The next time that we meet, let it be under better circumstances, yes?" Thorne hesitated, still annoyed, then nodded. Despite his conflicted feelings about Aristides, he had always liked him more than his brothers, Cyrus and Linus. *Especially* Cyrus.

"I will take my leave, then," Aristides said, then promptly vanished.

Thorne sighed heavily as he sank deeper into the settee and stared up into the gray haze of clouds above him, gnawing at the inside of his cheek thoughtfully. He had been telling the truth, however slightly, when he'd told Aristides that he had saved that girl out of boredom.

Then again, he had been bored for *centuries,* and never once had he done something like *this.*

At any rate, regardless of his personal feelings on the matter, Aristides was probably right—this needed to be fixed.

CHAPTER FIVE

GHOSTS AND FAMILIARITY

KAI

Ever since she had left her apartment that morning, Kai hadn't been able to shake the feeling that she was being watched. Maybe it was just that it had been the second night in a row where she'd been unable to get more than an hour of consecutive sleep, or that she still had the events of the other day playing on a constant loop in the back of her mind, but Kai had never felt so paranoid, every hair on her body standing on end as she took periodic glances over her shoulder as she walked the relatively short distance to Tanner's Grocery.

By the time she stepped through the automatic double doors, her knuckles were white with how tightly she was clutching her phone in one hand and her keychain mace in the other, the small metallic container not doing as much as she had hoped it would in giving her a sense of security.

She had hoped, desperately, that the feeling would go away once she clocked in and started her shift, but alas, the following seven hours did more to exhaust her than a night without sleep *ever* had, her head on a constant swivel, eyes relentlessly searching the aisles as she stocked. Not even Avery's steady stream of cheerful chatter could distract her, her friend's detailed retelling of the drama going on between two of her

Biochemical Engineering classmates going in one ear and straight out the other.

The instant that her shift ended, Kai clocked out and practically fled from the building, tossing her apron haphazardly into the basket by the break room door and bidding Avery a hasty goodbye, desperate to get home and out of sight of her seemingly invisible stalker.

As she moved to take the usual path home, something stopped her—a feeling deep inside, prompted by she knew not what, that she should take the route from the other day: the path that led to the tracks. If the stalker knew her usual route home and was waiting for her along the way, this would surely throw them off her scent.

Keychain mace in hand, Kai turned down the worn dirt path.

Never in her life had Kai seen a car using this path, this dirt trail that could barely pass for a road, but it seemed that the past couple of days were a time for firsts. So preoccupied with her thoughts, so focused on getting home alive and in one piece without being attacked by some mysterious invisible entity, Kai didn't notice the beaten brown sedan approaching rapidly behind her until it was too late.

Everything went dark.

She didn't particularly *feel* dead, and when she tried to wiggle her toes they did her bidding without hesitation, but...it couldn't hurt to ask.

"Am I dead?" From above her came an amused snort, and a familiar voice.

"Open your eyes, sunshine." Her brows furrowed, and her eyes flew open, instantly met with the brown-eyed gaze that had been haunting her every waking thought for the past forty-six hours. She was vaguely aware of arms on either side of her head, boxing her in, of hands cushioning the back of her skull, protecting it from the packed dirt she was now lying on, of a chest pressing solidly against her own, and a mouth less than six inches from hers.

"You," she breathed, staring wide-eyed up at him, feeling as though the wind had been figuratively, as well as literally, knocked out of her. One corner of his mouth lifted, and he raised an eyebrow.

"Me," he said, and at last the pieces clicked together in Kai's mind, sluggish with the shock of it all.

"*You!*" Roughly, she shoved him off of her, and he tumbled unceremoniously into the dirt. Ignoring his mumbled *oof!* of surprise, Kai scrambled clumsily to her feet, jabbing an accusatory finger in his direction. "Have you been *following* me? What the *hell* is wrong with you? I swear to absolute *fuck,* if—" Thorne winced, holding up a hand as he rose to his feet.

"A little less shrill, if you don't mind—*ouch!*" He glared venomously at her, rubbing the spot on his arm where she'd just landed a solid punch. "You're welcome for saving your life, jeez," he mumbled, and Kai scoffed, incredulous.

"*Please!* My life wouldn't have needed 'saving' if you hadn't been *stalking me!*" Thorne rolled his eyes, sighing deeply. *Mortals,* he thought, but didn't say it aloud.

"Whether or not I was stalking you is neither here nor there; the fact remains, I *did* save your life. From where I stand, that warrants at *least* a 'thank you.'"

"From where *I* stand, that warrants a *restraining order,*" Kai hissed, crossing her arms as she turned to observe the skid marks that the car had left as it had swerved, too late, to avoid her. She scoffed, shaking her head in utter disbelief. "Asshole didn't even pause," she murmured, brows pushing together as she realized that, indeed, the car and its careless driver were nowhere to be seen. *Strange,* she thought, that not only had a car come down this path at all, but that the driver hadn't thought to stop and make sure she was all right.

"That's people for you," Thorne shrugged, seeming not to think much of it. "Guess you're just lucky I was here to save you from becoming a human pancake."

"Again," Kai sighed, tilting her head to the sky in a brief plea for patience before turning back to face him. "*You* are the *reason* that I almost got hit—I wouldn't have even taken this path if I hadn't felt your creepy little eyes on the back of my neck all day." She paused, her own eyes narrowing. "Speaking of, why *were* you following me? And if you say it's because you fell deeply in love with me at first sight or whatever creepy, unrealistic bullshit, I'll mace you."

"With what, this?" He held up her keychain, spinning the braided, multicolored loop around his index finger, the mace container in question glinting in the light of the setting sun. Kai's jaw tightened as she shifted on her feet, her stomach clenching as she glanced furtively from side to side in search of a way out.

Thorne sighed again, tossing her the keychain with another slight roll of his eyes. "Calm down—I landed on them when you so *rudely* dumped me on my ass." Kai released the breath that had caught in her throat, clutching the keys tightly in her hands like a lifeline. "And as if I would fall in love with *you,* of all mortals. *Please,*" he scoffed, as though the very notion was absurd.

"What's that supposed to mean?" Unable to help it, Kai instantly took offense at his words, voice pitching higher as she crossed her arms over her chest. Thorne shrugged.

"Just that I'm not particularly wild for girls who throw themselves in front of trains for sport and are rude to guys who have saved their life *twice,* now."

"Maybe I wouldn't be so *rude* if you weren't so *creepy!*" Kai said defensively. "You still haven't even told me what you were doing here in the first place." Thorne faltered at that, seeming unable to come up with a feasible explanation, and looked as though he were contemplating simply vanishing into thin air again when Kai froze, eyes widening as someone appeared suddenly behind Thorne.

Turning quickly, Thorne nearly groaned aloud when he saw Aristides standing there looking profoundly unamused, unmasked irritation clear in his eyes and the firm set of his jaw.

"What the *hell* is going on here?" Kai burst out before either of them could speak, looking very much like her sanity was about to *snap* like a rubber band. "Who are *you?*" For the first time since Thorne had known him, Aristides seemed taken aback.

"*Excuse me?*" Thorne fought a smile at the offense in Aristides' tone, the way his hand rose theatrically to rest on his chest, as though he had been deeply disrespected.

"Is this some sort of elaborate kidnapping? Because I am *not* in the mood today, and if you think that I'm going down without a hell of a fight, you are *dead* wrong." Though she sounded bold, Thorne didn't miss the way that Kai's shoulders tensed as she took a nearly imperceptible step back, clearly preparing to run.

"Come now, let's not be dramatic," Aristides rolled his eyes, looking rather amused with Kai's show of bravery, and Thorne's own eyes narrowed sharply.

"Wait, you can *see* him?"

"Wait, you can *see* me?" Aristides repeated, as though he had just registered this fact himself, and Thorne had to close his eyes to keep from rolling them.

"Wh—*yes?*" Kai seemed angry and confused all at once, blinking rapidly as she tried to process what was happening. "'*You can see me?*' No *shit*, Sherlock!" She tossed up her hands in exasperation, shaking her head. "What are you meant to be, some kind of ghost or something? Of *course* I can see you, dipshit!" Thorne smothered a smile at her colorful language, evidently exacerbated by the stress of the situation.

"Mm, close enough, I suppose, though not *entirely* accurate," Aristides responded to her mostly rhetorical question, bobbing his head from side to side. His eyes narrowed as he looked her up and down in a considering manner. Kai seemed alarmed at this, and took another step back. "I wonder..." Aristides mused, then shook his head. "But—well, no, that's impossible—improbable, at the very least...I ought to consult with—then again, perhaps...hm...no, but—now, that *is* interesting..." With each mumbled half-sentence and incoherent unfinished thought, Kai appeared to be closer and closer to making a run for it, so Thorne held up a hand, deciding that this was as good a time as any to intervene.

"I think we can all agree that this is...unusual," he said, and Aristides ceased his muttering. "But let's just take a step back, here. Kai, go home—"

"How do you know my name?" Kai demanded, blatant panic shining through her features, and Thorne could have shouted to the high heavens in irritation.

"*Kai,*" he repeated with exaggerated patience. "Go home and wait for me there; I'll come when I can and...well, explain things to you, I suppose, to the very best of my ability." Aristides cleared his throat pointedly, and Thorne's eyes cut over at him in warning. "I need to speak with my...associate, first." Kai shook her head violently.

"I don't want anything to do with you—*either* of you," she added as she uncapped the metallic bottle of mace. She alternated aiming at Aristides and Thorne, neither of whom appeared particularly concerned with this turn of events, as she began to walk backward toward the train tracks, toward the path that would lead her home. "And if I ever see *either* of you again, I'm calling the police, okay? Stay away. Just—*stay away.*" Quickly, she spun on her heel and took off, running at a breakneck pace down the worn path.

Aristides and Thorne watched her leave, neither moving a muscle until, at last, she was out of sight. Aristides broke the silence.

"Thorne," he began in a tone bleeding with exaggerated sweetness, similar to the tone mothers use to scold their offspring in public. "A word?" Thorne sighed deeply, eyes fluttering slowly shut as he clenched his fists until his knuckles popped, then flexed them back outward, before nodding in assent and disappearing alongside Aristides.

Chapter Six
TELLE EST LA MORT

When he opened his eyes, they were back in the In-Between, in the clouded ruins where he and Aristides always conducted their meetings. Like the old office in which Thorne and his companions passed their time, it was a place between worlds, somewhere between the lands of the living and the dead, and separate from the Other Place where Aristides resided with his brothers. It was a place where Thorne and Aristides could meet without intruding upon each other's designated spaces.

"So tell me," Aristides began, already seated in the purple wing chair, back ramrod straight and legs crossed, hands resting delicately on the plush arms of the chair. "What was it about *the balance of Fate must be restored* that escaped you?"

"I..." Thorne trailed off, struggling to find an explanation that would satisfy the disappointed Fate in front of him. He swallowed, his mouth suddenly dry as cotton, and Aristides' brows rose as he clapped slowly, the sound echoing throughout the endless space.

"Impressive explanation," he said coolly, bitingly sarcastic in a way that Thorne wouldn't have expected from him. "But I am afraid I require a little more...*elaboration,* if you please." He paused, then, "I'm waiting." Thorne's fingers twitched, curling into fists of their own volition.

"I'm *thinking*," he snapped, taking a deep, unsteady breath. His thoughts were racing a thousand miles a minute, the gears in his mind working a frantic overtime as he tried to come up with something—*any-thing*—that could explain this newest setback. But how could he possibly attempt to explain something that he himself still did not understand?

"Look," he said at last, his shoulders slumping in defeat as he ran a hand through his hair, pushing it out of his eyes as he shook his head. "I don't know how it happened; I was going to do as you said—*truly*, Ris, but...I can't explain it. It was as if my body acted without my consent: one moment, I was a mere bystander, watching from a distance and wait-ing to do my job, and the next, I was saving her. I know it sounds...utterly mad. I don't understand it, myself. She just...she's different, somehow." He winced, realizing suddenly how completely ridiculous he sounded. From the expression on Aristides' face, he was thinking the same thing.

"*Different?*" Aristides shook his head, and Thorne averted his eyes, fixing his gaze on the dusty gravel beneath his feet with cheeks burning in humiliation. "Come now, Thorne, this is not *Romeo and Juliet;* this is not some terribly mortal adolescent film where a human and a vampire fall for each other at first sight and live 'happily ever after.' The things that I have seen, Thorne..." he trailed off, ancient eyes glazing over as he recalled the things that he had witnessed in Cyrus' mirrors over the millennia, the events that he had looked back upon in his own mind; it had been cheesy film upon cheesy film, terrible novel upon equally terrible novel.

Jolting suddenly out of his reverie, he continued. "The *point*, Thorne, is that she is not 'different,' she is merely *mortal.* A mortal that needs to die as she was destined, in order to restore the balance of Fate. It is what makes the world go 'round, as they say."

"But doesn't the fact that she can see us—see *you*—**prove** that she is different?" Thorne protested, voice rising as his confidence returned in a sudden burst. "From the way that you reacted, Ris, I would put money on this being the first time that a *mortal* has laid eyes on you." Aristides rolled his eyes, brushing a hand carelessly through the air.

"That is because I do not go gallivanting all over the mortal plane as you do."

"Come *on*, Ris! It means *something*—it *has* to." *It has to mean **something** that she can see me. That I can see her. This feeling, this...hope...it cannot be for nothing.*

"What it *means*," said Aristides as he rose slowly from his seat, long fingers flexing at his sides as his expression tightened, clearly growing hard-pressed for patience. "Is that you are tampering with things beyond your—or even my own—understanding, and you need to make it right." He sighed deeply, approaching Thorne with a gentler expression than he had been wearing the moment before. "Listen to me," he said quietly, softly, pausing until Thorne's eyes rose hesitantly to meet his own. "Clearly, there is something else going on here. I can see that. And it is understandable—centuries of reaping souls will do that to someone, I am sure, not that I am exactly an expert on the subject.

"*However,* despite whatever...*personal* feelings may be at stake, life goes on, Thorne, and so must death." The finality was back in his tone and his expression, and he placed a firm hand on Thorne's shoulder. "The next time that an opportunity presents itself, you *will* reap her soul, *regardless* of your personal feelings on the matter. Is that understood?"

Thorne nodded, saying nothing, and Aristides gave his shoulder a brief squeeze likely meant as comfort, but that felt more akin to a lock, sealing Thorne's fate.

"It is for the best," Aristides said quietly, and then he was gone.

Thorne knew that the Fate was right about this, but that didn't mean that he couldn't hate it.

What he hated the most, he thought as he turned to leave, appearing a split second later in his office and collapsing wearily into his desk chair, was the not knowing.

Not knowing why he had saved her again. Not knowing why he had saved her in the first place. Not knowing why she could see him. *Not knowing why he could see her.*

If only he had answers, he mused, staring thoughtfully at the large print of *The Swing* that hung on the wall to the left of his desk, perhaps he could move on; perhaps if he understood *why* he had done what he did, he could reap her soul without qualms and *move on.*

But as he had been learning since he was merely a child, answers were not something that he was likely to get—not in his life, and certainly not in his work.

Such is life, and such, it would seem, is death.

"I can do it," Minho offered immediately upon hearing Thorne's summary of the afternoon's events. "I'll do it."

"Min—" Thorne began, but Minho was quick to speak over him, his tone gentle, his eyes soft and serious.

***

"I said I'll do it. *I will do it.* I don't—" his voice dropped as he stepped closer to Thorne, speaking quietly so that Jai, standing to the side with his large ears straining to keep up with the conversation, couldn't overhear. "I don't know what is going on with you, but I do not have to understand to help; if it means that things can go back to normal, and that it keeps you out of trouble with the Fates, *I* will reap the girl's soul, and let us be done with it."

"*Min,*" Thorne said again, a grateful gleam in his eye as he placed his hands on Minho's shoulders, as if to physically restrain him from interrupting. "As much as I appreciate your offer, I'm afraid it doesn't quite work like that; for the Balance to be restored, it has to be *me* who reaps Kai's soul. *I* am the one who made the mistake, and *I* am the one who must fix it."

Minho's shoulders fell slightly, and he reached up to grasp Thorne's wrists, giving them a light squeeze in an attempt to convey his sympathy. Thorne smiled—faintly, but it was there, nonetheless, and one of the first that Minho had seen from him in a very long time.

Pulling away slightly, Thorne waved Jai forward, setting a hand on his shoulder. "I promise you both," he said, pausing to meet each of their eyes. "Things *will* go back to normal; my failure will have no effect on you. So *stop worrying,*" he added meaningfully to Minho, who laughed softly, his eyes bright. It was in his nature to worry, and Thorne knew it well.

Still, Minho nodded, and Thorne squeezed his shoulder briefly before exiting the room, ruffling Jai's hair playfully as he passed, and trying to act as though the confusion of it all wasn't beginning to tear him apart at the seams.

CHAPTER SEVEN

AN ILL-FATED TRASH RUN

KAI

As utterly exhausted as she felt, with her very bones crying out and muscles aching for rest, taking out the trash was the absolute last thing that Kai wanted to be doing just now. But in a valiant attempt to keep her mind off of the indescribably strange events of the afternoon, Kai had finally taken care of her sinkful of dirty dishes, even managing to clean off her crumb-littered counters and sweep the worn hardwood floors that had grown thick with dust and scattered tufts of Mister Sylvester's soft fur.

She had gone so far as to wipe down the empty mantlepiece that stood above the small, gas fireplace that she had never lit, and tidied her small bedroom, making the bed with fresh sheets and relocating the messy piles of laundry to the hamper. Even her bathroom gleamed and smelled of lemon-scented cleaning soap, so taking out her overfilled kitchen garbage was the finishing touch on her finally clean apartment.

Too tired to feel even the smallest sense of pride or accomplishment over the fact that her apartment was clean for the first time in months, she trekked with dogged determination down the stairs and out the back door of the building, wearily making her way to the secluded area where the large, blue communal dumpster was kept.

She had always hated coming back here; it was damp and dim and smelly and, more often than not, frequented by some of the building's more unpleasant residents.

"*Sanchez,*" a raspy, vaguely slurred voice greeted as the stench of week-old garbage filled her nostrils, her stomach turning violently as she struggled not to gag. "What a welcome surprise! I was *just* thinking about you."

Speak of the devil.

Kai pointedly ignored him as she yanked open the side window to the dumpster and heaved her bag into it with a light grunt of exertion, her skin prickling as she felt the man's stare on the back of her bare neck. Strands of hair had slipped from her bun and were brushing lightly against her skin in the gentle evening breeze, only serving to heighten her anxiety.

She shut the door to the dumpster and turned to leave, her spine stiffening as she heard him speak again, his gravelly voice like nails on a chalkboard to her already frazzled nerves.

"It's not nice to ignore people, you know—it's not *polite,*" he sneered, and Kai tried not to sigh aloud, pausing briefly to offer him a jerky nod.

"Hello, Kevin. *Goodbye,* Kevin." She turned again to make a hasty exit, gasping sharply as a severe, pinching grip closed suddenly around her upper arm.

"You know, I am so *sick* of being treated like I'm not worth the dirt under y'all's boots." The smell of booze and cigarettes slammed into her, nausea rolling in her stomach as her head lolled back for a moment, feeling as though she might pass out. When was the last time she had eaten? Breakfast? She wasn't sure.

"*Women,*" Kevin ground out through crooked teeth stained with nicotine. "Someone really ought to teach you your place." His eyes—one brown, one an electric blue that sent a shiver down Kai's spine—swept down her body, and Kai felt every cell of herself crawl in discomfort.

"You're drunk, Kev," she said calmly, trying desperately to keep her cool as she attempted to yank herself out of his bruising grip. "Let me go."

"*Stop telling me what to do!*" He exploded, and Kai jumped, eyes going wide at the force of his words, bits of spittle flying from his mouth and landing on her cheek. Genuinely panicking now, Kai slammed her fist against his chest, trying with renewed effort to free herself. This only angered him more, his pale, yellowing fingers tightening as he began pulling her back toward the dumpster.

"*Help!*" Kai screamed as loudly as she could, the words tearing painfully from her throat. "*Somebody he—*" her breath and her words swept from her sharply with a loud, resounding *crack!* as Kevin's knuckles flew across her face.

Blinking back tears of pain and terror, Kai mustered up what remaining strength was left in her tired, aching body and bolted forward.

Even intoxicated, Kevin was faster.

Kai hit the ground so quickly that it took a moment for her to comprehend what had happened, and by the time she had, there was another terrible pain—this time in her ribs, as his worn work boots met her side.

"Stupid, worthless, *disrespectful* piece of—" Kevin was muttering to himself in a frenzy, his cheeks red and his eyes wild, stumbling back a step after delivering another powerful, painful blow to Kai's ribs. She cried out, her fingers scraping against the pavement as she tried to pull herself away, crawling back toward the building in an attempt to escape.

Boots on the pavement approached, and out of the corner of her eye, she saw Kevin pull his foot back once more.

Everything went black.

Kai heard Kevin utter a weak, fearful cry, and something slammed loudly against the dumpster, sounding as though it were hard enough to leave a dent. Kai's heart threatened to beat out of her chest, the panicked organ racing so quickly that she worried it might give out as she continued trying to claw her way forward, though where she was going, she couldn't tell—it was so dark that she couldn't see an inch in front of her.

A sharp cry escaped her lips as she was pulled quickly to her feet, and all at once the light returned, and she found herself propped against the brick wall a short distance from the dumpster, where she could see Kevin curled in a quivering, whimpering heap on the ground.

There were hands on her shoulders, holding her up, supporting her, and blinking the light out of her eyes, Kai looked up to see just the familiar face that she had been trying to banish from her thoughts all day.

"Get off me," she mumbled, her voice coming out hoarse and raspy, unfamiliar to her own ears. She shoved weakly against his chest. Though he appeared unbothered by the gesture, he complied, dropping his hands slowly, as if making sure that she wasn't going to collapse, before taking a step back.

"Are you alright?" His voice was soft and gentle, and so concerned that it made her want to cry. Aside from Avery, she hadn't heard someone sound that concerned for her since—

She shook her head, then, realizing what she had done, quickly nodded.

"I'm fine," she said roughly, wincing as she tried to straighten her posture, her ribs throbbing in the spot that Kevin's boot had repeatedly struck. Her gaze shifted to the man in question, still slumped pathetically by the dumpster.

The boy in front of her seemed to understand what she was thinking, and his tone was careless, nearly spiteful, as he said, "He'll live." Kai's eyes snapped back up to meet his. "He'll just be in a world of hurt for a while." The corners of Kai's mouth twitched in spite of herself, her gaze darkening a little as she nodded. She didn't voice what they were both thinking: *he deserves it.*

"Well," she cleared her throat, shifting on her feet and looking away, feeling suddenly awkward. "Um...thank you, I guess. I'm not sure what I would've—what would've happened if..." Her teeth dug sharply into her lower lip, something wet glossing over her eyes.

She shook her head abruptly, clearing her throat as she blinked away the dampness. "Anyway, thanks. This doesn't mean we're cool or anything," she added sternly, though her mouth twitched again. "I still think you're weird and creepy, if not a complete stalker, so I wouldn't complain if I never saw you again, but..."

"Any time," he said softly, his brown eyes liquid in the light of the slowly setting sun, the sky above them a canvas of pale blues and pinks and purples as the day began to come to its close. Beside the dumpster, Kevin groaned as he made another vain attempt to rise to his feet, and the boy's jaw tightened, his eyes shuttering. "You'd better get back inside; I don't think he'll try anything with you after this, but—"

"Better safe than sorry," Kai agreed with a tiny, lopsided smile, hissing through her teeth as she pushed herself away from the wall. She stood crookedly on her feet as she bent slightly sideways to alleviate the burning pain in her ribs.

The boy took a half-step forward, hands already rising to help, but Kai shook her head. "Thanks again for the save, but I can take care of myself from here. Goodbye..." she squinted, then shook her head again, laughing under her breath. "Whatever your name is." She turned to leave, limping determinedly back toward the rear entrance of her apartment building, but before she made it out of sight completely, the boy called out,

"Thorne." Kai paused to glance over her shoulder, brows knitting together in confusion. "My name is Thorne." A beat of silence stretched between them, him standing awkwardly with his hands in the pockets of his black jeans, and Kai still craning her neck to look back at him, her gaze resting in his as the sun continued to set behind him, outlining him in the glow.

"Goodbye, Thorne," she said at last, so quietly that the words barely made it to his ears, nearly washing away in the almost nonexistent breeze.

Without waiting for a response—perhaps knowing that he did not have one to give—Kai turned and limped her way to the weathered back door of her building, pulling it open with a slight effort, as it had a bad habit of sticking to the doorframe. Unable to help herself, she turned to look over her shoulder again, but Thorne was gone, almost as if he had never been there at all.

***

Feeling thoroughly battered, and even more exhausted than she had been before she'd left her apartment, Kai sank shakily down onto her couch, her hands trembling uncontrollably as the adrenaline began to wear off, the brave front that she had put on in front of Thorne crumbling into nothing. Unbidden, tears sprang to her eyes, and Kai laughed humorlessly as they began to slide down her cheeks, realizing that this was the first time in recent memory that she had allowed herself to cry—the first time in longer than she cared to remember that she had even been *capable* of the act.

She wasn't even sure *why* she was crying; emotionally speaking, she felt numb, but also as though her entire reality had been completely shattered.

Ever since her family had died, she had been living with the guilt of survival, the bitter regret that she had been forced to live on without them weighing her down like an anchored chain around her neck. For the past thirteen years, she had been floating, purposeless, barely registering life as it just *happened* to her.

She couldn't begin to count the nights that she had laid in bed wishing, *praying,* that she could simply cease to exist, so that she wouldn't have to face the agony of another pointless day without them. It had been easier to shut down completely rather than face the reality: her family was gone, but she had to live.

She had the *chance* to live.

And she'd nearly squandered it—she had been so focused on what she'd lost that she'd forgotten that she had *lived.* So concentrated on surviving, on making it from one monotonous day to the next, that she hadn't realized she was practically wasting away.

She'd had dreams, once, and a desire to pursue them. Perhaps she could find that desire again; maybe, just *maybe,* she could muster up the desire to take advantage of the second chance that she had been given. Maybe she could still make her family proud, if they could see her wherever they were now.

With this realization came another wave of exhaustion, and she decided that seizing the day could wait until she had taken a nap; already her eyes were beginning to fall shut of their own accord, a yawn tearing from her sore throat. So, pulling the threadbare throw blanket from the back of the couch, Kai spread it over herself and curled up beneath it, losing herself nearly instantly to unconsciousness as her breathing evened out, her mouth falling softly open as quiet snores began to slip from her slightly parted lips.

When she awoke, hours later, from the first nightmare-free sleep that she'd had in longer than she could remember, her first realization was that she felt surprisingly *rested*. It had been a long time since sleep had made her feel that way. Usually, it only served to make her feel *more* exhausted—if not physically, from the effort it took to try and get to sleep in the first place, then mentally. For so long, sleep had been a battle rather than a solace, and to feel so rested was a pleasant change.

The second realization was that someone was standing over her.

She screamed.

CHAPTER EIGHT

A LINE IN THE SAND

They were in the In-Between, Thorne realized as he turned to lay eyes on his abductor, reeling slightly from the sudden change in scenery; one moment, he had been watching Kai hobble painfully back into her apartment building, and in the next instant, he had felt a hand on his shoulder, and had been unable to stop the subsequent disappearance.

With an internal groan, he realized that he should have known.

Aristides was already pacing. Hands clasped neatly behind his back and lips pressed tightly together, he kept opening his mouth as if he were about to say something, only to snap it shut again, shaking his head as though whatever he was going to say wasn't enough to convey the colossal disappointment that he was surely feeling in Thorne. Thorne, feeling thoroughly chastened already, shifted on his feet in discomfort, wishing that Aristides would just get it over with; Thorne would far rather be shouted at than stared at in disappointed silence.

Suddenly, Aristides stopped, turning swiftly on his heel to face Thorne, his cloak billowing out behind him as he did so.

"I was under the impression," he began, taking a measured breath through his delicately sloped nose. "That the task that I gave you was simple, my instructions clear. When I told you that you needed to correct your mistake, you said that you understood, that you would do what needed to be done. Were you lying?"

"Ris—" Aristides threw up his hand, commanding silence.

"Then were my words lost in translation? Did I leave something unsaid when I expressed the pressing *need* for you to restore the Balance? When I *explicitly* told you that there would be consequences should you not?"

"*No*, if you would just let me explain—"

"*Then explain!*" Aristides' voice thundered throughout the space, somehow filling the endless expanse with the force of his words, his golden eyes blazing in anger and disappointment, the text within them flashing darkly. "Explain to me how you could fail not once, but *twice*, in so straightforward a task as *reaping a soul*, something that you have been doing for *centuries*. Explain *that* to me, Thorne—go on, *explain*." Thorne opened his mouth, but no sound came out, his limbs feeling cold and frozen in place, a painful ache pressing against the confines of his chest. Aristides laughed humorlessly. "Enlightening, truly. *Thank you*, Thorne, for that clarification." Thorne's fists clenched.

"*Shut up!*" His chest heaved, nails biting sharply into his palms—a welcome sensation, the physical pain drowning out his emotional turmoil. There was too much happening. *Too many things were happening all at once*, and he could hardly stand it. He had just experienced one of the most startling, profound fears of his life, and he could not *take* dealing with an angry, disappointed Aristides, too. It was all *too much*. His jaw tightened, then relaxed minutely as he blew out a sharp breath through his nose, and he looked away, seething.

There was a long, tense silence, and Aristides pinched the bridge of his nose, his eyes closed as he shook his head, seemingly at an utter loss.

"Thorne—" he sighed abruptly and dropped his hands, his tone softening ever so slightly. "Just...*explain*. Help me to understand your thought process, here. Give me *something*." His eyes were wide, earnest, something like desperation in his tone as he awaited Thorne's response.

"I just—" An unwelcome, almost unfamiliar, pressure formed against the backs of Thorne's eyes. *Tears?* Surely not—he hadn't cried in what felt like too long to recall.

He bit his tongue, steadily avoiding Aristides' gaze as he tried to form the words on the tip of his tongue, to force them out of his throat and into the light, to voice them to someone who could possibly help him understand. *I am so tired. I wanted to have a choice, for* **once.** *I wanted to do something* **good.** *She can see me.* **I can see her.**

But he said none of that, the words refusing to come.

The faint, hopeful light in Aristides' eyes dimmed as it became apparent that Thorne was not going to respond, and his shoulders resumed their tense, angry set as he straightened.

"Well," he said, yanking his robes back into place where they had shifted and creased. "Regardless of your personal feelings, whatever those may be, this is something that *must* be done; it is not a matter of *if* you reap her soul, Thorne, it is the simple matter of *when.* It is a *choice*—of whether you will do this now, while you still have the chance to properly make things right, or whether you will force our hand. I know that you believe your life cannot get worse, Thorne, but I *assure* you, *it can.*" Thorne threw his head back with a loud, almost manic laugh, a small flicker of flame leaping to life in his eyes as he met Aristides' gaze.

"Somehow, I find that difficult to imagine." His expression hardened, and he took several slow, measured steps forward, his chin lifting as his eyes narrowed. "I'm willing to bet that this isn't even *about* the Balance—it's about Cyrus" the name was bitter poison on his tongue "and his desperate, *pathetic* need for control. He's just angry that I have a mind of my own, for once, instead of blindly obeying whatever task you set for me." Aristides exhaled sharply, as though he had been gutted, his eyes sad.

"Is that what you think?" He shook his head, and something in Thorne's chest clenched painfully at the Fate's defeated expression, at his quiet, wounded tone. Aristides took a breath, looking away. "You have *always* had a mind of your own, Thorne; ever since you were created, you have done everything in your power to prove that you cannot be controlled, and I have never tried to convince you otherwise. And I would not lie to you—when have I *ever* lied to you?" Thorne swallowed, avoiding Aristides' gaze, instead choosing to stare at the small pile of pebbles by his boot that suddenly seemed incredibly interesting. Aristides continued.

"This isn't about *control,* Thorne. It *is* about Fate, whether you choose to believe that or not. And whether you *like* it or not, it is *your* responsibility to fix it. So stop acting like a child and just—*fix it.* And *move on.*" Thorne's fists tightened at the phrase that he was tired—*so tired*—of hearing.

"You know," he began, his voice cold again as he moved slowly, deliberately, toward Aristides, who stood still, arms at his sides as he waited for whatever Thorne was going to say next. "I am *tired* of being told what to do by you people—you *Fates.* If it's such a big deal, *fix it yourselves.* I'm *done.*" He turned to go, and Aristides reached out, his hand wrapping around Thorne's forearm in an attempt to keep him from leaving.

Darkness exploded from Thorne's body, throwing Aristides violently back and into the floor, pebbles skidding across the ground with the force of the blast. Aristides' eyes were wide in astonishment, but he made no move to rise from where he had fallen. Thorne was equally as surprised, though he recovered quickly, eyes shuttering as his features smoothed back into that frigid mask of indifference. He rolled his shoulders back, his chest rising with a slow inhale of deliberation.

"Maybe I *should* move on," he said, and shrugged. "But then, doing what I was told was never an area in which I excelled—must be a family thing." His lip curled slightly, and then he smiled, a reckless gleam in his eye. "Tell Cyrus that he can reap his own damn souls. He can start with Kai, if he can take me out first." Aristides huffed a disbelieving laugh.

"You intend to protect her—a mortal? A *human?*" Aristides shook his head. "Why, Thorne?" Thorne lifted a shoulder.

"I don't owe you a reason." He hoped that Aristides had not caught the flicker of hesitation, of doubt, that crossed his features, masking it quickly with another slight sneer.

With a light sigh, he straightened his black hoodie, smoothing an invisible wrinkle as he took a step back. "I suppose this is goodbye, then." His tone was cold, but his gaze lingered on the Fate, still lying where he had fallen in the dust. Thorne's stomach twisted a little, and he promptly swallowed the lump that was trying to lodge itself in his throat. "Farewell, Ris."

As he turned to disappear, Aristides called out after him.

"They will come for her, you know." Thorne paused. He smiled grimly.

"Let them."

***

When Thorne reappeared in the bullpen, Jai fumbled instantly to his feet, his long limbs tangling amongst themselves as he rose quickly from the armchair he had been sprawled across, the comic he'd been reading fluttering forgotten to the floor.

As Jai pelted him with a billion questions that he had neither the brainpower nor energy to answer—or even pay attention to—Thorne briefly met Minho's questioning eyes, jerking his gaze quickly away as he ducked into his office, leaving the door slightly ajar behind him.

As he lowered himself into his chair, eyes falling shut at the infinitesimal relief, the door opened soundlessly, the latch clicking shut as Minho leaned against it, saying nothing. Despite his silence, Thorne could feel his steady gaze—patient, but intense, and burning with the same questions that Jai had been relentlessly bombarding him with only seconds ago.

"I didn't do it, if that's what you want to know." Thorne cracked an eye open to see Minho's reaction. His friend's expression didn't waver, beyond the minute raise of a thick brow. "You don't seem surprised."

"I find, at this point, that it is growing rather difficult to be surprised by you." A snort of laughter escaped Thorne, and a bitter, lopsided grin pulled at the corner of his mouth.

"Good to know that, if nothing else, I can consistently disappoint." There was an edge to his tone, his eyes glittering as he looked at Minho, waiting. He felt jittery, his fingers twitching sporadically, the clothes on his body feeling suddenly confining, irritating his skin and making him feel caged, trapped. Minho didn't blink.

"Did I say I was disappointed?" His voice was calm, quiet. Thorne's teeth ground painfully together.

"You didn't need to," he said, waving his hand dismissively. "I can tell—you were expecting me to fail. If only Ris had that same sense." Minho's brows moved upward again, eyes lighting in understanding.

"You spoke with Aristides." His gaze swept over Thorne, taking in his half-clenched fists, the way that his arms were twitching, as though his very bones were trying to escape the skin that covered them. "It went well, I see."

"As well as it could have gone, I suppose: he scolded, I lost my temper. He's disappointed, I'm a failure. *Reap the mortal, fix the balance, et cetera.* Nothing said that he hasn't told me already."

"If listening to him is so troublesome, why not do as he says?" Minho was irritatingly unwavering in his patience as he spoke. It made Thorne want to scream.

"They can't always have their way," he said, well aware that he sounded like a petulant child. His lip curled. "I'm so *tired* of them always getting their way, whilst *I* am the one to suffer for it." A ghost of a smile played on his lips as he idly turned the chair back and forth, casting a sidelong glance at Minho. "I told him as much, today—told him that from here on out, they can fix their own problems. I'm *done.*"

Minho pushed away from the door, his eyes wary. He rested his hands on the desk and leaned over it, seeming to measure his words more carefully than usual as he spoke.

"Thorne, what did you do?" Thorne's lips twitched, that sharp gleam back in his gaze as he noted the carefully contained anger simmering below the surface of Minho's mask of calm, just waiting to get out. It wouldn't take much, he knew; so, shrugging carelessly, he leaned back in his chair and set his booted feet on the desk, stacking one ankle casually over the other.

"I drew a line in the sand: they can reap their own damned souls, and if they want Kai, they will have to go through me." Minho exhaled sharply, and Thorne smiled. "Like I said, I am *done* playing by their rules."

"You—" Minho took a shuddering breath, fingers curling where his large hands lay spread on the desk. His jaw tightened, and he straightened abruptly, his eyes hard as he stood over Thorne, fists curled at his sides. Minho's was a quiet anger, all the more terrifying in its calmness, and Thorne had not seen him like this in well over a century. *Good,* he thought, ignoring the voice in the back of his head that told him that this was a horrible idea, that this was self-destructive and selfish and unwise, and that the last thing he should do was alienate the one person who had always been on his side.

"You have to take it back," Minho said. "Aristides is right: this needs to be fixed. You *need* to fix this." Thorne was on his feet in an instant, his eyes blazing.

"*I **need** to do **nothing**!*" The room nearly shook from the force of his anger, and *finally,* Minho met it in kind.

"*You promised!*" The words tore from Minho's throat with such unrestrained fury that, when he spoke again a moment later, his voice was slightly hoarse, raw with pain and quiet fury. "You promised us that your *failure*" Thorne tried not to flinch "would not affect us. You *promised.*" His chest heaved, a myriad of emotions swimming in his eyes—anger and hurt, love and disappointment, unfiltered betrayal like an open wound that Thorne had to resist the urge to look away from.

"Please," he waved his hand, and Minho's fists clenched tighter than ever at the dismissive gesture. "This won't affect you. This is my doing, not yours—Ris knows that."

"Did you ask? Did you tell him that we do not support this *foolish, childish* notion that you can rescue a mortal from an inevitable, fated death? Does he know that you are *alone* in this endeavor?" Each word chipped further into Thorne's stubborn heart, and his jaw trembled from the force with which he was clenching it.

"I'll be sure to let him know the next time that I see him, *friend.*" Thorne shoved roughly past Minho as he threw open the door to the office, a wide-eyed Jai nearly falling out of his seat where he sat curled with his comic in his lap, opened to the same page he had been on since Thorne had arrived. The way he jumped half-out of his skin at Thorne's reappearance, a guilty look in his eyes, suggested that he had heard everything. Thorne didn't care, barely sparing him a glance.

"Where are you going?" Minho demanded as he followed Thorne down the steps into the bullpen, Jai following several steps behind, looking confused and frightened.

"*Out,*" responded Thorne in a biting tone, and he disappeared.

CHAPTER NINE

AN APOLOGY, AN EXPLANATION, A PROMISE, AND A SUMMONS

THORNE

An instant later, Thorne found himself standing in a small apartment, and with a slight shock, he realized that it was Kai's. He didn't think that he'd meant to come here—he didn't know where he *had* meant to go, if he was being honest with himself. He was so on edge, and he had been thinking of her...somehow, he had ended up here.

And there she was, fast asleep on the just slightly too-small-for-her-to-stretch-out-comfortably couch. She looked, for the first time since he had met her, utterly at peace, her lips parted softly and her brow unfurrowed, her hair strewn messily across the pillow, several strands of it falling over her face, where a bruise had already formed on her cheek. Thorne's fists clenched of their own accord at the memory of how she had gotten it, of watching that...*filth* beat her half to death.

He had only just arrived on the scene when he had seen them—Kai, curled on the ground and crying out in pain, and the clearly intoxicated man standing over her, boot drawn back to land another kick into Kai's vulnerable body. Thorne had felt as though a fire had lit in his heart, blazing to life as, without fully meaning to, he had blanketed the area in darkness, appearing in an instant by the man's side and throwing him away from Kai, lifting her to her feet and trying to avoid the frantic blows she had tried to land on his body before realizing who it was that was holding her.

She had looked so *scared,* Thorne recalled with a sharp ache in his chest, and afterward, so tired. He wondered how long it had been since she had been able to sleep like this, peaceful and undisturbed by whatever it was that seemed to plague her so terribly. Quite some time, if her constantly-fatigued appearance was any indication.

Thorne realized belatedly that she had begun to wake, and before he could say anything, she screamed.

Aristides dragged a weary hand slowly down his face, feeling, more than he had in an eon, completely and thoroughly *exhausted.*

His encounter with Thorne had been, on every conceivable level, utterly draining; mentally, as his mind had worked overtime to hopelessly fathom the reasons the Reaper could *possibly* have for being so maddeningly obstinate. Physically, as Thorne's powers had emerged, flinging Aristides so hard to the ground that, if he had been capable of bruising, he would surely be black and blue from head to toe. And though he would never admit it—not to Cyrus, and *certainly* not to Thorne—the experience had been emotionally taxing, as well; he would never tell the little bastard so, but he truly did consider Thorne to be a friend. His *only* friend, really. To have Thorne turn on him so suddenly, so viciously...it had been unexpected, to say the least.

And all for a *mortal.*

Aristides sighed. It was in Thorne's nature, he supposed; though he was not exactly *human*—not anymore, at least—it was an innate part of human nature to fall for the wrong person. Over and over again Aristides had seen it happen, had heard the stories from Cyrus, who had spent lifetimes witnessing such tragic love affairs. Aristides had never *imagined* that it could happen to Thorne—after all, if Thorne could not even *see* mortals, how could he possibly fall for one?

But clearly, he had—or at the very least, was making it *seem* as though he had, and all to spite the Fates for something that had happened centuries ago.

Aristides could not even blame him for it, entirely. He knew that it had not been fair; had wondered, over the years, if perhaps it had not been completely the right decision. Not that he would dare question Cyrus, and after all, Aristides was not entirely blameless: after all, he had been present when Thorne was handed his sentence.

Turning a corner, Aristides found Cyrus waiting for him, as if he had known that Aristides was thinking of him.

"Brother," Aristides greeted wearily, mustering a slight smile as he approached. Cyrus was stone-faced, and Aristides was surprised to see something like—or *exactly* like, he realized with a slight start—carefully contained rage brewing in his eyes. "Brother, what is it?"

Cyrus took a carefully measured breath and exhaled it slowly through his nostrils, his furrowed brows twitching, as though the question itself irritated him.

"The boy," he said slowly, releasing his hands from where they were, as usual, clasped behind his back, flexing his long fingers. "Is out of control." Aristides sighed and nodded his agreement, running a hand over his face again, as though he could physically scrub the exhaustion from his pores.

"I know. I am trying, but he is being...stubborn; I cannot seem to get through to him. I have hope that, over the course of the next few days, his temper will fade and allow him to see reason. Fear not, brother—I will *make* him see reason, if it is the very last thing that I do."

"I fear it may be too late for that," said Cyrus gravely, and Aristides straightened, suddenly wary. A chill ran down his spine.

"What do you mean by that?"

When Thorne returned to his office, he collapsed into the worn desk chair with a relieved sigh, his eyes falling shut as he pressed his fingers to his temples. He couldn't remember the last time he had been this exhausted; not *sleepy*—he had no use for sleep anymore—but physically drained after the events of the day. Bone-tired, the mortals called it.

And he felt *guilty*. In no small portion for the way his talk with Aristides had gone (he did, after all, consider Aristides to be someone he didn't entirely mind being around), but more so for the way that he had treated Minho, who was, though he had never said it aloud, like a brother to him. Better than a brother, because Minho had *chosen* him.

Movement outside the halfway-open office door caught his eye. *Minho.*

"Min?" Thorne called tentatively, and he saw the figure stiffen. Minho was angry. And he had every right to be; Thorne had been a complete and utter *dick,* and he knew it. "Could you come in here for a minute? Please?" He added for good measure, knowing it was a word that he said all too rarely, and would hopefully work in his favor. He saw Minho's broad shoulders rise and fall as he sighed deeply, hope daring to flicker to life in Thorne's chest as he watched his friend turn to enter the office.

Minho stopped just inside the doorway, arms crossed over his chest as he refused to meet Thorne's eyes.

"What is it?" He asked flatly, and Thorne swallowed.

"I'm..." he faltered, words failing him. Apologizing had never been a talent of his; he imagined that he could count on one hand how many apologies he'd made in the last...well, ever, to be truthful. But this situation *definitely* called for one—Thorne had gotten snippy and short with Minho before, but never like this. *This* was a new low for his treatment of his closest friend, and only an explicit apology would do. "I just...I wanted to say—" Minho waited, saying nothing, his expression distant and resigned. "Earlier..." Thorne huffed, running a hand through his messy hair, tugging it loose from its tie. "I'm sorry," he said at last, the words foreign, unfamiliar on his tongue. "I shouldn't have blown up at you like that. You were right—I wasn't thinking about how my actions could affect you. I...I'm sorry." Minho released a breath, his brows lifting in surprise.

"Well," he remarked, unable to resist the small smile tugging at the corners of his mouth. "I have to admit, I didn't think that you had it in you." Thorne laughed, relief rushing over him like a cool wave of water on a hot day, the tightness in his chest dissipating as he felt the frigid air between them thaw.

"I didn't either, but...I mean it. I'm sorry, Min." Minho finally met his eyes, and Thorne understood; it didn't need to be said in words—he was forgiven.

With a light sigh, Minho dropped into the leather armchair opposite Thorne, the tips of his fingers absentmindedly toying with the tear on the right arm of the seat.

"So," he said, gaze rising to meet Thorne's, the smile still playing on his lips.

"*So,*" Thorne repeated. He chewed the inside of his cheek for a long, silent moment, torn between one thought and the other. *Fuck it,* he decided, pushing past the wave of nerves to say, "I told her." Minho's brows shot up to his hairline, his eyes widening as his fingers abruptly stilled. He leaned forward in his seat, clasping his hands cautiously together between his knees.

"You—" Thorne gave a short, jerky nod.

"Everything."

"Just—hold on for a second." Kai was pacing, as she had been for the fifteen minutes since Thorne had managed to convince her to stop screaming bloody murder when she had awoken to find him in her apartment. He leaned against the empty mantlepiece, hands resting loosely in his pockets as he waited patiently for her to calm down. *"You're saying—like you **actually** expect me to believe—that you're the **Grim Reaper?** Like, with the cloak and the scythe and the death—"*

"No scythe," Thorne interrupted, and she paused. *"Not for a while, anyway; no cloak, either."* Kai narrowed her eyes.

"How long is 'a while'?" He shrugged, tilting his head in consideration.

"A couple hundred years, give or take. Probably give a bit, actually—I can't recall the last time I used the thing, to be honest." Kai huffed a short laugh of disbelief, shaking her head.

*"But that—it's not **possible.**"* She shook her head again, and Thorne tilted his own, his brows furrowed. She clarified. *"I mean, Reapers and Fates and those...sorts of things...they aren't **real.**"* He resisted the urge to snort. The Fates were all too real—real pains in his backside.

"Says who?" She looked up at him, eyes narrowing at the challenge in his tone. *"For hundreds of thousands of years, mortals have been telling stories of the Fates, of the Greek deities, of the nine muses, of the 'Grim Reaper.' Why is it so hard to believe that those stories might have actually **come** from somewhere?"*

"Because—" she faltered, blinking rapidly for several seconds before shaking her head again, refusing to give in. She tipped her chin upward, taking a short, determined breath. *"It's not **possible.**"*

*"**Why not?**"* His voice was firm, but soft, gentler than she had yet heard it. He smiled slightly. *"Is it so hard to imagine? To adjust your belief system and make room for the idea that the stories you had chalked down to myth and legend might be true?"* Kai's chest rose sharply as she heaved several deep breaths, looking frozen, and very much as though she might cry.

She dropped suddenly back onto the couch, her face falling into her hands. She shook her head again. It seemed as if it was all she could bring herself to do, unable to form a coherent thought or sentence, utterly overwhelmed by Thorne's revelation. Her hair, dark and thick and probably soft—it looked soft—fell around her hands and face like a veil as she continued to shake her head in disbelief.

When she spoke again, her voice was muffled. "It's not—" she pulled her face away from her hands, mascara smudged beneath her eyes. "It **can't** *be real."*

"Why not?" He asked again. Kai opened her mouth, faltered for a moment, then shut it.

"You—" Minho exhaled sharply, cheeks puffing out as he shook his head once. Thorne couldn't help his slight, albeit sheepish, grin.

"What can I say?" He shrugged, laughing a little as Minho met his eyes. "I'm full of surprises."

"Yeah, you're full of shit," Minho said dryly, though his tone lacked any real bite. He scoffed a laugh and relaxed further into his chair. "Well, how did she take it?" Thorne tilted his head thoughtfully.

"Let's say you're telling the truth." Kai had pulled herself together slightly, hair tucked behind her ears and hands folded neatly in her lap. She licked her chapped lips, her right leg bouncing incessantly. "For like, five seconds, let's say that I believe you. What does it **mean?"**

"I don't follow." Thorne's forehead creased, not fully understanding the question.

"Well, in **theory,** *assuming that I* **do** *believe you, I now know your big secret. Why? What's the point of telling me all this? Why* **now?** *Why...ever, if it's all so hush-hush?"*

"Ah." He took a deep breath, uncrossing his arms and flexing his fingers, cramped slightly where he had been unconsciously holding them in fists around his sleeves, his body tense with stress. He moved forward and took a

seat in the armchair to Kai's left, having not dared move too far from the doorway until this moment. He tilted his body toward her, mimicking her body language and leaning forward slightly.

"Well, you were **supposed** to die." Kai's leg paused briefly in its anxious bouncing, and she leaned away from him slightly, her brown eyes widening a little. Thorne couldn't help but laugh. "I'm not saying that out of malice or to threaten you, it's just a fact: that day at the tracks when we first met, it was your time to go. Nobody knows why—well, the Fates might, I've never thought to ask. If they do, I highly doubt they would feel obligated to share that knowledge if I **did** ask. It's just the way of things; when your time is up, it's up."

"So..." Kai thought for a moment, her thick dark brows knitting together as she struggled to piece together the information she had been given. "If I was supposed to **die**, then...why am I still here?" Thorne winced.

"That's the tricky part," he said reluctantly. "It's because I saved you." Her eyes snapped up to meet his hesitant gaze.

"Why?" It wasn't a demand, just curiosity, almost astonishment. Thorne shrugged a shoulder.

"I don't really have an answer for it myself, to be honest. I don't typically do that—save mortals, I mean. I don't interact with humans very much, not until they're dead, anyway, and even then, it's not usually much more than a routine **you're dead, I'm your personal tour guide to the afterlife** kind of thing. You...are different, somehow." He cringed as he said it, not having any other way to describe it, and she scoffed, rolling her eyes as she used her palm to swipe at a tear that had leaked from the corner of her eye. She looked away, avoiding his gaze.

"Right."

"I mean it." He leaned forward, his eyes and tone earnest, desperate to make her believe him—to make **someone** believe him. "I have no idea why, or **how,** for that matter, but I-I **have** tried. Remember the car that didn't *even bother to stop, and—earlier?" He was loathe to bring up the incident, his gaze briefly focusing on the darkening bruise below her eye, and his nails bit into his palms at the reminder.*

He pressed on. "I was supposed to let you die; I was only there to reap your soul and fix the mistake I had made by saving your life the first time. I was **supposed** *to let you die. But I didn't—I* **couldn't.***"**

"Why not?" This time, it **was** *a demand. "What is so special about* **me?***"*

"What *is* so special about this girl?" There was no judgment in Minho's tone, only a genuine wonderment. He did not seem to doubt Thorne, but it was a fair question, though one that Thorne did not have the answer to.

All he could do was lift his shoulders briefly, helplessly, and shake his head.

"I truly have no idea," he said. "I would give anything to find out, but I wouldn't even know where to start." Minho said nothing—likely, he didn't know what *to* say. He had no solutions, either.

"I wish I knew," he responded at length, staring down at his hands. "But whatever the reason, I couldn't just stand there and watch you die. I've done it before, you know," he said, his stomach turning slightly as fragments of memories flashed across the forefront of his mind. "I can handle a bit of blood. I have seen more death than I can recall." Kai grimaced a little at that, but he would not sugarcoat it for her; he had promised to tell her the truth, and that's what he was going to do. "But you're..."

"Different," Kai finished, her eyes narrowed skeptically.

"I know that it sounds ridiculous," Thorne said, feeling his face flush hotly as he avoided her gaze. "But I just...can't seem to let you die. Not when I know that you can see me. When I can—" He stopped short, teeth catching on his lower lip so hard that he absently wondered if it would bleed.

"When you can...?" Kai prompted gently, patiently. Thorne's heart pounded, the blood rushing through his veins sounding like a violent flood in his ears, and he took a deep breath, willing away the blind panic, lifting his eyes hesitantly to meet hers.

"When I can see **you**." Kai's brows snapped together, confusion clear in her eyes.

"What do you mean?" Thorne expelled the breath that he had been holding, remaining silent for a long moment as he tried to gather his thoughts enough to form a coherent explanation.

"I used to be mortal," he began, and Kai's brows lifted, her lips parting softly in surprise. Thorne's eyes caught the movement, lingering there for only a second before he hastily jerked his gaze back up, pushing quickly forward. "When I became...this," he gestured to himself, "I stopped being able to see humans the way that I'd used to. It's like...staring out of a foggy window: I can see vague shapes and colors, but the sounds are dim, the outlines undefined. I cannot see humans clearly, and I am completely invisible to their eyes; if I am in their path, they can walk right through me, without ever having the slightest inkling that I exist at all.

"It isn't until they die that I can finally see them clearly—well, clearly enough, though their spirits don't look like that of a **living** soul—and they can see me, in turn. You are the first mortal who is living to see me since...well," he lifted the corner of his mouth and shook his head slightly. "It's been a very long time." He paused, expression going serious again. "You are also the first mortal since I was mortal, myself, who **I** have been able to see clearly before they are dead." Kai exhaled a long, slow breath, wiping her palms—damp from where she had been clasping them tightly together during Thorne's revelation—on her jeans. Her right leg was still bouncing. She tilted her head.

"Who was that man with you that day, after you...after that car almost hit me? He seemed awfully surprised that I was able to see **him,** too."

"That," Thorne responded with a rueful smile. "Was Aristides. He is one of the Fates." Kai's eyes went wide.

"He—" She stopped short, falling back in her seat and staring dazedly ahead at the coffee table. Her leg had stopped bouncing. She met his eyes again. "So, what do they think about all this—the Fates? Are they super pissed?" Thorne laughed, and Kai looked a little wistful at the sound, like she was drinking it in.

"Well, they aren't pleased, I can tell you that much for certain. I suppose I can't really blame them—maintaining the balance of Fate is what their entire existence revolves around, after all."

"So they want me dead," Kai surmised, and shook her head. "The **Greek Fates** want me dead." She laughed abruptly, a scoff of disbelief. "I never in a million years thought I would say something like that."

"It isn't—I don't think that they **want** you dead, specifically," Thorne said, finding it difficult to explain. "Not if Ris is to be believed, anyway, and he...he's never lied to me." Regret pooled in his abdomen, and he swallowed the guilt, shoving the shame of how he had treated Aristides to the darkest recesses of his mind. "It's just...their **job.**"

"Like it's **your** job to reap my soul." Thorne nodded, and Kai shook her head, hard, like the concept was too much for her to handle. "So, why **can** I see you? And why can you see me?"

"I haven't the slightest clue," he admitted as he flexed his fingers, and she smiled crookedly.

"For a guy that's been around for hundreds of years—if I believe you, that is, and I'm still not entirely sure that I do," she added quickly, though he could tell from the way she was avoiding his eyes as she said it that she was at least **beginning** to believe it. He stifled a smile as she finished, "You sure don't have many answers, do you?" He laughed, unable to help it, knowing that she was right.

"No, I guess not."

"Hmm..." Minho was thoughtful, his brows drawn low as he leaned forward in his seat, elbows on his knees and thumbs supporting his chin, his index fingers brushing against his mouth as he mused. "Could it be because you touched her?"

"What?" Thorne blinked, startled.

"It would make sense." One of Minho's shoulders lifted briefly. "Presumably, none of us have ever touched a *living* mortal—not skin to skin, anyway, not with intent—so we don't really know the effect that a Reaper's touch could have on a mortal. It would be a simple enough explanation—you touch her, and she gets a glimpse into the world of death."

"That would make sense, I suppose," Thorne twisted his lips, considering it. "But what does that mean for *her*?" Minho shrugged. He couldn't be expected to have *all* of the answers.

She was back to denial.

"This is all just too insane to be **real***,"* *Kai said, rising from the couch to resume her pacing. Mister Sylvester, emerging from the bedroom in search of food and company, seemed to quickly think better of his decision. As the cat retreated into the dark room from whence he had come, Kai tugged on her hair, looking as though she were about to cry; Thorne didn't blame her.*

"I know that this must be incredibly overwhelming," he said gently, and Kai scoffed, nodding as if to indicate that his words were an understatement, but saying nothing. She sniffled. "And I understand if you have trouble believing it. But I wouldn't lie to you, Kai—I know you have no reason to believe it, to believe **me***, but I would not lie to you." She met his eyes, looking unsure. She gnawed at her lower lip, her expression torn, and slowly, she sank back down onto the couch, covering her face with her hands again.*

"I feel like I'm going crazy," she whispered. A tear slipped through her fingers.

Thorne leaned forward, and gently, he wrapped his fingers around her slender wrists, pulling her hands away from her face. She looked up at him, her lower lip trembling as another tear trailed down her cheek.

*"You are not crazy," he said firmly. Kai laughed weakly, but Thorne didn't smile; he held her gaze steadily, waiting. He said it again. "You are **not** crazy." She swallowed, looking terrified as she asked, lower than a whisper,*

"Am I going to die?"

*"No," he said before he could stop himself. He found that he meant it, and he said it again, with more conviction this time. "No, you are not going to die. I promise—whatever it takes, I will **not** let you die. I swear it."*

"Thorne—" Minho sighed deeply and shook his head. "I get it, okay? You miss being mortal—you miss having that sort of *human* connection, and now you've found one, so I *understand* why you want to cling to it no matter the cost. But is it truly worth it—is *she* worth it? A mortal girl whom you have just met who will likely die in a handful of decades anyway? Is she *really* worth invoking the full fury of the Fates?" Thorne took a shaky breath, tears pressing against the backs of his eyes. He stared down at his clasped hands and shrugged helplessly,

"I can see her, Min." His voice broke, and when he looked up, his eyes were damp, and Minho's lips had parted softly in surprise. Thorne laughed weakly. "I had gotten so used to it—the blurred, foggy outlines of the living; the faint, gray souls of the dead...I had almost forgotten what it was like." He swallowed, unable to rid himself of the thick lump that had lodged itself in his throat. "I don't know why all of this is happening, but I can't—I *can't* just let her die. I can't be the one to reap her soul. I can't *do* it, Min."

Minho had never seen him like this—broken and pleading, desperate and brought nearly to his knees. His expression softened, and he sighed, nodding. "Alright," he said quietly. "Then I will help you."

Aristides was stunned, feeling as though he had been struck three times over with a lightning bolt; then he was furious, fists clenching tightly as he took several deep, measured breaths to try and stifle the hot rage coursing through his veins.

"I truly do not know what has come over him—that *stupid* boy." He would strangle Thorne and shake him silly the next time that he saw him, he was sure of it. Knock some sense into his thick skull, that was what he would do; he should have done it far sooner. Perhaps if he had, they would not have gotten to this point. He sighed. "I will...I will speak to him again. I will send for him immediately—perhaps this can yet be fixed."

"I do not think—" Cyrus began, stopping short as a third figure appeared soundlessly by their sides. His face was shadowed by his hood—identical to those that Cyrus and Aristides wore—though his mouth, sewn neatly shut, was fully visible.

I am afraid that this conversation must wait, my brothers, his voice materialized in their heads as clearly as if he had spoken aloud. His eyes, narrow and brown and intensely serious, moved from Aristides to Cyrus. ***We have been summoned.***

S he had never been so completely and utterly *drained.*

Every bone in her weary body ached, and her eyelids felt as though there were heavy weights tugging at her lashes, enticing her into unconsciousness; all she wanted was to curl up in a ball under her blankets and lose herself to sleep. But even after drinking a steaming mug of lavender chamomile tea and bundling herself under her soft, thick comforter, Mister Sylvester curled comfortably at her feet, Kai couldn't seem to silence her racing mind, her thoughts louder than a radio at full volume. She couldn't stop thinking about *him:* Thorne.

*"Whatever it takes, I will **not** let you die. I swear it."*

For a long, silent moment, she had simply stared at him, dumbstruck, shaken to her core by the intense determination burning in his eyes. Another tear slipped down her cheek, and she moved to wipe it away, almost forgetting that he still had a hold on her wrists. Her gaze dropped to his fingers.

They were long and slender, and painfully gentle in the way that they gripped her. A musician's hands, she thought absently, all delicate bones and sharp knuckles; she had always been envious of such graceful, elongated bone structures, her own hands soft and round, with short fingers and nails bitten into unattractive stubs. His plethora of rings glinted in the low light provided by the lamp on the end table, the silver cool against her overheated skin.

She sniffled, her nose cold and damp.

*"I mean it," Thorne said, and she looked up. "You are **not** going to die."*
As his eyes gazed deeply into hers, Kai was once again struck by the odd familiarity of his eyes. She couldn't quite place her finger on where or when, but she had seen those eyes before that day on the tracks—she could feel it,

somewhere deep in her bones, like a movie or TV show that you might have seen as a child, forgotten until you see a prop or hear a phrase that makes you remember it in a wave of sudden nostalgia.

Realizing that he seemed to be waiting for an answer, Kai managed a nod, afraid that if she attempted to speak, her voice would come out embarrassingly shaky and small. Even if she didn't fully believe that he could do as he promised, she had no choice but to trust him; she might die if he failed, but if he did not at least try, it would be a certainty.

Almost reluctantly, he released his gentle hold on her wrists, brushing his palms lightly against his jeans as he rose to his feet.

"It's getting late," he said, seeming suddenly awkward as he stood in the middle of her tiny living room. "I'm sure you have a lot to...process, and to consider, and you're probably tired, so I should—I should go." He gave a single, jerky nod, as though it was himself that he was trying to convince. "Will you—" he paused, worry in his eyes and in the furrow of his brow as he tried again. "Will you be alright?" Kai smiled a little—part of it forced, to try and reassure him, but part of it genuine, prompted by the small flame that ignited in her chest at the feeling of having someone worry over her. It made her feel warm, and comforted, yet at the same time, slightly queasy at the unfamiliarity of having someone who wasn't Avery care about her.

She nodded.

"I'll be fine." He turned to go, and she flew to her feet, lurching slightly forward. "Will I see you again?" He turned back to her, his own lips curving upward.

"Soon," he promised with a nod, his hand rising to turn the knob of her front door. "Get some sleep, sunshine."

*"You, too," she said out of habit, flushing slightly at the nickname, and he laughed softly, shaking his head. It struck her suddenly that perhaps he did not **need** to sleep, and her face burned a little more at the thought.*

"Goodnight, Kai."

Restlessly, Kai flipped over, curling her right arm under her head as she gazed out of her bedroom window, the star-filled night sky just visible through a crack in the curtains. The moon was full tonight, and she forced her eyes shut, trying her best to imagine that it was watching over her as she slept, protecting her.

Kai had always known that death was something that you couldn't control—the accident had taught her that lesson better than any textbook or novel ever could. But knowing that, at this very moment in time, *she* was supposed to be dead...it changed things, somehow; anxiety swam in her stomach like something living, and her skin felt as though every nerve ending was on high alert, every shift in the sheets caused by Mister Sylvester's attempts to get more comfortable causing Kai to clench her teeth at the almost painful sensation. Her head hurt, exhaustion pounding at her temples like the steady beat of a drum.

But those *eyes.*

She didn't know how long it took for sleep to claim her—she didn't even remember it happening. One moment, she was once again replaying her conversation with Thorne in her mind, analyzing his words and dissecting her own responses, and in the next breath, she was dreaming.

Remembering.

It began as it always did—her family, dangling still as statues from the ceiling of the wrecked SUV. Her tears, streaming down her face and dampening the roots of her braided hair as she stretched out her fingers in search of her stuffed rabbit. The reflection, a dark figure crouching by the passenger window, a pale, delicate hand with long, slender fingers adorned with silver rings brushing gently against her mother's face. Kai's own gasp of horror and fright that drew the attention of the figure as a pair of dark brown eyes—nearly black—stared at her in something like bewilderment. They gazed into her very soul, burning, a flicker of surprise, and—

Familiarity.

Kai awoke with a sharp gasp, bolting upright in her bed so quickly that she dimly registered Mister Sylvester's nails scratching against the hardwood as, terrified, he leaped from the bed and scrambled to safety beneath it.

Kai's chest heaved as she fought to catch her breath, her throat burning and her eyes as wide as the full moon outside her window, tears pressing painfully against them and forcing their way to the surface. She was cold, and her hands were trembling, she noticed, then realized that it wasn't just her hands, but her whole body, knees bumping sporadically together beneath the covers. She felt light-headed and weak, nausea rolling in her stomach and beads of sweat dotting her nose and her forehead, her shirt sticking to her back and arms. There was a damp imprint on the pillow where her head had been.

Normally, she would be disgusted, moving immediately to rip the sheets off of the mattress before jumping into the shower to scrub herself clean of the perspiration. Right now, though, her thoughts were on the dream—on the *memory*.

*Those eyes...*those familiar eyes.

She shook her head in denial, clamping a hand over her mouth to stifle a sob. It couldn't be true—it *couldn't*. It would be far too cruel a joke for life to play.

But those eyes—*his* eyes, the ones that, only a few hours ago, had looked into her own and promised her that she was not going to die. The eyes that had reassured her, had gazed at her in comfort and concern. The eyes that had haunted her dreams for the past thirteen years, that had been right in front of her all along.

The eyes that had stolen the lives of her family.

Chapter Ten

AN UNWELCOME SURPRISE

KAI

It had been two days.

Two days since she had learned the truth about the invisible world that she had always thought was the stuff of myth.

Two days since Thorne had promised her that he would do everything in his power to save her life.

Two days since she had been startled awake with the realization of why his eyes were so familiar, as though she had seen them before, though the idea had seemed impossible.

It had been two days, and Kai had spent them isolated in her apartment, curled under her covers and barely moving from her bed save to feed and water Mister Sylvester. She wished that she could stay like this forever, alone and miserable and hating the world.

But alas, she had a shift at the store today and rent due in two weeks, so dragging herself out of bed with a long, whining groan of reluctance, she padded heavily into the bathroom, narrowing her eyes at the mirror hanging over the sink. The reflection that stared back at her was, to put it simply, *gross*—her hair was greasy and tangled, the bags beneath her eyes dark and pronounced, and the t-shirt that she was wearing had a stain on it from where she had spilled tea on herself two nights ago. Or maybe it was sauce from the chicken katsu that she had pulled from her freezer yesterday, desperate for a comfort food that wasn't mac and cheese, which she had devastatingly run out of. Either way, she looked...

Like her life had fallen completely and utterly apart.

Perhaps it had, she mused as she stepped out of a scalding shower, running a brush through her wet curls. She thought her life had sucked before, but finding out that your new ally—the only person who stood a chance at saving your life, which was an odd sentence in and of itself—had reaped the souls of your entire family on the worst night of your life...*that* took the cake. This, Kai decided, was *officially* rock-freaking-bottom.

She dressed comfortably in a pair of faded jeans and her mom's oversized college pullover, an old favorite—it was navy blue, with the faded emblem of a bear on the front, the symbol of the university where her parents had met. Kai pulled the collar up over her nose and took a deep breath, letting her eyes flutter shut. It didn't smell like her mom anymore, she knew, but the act itself was still somewhat comforting; for months after the accident, she had refused to wash the thing, determined to cling to the remnants of her mother's fruit-and-floral scent.

It wasn't until Kai realized that it had grown to smell more like dinosaur chicken nuggets and Top Ramen that she had finally allowed her Aunt Camila, Kai's only living relative and the elder sister of Kai's father, to wash it. Kai had cried when Camila had pulled the shirt from the dryer and returned it to her, feeling as though her mother had died all over again when, no matter how hard she tried, she found that she could no longer smell her mother's perfume.

Kai shifted the pullover back into place with a light sigh, pulling on a pair of mismatched socks before heading to the kitchen to see if she could find something to eat for breakfast. The fridge was empty aside from a half-gallon of milk and a large container of expired yogurt, and she had run out of bread yesterday.

Oatmeal it is, then.

She discovered halfway through making the oatmeal that she had already run out of bowls, and as the thought of having to clean the small mountain of dishes that had once again accumulated in the sink pitted her stomach with dread, she ate her breakfast straight from the pot with a slightly crooked fork, as she was also out of clean spoons.

As she ate, leaning comfortably against the still-warm stove, she caught sight of the couch, and she felt a sudden cold, the oatmeal turning to lead in her stomach as her fingers twitched involuntarily. Two nights ago she had sat on that very couch as Thorne told her all of his secrets—all but the one that mattered most, at least to Kai.

She wondered if he remembered her family at all—if he remembered *her*. Probably not; after all, he had likely reaped millions of souls by now, stolen hundreds of lives, just as he had stolen the lives of Kai's family.

Shaking her head abruptly to banish the thoughts from her mind, not wanting to think about it a minute longer, Kai's eyes widened as she realized the time.

"*Shit,*" she hissed, shoveling the last lukewarm bite of oatmeal into her mouth and dropping the pot back onto the stove, knowing that it would be a bitch-and-a-half to clean later, but running too behind to care. She dashed into the bedroom for her bag and a pair of sneakers, hopping back into the living room on one foot as she struggled to pull them on, nearly tripping over Mister Sylvester in the process.

"Sorry!" she called to the offended kitty, who glared at her out of the corner of his narrowed yellow eyes. Snatching her keys from the coffee table, Kai yanked open the door, nearly slamming right into a broad, solid chest.

She stopped short, unable to breathe as her shocked gaze met Thorne's, who stood over her with one brow lifted upward in faintly surprised amusement. She could feel her heart threatening to beat out of her chest, could hear every loud, panicked beat as electricity held her spine in a painful grip. She felt frozen, cold, unable to move, to even lift a finger to steady herself against the door.

It had been two days.

"What are you doing here?" She blurted, wishing desperately to take a step back, to not have to breathe in his scent—pine, worn leather, and something else that she couldn't quite place—as she looked up at him. Her knees were locked, refusing to budge, so she clenched her jaw and her fists, trying to act like that didn't both anger and despair her all at once, like she wasn't staring the thief of her family's souls in the face as though nothing was wrong.

Thorne seemed to notice that there was something off about her, and his eyes narrowed slightly, brows pushing together in confusion as he took in her frozen expression and rigid posture, noting the way that her nails were biting white crescents into her palms. He shifted on his feet as he glanced behind her, likely wondering why they were standing in the doorway of her apartment like this.

"I, uh," his tongue poked out to wet his lips as he forced his gaze back to hers. "I just wanted to check in. After the other night and everything, I just...wanted to make sure that you were okay." His voice had dropped, and Kai tried to ignore the way her stomach tugged at the softness in his tone. *He took your family,* she reminded herself. *He's not your friend, he is a fox—a wolf in sheep's clothing. A Reaper of souls, disguised as an innocent boy.*

"I'm fine," she said in a clipped tone, pretending not to notice the bewilderment—the hurt—forming in his eyes. She shifted her bag higher on her shoulder, feigning nonchalance. She raised her brows. "Was that all?"

"Did—" he swallowed, and her eyes inadvertently followed the motion of his Adam's apple beneath the golden skin of his throat, delicate collar bones peeking out beneath the thin material of his black knit sweater. "Is something wrong?" She jerked her gaze sharply back up to his, a fire igniting in her chest at the question, fists curling tighter at his utter obliviousness of her inner turmoil, of the mental hell that she had been trapped in for the past two days.

She forced a thin smile and shook her head. "Why would anything be wrong?" He faltered and shifted on his feet again, clearly uncomfortable. *Good,* Kai thought viciously. Her conscience twinged, but she quickly smothered the feeling. Thorne's lips parted briefly, then clamped shut, obviously at a loss for something to say.

Kai sighed impatiently. "Look, I have to go—I'm late for work." She waited a moment, raising her brows expectantly. "*Excuse* me." Hesitantly, Thorne stepped aside, and she pointedly ignored him as she pulled the door shut and locked it.

"Did—are you—?" he paused as she turned slowly, reluctantly, to face him. Something shuttered in his eyes, and he sighed, shaking his head. "Never mind. I'll...see you later?" He posed it as a question, and she gritted her teeth.

"Maybe," she responded noncommittally as she brushed past him, practically running down the dimly lit flight of stairs and out the front door.

Leaning against the cool brick wall of the building, Kai closed her eyes and took several long, deep breaths of fresh air, the gentle breeze washing over her like water to a parched tongue, soothing her warm, agitated skin and brushing the stray hairs away from her heated face. She felt as though she had been suffocating for these past moments with Thorne, her lungs starved for oxygen, her fingers trembling almost imperceptibly at the effort of trying to hold herself together, to not scream at him and slam her fists against his chest and ask *why*.

There wouldn't be a point.

Because no reason that he could give could even come close to explaining why she'd had to grow up without her family.

Feeling drained, and wanting nothing more than to go right back up to her apartment and crawl back into bed, Kai pushed herself away from the wall, squared her shoulders, and began to walk, determined to banish any thoughts of Thorne far from her mind.

Chapter Eleven

THE KEEPER

I t was painfully bright.

That was the first thing that Aristides noticed when they entered the foyer of the palace. The second was that it was incredibly *white*, and so large that, if he were to speak in an even slightly elevated tone, his words would echo back to him.

Oil paintings in ornate gold frames lined the walls of the endless hallways, and through the gaps of the gigantic, rounded pillars, Aristides caught glimpses of other equally large, equally white rooms as they passed.

The palace was vast, and the hallways that they were currently being led through by their silent, stoic guide seemingly endless; already they had been walking close to ten minutes, and their guide wasn't showing any signs of stopping.

"It would behoove you to not have such a sullen expression," Cyrus said lowly, turning his head slightly so that Aristides, who was walking several paces behind him, could just hear him.

"This place hurts my eyes," Aristides responded sourly, lips pressed together in an expression of mild distaste. His eyes narrowed at the back of their guide, Alastair, who either couldn't hear them or was pretending not to. He had not said a word upon their arrival, merely giving them a cursory once-over before turning and showing them the way.

Aristides spoke again, this time at a considerably louder volume. "I say," he called, ignoring the deadly look of warning that Cyrus shot him. "Are we nearly there?" There was no response, and Aristides clicked his tongue in irritation.

"Aristides, that is enough," Cyrus murmured, and though his tone was cool, features smoothed into an unbothered expression, his eyes—all three of them—were unamused. Aristides rolled his own.

"He probably can't even hear us—*can you hear us?*"

Aristides! Aristides winced as Linus' voice reverberated in his head like a shout, and he cut his eyes narrowly at the mute Fate by his side.

"*What?*" Aristides hissed, and ahead of them, Cyrus' shoulders tensed.

"That is *enough*," he said in a tone that left no room for argument. Aristides fell silent, and they followed Alastair down several more high-ceilinged corridors before coming to a halt at last in front of a large, arched entryway. There did not seem to be any doors here, Aristides noted, but this observation was quickly forgotten as they stepped through the arch, and a painful light from above nearly blinded him.

And here I had thought that it could not get any brighter, he thought, frowning in annoyance.

"I apologize for the luminosity here," said a light, musical tone to their left. Squinting and trying to ignore the searing pain in his retinas, Aristides searched for the source. "Like myself, the sun here is reborn every couple of millennia; I am sure that, given the dim world that you hail from, it must be quite painful."

"Only like needles stabbing into my eyes," Aristides muttered darkly, and Linus stepped on his toes. Cyrus pretended not to notice.

"My lady," Cyrus inclined his head in respect. "Though the circumstances are certainly regrettable, it is a true pleasure to see you again." As Aristides' eyes began adjusting to the light, he was finally able to get a good look at their surroundings.

They were in a garden, lush and magnificent and bursting with color, nearly overflowing with bushes and vines and trees that stood as tall as the sky, with flowers of every variety bursting freshly into bloom. The color was a startling contrast to the stark hallways that they had just traversed, but Aristides wasn't complaining.

In the center of the garden, just ahead, stood a grand stone fountain with clear, glistening water bubbling out of the top and flowing smoothly over the edges, spilling downward into a round pond filled with large, colorful fish of various patterns and sizes.

Beside the fountain stood the source of the musical voice: a woman with dark brown skin that gleamed in the sunlight, smiling graciously as she tipped her head ever so slightly in acknowledgment of Cyrus' statement. A delicate crown of glittering silver and gold stars hovered atop her head, where hair as black as midnight fell to her waist in perfect, shining waves; she wore a white dress that left her arms bare, and stacks of thin, golden bracelets that chimed musically whenever she moved lined her slender wrists. Physically, she had changed much since Aristides had last seen her.

Except for her eyes.

Her eyes were white. Not a bright, stark white like her dress, but rather a pale, frosted white, as though made of ice so thick that you could no longer decipher whether her eyes had once had color.

Aristides shivered. In no small part because, given that her eyes had neither iris nor pupil, one could barely tell whether or not she was looking directly at you, but also because he knew that those eyes—the eyes of the Keeper, for that was her title—could see *everything*. Or nearly so; like Cyrus, her gaze could not penetrate the In-Between, as it was a realm of existence between existences, and like Cyrus, she also could not see into the Underworld. *Unlike* Cyrus, however, she did not need a wall of mirrors to pinpoint exactly what anyone in the universe was doing at any given time; also unlike Cyrus, she could see into Olympus and other such places that the deities and their ilk called home.

Linus nudged him in the ribs with a bony elbow, and Aristides realized that he had become distracted. He shook his head and blinked rapidly to clear his mind as he tuned back into the conversation at hand.

"—sure that you are aware of what is happening," Cyrus was saying. "But we had hoped to handle it ourselves. Aristides has an established relationship with the boy, and has been trying—in vain, I am afraid, though by no fault of his own—to make him see sense."

"Perhaps it *is* time that I get involved, then," mused the Keeper, her plump lips pursed thoughtfully, one hand resting lightly on the stone ledge of the fountain as her long, pointed nails tapped a slow rhythm on its surface. Aristides cast a subtle glance toward Cyrus, who was maintaining steady eye contact with the Keeper, his expression as stoic as ever. His hand flexed almost imperceptibly by his side, signaling Aristides to remain silent.

"I do not believe that the need has quite arisen for that, my lady." Ever the diplomat, Cyrus' tone was cool and even as he attempted to reassure her. "We have one approach that we have yet to try, and we believe—*I* believe—that it will have the desired effect." The Keeper was silent as she regarded Cyrus thoughtfully, her fingertips continuing that slow, rhythmic tapping that was beginning to both grate on Aristides' nerves and attempting to lull him into a deep slumber. Cyrus did not flinch.

"Very well," she agreed with a slow nod. "However," she said, something deadly and serious in her tone, chilling Aristides to his core. "Know that should you fail, I will have no choice but to step in; I have no doubt that the boy remembers how unpleasant I can make things for *everyone* involved, should he fail to comply." Aristides' fingers twitched as he tried to refrain from curling his hands into fists. The Keeper smiled. "This is not a threat, my dear boys, but merely a warning. Fate itself hangs in the balance, and we can afford no further mistakes."

"I understand. Thank you, my lady." Cyrus bowed his head low, and after another sharp nudge from Linus, who was already doing the same, Aristides grudgingly mimicked the gesture.

"That will be all then, gentlemen; hopefully we need not meet again for some time." She turned to pick up a pair of golden shears that Aristides had not noticed before, and began to prune a twilight-colored rosebush, signaling in no uncertain terms that they were no longer welcome here.

"Cyrus—" Aristides began as they reentered the hallway of the palace, where their guide was waiting to escort them back to the entrance. Cyrus shook his head sharply.

"We will discuss this upon our return," he said, and Aristides fell silent. Cyrus appeared to be deep in thought—indeed, they all were. Even Linus seemed more somber than usual, and Aristides' stomach kept turning, a feeling of profound unease settling over the whole party, aside from Alastair, who seemed not to notice. But Aristides did not nettle at their guide on the return journey to the palace entrance, too focused on the Keeper's warning. He simply *had* to make Thorne see sense. If he did not...

He shook his head, banishing the thought. He *would* make Thorne see sense. He had to—for all of their sakes.

Chapter Twelve

ACCUSATIONS AND THE LAST OPTION

Kai's shoulders dropped as she pushed open the door to her apartment building, every cell of her body aching, longing to take a hot bath and drink a steaming cup of tea before burrowing beneath her covers and losing herself to sleep.

It had been a long day of stocking shelves and cleaning, and the break room of Tanner's Grocery was now shining and spotless. Kai hadn't even had Avery to make it fun, as the cheerful blonde had been busy with a full day of classes, leaving Kai with the new kid: a lanky, freckled redhead with a chatterbox mouth and a tendency to drop things. He was kind of adorable—only a sophomore in high school, new to the joys of adulthood and employment. He had been polite, at least, and eager to help; and the talking wasn't *so* bad, Kai admitted with a mental grumble, considering that she hadn't had to do much of it herself.

As she ascended the stairs, she nearly groaned aloud at the sight of Thorne sitting on the floor outside of her apartment.

"What are you doing here?" She crossed her arms as she stopped in front of him, something within her crying out at the delay, wanting nothing more than to brush past him and get on with her preparations for bed. He looked up at her, and she fought the guilt stirring in her chest.

"

He looked like a lost puppy, his brown eyes gazing up at her imploringly, strands of messy black hair slipping from its tie and falling around his face, his bitten lips parting softly, though no words came out.

Kai shook her head a little, feeling disgusted with herself. He had stolen her family, and here she was, feeling sorry for him and looking at his lips. Her jaw tightened, her resolve hardening as she waited for his answer.

"I..." He licked his lips, drawing her attention momentarily back to them, and she wanted to smack him over the head with her bag for it. "You didn't seem like you were entirely okay this morning, and I just wanted to check in and make sure that everything was alright—that *we* are alright." His cheeks flushed, and he seemed awkward, almost embarrassed, his eyes barely able to hold contact with hers for more than half a second. Kai's skin prickled, her spine stiffening as she shifted on her sore feet. She wanted to scream at him, *there is no **we**.* Who did he think he was, staring up at her so innocently, while her family was dead and she was alone?

So alone.

"We're fine," she said shortly, looking away from him. She heard him rise from the floor, felt his body heat as he stepped closer.

"Kai..." he paused. She swallowed. "I know that all of this is probably a lot to take in, but I *swear*, I am going to do whatever it takes to save you. And after that, if—if you never want to see me again...I'll understand." He looked as if the words physically pained him to say. Kai scoffed lightly, shaking her head.

"If only," she murmured, and in the corner of her vision, saw his brows push together in confusion.

"What?" She clenched her fists so tightly that her hands trembled, bitten nails digging into her palms. Thorne touched a hand lightly to her elbow, and she jerked away sharply, heart slamming against the confines of her chest with the electric shock of his touch.

"*Don't.*"

"Kai, what's wrong?" She detested the look of concern on his face, the way that he reached back out for her before stopping short, as if thinking better of it. "What did I do?"

"As if you don't know." The words were out before she could stop them.

"I don't. I *promise* you that I don't. If you would just tell me, maybe I can—"

"What, bring them back?" Kai turned on him, eyes blazing and cheeks red hot, her body feeling overheated and on edge, the narrow hallway and her proximity to Thorne suddenly stifling. "*You can't. They're dead.* **You** *took them, and I am here, alone.* **You did that.**" Thorne took a step back, his brown eyes wide and confused.

"What—*who...?*"

"My *family,* you clueless asshole!" Kai's chest heaved, her eyes stinging with tears, the edges of her vision beginning to blur. When Thorne was silent, still standing there with that bewildered look on his face, Kai ground her teeth together and explained. "A car accident, about thirteen years ago. A family of five. Two parents, and a brother, and a sister, and in the backseat—all alone—a little girl, terrified out of her mind. Anything clicking yet?" She waited for a beat, then laughed, a single tear spilling from her eye and trailing down her cheek. She shook her head, not sure how she ended up here—in this situation, in this building, in this *life.*

Thorne looked torn, helpless, the pain written across his face an echo of her own.

"I'm sorry, I don't—"

"*Remember?*" She finished bitingly. Her lower lip trembled as her nostrils flared, hating this, hating *him,* hating that she was completely falling apart in the middle of the hallway where anyone could see. Not that they would— there was only one other occupied apartment on this floor, and the occupants were both deaf, so there would be no nosy neighbors stepping out to see what was going on outside their door.

"I realize it must be hard for you, considering how many lives you must have stolen by now, but *I* remember. Every night in my dreams, every time I *blink,* it's *your* eyes that I see. *Because you took them!*" She practically screamed it, slamming her palms against his chest. He stumbled back a step, swallowing hard as he stared down at her, seemingly at a loss.

"Kai—"

"*Don't* say my name! **Murderer!**" Thorne's eyes flew wide, and he backed away so quickly that he slammed into the wall, his expression frozen in shock. A sob ripped violently from Kai's throat, one hand flying to cover her mouth as if the words had caught her by surprise, and she surged forward, trembling fingers struggling to insert the key into her door. She had to—she couldn't be out here anymore, with *him,* with the memories that were threatening to drown her.

"Kai, please, *wait*—"

"Just leave me alone!" At last, she got the key into the lock, turning it quickly and slipping through the door, slamming it shut before he could say another word. She turned the locks, and her knees finally gave out as she slid to the floor, clamping both hands over her mouth so that, if he was still out there, he couldn't hear her sobs.

On the other side of the door, Thorne's hand shot out for the handle, then stopped short, fingers curling into a fist that he laid softly against the wood. His head bowed against the door as his eyes fluttered shut in defeat, stomach twisting painfully as he heard Kai's muffled sobs from the other side. Every fiber of his being wished for nothing more than to burst through that door and sweep her into his arms, whispering words of comfort.

Not that she would let him.

He raised his hand hesitantly to knock, then stopped again, feeling an insistent tug from somewhere deep within his chest. His jaw clenched. Of all the times to summon him, it *had* to be now.

With a heavy sigh, he stepped back from the door and let himself disappear.

"I'll threaten him," Aristides suggested the moment that they reappeared in Cyrus' room of mirrors.

And how do you suggest threatening someone who is already cursed? Linus' voice questioned in his head.

"I'll tear out his spine." Linus tilted his head, then narrowed his eyes.

I highly doubt the effectiveness of that tactic. Though his words were transmitted mentally, he still somehow managed to make them sound sarcastic and dry.

"I will curse his friends, then; I know for a *fact* that he cares for them."

They are already dead, and Reapers, at that; how much more can you really curse them?

"I don't see *you* offering any grand ideas!" Aristides snapped, and Linus fell silent. With a deep sigh, Aristides pushed back his hood, reaching up and freeing his hair from its tie and letting it fall loosely over his shoulders. He ran a hand through the silken strands. "I will speak with him again, try to make him see reason. Surely he will, now that *she* is involved...yes," he nodded firmly, his eyes distant. "Yes, that is all I *can* do, I suppose."

"No." Cyrus turned away from his mirrors to face his brothers, and Aristides' brows rose in surprise. "You have tried several times already, and you have failed. I am not blaming you, Aristides," he said, holding up a hand as Aristides opened his mouth to defend himself. "I know that you did your best. But the fact remains that your tactics were ineffective. It is time that we tried another approach." Aristides narrowed his eyes warily.

"Another approach?"

"Yes," Cyrus mused, looking thoughtful. "It occurs to me that *I* have yet to speak to the boy—perhaps that is what is needed to make him do what is necessary."

"All due respect, Cy," Aristides began with a sidelong glance at Linus, who seemed, as always, entirely unsurprised. *Future-seeing bastard.* "But what makes you think that he will listen to *you,* of all people? He hasn't even *seen* you since we—"

"Cursed him?" Cyrus finished lightly, arching a silver eyebrow. "Perhaps that is exactly *why* this approach may be effective. Nevertheless, it is as you said: it is all that we *can* do. We have exhausted every other peaceful option. In the event that it does *not* work..." There was no need for him to finish his sentence; they all knew what was at stake.

"Very well," Aristides sighed. "I shall summon him, then. He is more likely to show up if he believes that he will be meeting with me—no offense."

"None at all taken," Cyrus smiled easily, all three of his eyes blinking slowly in unison. "Be sure that he knows to come immediately—there is not a moment to waste."

"Of course," Aristides bowed his head briefly, then turned to leave the room. Linus lingered, hands clasped behind his back, and though his back was turned, Cyrus felt the weight of his brother's gaze.

"What is it, Linus?" There was a slight edge to his tone, as if daring Linus to challenge him. Linus shrugged.

I hope that you know what you are doing, was all that he said, before noiselessly slipping from the room.

"And I, as well," Cyrus murmured.

Chapter Thirteen
A CHALLENGE

THORNE

Once again, Thorne found himself waiting for Aristides in the In-Between. As was his habit, the Fate was running fashionably late, and after the events of the evening, Thorne was simply not in the mood. He felt jittery and on edge, like he wanted to tear his skin off or scream into the abyss until he went hoarse or...punch something. Aristides' face, if he did not arrive soon.

"*Honestly,*" he muttered through clenched teeth as he kicked a stray pebble with the toe of his boot, watching as it rolled one, two, three times before coming to a stop. "Would it kill the guy to be on time for *once*?"

"I apologize for my tardiness," came a voice that was unmistakably *not* Aristides' from behind. Startled, Thorne spun on his heel to face the newcomer. At the sight of the person in front of him, his heartbeat stuttered, then resumed with a vengeance, threatening to beat right out of the confines of his chest. Without quite meaning to, Thorne clenched his fists. "Please do not blame Aristides—he was merely the messenger for this meeting."

"Cyrus," Thorne ground out, his boot starting to tap against the ground of its own accord, an action that did not go unnoticed by Cyrus. His three eyes made swift note of the movement, then swept back up to meet Thorne's gaze. "To what do I owe the pleasure?" The words felt like acid on his tongue, and he choked down the wave of nausea that roiled in his stomach at seeing the Fate.

Cyrus summoned a brown, high-backed leather armchair and took a seat, leaning back with a regal air and crossing one long leg over the other, hands resting lightly on the arms of the chair. He observed Thorne silently for a moment, his trio of eyes making the hairs on the back of Thorne's neck stand on end.

At last, he spoke.

"You are a clever boy, Thorne; have you not the slightest notion of why you have been summoned here?" Thorne rolled his jaw and met Cyrus' gaze unflinchingly, his eyes hard and cold.

"I can guess." Cyrus waited, unblinking. "You want me to reap Kai's soul, am I right?" Shoving his shoulders back, his expression shifted, one brow arching upward as an arrogant smirk played on his lips. He shook his head once, his eyes narrowing slightly. "That's not happening."

"Come now, Thorne." Cyrus' voice was low and soothing, emanating like a hum from his broad chest. Cold revulsion rolled over Thorne's body, centuries of festered bitterness and hatred urging every fiber of his being to launch himself at Cyrus. He resisted, keeping his feet firmly planted; he could feel blood leaking where his nails were biting into his palms. "Surely one little mortal is not worth all of this fuss. Surely she is not worth a *war*."

"Wars have been waged for less."

"What you say is true," Cyrus admitted, a subtle glimmer of calculation lighting in his eyes. "I must admit, I am rather curious to know what the drive is behind this little rebellion—why you are prepared to risk *everything* to keep a complete stranger, an inconsequential mortal who would likely die in another sixty-odd years anyway, alive." Thorne didn't have an answer, and he had a feeling that Cyrus knew it. *Bastard.* He threw all of his focus into staying still, into not letting his body betray how agitated he was becoming, how much Cyrus was getting to him. He would refuse him, at least, this one small satisfaction.

"Maybe I'm just bored." Cyrus clicked his tongue at that, the corners of his mouth turning upward slightly as he shook his head, a knowing expression in his eyes. Thorne tilted his chin upward, his lips pressing into a thin line of stubborn refusal to say anything further, and Cyrus sighed lightly in disappointment.

"Very well, then—keep your reasons to yourself. But you cannot *truly* believe that all of this—waging war against Fate itself—is worth it to save a single mortal. She cannot possibly be worth losing everything that you care for."

"I have nothing else to lose," Thorne said with a note of bitterness. "And she is—worth it. She is worth it to me."

"I see," Cyrus mused, his eyes narrowing thoughtfully at Thorne, studying him, searching his eyes and expression intently as if trying to detect the barest hint of deceit, of false bravado, of doubt. The Fate's expression sharpened suddenly as though he had found something that displeased him, and he uncrossed his legs, leaning slightly forward as his brows pushed together. "And you are prepared to risk everything—every*one*—that you know, for a mortal that you have just met?" Thorne's jaw clenched, and Cyrus pressed on. "I urge you to reconsider; I know that you must believe that things cannot possibly become worse for you—"

"*They can't,*" Thorne ground out through clenched teeth. Cyrus opened his mouth to continue, and fire burned in Thorne's eyes as the words began to burst forth. "You don't know what it's like being...*this.* You have always been what you are, but I *wasn't.* I wasn't *born* like this!" His voice cracked, the hopeless sound echoing throughout the endless space, and he blinked away the dampness that had arisen in his eyes. "*You made me into this,*" he snarled, his tone venomous and laced with hate.

Cyrus was quiet for a moment.

"But I *assure* you," he continued gently, as though the interruption had never happened. "They *can.* Perhaps not for you, but surely for those *around* you." Thorne looked away, guilt making an uncomfortable home in the cracked crevices of his chest.

Cyrus rose from his seat and approached slowly, his expression soft, his voice quiet, though not quite gentle, when he spoke again. "It may be true, Thorne, that you did not *choose* this path for yourself, but it is the one that was laid out for you, and the one whose rules you *must* adhere to. This bout of...spite, or boredom, or whatever you would like to call it, must *end.* And it *will* end, be it peacefully, or in heartbreak and destruction."

"You're wasting your breath, Cyrus," Thorne scoffed, and turned to leave.

"She knows, Thorne." Cyrus' voice was as low and even as ever, but the words carried. Thorne froze. Slowly, he turned back to face the Fate, his expression guarded.

"'She' as in...*she?*" Cyrus nodded, and Thorne fell silent, his heart beginning to pound again, sweat dampening his palms as he felt the sudden urge to empty the nonexistent contents of his stomach into the dust.

He had never met the Keeper, as the last time that she'd had a reason to interact with the mortal world, the Fates had stepped in to carry out the task for her. He knew very little about her, but he knew enough for the vaguest mention of her to make every cell of his body instinctively want to run and hide.

Pushing past the lump in his throat, Thorne walked slowly back to where Cyrus was still standing. "What does this mean?" Cyrus expelled a short, sharp breath, and shook his head.

"I cannot say for certain," he admitted, catching Thorne by surprise. The Fates seemed to know everything, *always.* "But no good can come of it. The Keeper and the mortal world are not meant to interact, and she knows it, otherwise she likely would have intervened sooner. *Her* duty is to observe from afar, to keep order amongst the deities; if she were to step foot on the mortal plane, I cannot imagine that it would not result in disaster." The gravity of his words weighed on Thorne like the heavens on the back of Atlas, and he nearly staggered back.

When he spoke again, his voice was quiet and small, betraying the tears still pressing heavily against his eyes.

"She doesn't deserve to *die,* Cyrus."

"Many do not," Cyrus said solemnly. "But if Fate wills it, so it must be done." The flame that had dimmed to a faint flicker inside of Thorne roared back to life at that, burning a fire so hot in his chest that he would not have been surprised to remove his shirt and find the very skin melting off of his bones.

"*Fuck* Fate," he said lowly, his hardened gaze rising to meet Cyrus' surprised trio of eyes. "And that goes double for the Keeper. If she wants Kai dead, then she can come and tell me so herself." He turned to leave, not turning back even as Cyrus called out his name.

"*You cannot do this!*"

At that, Thorne paused, glancing over his shoulder to see the Fate standing where he had left him, his expression angry and...was that the faintest glimmer of fear? Thorne grinned.

"Watch me."

Kai wasn't sure how long she stayed there like that, curled in a messy, wet-faced heap on the floor, sobs wracking her body in a manner that left her gasping for breath, her lungs and ribs aching for respite. At some point she must have fallen asleep, because when she forced her swollen eyes open again, the apartment was dark.

It was a knock that had awoken her, harsh and loud and sudden, and as memories of the day's events flowed back into the forefront of her mind, Kai groaned audibly, pushing herself slowly to her feet with a pained wince. Falling asleep on the floor had been a terrible idea.

"I thought I told you to *go away,*" she said, her voice coming out hoarse and thick with sleep as, without pausing to glance through the peephole, she opened the door.

It wasn't Thorne.

Chapter Fourteen
IRON AND MACE

KAI

She didn't get the chance to scream as the masked man surged forward into her apartment, slamming the door swiftly shut behind himself as Kai stumbled back, her mind, dazed and clouded from sleep, reeling at the sudden intrusion. She tripped over her bag and fell to the floor, her head barely missing the corner of the coffee table as she landed painfully on her left wrist, using the other hand to drag herself further back toward the couch as the intruder approached, his boots landing heavily on the scuffed hardwood.

"Please." Kai's voice was low and shaky, and utterly pathetic to her own ears. She should be screaming herself hoarse for help right now, but she found that she could barely urge her voice louder than a whisper. Her limbs locked, her heart racing as fear washed over her in a cold flood, scrambling the parts of her brain that would allow her to make logical or strategic decisions, anything that wasn't merely pleading helplessly for her life. "Please," she said again, her eyes wide as her back hit the armchair, preventing her from backing away farther as the man continued his approach. "I have some—some money in my wallet, i-it's in my bag, *please—*"

"*Shut up,*" the man growled, dark eyes glaring hatefully from the mask that obscured the rest of his features. He drew a large knife from a sheath

101

on his belt, and Kai's heart stuttered, her stomach clenching. This was it; it had been two days since Thorne's promise, and she was going to die.

Maybe it's better this way, she thought briefly, the thought flickering unprompted into her mind. She could hear her mother's scolding tone in her head. *Kailani Sofia Sanchez, our family does not give up when things seem difficult. We fight, and we persevere. Do you understand?* It was about some argument that Kai was having with her older brother, Makani, during which he had said something about how he would never, ever, not in a *bajillion years,* forgive her. For what, she couldn't remember now, but back then, she had apologized countless times for whatever offense had been committed, before exasperatedly deciding that she was going to give up. *"If he never talks to me again, I won't care,"* she had declared with a toss of her dark pigtails.

It was a different situation entirely than this, but Kai was sure that if her mother were here now, the general sentiment would still stand.

Her eyes snapped open as the man tightened his grip on the knife, and Kai brought her legs to her chest and kicked as hard as she could in his general direction. With a surprised grunt of pain, the man stumbled back, the knife clattering to the ground and skidding across the floor. Kai wasted no time, lunging forward with hands outstretched for her keys, lying by the door where she had dropped them earlier.

She fumbled with the cap of her keychain mace as she heard him approaching, curses spilling profusely from his lips, and turning quickly back around, she pressed down.

There was a brief pause as the man flinched, and Kai's stomach sank, her limbs going cold with terror as the mace that she'd never had cause to use failed her. *No,* she thought in horror, her eyes rising slowly to meet the cold, vicious gaze of the man standing over her, who seemed to be belatedly realizing what had happened.

"You little bitch," he hissed, and attacked. A brief shriek of terror escaped Kai's throat as she was thrown brutally across the floor by her hair. He was on top of her before she could make any attempt at escape, his large hands enclosing her throat and squeezing tightly, cutting off her airway as the heavy weight of his body crushed her beneath him. Her hands clawed in vain at his wrists, bits of his skin finding their way under her nails, to no avail; unable to shake off his strong, determined grip, her fingers desperately searched the floor for what she knew must be nearby.

Her vision began to spot, thoughts growing hazy as she began to feel lightheaded, and her throat ached, her chest heaving helplessly as she fought for the smallest gasp of air, her lungs burning. She could feel death, at last, begin to close in, cold fingers brushing at her skin in eager preparation for her dying exhale.

Kai's heart soared as her fingers closed weakly around the handle of the knife, and grasping it firmly, she brought it around in a swift, hard arc, knowing it had found its mark in the man's thigh when she felt it sink into the soft flesh, a scream of agony immediately following as she twisted the knife viciously before yanking it out and throwing it as far as she could manage. She barely heard it skitter across the floor and under the couch over the man's howls of pain. His hands finally released their hold on Kai's throat, and she gasped sharply as her lungs welcomed the flood of fresh oxygen.

Still dizzy, Kai barely had the presence of mind to take advantage of her attacker's weakened state and push him off of her as he clutched at his wound, which Kai faintly registered was bleeding profusely through his fingers and onto the floor. She thought she could feel some of the sticky substance on her own hands, but she didn't stop to check as she crawled away, stumbling to her feet and reaching for one of the heavy bookends that sat atop a small shelf by the fireplace. She could hear the man mumbling slurred profanities as her shaky fingers closed around the bookend.

Behind her, she could hear the man clambering clumsily to his feet, heavy footsteps beginning an unsteady approach. Kai spun around, involuntarily squeezing her eyes tightly shut as she swung her makeshift weapon.

Crack! The man fell heavily to the floor and didn't move. Kai dropped the bookend, not caring that it would likely dent the floor, and sank quickly to her knees, her chest heaving. A feeling of numb nothingness settled over her, and the rush of adrenaline that had swept from her the instant the bookend had made contact with the man's body left her feeling shaky and faint. There was something damp on her face. She lifted a trembling hand to investigate the source. Was she crying?

She brought her hand back down, brows pushing together in confusion as, through her blurred vision, she saw something dark and sticky and wet coating her fingers. It smelled like rust and copper. Her stomach lurched with dread as she realized that it was blood—not her own.

Kai scrambled away from the man as if he'd shocked her, though he was still lying motionlessly on the floor, and she pushed herself to her feet, stumbling into the bathroom and falling hard back onto her knees in front of the toilet just in time to empty the few contents of her stomach into the bowl. The sounds of her retching echoed loudly in the tiny bathroom, and by the time it was over, she felt hot and sweaty and so, *so* tired.

Reaching briefly up to flush the toilet, Kai lowered herself back down to lie on the floor, her eyes fluttering shut in relief as her burning cheek met the frigid tiles, the cold soothing the overwhelming, nauseating heat. Distantly, she thought that she should get up; the man was still out there, lying in a growing pool of his own blood in the middle of her living room, and if he was...if he was still alive, she thought, feeling sick again as it occurred to her that she might have killed him, he could wake at any moment. She should get up. She should push herself up from the floor and go back out there. She should get up.

But there was no strength left in her quivering limbs, her body completely and utterly drained, barely left with enough energy to slowly blink her heavy, swollen eyelids. So she didn't move.

She wasn't sure how long she laid there like that. It could've been an hour, but she thought it must have been closer to ten or fifteen minutes, given that she had yet to hear movement from the living room. She tried not to think of what that could mean.

Dimly, she became aware of footsteps, and a panicked voice calling her name. Who could be calling her? Avery was the only person who ever checked up on her, but she was probably holed up in her apartment studying for her midterms.

The footsteps were getting closer. Kai managed to push herself into a seated position, sliding back on the tile until her back met the wall. For what, she wasn't quite sure, but it felt safer than lying prostrate on the floor, even if it did make her head ache terribly to move.

"Kai!" Thorne appeared in the doorway, and she could practically feel the relief emanating from him as he laid eyes on her, though his expression quickly morphed into one of concerned horror as he took in her pale, shaky state, saw the blood covering her face and hair and clothes, the red handprints smeared across everything that she had touched. "What happened," he breathed, stepping slowly into the bathroom, his gaze rising slowly back up to meet hers.

"I..." she trailed off, unsure of where to begin. Her mind felt dazed and clouded, as though she had just awoken from a heavy slumber in a strange place. Thorne lowered slowly, carefully, as though she were a wounded animal that he was trying not to frighten, into a crouch, waiting patiently for her to find the words. He said nothing as Kai swallowed the lump in her throat, as she glanced down at her involuntarily twitching fingers, twisting her sweatshirt—her mom's sweatshirt, she realized, her heart breaking a little more—in her blood-stained fists.

"He caught me by surprise," she said finally, her vision unfocused as she stared straight ahead at the delicate gold chain hanging from Thorne's neck, resting on his chest between the lapels of his black leather jacket. "I thought he was you, and I...he never even—" her voice broke, tears springing, unbidden, to her eyes. She licked her lips, more cracked and chapped than ever. "He never even said what he wanted, just...went straight to trying to kill me." She laughed weakly, and sniffled, using her sleeve to wipe her damp nose.

"Looks like you foiled his plans," Thorne said, his voice soft as he tilted his head in an attempt to meet her eyes, a faint smile tilting the corners of his mouth upward. Kai froze, and it took several tries for her to make her vocal cords cooperate, to get out the words.

"Did—is he—did I...?"

"He's alive," said Thorne reassuringly, but his eyes darkened, the slight smile disappearing. Kai sensed that he was none too pleased to relay this news, but a wave of relief washed over her at the confirmation that she was not a murderer. She leaned her head back against the wall and closed her eyes, nodding.

Neither of them spoke again for several long, quiet moments, and Kai wondered how in the world she had ended up here, sitting in a broken, bloody heap on her bathroom floor with—

Her eyes flew open, and Thorne jumped slightly, taken aback by the hard, angry expression on her face. As Kai pushed herself quickly to her feet, Thorne followed suit, brows lowering in confusion as she brushed roughly past him. She rubbed her wrist, still aching from where she had landed on it earlier, but not badly enough to make her fear a break or serious sprain.

"Kai?" Thorne called hesitantly as he followed her back out into the living room. He watched in bewilderment as she turned this way and that, searching the floor, trying to figure out where her phone had disappeared to. 911—she should call 911. That's what people did when other people broke into their apartments and tried to kill them.

"Where *is* it?" She murmured, stooping to look under the couch. She saw the knife, and her stomach clenched. She ignored it, moving on.

"Kai?" Thorne asked again, and her jaw tightened, irritation flaring in her chest at the sound of his voice.

"What?" She plucked her bag from the floor and rifled through it, narrowing her eyes as she came up with nothing. She made to walk back toward the bathroom—maybe she had dropped it on her way to hurl her guts out—and nearly bumped into him as he stepped in front of her, effectively blocking her path as he looked down at her, questions in his eyes. Kai rolled her shoulders back and forced herself to look up, to meet his gaze. "*What?*" She repeated in a hard, snappy tone, feeling almost guilty at the hurt that flickered across his expression.

"It's just a job," he said softly, so quietly that she barely heard him, the hurt plain in his tone and in his eyes, and whatever guilt she had been feeling instantly dissipated. She scoffed, shaking her head. Her lip curled.

"*Just a job?*" That was my *family.*"

"I have reaped hundreds of families." He was expressionless, his detached tone and smooth features betraying nothing, and Kai wanted to slam her fists against his chest and force him to feel some small measure of the impossible pain that she had been feeling for the past thirteen years, as futile as she knew it would be. "I don't like it," he said. "But it's my job—*just* a job. I didn't choose it." Something seemed to break in that cold, distant expression of his, his voice faltering on the last sentence. Kai couldn't bring herself to care.

"I want you to get out," she said, taking a step back. She waited. "*Leave!*" She all but screamed it, the word tearing from her sore throat and making her wince. She let out a short, frustrated sound that fell somewhere between a shriek and a sob, and went back to her search, electing to ignore the Reaper standing frozen in her living room. "*Where the **fuck** is it?!*"

"What are you looking for?" Thorne asked, still standing where she had left him, his voice soft, barely audible, as though he were afraid to speak too loudly. Kai's fingers twitched reflexively, and taking a slow, deep breath through her nose, she forced herself to respond.

"My phone," she replied evenly, refusing to look in his direction. He approached her slowly, and her eyes widened as he reached around her and slipped something out of the back pocket of her jeans. Tearing her gaze away from where it had snapped up in surprise to meet his, she looked down. "Oh." She took the device from his hand, and he stepped back. "Thanks," she said before she could think about it, staring numbly down at the cold, dark rectangle. She swallowed. "You can go now."

"Okay," Thorne said simply, sounding tired, and when Kai looked back up, he was gone, and the body of her attacker with him.

CHAPTER FIFTEEN

MARY POPPINS HAVE MERCY

THORNE

Thorne sighed deeply as he kicked at a stray pebble, glancing periodically back toward the small grocery store across the street as he waited for Kai's shift to end so that, from a distance, he could see her safely home.

Several days had passed since the incident at Kai's apartment, and since then, she had seemed utterly determined to ignore him. The first day, he had been waiting outside of her apartment when she got home from work, desperate to apologize—to *explain,* in a way that didn't make him seem so cold and uncaring of the event that had defined the last decade of Kai's life. She had looked surprised to see him there, her expression hardening as, without a word, she brushed roughly past him and shut the door in his face.

The second day, she had walked wearily up the steps after a double shift and seemed not to even notice him sitting by the door. She hadn't spared him a glance as she turned the key in the lock and entered the apartment, securing what sounded like a half-dozen locks behind her.

The third day, she came home with jeans scuffed at the knees and scraped, bloody palms, shoving past him as he asked what had happened and slamming the door loudly shut, hellfire blazing in her eyes when he made the mistake of asking, *"Are you okay?"* He had realized, belatedly, that there must have been another attempt on her life, and had made the decision to start following her to and from work, watching her like a hawk from a safe distance and intervening whenever it looked as though she might be in danger.

There had been only two times of note, thus far—once when a boy lost control of his bike and went crashing into Kai, who was holding several bags of groceries and stumbled back into the busy street, where Thorne had yanked her out of the way of a rapidly passing car. The other time, someone had dropped a sheet of newspaper on the stairs leading to Kai's apartment; she had slipped, tumbling painfully down several steps before Thorne had caught her, just before she could land face-first against a large nail that had *conveniently* pulled loose from one of the creaky wooden stairs.

Both times, though shaken by the experience, Kai had quickly pushed him away from her and rushed off without a word, her shoulders tight and jaw set angrily, as though his very touch incensed her with anger and grief.

"You're stalking her after she specifically told you to leave her alone," Minho, who was sympathetic to both Kai's tragedy and the unfortunate predicament Thorne now found himself in, pointed out. *"Of course she is angry."*

"If I wasn't watching her, she would be dead half a dozen times over by now," Thorne had argued. *"It's protection, not stalking. Besides, it's not like I'm watching her change through her window—I'm just making sure she makes it safely to and from work each day."*

"Mild stalking," Jai amended, returning his gaze studiously to his comic book when Thorne shot him an irritated glare, then smothering a snort of laughter when Minho said,

"Well-intentioned stalking." It was only because Thorne appreciated that the pair had largely taken over his Reaping duties so that he could watch over Kai that he did not thump them each over the head with their respective books. Still, he had held up two middle fingers as he disappeared from the bullpen, their laughter ringing in his ears.

Every day had been more of the same: Thorne watched over Kai from a distance as she made the trip to and from the store each time she had a shift, and waited outside her door during the night to ensure that there were no more break-ins. She had nearly tripped over him several times when leaving early for her shift or making a trash run, but she had thus far stoically ignored him, the tense set of her jaw the only indication that she even noticed his presence. He could feel the anger emanating off of her in waves, noticed the way that her fingers would twitch into fists every time she realized he was nearby, and it took everything in him to not just start talking, to make her hear his explanation for at least the time it would take her to unlock the door before slamming it in his face.

He knew that it would be a fruitless effort.

So he let her ignore him in silence, waiting—hoping—for the day that she would finally look at him without malice and allow him to explain. To *apologize. To...anything.*

He knew that she could feel his presence the second that she stepped through the automatic double doors of the storefront, her eyes scanning the street and finding him easily. Thorne pushed off of the streetlight that he had been leaning against, daring to feel the slightest bit hopeful, his heart dropping in his chest when Kai rolled her eyes in unmasked irritation. He had anticipated the reaction, but still, he couldn't help but feel the sharp sting of rejection.

But he couldn't give up. Not when he had promised to protect her, to *save* her; not when he knew that forces larger than anything he had ever dealt with were likely conspiring at that very moment to take Kai's life.

She could hate and despise and loathe him forever if she liked, but he was determined that she would at least be alive to do it.

His brows rose in faint surprise as he saw another girl join Kai, walking in step with her as they made their way down the sidewalk. She was pretty, her small nose wrinkling as she threw her head back in laughter at something that Kai had said, using a pale, delicate hand to toss her shiny blonde hair over her shoulder. Thorne had never seen her before, and he wondered who she was—a friend of Kai's, it would seem. He hoped so. Kai seemed so very lonely, and if Minho was to be believed, everyone deserved *someone* to share their burdens with; as much as Thorne had found himself wishing that *he* could be that person for Kai, he was glad that, if not himself, she at least seemed to have *someone.*

He hoped that the blonde girl would keep her safe; perhaps if Kai was in the company of another person, she would be protected. It would be difficult for the Fates—or even the Keeper herself—to orchestrate something like a car accident or a robbery gone wrong without also harming the blonde, and surely *that* would go against Fate just as much as Thorne saving Kai's life had.

Still, one could never be *too* careful, so, keeping a safe distance, Thorne watched them walk to what he assumed must be the blonde girl's apartment building. As they disappeared inside, engaged in lighthearted conversation, Thorne sighed lightly and settled himself on a bench across the street, lying on his back with his hands cushioning his head as he stared up at the stars and wondered if somewhere, someone saw what he was doing and believed that it was the right thing. He wondered if the stars could see the future, as they saw the past and present; he wondered if they knew whether or not Kai would ever forgive him, and if he would succeed in saving her life. He wondered if they knew what it meant that Kai could see him—that he could see *her.* He wondered if they remembered the night that, for the life of him, he could not: the night that he had reaped the lives of Kai's family.

She had *blamed* him.

He couldn't blame her; after all, whilst there were many myths surrounding the origins of the Grim Reaper, many depictions didn't make it clear that he didn't actually *do* the killing. That he had no control over who lived or died, that he did not pick the method or the person or the time, that all he really did was guide souls from the In-Between to the land of the truly dead.

He hadn't *chosen* this—who would? Well, Minho, he supposed, but that was different. In a million years, Thorne would never have chosen this path for himself. It had been forced on him—*cursed* on him. But Kai didn't know that. Even if she did, he doubted that it would make much of a difference.

And the only defense that he had managed was, *"It's just a job."*

"Just a job," he muttered with a scoff, self-loathing gnawing at his insides. "*Idiot.*"

"Well, *that's* rather rude," came a voice to his right. Startled, Thorne nearly fell off of the bench in his haste to sit up. He turned to lay eyes on the newcomer, and was only faintly surprised to find Aristides standing with his back to a streetlight, hands hidden within the depths of his cloak. "I've not even said anything yet."

Thorne wasn't in the mood for jokes.

"Let me guess," he drawled, resting his elbows on his knees, feeling weary. "Cyrus sent you to try and convince me to see sense."

"He didn't need to," Aristides said, and sighed. "*Honestly,* Thorne, what were you *thinking?* Challenging the *Keeper?* Have you gone completely mad?" Thorne rolled his eyes.

"Give it a rest, Ris; I'm not feeling up to our usual witty banter tonight. Besides, don't you have better things to do than nag me? Like, I don't know, your *job.*"

"Of course I do," Aristides snapped. "But thanks to you, I *cannot,* not until you give up this foolish, infernal venture of trying to save somebody who *cannot* be saved." Thorne didn't respond, staring at the ground before him for several long, silent moments, and Aristides huffed a harsh sigh of irritation.

"Her name is Kai, you know," Thorne said suddenly. He felt, more than saw, Aristides' start of surprise. "She's just a *girl*—a girl who has lost *everything,* who just wants the chance to live her life." His heart ached at the reminder that he and Kai were more alike than they might, at first glance, seem.

When Aristides spoke again, his voice was soft and gentle and quiet, but easily heard in the silence of the dark and otherwise empty street.

"Thorne, as much as I feel for you—and I *do* feel for you—do you not think that it is time that you let this *go,* before it gets any worse? The Keeper is not someone to trifle with, and if you continue, she *will* get involved—"

"Then let her," Thorne said harshly, his eyes flashing, and Aristides' eyes widened a fraction. "I meant what I said, Ris—whatever she's got, *bring it on.* I'm waiting, and I will be ready for her if she does decide to show her face." Without another word, he turned and laid back down on the bench, gazing up at the stars in silence until, once again, he knew that he was alone.

Kai's shoulders dropped minutely the moment that she entered Avery's apartment, glad to be, at least for now, away from Thorne's watchful eyes. She knew that he had been following her, and as much as she knew she should probably be grateful that, despite her flat-out accusation that he was a murderer, he was still trying to keep his vow to save her life, every time that she felt his gaze on her she wanted to rip out her hair and scream, to walk up to him and kick him in the shin as hard as she could manage. *Something.*

She had resigned herself instead to ignoring him, and for now, at least, he seemed to be accepting of that fact. If he had tried to approach her directly again to try and explain how the deaths of her family could *possibly* be justified, Kai wasn't sure what she would do.

So intent on avoiding Thorne, and not particularly wanting to be alone, Kai found herself still at Avery's by the time the clock hit twelve, sprawled on her stomach across the floral bedspread, half-dangling off of the full-sized mattress every time she reached for the snacks that surrounded Avery, who had been studying diligently on the floor for the past several hours. The blonde displayed a truly astounding talent for ignoring the noise of the television, which was currently playing *Mary Poppins*—Kai's selection. She had adored the movie as a child, and with everything that had been happening to her recently, she felt a painful ache for something comforting and nostalgic.

"Julie Andrews," said Kai, pausing as she strained for a pretzel, the nearly-empty bowl that had earlier been filled to the brim with the salty snacks just beyond her reach. Without looking up from her textbook, which was alight with color from the pastel highlighters scattered messily amongst the papers around her, Avery moved the bowl closer to Kai. "Thank you." Satisfied, Kai scooted back onto the bed, her legs idly kicking the air behind her. She continued, waving the pretzel toward the screen. "Is an international *treasure*. I hope that woman never dies." Avery snorted.

"I think you're safe there," she said. "Between her talent and the fact that she's in her eighties and hasn't aged a day in over twenty years, that woman made a deal with *something*."

"Queen Clarisse Renaldi would *never*," Kai said strongly, staunchly defending her longtime favorite actress. Her brows pushed together as she suddenly wondered if selling your soul for deals was actually a thing. She should ask—

Her expression darkened at the thought of him, and she picked at the stray threads of the worn baby blanket at the foot of Avery's bed.

After a few moments, Avery noticed her companion's quiet, dampened demeanor, and finally looked up from her books.

"Okay," she said, removing a highlighter from between her teeth and turning her body so that she could more easily look her friend in the eye. "What gives?"

"Hm?" Distracted, Kai nearly jumped out of her skin when she found the blanket suddenly snatched away from her fiddling fingers. When she looked up, she found Avery glaring at her, the blanket bundled protectively in her arms. "Sorry," Kai grinned apologetically. Avery was incredibly attached to the sentimental object and did not take kindly to Kai's unfortunate habit of playing with the loose threads whenever she got her hands on the thing.

Avery had always been quick to forgive, however, and lowered the blanket onto her lap with a light sigh, her expression easing. She grabbed a sour gummy worm from one of the bowls on the floor and offered one to Kai, who accepted it, promptly biting it in half where red met blue.

"So, what's the matter?" Avery asked again, and chewing the multi-flavored worm thoughtfully, Kai pondered how best to respond to the question without guaranteeing a 72-hour hold in the psychiatric ward of the local hospital. The odds of Avery subjecting her to such a thing were slim to none, but Kai would rather not cause her closest—and only—friend to believe that she'd gone completely insane.

Uncomfortable with the attention, Kai searched for something else to fiddle with. She settled for the stuffed bear by the top of the bed—another relic from Avery's childhood—and amused herself with making its arms move.

She could feel Avery's patient, persistent gaze resting on her, so finally, Kai sighed deeply and relented. "I'm just so *tired*," she said. "I haven't been sleeping, and I've been so stressed out with this...bad luck." Before Kai had taken to wearing long-sleeved turtlenecks under her sweaters and tees, Avery had caught glimpses of her bruises and demanded to know what had happened. Kai had decided on a watered-down version of the truth—a run of bad luck that had resulted in her falling more than usual. Nothing to worry about.

"And on top of it all," she continued, "I keep feeling like I'm being *watched*. I'm so paranoid, and so tired, all of the time, and I feel like I'm going insane." It was all the truth, albeit a censored version of it, and it felt surprisingly good to let it all out, as though a colossal weight had been lifted from her shoulders. She wished that she could say more, that she could tell Avery about everything that had been going on—about Thorne and the Fates and the man who had broken into her apartment and how Kai wasn't even supposed to be *alive* right now. But she couldn't—who knew what kind of danger that might put Avery in?—and so she held it in.

"Oh, *honey*," Avery sighed, leaving the baby blanket on the floor as she climbed up onto the bed beside Kai, laying her head sympathetically on one of Kai's broad, sloped shoulders and clasping one of the brunette's icy-cold hands in both of her warm ones. Kai stared down at their intertwined arms, noting the contrast between her golden skin and Avery's porcelain complexion.

It felt nice, sitting in comfortable silence like this; Avery's frame tucked against her own was a surprisingly soothing weight, her body heat warming Kai like a furnace. Somehow the blonde had tangled her legs with Kai's, effectively blanketing Kai in her warmth, and the tension began to ease from Kai's aching body. It was nice. Until Avery, Kai had never realized how starved for touch she had been; her aunt was not a touchy-feely sort of person, and as the years went by, Kai had become increasingly uncomfortable and unfamiliar with physical contact.

Until Avery had entered her life like a ray of sunshine. A bubbly, energetic ray of sunshine who gave hugs as freely as she gave her smiles, and who had a heart bigger than anyone Kai had ever seen. It had taken some getting used to, but Kai no longer tensed whenever Avery threw her arms around her, no longer waited uncomfortably with arms stuck rigidly to her sides as she waited for the embrace to end.

She leaned into Avery's warmth now, tilting her head so that it was resting on top of the blonde's, and they said nothing more until the credits of the movie began to roll, when Kai rose reluctantly from the bed and bid her goodbye. She could tell that her friend wanted to ask Kai to sleep over, but Avery needed to study for her midterms and Kai needed to feed Mister Sylvester his evening meal, so plucking her backpack from the floor and giving Avery one more warm, bone-crushing hug and accepting a kiss of encouragement on her temple, Kai went home.

She resolutely ignored the presence that she felt on the other side of the street as she paused to wave at Avery, who was watching her from the window above, and continued to disregard the hairs-on-end feeling of being followed as she continued home.

When at last she reached her apartment, she paused with her hand on the doorknob.

"You can stop following me," she said, not turning to check if he was behind her; she knew that he was, could feel his steady gaze on the bare nape of her neck. "I can take care of myself."

When no response came, she huffed in irritation before slipping through the door, shutting and locking it behind her without a backward glance.

As the door clicked shut between them, Thorne sighed as he leaned wearily against it, sliding down to sit on the threadbare carpet and resting his arms on his knees. *I can take care of myself.*

"It may not be up to you," he whispered in the dark, quiet hallway. He wished more than anything that he could believe her, that he could leave her alone as she clearly wanted him to, no matter how deeply it would pain him to do so; he wished that there weren't things more powerful and ancient than either of them knew trying to take her life. More than any of it, he wished that she didn't hate him.

Once again, Cyrus found himself standing in the large, bright halls of the white palace, though this time he was alone. He had been summoned, and with Aristides away from the fortress and Linus diligently at work spinning the delicate golden threads that gave mortals life, he had thought it best not to wait.

There was no guide waiting for him this time, so Cyrus found his own way through the long, impossibly tall hallways, not pausing to stare at the art or catch a glimpse of himself in the countless mirrors that lined the walls in heavy golden frames.

He did not hesitate as he entered the garden, where he found the Keeper waiting for him. She wore that same white dress, though she was missing her shimmering crown, not that it made her look any less regal; tonight, she sat perched lightly on the edge of the stone fountain, her fingers idly trailing through the water, which glittered with invitation under the light of the full moon.

She looked up as he entered and smiled serenely in welcome. In the shadowed darkness of the evening, her eyes were a stark contrast to her gleaming midnight skin, and Cyrus could physically feel the weight of her penetrating gaze. He did his best not to let it show, inclining his head as he approached.

"Cyrus." Her voice was as light and musical as ever, dancing over the flagstones and effortlessly to his ears. "I believe that you have news for me."

"Yes." Though he felt reluctant to divulge the information that he had come to share, he had no real qualms about doing so; the consequences that Thorne might reap were a result of his own stubborn actions. Cyrus only regretted that he had been unable to solve this problem himself. And perhaps he felt some trepidation at the Keeper's impending presence in the mortal realm, a thing that had not been seen since the days that the deities roamed freely amongst the humans who worshiped them as gods. He reminded himself that this was the only way—the balance of Fate *had* to be restored, lest reality as they knew it come to an end.

So, straightening his shoulders, he delivered his report. "I regret to inform you, my lady, that we have been unsuccessful in our attempts to make the Reaper see sense. We no longer have control over his actions." With a reflective sigh, he added, "Perhaps we never did." The Keeper nodded, seeming unsurprised at the news.

"I applaud your efforts, Cyrus, and I assure you that *I* will not fail. This matter shall be resolved, and quickly." Her gaze moved to someone behind him, and turning, Cyrus found Alastair standing at attention. He had not noticed the Guardian's appearance, and wondered how long he had been standing there.

"Do what you must," instructed the Keeper, rising to her bare feet. "At any cost, the balance of Fate *must* be restored." Alastair nodded, leaving as silently as he had come. The Keeper turned back to the fountain, and Cyrus knew that it was time to take his leave. He bowed low once more before exiting the way that he had come, something in the depths of his ancient heart wondering if this had indeed been the right choice—hoping desperately that it was.

Whether it was or not, Cyrus could feel in his bones that things were about to change.

And Fate have mercy on us all when they do, he thought grimly.

Chapter Sixteen

TALL, DARK, AND TERRIFYING

When Cyrus returned to the sanctuary and shared the details of his meeting with the Keeper, the news was met with relative silence. Aristides was grim, and Linus, as always, was expressionless, his features a smooth mask of calm. Though he said nothing, his brothers knew that he had seen this coming.

"What do you think will come of this?" Aristides wondered aloud, and Cyrus sighed deeply, shaking his head.

"Nothing good, I fear," he said. "But it is out of our hands, now—Thorne left us with no choice. Things must be made right, and it seems as though this is the only way."

"I find myself unfortunately in agreement," said Aristides, looking resigned. He sighed. "Very well, then." He smoothed the folds of his cloak as he straightened. "I suppose I will relay this news to Thorne; perhaps now that *her* arrival is imminent, he will—"

"No," interrupted Cyrus firmly, and Aristides blinked, taken aback. "He has run out of chances; he knew that this was coming, and now he must face it. No more warnings. No more chances. Whatever happens from here, we can no longer involve ourselves—it is up to Fate and the Keeper, now." There was a note of finality in his tone, and reluctantly,

123

Aristides nodded. "Good. Then let us put this matter behind us and get back to work; this mess has taken up far too much of our time."

As his brothers started down the hallway that led to Cyrus' room of mirrors, Aristides lingered behind, guilt tugging at his heartstrings as regret pooled in his stomach. He had rarely questioned Cyrus' decisions before this, but he could not help but wonder if this was the right thing to do—whatever Thorne's faults, Aristides very much doubted that the boy deserved what the Keeper likely had in store for him.

But Cyrus had spoken, and Aristides had little choice but to follow him down the dimly lit hallway and return to his eternal task.

"I think I left my name tag at your place," Kai said when Avery arrived, fifteen minutes late and out of breath, to work several days after their *Mary Poppins* movie night. Kai's brows pushed together as she noticed Avery's frazzled state. "Where were you?" Avery's fingers froze momentarily as she tied her apron snugly around her slender waist, and she flushed deeply, avoiding Kai's gaze.

"What do you mean?" Kai's eyes narrowed in suspicion, and she watched as Avery snatched up several boxes of cereal from the stocking cart and turned to shove them onto the shelves.

"You're late."

"I'm always late," Avery said, putting a box of family-sized Fruit Loops in the Cheerios spot. It did not escape Kai's notice that Avery's gaze kept shifting up and down the aisle, or that she kept tucking her shiny blonde hair—freshly washed, from how strongly she smelled of her strawberry-scented shampoo—behind her ears, which sparkled with a set of earrings that Kai knew for a fact had been sitting unused in Avery's jewelry box since September. Avery always complained that it took too much time and effort to change out her multiple lobe piercings, and rarely made the effort to do so, yet here she was, late to work because she had spontaneously decided that today was the day to make a change.

"You're never late," Kai countered. "And," she added, as though it were concrete proof of Avery's deceit. "You're wearing the earrings that I got you for your birthday."

"So?" Avery said defensively, the pink on her cheeks deepening to crimson as her voice rose to a near-squeak. "I can't wear the *beautiful* set of earrings that my best friend so thoughtfully gave to me?"

"You're a terrible liar," Kai said. Avery paused as she reached for another box of cereal to stock, biting guiltily on her glossy lower lip. Her eyes met Kai's, and a sheepish grin dimpled her rosy cheeks.

"Okay," she gave in, practically vibrating as she stepped closer to Kai, lowering her voice as though she were about to share an important secret. Kai blinked at the sudden change, feeling whiplashed. "So, there's this guy that's been coming in for the past couple of days—I've never seen him before, and nobody else I know has either, so he has to be new to town, and *Kai*," her eyes rolled back dramatically in her head as she gripped Kai tightly by the shoulders and shook her. "This has got to be the most downright *gorgeous* man I have ever seen in my *life*. He's tall and dark and mysterious, and he keeps ending up on the aisles that I just *happen* to be cleaning or stocking, and Stacey said that he never even *buys* anything, and—well, he hasn't exactly *spoken* to me yet, but he keeps stealing little glances in my direction like he *wants* to." She squealed, bouncing on her heels as she grinned from ear to ear. Kai couldn't help an amused, albeit slightly confused, laugh as she watched, shaking her head fondly at her giddy-in-love best friend.

Avery froze, cheeks flushing again as her eyes fixed on something behind Kai, who turned instinctively to look.

"What—?"

"*Don't look!*" Avery hissed, hands flying to Kai's cheeks and pulling her face back around, her tone panicked. Kai smacked her hands away.

"Okay, *okay*, I won't look! What is it?"

"*He's here,*" Avery said under her breath, trying—and failing—to keep her gaze from straying from the boxes that she threw herself back into flinging onto the shelves, not noticing or caring that hardly any of them were ending up where they were actually supposed to go. "Don't just *stand* there—make yourself look busy." Kai began rearranging the boxes that Avery was haphazardly stocking, moving them to their rightful places. She put a box of spaghetti, which belonged three aisles over, back on the cart.

"Can I look now?" She asked quietly, and, biting her lip, Avery chanced a glance down the aisle. She nodded.

"Quickly—don't let him see you." Trying to be subtle, Kai glanced over Avery's head, and instantly froze. The blood seemed to drain from her body, the hairs on her arms and the back of her neck standing suddenly on end, and something deep within her bones warning her: *run.*

But she couldn't move.

As if he could sense her eyes on him, the tall, dark-haired man at the opposite end of the aisle paused as he perused the oatmeal selection, and he turned his head.

Kai's eyes flew wide, and she ducked quickly behind Avery.

"Did he see you?" Avery asked in that same whispered tone, and though her stomach clenched at the thought of doing so, Kai dared to peek back down the aisle to see whether he was still looking at her.

But the man was gone.

Kai felt as though she had just been sick, her skin clammy and damp, her limbs trembling imperceptibly. She found that her lungs refused to suck in more than the slightest bit of air, and her heart seemed to be attempting to pound itself out of her chest, the organ beating faster and faster with every passing second, the beats like a drum in her ears.

"Isn't he *dreamy?*" Avery sighed happily as she stared down the aisle at the spot where the man had been standing, oblivious to Kai's inexplicable terror. She turned back to look at her friend, and Kai forced a shaky smile.

"He was very handsome," she said with a nod. In truth, she had barely noticed his appearance, so overcome by the strange, horrifying feeling that had washed over her upon seeing him. But how could she explain something like that to Avery, who so clearly had the world's most gigantic crush on the guy?

You're just being paranoid, she chided herself harshly, turning back to the cart as Avery began talking a mile a minute about something that Kai couldn't quite focus on. *The past couple of weeks have been traumatizing and strange, to say the least, but not everyone is out to get you. Not every stranger is something...supernatural.*

It was a convincing argument, but still, she couldn't quite make herself believe it, and she couldn't help but look over her shoulder for the remainder of her shift, feeling as though something terrible could happen at any given moment.

He watched as the pair stepped out of the store, the brunette seeming to be in some sort of stunned trance whilst her blonde friend chattered in a blithe, animated fashion, then threw her arms suddenly around the silent brunette, squeezing briefly before stepping back and saying something else. Her smile dimmed momentarily, her expression morphing into one of concern as the brunette shrugged noncommittally. The blonde nodded, and her friend smiled faintly before turning and walking away, hiking her bag farther up her shoulder.

The blonde turned to walk in the opposite direction, a cheerful skip in her step as the smile returned to her face, brightly calling out greetings to people that she knew as she passed them on the busy sidewalk.

He crossed the street, his long legs making it a quick journey, and as he stepped up and out of the street, he stumbled into the distracted blonde.

"Oh!" She gasped as his large, strong hands caught her narrow shoulders to stop her from falling, their chests brushing as she teetered back on her heels, her silky hair brushing lightly against his skin. She smelled pleasantly of strawberries and vanilla, her pale skin soft beneath his calloused hands.

"I am *so* sorry, miss," he said earnestly as he steadied her, and she was halfway through what seemed to be an automatic *"don't worry about it"* when she looked up, her body stiffening in surprise as their eyes met, hers going as wide as saucers as the words died on her pink, faintly glossy lips. He smiled as he slowly released his steadying hold on her, one hand sliding down her arm and lifting her hand, which he bent to press a brief, tender kiss to.

"Please accept my most sincere apologies," he said as he straightened. Her hand fell limply back to her side as he let go of it, and that seemed to jolt her out of her trance. With a flustered laugh, she tucked her hair behind her ear, a light shade of pink dusting her dimpled cheeks.

"Apology accepted," she said with a smile that seemed to light up the entire street. Had he been a weaker man, he might have taken pause, but nothing could distract him from his task, his holy mission. "Are you new to town?" She asked, and he nodded, the corners of his lips turning upward in a charming smile.

"Yes," he said. "Yes, I am. My name is Alastair."

Chapter Seventeen
A BAD FIRST DATE

It had been another night of restless tossing and turning, and an already-grumpy Kai was halfway to the door when she remembered, smacking her palm to her forehead, that she had never retrieved her name tag from Avery's apartment.

"*Damn it,*" she swore under her breath as she pulled out her phone to check the time. She was going to be late. With a frustrated sigh, she pulled up her contacts and dialed Avery.

Blowing a brief kiss to Mister Sylvester, who was settling comfortably into the couch for his afternoon nap, Kai stepped out of her apartment with her phone in hand, pinning it between her shoulder and her ear as she locked the door. She tried to ignore the wave of nostalgia as she remembered seeing her mother do the same thing when she would talk on the phone to her own mother, Kai's *tūtū,* as she cooked dinner or cleaned the house.

Trying not to let the sudden grief overcome her as she turned away from the door, Kai let out a sharp cry of surprise as she nearly slammed into an all-too-familiar chest.

"Sorry," said Thorne, sounding far more apologetic than the situation called for. *Of course,* Kai thought with a bitter scowl, *he's not apologizing just for* **this.**

"What do you want?" She asked bluntly, her eyes narrowing. She was in no mood for this.

*"Um, you called **me**,"* Avery's voice said through the phone, sounding more than a little confused.

"Sorry," Kai said, then to an equally surprised Thorne, she silently mouthed, *not you.* He opened his mouth to speak, and she held up a finger as she turned away. *I really am turning into my mother,* she thought, turning her attention back to her phone. "Sorry, I'm here."

"Who are you talking to?" Avery asked curiously, and Kai hesitated. She glanced briefly back at Thorne, who stood with his hands behind his back, bouncing on the steel toes of his boots as he waited for his turn. The sight of him grated on Kai's nerves, and it came through in her tone as she said,

"It doesn't matter. Nobody important."

"Somebody's cranky," Avery observed, and Kai winced, wanting to bang her head against the wall as guilt settled in her stomach.

"I'm sorry," she apologized, taking a deep breath. "I'm just tired, and one of my neighbors is on my case about...something." She shook her head. "What's up?"

"You called me, remember?" Avery reminded her patiently. Kai bit her tongue, internally blaming Thorne for this entire fiasco of a phone call.

"Oh, yeah, sorry," she apologized again, sounding like a broken record to her own ears. "Um...yeah, I think my name tag is still at your place."

"Sure is!" Avery chirped brightly, and Kai could hear things clattering around on the other end, like Avery was rifling through the entirety of her jewelry box. "It's right here on my dresser. You work today, right?"

"Heading in now," Kai nodded, even though Avery couldn't see her. "Is it alright if I stop by to grab it? Chrissy works today, and I just know she's going to give me a hard time if I don't have it." Christina was their assistant manager, and was annoyingly strict about the unbendable laws of dress code. Kai wondered whether the stick up Chrissy's ass was part of that dress code, or if the rules simply did not apply to her, but she didn't dare ask. She needed this job.

"Sure thing!" It sounded like Avery had put her on speaker and set the phone down several feet away. "See you soon?"

"See you soon." Kai ended the call, and Thorne raised his brows in question. Kai rolled her eyes. "What do you want?" She repeated her earlier question, then held up a hand. "If it's an apology or an explanation, you can save it—I don't have the time to listen, nor do I really care to hear it." She sighed, her loose, comfortable clothing feeling suddenly itchy and tight. There was a headache brewing in her temples. "You know what, I have to go. I'm already late." She brushed past him then, sensing his presence behind her, spun on her heel, another snarky remark ready on her lips.

He was closer than she expected, and her eyes widened, a sharp gasp escaping her as the heel of her shoe slipped off of the top step and threw her off balance, her body falling backward. She felt an arm lightly corded with muscle wrap around her waist, long fingers splaying wide against the small of her back and pulling her to safety.

She took several deep, shaky breaths of relief before realizing that she was clutching the front of Thorne's shirt tightly in her fists and, eyes snapping sharply up to glare at him, she pushed him roughly away.

"Thanks," she said reluctantly, averting her gaze. She huffed, kicking the worn, red carpet of the hallway with the toe of her shoe.

"Kai—" he sighed, and in the corner of her vision, she saw his shoulders drop. "You should get going."

"Yeah." She waited a minute, then said, "I can take care of myself, so...you don't need to follow me around anymore." It was true enough—whilst her apartment had once more fallen into a state of chaos, she had been fending off the continuous 'accidental' attempts on her life *without* his help for the past several days. At least, she was pretty sure he wasn't involved, as she'd not seen hide nor hair of him since the night when she'd told him to stop following her. "In fact, I'd prefer it if you didn't," she added, and he laughed a sad, quiet laugh.

"I promised that I would keep you alive," he said. "And I don't intend to break that promise."

"It's not breaking it if I release you from it." He shrugged, expression unchanging, and she rolled her jaw, nails biting viciously into her palms. "Look, I said I don't want you following me around anymore, okay? Just leave me alone. *Please.*" When he said nothing, silent and still and immovable as a stone statue, Kai scoffed, shaking her head as she rolled her eyes in irritation. "Whatever. I don't have time for this." She turned and descended the stairs, taking them two at a time to more quickly escape his presence before pushing roughly through the front door, not letting herself look back to see if he was still following her.

***

When she finally arrived at Avery's apartment, Kai felt more jittery and on edge than she ever had, the tips of her nail-bitten fingers tapping a rapid rhythm against her thigh, her right knee bouncing of its own accord as she waited for Avery to answer the door.

She was *burning,* her cheeks flaming as the blood coursed through her veins like fire, her heart pounding faster and faster with every second that she was unable to banish Thorne from her mind.

The door before her flew open, and a rosy-cheeked Avery spun for inspection, the skirt of the light blue sundress that she was wearing billowing around her like a cloud before settling mid-thigh as she came to a breathless stop, her eyes sparkling as her face lit up in a dazzling grin.

Her shiny blonde hair fell around her shoulders in loose waves, and Kai could see makeup glittering subtly on Avery's eyelids.

"*Well?*" Avery asked, extending her arms expectantly and lifting one kitten heel-clad foot for effect as she twisted and turned. "How do I look?"

"Wow," Kai said, stunned to silence. Her eyes were threatening to fall out of their sockets with how wide they had flown upon Avery's appearance, and her mouth had gone dry. Avery was *always* pretty—she was one of those people who always looked *clean,* with soft hair and perfectly clear skin that radiated with a natural glow—but this was...

"Wow," she said again. Avery lowered her foot to the floor and bit her lower lip, which had been painted with a light sheen of clear gloss.

"Is it too much?" She asked, sounding nervous. Her forehead wrinkled as the corners of her mouth turned down, and she tugged anxiously at her dress, fists wrinkling the fabric as she stomped her foot. "I *knew* it. It's just a coffee date, but I wanted to look pretty, and—" Kai's eyes widened further, and without thinking about it, she surged forward, hands wrapping around Avery's to stop the havoc that she was wreaking upon her dress.

"Wait, that's not what I meant." The words tumbled out of Kai's mouth faster than she could think them. "You look *gorgeous*—stunning, honestly. *Honestly,*" she repeated, desperate to make Avery believe her, and the blonde girl's hesitant gaze slowly rose to meet hers. Kai smiled, and after a beat, Avery's grin was back in full force.

"Really?" Kai nodded enthusiastically, and Avery squealed in excitement, her hand wrapping around Kai's wrist as she dragged her forward into the apartment.

"I can't *believe* it, I haven't been on a date in *ages,*" she said as she spun in another circle. Kai couldn't help but laugh, her shoulders feeling lighter and her troubles seeming far out of reach as she watched her best friend twirl across the room.

"*So...?* Who's the lucky guy?" Kai asked, dropping her backpack to the floor and perching herself on the arm of the pale blue sofa. Avery flushed as she stopped spinning, her chest heaving with breathless pants of exertion.

Almost bashfully, she said, "That hot guy from the store...the one we saw yesterday, remember? Who's been coming in a lot?" Kai's smile froze as her heart skipped a beat, but Avery didn't seem to notice, blissfully recounting her story with giggles and swoons. Kai couldn't explain the feeling brewing in her stomach, anxiety rolling over her like a freezing tidal wave. She felt as though she was going to be sick.

"...and then he asked me out! *Me!*" Avery exclaimed, bouncing on her heels. She looked happier than Kai had ever seen her, and she felt a pang of guilt at the inexplicable dread she was feeling. *You're just being paranoid,* she reminded herself, and forced her smile a little wider as she nodded to show that she was still listening. "I mean, I've been asked out before," Avery said, twisting her skirt in her hands in something like embarrassment. "But this guy is so *gorgeous,* and he's charming and flirty and polite, and there's just no one around here who really measures up. And—" Kai nearly jumped out of her skin as someone knocked on the door. "Oh! You can see for yourself—that's him!"

Kai wanted to protest, but Avery was already opening the door. "Alastair!" She greeted with another of her dazzling smiles, and Kai heard a low voice respond with what sounded like Avery's name. "Please, come in. This is my best friend in the world, Kai. Kai, this is Alastair." Avery was flushed with excitement, her cheeks dimpling as she glanced between her best friend and the tall, broad-shouldered man towering over her. Not wanting to be rude, Kai sucked in a deep breath, rising from the couch and lifting a hand awkwardly.

"Hey, there." Alastair met her gaze evenly, and Kai felt as if a great weight was pressing down on her from her head to her toes, threatening to crush her with its slow, steady force. Though Alastair appeared to be in his mid to late twenties, his eyes—amber and narrow—look as though they could be far older.

"It is a pleasure to meet you," he said, his voice deep, and Kai swallowed. She nodded.

"You, too," she said hoarsely, her mouth suddenly dry as a bone. She gestured behind herself in the direction of the bedroom. "I, um, I'm gonna grab my name tag and get out of your hair, Avery." Avery nodded, her forehead creasing as she mouthed, *you okay?* Kai nodded minutely, forcing a bright smile directed at Alastair as she made a hasty escape from the room.

She leaned heavily against the dresser as she took several deep, shuddering gasps of breath, the weight that had been crushing her suddenly lifted, and she paced the floor as she struggled to understand what was going on. It was perfectly possible that Alastair was a completely normal man, nothing out of the ordinary about him aside from his admittedly stunning looks, but...

Kai's fingers twitched, and she glanced toward the window. She suddenly hoped that Thorne hadn't listened to her—that he was outside after all, keeping his promise to keep her safe. *The promise that I tried to release him from.* She hoped desperately that he had not listened; if she could make it outside before Alastair and Avery did, maybe...maybe he knew Alastair? Or could at least tell from looking at him whether or not he was someone—some*thing*—not entirely ordinary?

Snatching her name tag from the dresser, Kai walked back out into the living room, ready to bid her goodbyes and run like hell to find Thorne.

The name tag fell to the floor with a quiet clatter as she stopped short.

Alastair's hands slipped from Avery's pale cheeks as she crumbled to the floor, her mouth open in a silent scream and her eyes falling shut as her head hit the hardwood. She went still, and from this distance, Kai couldn't tell if she was breathing.

Her senses returned to her all at once, everything snapping into focus.

"Avery!" Kai surged forward, dropping roughly onto her knees as she rolled Avery onto her back, shaking her body—cold and pale and deathly still—urgently in an attempt to wake her. "Avery, wake up, *please,* wake up!" Tears threatened to pour from her eyes, and her words ended on a strangled half-sob.

She turned, leveling a venomous glare at Alastair. "What did you do?" She pushed herself to her feet and shoved his chest, hard. He didn't budge. "*What did you do?!*" An enraged scream tore from her vocal cords at his silence as she beat her fists on his chest, painful, ugly sobs wracking her frame, and for a moment, he let her, not flinching as she kicked his shin and scratched at the flawless skin of his face and neck in her fury.

After a moment, his hands snapped up and clasped her wrists in an iron grip. He waited calmly for her tear-filled eyes to meet his cold, detached ones.

"I am sorry," he said, his voice as cool and clear as crystal. "This is the price that must be paid if what must be done is left undone." Dropping her wrists abruptly, he disappeared as the room flashed, leaving a wide, black imprint on the floor in his wake. Kai exhaled a long, ragged breath, sinking back onto her knees.

Through blurred vision, Kai crawled to her friend and pulled her limp, lifeless body into her arms, pressing her quivering lips against Avery's cold temple. Quiet sobs escaped her as she tightened her hold, and a pained, grief-stricken scream began to build in her throat. When she let it loose, it felt as though it shook the building, the world crumbling to ash around her.

CHAPTER EIGHTEEN
A GUARDIAN AND A LULLABY

K ai listened dazedly as the doctor explained in a tone filled with compassion and regret that, despite running every test they could think of to try and explain what had happened, they had come up with nothing. They had no idea what had caused this. *A medical anomaly,* the doctor had said.

Kai's chest felt like it was going to cave in as she turned her eyes to the hospital bed where Avery lay connected to a plethora of multicolored wires and tubes, monitors blinking and beeping steadily around her. She looked peaceful, as though she were only sleeping, but every attempt to rouse her from her slumber had been unsuccessful. The doctor explained that she still displayed normal brain activity, her chest still rising and falling of its own accord and her heart beating just as strongly as it ever had, so she wasn't *dead* in any sense of the word; she was simply...unconscious. Gone—lost to a coma that nothing and no one could explain.

Kai had told nobody of what she had seen in the apartment, of the events that had led to Avery's collapse. She *couldn't* have told them—who would believe her?

"She just collapsed," Kai, sobbing hysterically, had told the paramedics when they'd arrived. She wasn't sure who had called them—one of the

"

neighbors, most likely, frightened by Kai's horrified screams. *"I don't know what happened."* They had pulled Avery from her arms, and although she was now standing mere feet from the bed where her best friend lay, Kai had not touched her since. She was afraid—*terrified*—of the unresponsive cold that she knew would greet her if she reached out to touch Avery's hand.

All around her, Avery's family sat or stood in varying degrees of shock and grief. Carrie, Avery's mother, sat with one of Avery's pale hands clasped in both of hers, blue-green eyes rimmed with red. The hands resting on her shoulder in comfort or for support, perhaps both, belonged to her husband, Alan, who looked as destroyed as Kai felt.

One of Avery's cousins sniffled, and Kai suddenly felt like she was suffocating, the crowded room closing in on her so quickly that she felt as if the remaining air in her lungs had been sucked suddenly out with a vacuum. She stumbled back, nearly falling into Avery's aunt, who was standing with a tissue pressed to her red nose, and Kai mumbled an unintelligible apology.

"I need some air," she managed to choke out, and the sea of Avery's grief-stricken relatives parted for her to flee the room. They were all too focused on whatever the doctor was still droning on about to question her, and Kai was grateful for that. She didn't know if she could stomach another one of Avery's aunts or uncles or, heaven forbid, her grandfather, the man who employed them both at his grocery store and treated Kai as another grandchild, meeting her eyes again with their tear-filled ones. She couldn't take their questions or their concerns or their *sympathy* that she had been the one to find Avery like that; couldn't fathom what she would say if one more person asked her if she was *okay*. She wasn't. It was *her* fault that this had happened to Avery, and the guilt was already eating her alive from the inside out.

She found herself in a small, dimly lit hallway, occupied only by herself and three large vending machines. She sighed deeply, her eyes falling shut as she rested her forehead against one of the machines, letting the coolness of the acrylic viewing window soothe her overheated skin.

She wished that she could scream, or kick something, or punch her fist through a wall over and over again until it bled, but her traitorous body wouldn't let her, her shoulders sagging with exhaustion and her very bones aching to curl up in some forgotten corner and fall asleep.

She felt numb.

Staggering back from the machines, her back hit the wall opposite, and she let her knees give out, sliding down the faded green wall and onto the cold hospital tile. She dragged her legs to her chest and wrapped her arms around them, resting her forehead on her knees and letting the chill of the floor seep into her bones.

She didn't know how much time passed as she sat there, desperately fighting the urge to fall asleep and trying to shut down the images racing through her brain. Images of Avery in the moments before she collapsed, smiling and excited to go on her date; Alastair, looking gravely at Kai as he disappeared; Avery's body in the hospital bed, an IV slowly dripping fluid into the hand that her mother was clutching like a lifeline; *the car, upside down with windows shattered, her family hanging limply around her, crimson blood dripping from her sister's fingertips and onto the beige carpeted ceiling—*

Kai jerked awake, the back of her head slamming into the wall behind her and jerking her back to reality. She sucked in ragged, gasping breaths as she dug her fingers into her hair, nails scraping against her scalp, eyes burning as she shook her head in an attempt to shake off the remnants of the nightmarish memory that she had somehow fallen into. Her chest began to heave, blood rushing in her ears like a tsunami as it all became too much. She was going to die. She was going to—

"Kai." It felt as though a bucket of cold water had been dumped over her, and Kai froze, hands falling from her head as she looked up to find Thorne standing over her. Slowly, he crouched in front of her, brows drawn low over eyes shining with concern. He licked his lips nervously, then, after a split second of hesitation, placed his hand on her knee.

"I'm so sorry." Kai wasn't sure why the words surprised her so much, but as she met his eyes, wide and brown and painfully apologetic, she broke.

Stifled, painful sobs tore from her chest, hot tears pouring down her cheeks as she rocked back and forth, hugging her knees tighter to her chest in an attempt to keep from shattering to pieces on the floor, feeling as if the world was caving in and whatever scraps of her were left might blow away at any given moment. Thorne didn't move, remaining completely still save for the thumb that began to rub gentle, soothing circles into the side of her knee. He said nothing as her tears fell onto his skin, even as she began trying to gasp out words, her throat constricting whenever she attempted to force them out.

Under his breath, Thorne began to hum something in a language that Kai was unfamiliar with. It sounded like a lullaby, and it reminded Kai of the songs that her mother would sing to put her to sleep as a child; another tear slipped quietly from the corner of her eye at the thought.

Thorne's voice was soft and low, and the slow, consistent cadence of the lullaby washed over Kai like a warm blanket, soothing her and slow-ing the sobs that wracked her body. By the time Thorne was finished, the only sound remaining in the empty hallway was Kai's occasional sniffle as the tears began to dry on her cheeks.

"It's my fault," she whispered, and when he didn't respond, she half thought that he hadn't heard her. She looked up and found him staring at her. He showed no reaction to her flushed, damp face, and she sucked in a quiet breath of surprise when he reached out to tuck a strand of hair behind her ear. He seemed in no hurry to speak, and at length, he said firmly, maintaining steady eye contact with her,

"No, it's not." Kai laughed quietly, but he didn't smile. "This is *not* your fault."

"This wouldn't have happened if it wasn't for me," she countered as his hand caressed her temple, smoothing over the hair that he had just brushed away.

"You could never have expected this to happen—"

"Did you?" She asked before she could stop herself. Thorne paused, then shook his head.

"No," he sighed heavily. "I knew...I had been told that someone very powerful would be getting involved if I didn't comply with her demands to reap your soul, but I never—I had never imagined that she would put a mortal in harm's way. A mortal who *isn't* supposed to be dead, that is."

"She?" Kai's brows furrowed and, after seeming to struggle briefly with some silent internal debate, Thorne nodded.

"The Keeper," he said with another sigh. "She is very old, and even more powerful than you can imagine—even more so than the Fates. I have never had the misfortune of meeting her myself, and from what I've heard of her, I thank my lucky stars for that."

"Alastair—does he work for her?" Thorne pressed his lips together in obvious distaste.

"He does," he said dryly. "*Him* I have met, and while he isn't overly powerful, he's not exactly a treat for company, either."

"Not overly powerful?" Kai echoed in disbelief. She found herself unable to move her gaze from his. "He put my best friend into a coma just by *looking* at her."

"I meant in comparison to the Fates or the Keeper," Thorne clarified. Kai began to gnaw at her lower lip, and the hand still cupping her knee gave a brief, reassuring squeeze. "I'm sure that your friend will be alright," he said gently. "It's just a scare tactic—I find it hard to believe that they would kill her and go against Fate just to prove a point."

"Do you know that for sure?" The words came out sharper than Kai intended, and Thorne was quiet. She shook her head, letting his hand slide off of her knee as she pushed herself from the floor to stare pensively down the hallway. "I appreciate what you've been trying to do," she said, sounding hollow, her eyes dull. "But maybe it would be better if...if I..." She swallowed.

Thorne rose to his feet as well, and she felt his presence looming over her.

"It wouldn't," he said firmly, in a tone that left no room for debate. Kai continued to stare down the hallway. Thorne sighed, looking down, and she felt his fingers brush feather-light against her palm. Her own fingers twitched in response, and she pulled away, crossing her arms over her chest like a shield as she took a small step back.

"I think I'd like to be alone, now," she said, and didn't wait for a response before walking away from him, her shoulders curling inward as she wrapped her arms around her body and exited the dim hallway back into the light.

Thorne's heart ached as he watched her go, and he sighed deeply as he stared down at his hand. It was warm where it had brushed, just slightly, against hers, and his thumb caressed the tips of his fingers where their skin had touched.

Something moved on the floor below his hand, and he froze, his eyes narrowing, then widening infinitesimally as a shadow slid across the speckled white tiles. From behind him came the whispered sound of wings crisply folding and, flexing his hands briefly as he wondered how long it would take for him to snatch the dagger that he kept stored in his right boot, Thorne spun to face the newcomer.

A familiar, if incredibly unwelcome, figure stood at the opposite end of the hallway, broad shoulders pushed back and handsome features smoothed into an eternally stoic expression.

"Alastair," Thorne said, the name leaving an unpleasant taste on his tongue.

"Thorne," Alastair greeted similarly, and he approached slowly, his shoes making scarcely a sound as he advanced. Thorne resisted the urge to back away.

"I thought that I recognized your handwork; it's been a while—what, a couple hundred years, give or take?" Alastair sighed lightly as he finally came to a stop just in front of Thorne. He looked bored.

"Let us skip the formalities, Reaper. I presume you know why I am here?"

"Well, you know what they say about—wait, no, that's *assume*." Alastair was unamused, and Thorne rolled his eyes lightly. "Yes, I know why you're here, *Guardian*." His eyes darkened, and a smirk twisted his lips as he stepped closer to Alastair. "I've been expecting you," he said, and taking a sudden hold of Alastair's collar, he turned to push him into the wall.

They reappeared in the In-Between, and Alastair's back slammed roughly into a high wall of adamant. Dust fell at the sudden impact and, though he raised one thick, angular black eyebrow, Alastair appeared otherwise unphased at the turn of events.

"Is that all?" He chuckled, the sound deep and dark with amusement. "I did not come here to exchange petty insults or weak threats—merely to relay a message." Thorne's fists curled tighter around the pressed fabric of Alastair's shirt, and he waited. "Reap the girl's soul. Let her die, and her friend will live."

"And if I refuse...what, you'll kill Avery?" Thorne scoffed, and shook his head. "I don't think so—that's not exactly your style."

"While it is true that we cannot kill your little human's friend so long as her time in the mortal realm is not expired, we *can* ensure that she remains sleeping for the rest of her natural life. Do you believe that your mortal pet would find those terms acceptable?" He tilted his head slightly, not blinking as his eyes lazily searched Thorne's.

"Here's a counteroffer," Thorne said, leaning in so that his face was mere inches from Alastair's, his gaze unflinching. "You wake Avery up, crawl back to whatever dark, damp hole that you spawned from, Kai lives, and we all go on with our lives as we see fit. Deal?" He released Alastair abruptly and brushed the dust off of his sleeve as he took a step back. "We really should do this more often," he said with biting sarcasm. He turned to walk away.

"You think that Avery is the only person that means something to your mortal?" Alastair called from behind him, and Thorne's footsteps stuttered. "True, she may be the only person that your human calls *friend,* but what of her grandfather, that kindly old man who employs them both?" Thorne's jaw tightened, and Alastair continued.

"And *you*. Your newest addition—Jai, is it?" He cocked his head, not missing the way that Thorne stiffened at the mention of the younger Reaper. Thorne wondered if the Guardian could hear his heart pounding in his chest. "He still has unfinished business, does he not? How do you think that he would feel if that business *remained* unfinished?"

In a flash of blazing fury and glinting silver, Thorne had Alastair pinned back against that wall of adamant, one hand fisted around his collar and the other holding the dagger he'd seized from his boot against the Guardian's golden throat. Alastair laughed, the tip of the knife pressing a little closer beneath his jaw.

"I see I have hit a soft spot," he said, and his amused expression dissipated. "However, if you believe that you can threaten me—" He froze in surprise as he found himself unable to step forward, and he looked down, eyes widening slightly as he saw that the stone ground beneath him had somehow cemented over his shoes, holding him securely in place.

"You're in *my* domain now," Thorne hissed, flames leaping behind his dark eyes. "*I* make the rules here." As if to prove his point, the ground rose with a crack over Alastair's shins, stopping just below his knees. Alastair lifted a brow, seeming unbothered.

"And what do you think that this little display of yours is going to accomplish? You cannot kill me; and besides, if you are here with *me*, who will protect your mortal?" Thorne didn't flinch.

"I have no intention of killing you," he said. "But I wonder how many humans I can rescue from the jaws of death by the time that you manage to get out of this?" As the ground rose higher, the corners of Thorne's lips twitched upward as he made a show of imagining it. Alastair's eyes narrowed.

"What is it that you *want*, Reaper?" He asked, and Thorne shrugged.

"Just a meeting with your boss." *That* seemed to catch Alastair by surprise, his dark brows shooting upward, and Thorne couldn't help but feel a twinge of satisfaction.

"You cannot *possibly* imagine that such a thing will end in your favor," Alastair said incredulously, and Thorne arched a brow.

"Do we have a deal?"

CHAPTER NINETEEN
YOUR DEEPEST DESIRE

MINHO

"What happened?" Minho swept into the office and stopped short, hands catching the doorway for support as his breath caught in his throat, his eyes widening slowly as he took in the state of the room.

The papers and trinkets that had covered Thorne's desk were scattered across the floor, the armchair unceremoniously overturned, and there was a sizable hole in the wall behind Thorne's desk chair, where he was now sitting with hunched, heaving shoulders.

"Dear lord," Minho breathed, taking in Thorne's disheveled appearance—the messy hair that had fallen from its tie, the red, bitten lips resting against his knuckles, bruised and bloody.

Every fiber of Minho's being itched to surge forward—whether to shake Thorne to his senses or to pull him into his arms and offer him a shoulder to cry on, he wasn't sure—but he resisted, something within him whispering that it was best he keep his distance.

"Are you alright?" Thorne mumbled something unintelligible under his breath, and Minho strained to hear. "Thorne."

"I fucked up," Thorne repeated, barely audible. His voice was quiet and hoarse, his vocal cords sounding strained. He shook his head. "I fucked up so bad, Min." His voice broke on the whispered words, and when he looked up, Minho nearly stumbled back at the devastation painted across his face, feeling as though he were staring into an open wound. In all his years of knowing Thorne, Minho had never seen him wear such an expression.

Slowly, he moved forward, clicking the door quietly shut behind him and lifting the armchair from the floor, setting it right side up so that he could take a seat. He leaned forward and rested his elbows on his knees, steepling his fingers.

"Tell me everything."

"Y*ou should really think this through,"* Alastair repeated for what seemed like the hundredth time as they walked through the palace, his voice echoing off of the walls in the absurdly spacious, alarmingly high-ceilinged hallway. Thorne, walking just behind him, hummed thoughtfully for a moment, pretending to mull briefly over the suggestion.

"Just did," he said. *"Still haven't changed my mind. Keep it moving, Guardian."* Alastair's jaw tightened as Thorne shoved him forward, but he picked up the pace slightly.

"Then let me advise caution from here on out, Reaper—we are no longer, as you so eloquently put it, in **your** *domain, and whilst* **I** *am not permitted to kill you, I am sure that My lady would not hesitate to inflict upon you a fate worse than death, should she decide that your audacity outweigh your worth."*

"She'd be a bit late for that," Thorne said grimly, staring straight ahead as they continued on. They fell silent, and Alastair led them down several more long, equally bright corridors. Thorne was just about to ask how much longer their journey would take when Alastair came to a sudden stop before a large, arched doorway.

"This is as far as I go," he said, and Thorne narrowed his eyes, preparing to protest. *"I would imagine that she is expecting you,"* Alastair interrupted. *"But this meeting is between you and her—I will remain here."* Thorne huffed in mild irritation and rolled his eyes, but shoved back his shoulders, nonetheless, tilting his chin upward as he took a deep, steadying breath, trying to quell the sudden nervous hesitation bubbling in his stomach.

Onward and upward, *he thought, and stepped through the doorway.*

He found himself in a large, open garden, and his eyes automatically fell on a tall, bubbling stone fountain to his right. The water sparkled as it moved fluidly over one ledge to the next, and it took him a moment to finally notice, with a start of surprise, the still-as-stone figure standing beside it.

His legs buckled slightly as something deep inside of him sensed her power, urging him to fall to his knees and pay respect, but he resisted, his jaw tensing as he fought off the impulse. She was ethereal, delicate golden bands winding their way up and around her arms, glistening in the bright light of the sun overhead. A crown of silver and gold stars that seemed to float sat atop a head of gleaming black tresses, and her dark lips curved into a welcoming smile, contrasting eerily with her white, frosted eyes.

"Thorne." Her voice was light and musical, a siren luring him to his death. "What a pleasure it is to finally meet you."

"Is it?" He asked flatly, arching a brow. She threw her head back and laughed, and he blinked in surprise, her reaction throwing him off-balance.

She stopped, her steady gaze leveling on him suddenly, and though a slight smile still played faintly on her lips, there was a darker energy radiating from her than there had been the moment before.

"Not really," she said as she tilted her head, looking him up and down. "But, niceties—I cannot very well be rude to my guest, can I, now?" She did not seem to expect an answer, and smoothing the stark white fabric of her dress, she took a seat on the edge of the fountain. "And what business brings you to my estate, little prince?" Thorne's chest tightened, and he had to make a conscious effort to keep his breathing even as he forced his hands to flex, his fingers trembling slightly as they ached to curl into fists.

"I have a feeling you know the answer to that," he responded evenly, and she smiled a little wider.

"You want me to save your little mortal pet, am I right?" She guessed, tapping a long fingernail thoughtfully against her full lower lip.

"She isn't a **pet.**" Thorne struggled to keep his tone light. "Just a good person, who doesn't deserve to die."

"Oh, darling." She was suddenly behind him, and a shiver ran down his spine at the feeling of her warm breath on the nape of his neck. Understanding dawned on him that, whilst she looked very much the part of an angel, she was more akin to a deadly snake—venomous, and waiting to strike until you least expected it. "They rarely do."

Thorne slumped in his chair, exhausted, a defeated expression on his face as he stared bleakly down at his hands, lying uselessly in his lap. Minho waited patiently for him to continue, saying nothing, though he looked pained and sympathetic.

After a moment, Thorne sucked in a breath, pressing on with his story.

Seated once again on the edge of the stone fountain, the Keeper reached out a hand, her fingertips breaking the surface of the water and creating small ripples that she seemed to be utterly mesmerized by. Thorne was beginning to think that she had forgotten he was there when she suddenly broke the silence.

"Now, then," she said as she cocked her head slowly to the side, her foggy eyes assessing him thoughtfully, like a cat sizing up its prey. The corners of her mouth turned up ever so slightly, and her voice was light again. "Surely we can come to some sort of agreement."

"If it involves me reaping Kai's soul, I'm not interested," Thorne said coldly, and the Keeper laughed. Slowly, she rose from her seat, her eyes locked intensely on his, staring deeply into his soul and laying it bare.

*"Silly boy," she crooned softly. "If there is one thing I have learned in the time that I have lived, it is that **everyone** has a price. And I am willing to wager," she continued, drawing closer, a wisp of a breath hitting Thorne's ear as her lips hovered beside it. "That I know yours." She smiled as she pulled away, and he swallowed, resisting with difficulty the urge to shiver and flinch, to show any sign of discomfort in her presence.*

"Are you?" His voice was surprisingly steady, and he scoffed a short, mirthless laugh as he shook his head. "All due respect, Your Royal Ladyship, but I must disappoint you—there is nothing you can offer that will sway me." The Keeper arched a brow.

"Is that so?" She hummed, moving back toward the fountain. "Desire..." she murmured, her eyes half-lidded as she seemed to lose herself momentarily in thought. "No matter how desperately people try to hide it, it is always so obvious to those around them—they simply cannot help it. Yours, my boy, is painfully clear." Her gaze snapped abruptly back to his, and he nearly jumped out of his skin at her sudden change in demeanor. "You wish to be free of your curse, do you not?"

Thorne's heart stopped, and it was as if all the air in the spacious garden had dissipated, leaving him suffocated and faltering for a response. His mind raced, the thoughts rushing by too fast for him to properly think or consider them. It was too cruel—the words that he had always wanted to hear, the possibility that he had always longed for, dangling just within reach, but with far too heavy a price.

He shook his head, tongue feeling dry and heavy in his mouth, his lips numb and hands still dangling uselessly at his sides.

"You're lying," he forced out at last, shaking his head again, refusing to believe the words dripping from her lips like poisoned honey. "You're **lying.**" She laughed, sounding almost gleeful as she stepped back to observe the mess that she had made of him.

"Is that so?" She cocked her head with an arched brow, her eyes seeming to darken as she looked at him, no longer the cat assessing its prey, but the hawk who knew she had him caught. **Checkmate.** "There is only one way to find out." She held out a hand invitingly. His lip curled.

"It's not possible," he said, the words like acid on his tongue. "It isn't in your power."

"Is it not? It may not have been my finger on the trigger, as your mortals like to say, but I was the driving force behind the bullet. You have the Fates to thank that you still **breathe,** little prince." She was no longer soft, no longer gentle or cajoling, the facade that she had been wearing falling away completely. **Now** she was the Keeper that he had heard about, cold and hard and unforgiving; vengeful, and fatally determined. "It may have been **their** curse, Thorne, but **I** have more power than they could ever dream of possessing—at your request, I could undo it."

For the fleetest of moments, Thorne allowed himself to believe that what she was saying wasn't entirely impossible or insane, that it wasn't so utterly out of the question that it pained him to even **think** about. For a moment, he let himself imagine what it would be like to **finally** get what he wanted—for his curse to be broken, for him to live the mortal life that he had always been meant to live. To be, at long last, human again. To feel the air that mortals breathed filling his lungs; to know that when he heard his heartbeat, it was not merely out of anger or fear, but from the simple need to **survive**; to be, after all this time, **seen** by the very humans that he had spent so long observing from the shadows.

For a moment, he imagined what it would be like, and a long-dead hope began to bloom in his chest.

Then came the cold realization, rushing over him like a tidal wave, dread filling every crevice in his chest and drowning out the hope as quickly as it had arrived. What lay for him in the human world? His only friends existed in the In-Between—he would never see them again if he were mortal. He had no skills or talents that he could use in a mortal life, no family to turn to when he needed a helping hand. And Kai...the bargain was obvious: his mortality in return for her soul. She would be dead, and he would be mortal at last, but alone.

His choice was clear.

"You turned her down?" Mouth agape, Minho stared at his friend in wide-eyed disbelief, looking physically stunned by the revelation. "Thorne..." he trailed off, at an utter loss for words, for there was nothing that he could say—what comfort could you possibly offer to someone who had just given up their lifelong wish, the one thing that they had dreamed and hoped and lived for for half a millennium?

"Please," Thorne scoffed, rolling his eyes as he brushed off his friend's sympathy, skin crawling with discomfort at the pity that he could see glistening in Minho's eyes. His voice was rough. "It was an easy decision; even if she *was* telling the truth, what makes *me* more deserving of life than Kai?" Minho didn't answer, and Thorne huffed a laugh tinged with bitterness.

He continued.

"You...refuse?" The Keeper blinked, flustered, seeming genuinely stunned by his response. Thorne nodded once, his gaze unwavering.

*"I refuse," he repeated, and shrugged. "I say no. I **reject** your offer." The Keeper's slender brows lifted, and she sighed lightly as she turned away to rest her hands on the edge of the fountain, her nails tapping slowly against the stone.*

"I cannot say that I am not surprised," she said, and he saw her spine straighten, the delicate bones in her shoulders shifting as she pushed them back, her chin tipping upward. "However," her tone grew hard once again. "It changes nothing. The girl's soul must be reaped, as was her Fate, and as for you...well, you had your chance, little prince. You may continue your eternity of misery, since that is the option which you so dismissively selected. But do not say that I never offered you a way out."

"Your offer was a double-edged sword," Thorne said vehemently as he stepped forward, eyes blazing, finally throwing out any semblance of respect for the being standing before him. "It is true that I desire to be mortal again, to be free of my curse, but I know very well what the price would have

been—Kai's life. And that is not something that I am willing to bargain with."

*"And while I can almost respect your obstinate loyalty to the girl—though I will not pretend to understand it—I cannot and **will not** sway from the duty that has been bestowed upon me. I **will** see the natural order of things carried out. My job, little prince, is not to make Reapers happy—it is to keep the world balanced."*

"Bring it on, then." Thorne snarled. He knew that he was getting ahead of himself, threatening the Keeper so boldly when she so clearly held all of the power, but there was no more room for begging or bargaining. This was war.

Her expression was stone, and he knew the instant she opened her mouth to speak that he had made a grave mistake.

"Very well, Reaper," she said in a voice carved from ice, looking down on him as though he were an ant beneath her boot, an obstacle that she must swiftly and unforgivingly crush. "The time for bargaining has passed; you have made your decision, and so must I. You have thirty-six hours to reap the girl's soul, or I will unleash hell on you and your kind. I will rain misery on anyone that any of you have ever known or loved, and that includes that beloved mortal of yours. Think me cruel if you will, Thorne," she said, and he couldn't help but flinch slightly. "But if you threaten what has been the effort of my eternal life to maintain, you mark yourself as my enemy."

"I think we both know that I have always been your enemy," said Thorne. "Or at least, I represent who it is that you truly despise. But if war is what you want, war is what you will get."

Stunned silence echoed throughout the small office as Thorne finished, and he hung his head, pressing his palms harshly against his closed eyes.

"I should never have gone there," he said, his voice muffled and broken. "I've fucked everything up. Any hope that we had...it's all gone, now. I have *nothing*—no cards to play, no tricks up my sleeve. I have *nothing* that I can bargain with. I've just made everything worse. *Fuck!*" He slammed a fist on the desk. "And to make matters worse, she threatened you and Jai—after I *promised* that my actions would not affect you. I don't know what to do." His voice was thick, something wet pressing at the back of his eyes. He pressed his palms against his face again, as though it could stop the tears from coming.

"Shit," Minho breathed as he leaned back into his seat, looking nearly as defeated as Thorne felt. "Listen," he said, sitting forward and licking his lips, seeming to consider his words carefully before speaking them into existence. "I do not fully understand why she means so much to you; I know that you can see her, and she can see you, and you feel a connection there, but I cannot completely comprehend what it is about this girl that makes you so willing to damn everything to save her." He paused, then, "With that being said...I haven't forgotten what it feels like. That connection." Thorne looked up to meet his eyes, and Minho smiled a little sadly, his eyes shining before he blinked the dampness rapidly away and continued. "And you are my friend. I suppose what I am trying to say is...I will stand by you. No matter what happens, I am on your side, Thorne." Thorne's red-rimmed eyes filled with relief, and he nodded.

"Thank you, Min," he said gratefully, and a smile wavered on his lips. "I...I don't know what I would do without you."

"Oh, get yourself into an even worse mess than you're already in, most likely," Minho responded cheerfully, a twinkle in his eyes as he grinned. Thorne snorted softly, rolling his eyes.

"Probably," he agreed. With a sigh, he leaned forward to rest his elbows on the desk and ran a hand through his messy hair, pushing it out of his face. "I just...I don't have any solutions," he admitted, his shoulders sagging in weary defeat. Minho gazed deeply at him in silence, sadness and something like surprise in his expression, as though he had never seen Thorne looking so completely *exhausted*, so utterly destroyed, as if something had been torn out of him. Perhaps something had.

They sat in silence for several long moments, Thorne in weary defeat, and Minho with brows furrowed and lips pursed slightly, as though he were wracking his brain for something that could possibly solve this. Out of the corner of his eye, Thorne saw his friend's expression suddenly brighten, like the bulb had switched on in his mind. He eyed Thorne hesitantly.

"There might be *one* way," he said slowly, and Thorne raised his head, brows pushing together at Minho's somewhat guilty expression. It dawned on him quickly what Minho was suggesting, and he shook his head.

"No." He rose from his chair so swiftly that it slammed back against the wall, nearly toppling from the force. "Absolutely not. *Not an option.*"

"If it is the only way—"

"It's *not*," Thorne said vehemently, his teeth flashing. "It *can't* be—there *has* to be another solution. Some other option."

"Thorne." Minho's tone was hard, unyielding. "This *is* the other option. I know that you don't want to, that it might be one of the hardest, most unpleasant things you will ever have to face," *A massive understatement if there ever was one.* "But if you want to save Kai as badly as you say that you do, *this* is how you can do it." Feeling chastened and sullen, Thorne was silent, refusing to meet Minho's eyes as he took in his words. Though he was loathe to admit it, he knew that his friend was right—this probably *was* their only option.

Several long, tense moments passed before either of them spoke, one waiting for an answer and the other trying to come to terms with what had been said, searching desperately for another solution—*any* other solution.

"Well, then," Thorne sighed deeply, dropping heavily back into his chair and pulling an old, dusty bottle from his bottom desk drawer. The label was faded, but Thorne flicked the top off and took a long sip, hissing at the burn that followed as the liquid slipped down his throat. He slid the bottle across the desk to Minho, who took a small, dubious sip and winced. Thorne met his eyes fully, seeming resigned, but freshly determined. "Looks like I'm going to the Underworld."

Chapter Twenty
WARMTH

KAI

When Kai arrived home, it was with a heavy heart and a guilty conscience, her shoulders sagging and eyelids drooping heavily with exhaustion. She dropped her bag by the door and collapsed onto the couch, the small, nagging voice in her head whispering that she was selfish, that this was all her fault, that she should still be at the hospital right now, waiting alongside Avery's family for her to wake.

I know, she thought wearily, lowering a hand to pet Mister Sylvester as he walked by on the way to his water bowl.

She hadn't been able to take it anymore—the devastated expressions painted across the faces of Avery's family; the way that Avery's mother kept insisting that she had seen Avery's finger twitch, paging the nurse over and over only to be informed that there was no change in Avery's brain activity, that she was still, in fact, hopelessly unconscious for reasons beyond human comprehension; the way that Avery's dad just sat there in silence, head bowed and one hand lying on the hospital bed. She hadn't been able to stomach the way that Avery's youngest cousins kept asking when Avery was going to wake up, or the way that Avery's grandfather looked frailer than Kai had ever seen him, as if the stress and grief of it all was going to do him in at any given moment.

She hadn't been able to pretend that this wasn't all her fault, or that she believed Avery was going to wake anytime soon, or that she wasn't about to collapse from grief and exhaustion. And of course, *of course* Avery's mother, the kind soul that she was, had noticed the way that Kai had been leaning against the wall like it was the only thing keeping her on her feet, and had insisted in a tone bleeding with maternal concern that Kai should go home and rest, that they would let her know if there was any change.

Kai knew that she should have smiled and shaken her head, should have downed another energy drink from the hospital vending machine and insisted that she was okay, that she wanted to stay. Should have rolled her shoulders back and lifted her chin and pretended that this wasn't absolutely killing her from the inside out.

Instead, she had simply nodded, offering a half-hearted smile that had come off as more of a grimace, and slipped quietly from the room as Avery's mother exclaimed for the fifteenth time that she could have *sworn* she'd just seen Avery's eyelids move.

Selfish, the voice in Kai's head reminded her with a hiss. *Weak.*

I know.

With a huff of frustration, she flipped onto her side and reached for the worn, woven blanket at her feet, yanking it up to her ears and screwing her eyes shut in determination. If it killed her, she was going to get some sleep so that she could feel, if not exactly well-rested, at least not quite as exhausted as she felt now, so that when she returned to the hospital she could sit by Avery's bedside without feeling so completely panicked and suffocated and drained.

She was nearly asleep when she heard a knock at the door. *No,* she thought, feeling a sudden desperate urge to burst into tears. She was so *tired.* Another knock and, dully, she opened her eyes. Slowly, her head feeling unbearably heavy, she swung her legs off of the couch and onto the cold hardwood, sighing deeply as she pushed herself to her feet and padded heavily to the door.

"If this isn't important," she said as she flipped the lock and turned the knob. "I will kill you and everyone you've ever met." She yanked the door open and promptly froze, eyes going wide.

"So," began Thorne, looking nearly as guilty and exhausted as Kai felt. "I may or may not have screwed everything up."

He wasn't sure if Kai was going to kill him, burst into tears, collapse into an exhausted heap on the floor, or all three at once—or at least, in very quick succession. He saw her fists clench at her sides, her shoulders tensing as her expression morphed from shock to anger to confusion and back to anger again, her brown eyes burning as she looked at him.

She moved suddenly to close the door and, his eyes widening in panic, Thorne bolted forward.

"Wait!" Instinctively, he shoved his boot into the doorframe, wincing as his foot was crushed by the slamming door. Kai scowled, and opened the door just enough to try and slam it shut again—once, twice, three more times before Thorne swore, raising a hand to forcibly stop the door from moving any further. "*Ouch.*" Kai glowered at him, the dark bags beneath her eyes and the tangled waves falling messily around her face giving her the appearance of a woman unhinged. Thorne couldn't help but shift on his feet slightly in discomfort, swallowing hard as he tried to find his next words.

"Look," he sighed, pausing to blow a strand of hair out of his eyes, the messy ponytail that he'd shoved his hair into just before leaving his office already beginning to come undone. "I know that you're pissed at me, and I've accepted that, but there's something you should know." Kai's jaw tightened, and slowly, she looked up at him, lifting her brows expectantly. "Can I come in?" He waited as she exhaled sharply in irritation, seeming to briefly consider her options before rolling her eyes and walking away.

He took that as a grudging *yes* and cautiously stepped into the apartment, shutting the door quietly behind him and turning the lock. Kai said nothing, looking away from him as she sat down on the couch with her legs tucked underneath her, seeming determined to ignore him even as he took a seat in the chair beside her.

Thorne couldn't fight the nerves that skittered across his atoms, his stomach feeling as though it had been turned inside out and upside down, fingers tapping anxiously against his thigh as he licked his lips, wondering how best to deliver his news.

"So," he said, trying in vain to swallow the lump that seemed to have lodged itself permanently in his throat.

"So," Kai repeated blankly. A small, breathless laugh escaped Thorne, but he quickly smoothed his features back into a serious expression.

"Sorry." He cleared his throat. "Um...well, like I said, I, uh, I may or may not have made things catastrophically worse." He winced, reaching up to scratch behind his ear, pausing to play anxiously with the silver hoop dangling from his cartilage. His nose twitched, and every sound in his body seemed to magnify in his ears as his heel started to tap a quick rhythm on the floor, his knee bouncing anxiously. Kai's eyes cut over sharply at the movement, and as the minutes dragged on, she seemed to grow increasingly annoyed, her jaw clenching and unclenching as she kept opening her mouth to speak, then seeming to think better of it.

Finally, she lunged across the space between them to slam a palm on his knee, glaring up at him in profound irritation as she said in a tone that left no room for argument, "*Stop.* Speak." Thorne's Adam's apple jerked sharply as he swallowed, and her eyes followed the movement.

"Sorry," he said again, sounding slightly hoarse. Kai nodded and withdrew back to her seat, with cheeks that seemed just slightly rosier than they had been the moment before. "Right—where was I?"

"You somehow managed to make everything worse than it already is," Kai prompted flatly, and he nodded, smoothing his palms against his jeans as he took a deep breath.

"Right. So...you remember the Keeper?"

"You mentioned her—terrifying immortal being that really, really wants me dead?" Thorne nodded.

"That's the one. I...may or may not have demanded a meeting with her." Kai's brows jumped a little in surprise, and Thorne pressed quickly forward. "It didn't go well, to say the least—she doesn't like to negotiate, it seems, and she...she gave me thirty-six hours to...well, to reap your soul." Kai exhaled sharply, and her entire body seemed to deflate, making her look small.

"Wow," she scoffed, shaking her head a little as she stared down at her hands, lying still and open in her lap. "Well...thanks for telling me, I guess." She swallowed, avoiding his gaze as she began to absentmindedly pick at the skin around her nails. Thorne reached over to cover her hands with one of his own, and she flinched, jumping slightly at the unexpected physical contact.

"I'm not going to let you die," Thorne said, and when, slowly, she looked up to meet his gaze, he smiled, his eyes shining earnestly. "I made you a promise, and I intend to keep it; I'm not giving up on you just yet, Sanchez."

"How do you—?"

"I spent a lot of time sitting outside your apartment," Thorne grinned, shrugging a shoulder. Kai tilted her head, and Thorne gestured to the pile of mail scattered haphazardly across the coffee table. Her forehead smoothed in understanding and, unable to help herself, she laughed.

It was a contagious sound, though Thorne found himself too in awe of her to join in, caught utterly by surprise by the way that her eyes lit up in unguarded amusement, her smile so wide that dimples appeared in her rounded cheeks. Something warmed inside of Thorne's chest, and he couldn't help but stare with softly parted lips as she sank back into the couch cushions.

As her laughter dissolved into soft, breathless giggles, she noticed his captivated expression and flushed slightly.

"What?" She asked, crossing her arms over her chest self-consciously.

"Nothing." Thorne shook his head a little, then shook it again to fully jolt himself out of his trance. "So..."

"*So...*" Kai grinned crookedly, rolling her eyes as she grabbed a pillow and set it on her lap, absently playing with the braided tassels that lined the edges. "Do you have a plan, then?" Thorne's eyes widened.

"Oh! Yeah—*yes,* of course. It's kind of dangerous, and it more than likely won't even work, but...it's our best option. Our *only* option, really." Kai's brows lifted expectantly, and Thorne took another deep breath.

Chapter Twenty-One
HYPOTHERMIC

For the fourth time in as many minutes, Minho voiced his concern about the plan, a frown having taken up a seemingly permanent residence in his expression. His arms were crossed, and when his eyes shifted briefly to Kai before casting another sidelong glance at Thorne, she shifted uncomfortably in her seat.

"I think he hates me," she murmured to Jai, who laughed brightly, his long, aquiline nose wrinkling as the corners of his dark brown eyes creased.

"Nah, he's just worried," he reassured her before jerking his head, violently and abruptly, to the side in an attempt to flick his wavy black bangs out of his eyes. He turned his attention back to Kai. "It's kind of what he does—he's a worrier. And he thinks this plan is reckless." Kai glanced dubiously back at Minho, who stood several feet away absorbed in a quiet conversation with Thorne. She sighed.

"Is it?" Jai's brows lifted, and she clarified. "I mean, how big a deal is this, exactly?" She gnawed at her lower lip nervously, her fingers tangling themselves in the hem of her knit sweater as her stomach began to wind itself into a series of tight knots.

"You're going to the Underworld," Jai said, as if that answered everything. Kai nodded, releasing the air that she had been holding in her chest, though the tension remained.

"Right," she said, her eyes glazing over slightly as she recalled the conversation of the previous evening.

*"The Underworld?" Kai's eyes were wide, her tone echoing her disbelief. "As in, the **Underworld?"** Thorne nodded, looking more than a little nervous as he watched her digest the news. Expelling a sharp breath, Kai dropped back onto the couch.*

"Wow," she said, and Thorne snorted.

*"Yeah." They sat in silence for a moment and, after casting several furtive glances in his direction, Kai turned to face Thorne fully, hands clasped neatly in her lap. She felt **awake,** a fire igniting in her chest at the possibilities—not only of saving her own life, but also of waking Avery.*

"Okay, tell me one more time exactly what it is you're doing. Just so I have everything straight."

"I'm going to pay a visit to an...acquaintance of mine in the Underworld. There's a chance—and I cannot stress enough just how slim that chance is—that he can help us." Kai nodded, considering his words. After a moment, she nodded again, firmly. She had made her decision.

"Alright," she said. "I'm coming with you."

"This is a bad idea." In the corner of the small hospital room, Thorne and Minho were engaged in a murmured conversation, both standing with their shoulders hunched and arms crossed, as if being physically closed off from the rest of the room would somehow make their conversation more private. "This is a bad idea," Minho repeated, his eyes shifting once more to Kai, who had her head thrown back in laughter at something that Jai had said. The two seemed to be getting along surprisingly well for two people who had met all of exactly twelve and a half minutes ago.

Minho sighed, shaking his head. "This is a bad idea." Across from him, Thorne's fists clenched so tightly his knuckles went white.

"If you say that one more time, I'm going to send *you* to the Underworld," he threatened under his breath, and Minho cut a narrow-eyed glare at him before rolling his eyes.

"Very well," he acquiesced, then, "Are you *sure* about this?" Thorne winched slightly.

"No," he admitted, reaching back to rub the nape of his neck in discomfort. "Honestly, I *know* this is a bad idea that's likely to go horribly wrong, but..."

"No," Thorne said immediately, rising so quickly from his seat that Mister Sylvester, napping peacefully in the corner of the room, started abruptly awake to see what the racket was about. "No, absolutely not." Thorne shook his head in firm denial of her request, and Kai pushed herself to her feet as well, looking him resolutely in the eye.

*"It's **my life!**" She protested vehemently, and the fire in her eyes burned so bright that Thorne shut his mouth, waiting for her to continue. She exhaled sharply and returned to her seat on the couch. Slowly, reluctantly, Thorne did the same, reseating himself in the worn armchair adjacent.*

"Thank you," she said, and sighed. "Look, I know that you have no reason to do this for me, and it would probably be much easier for you to just agree to do this and then ditch me at the last second," Thorne averted his eyes guiltily. "But it's **my** *life, and I can't just sit here and do nothing but go crazy with anxiety while you go to the literal Underworld to plead my case. And if I die..." she lifted one shoulder, her expression one of steely resignation. "Then at least I'll die fighting for something."*

"She's right," Thorne said, and sighed deeply, pressing his thumb and forefinger to the bridge of his nose in an attempt to alleviate the pain currently wreaking havoc on his skull. "It is *her* life." He laughed a little and shook his head ruefully. "I just hope that this doesn't all turn out to be for nothing." Minho placed a sympathetic hand on Thorne's shoulder. He said nothing, but the gesture was enough; Thorne smiled gratefully and covered Minho's hand briefly with his own, and the pair turned around.

"So..." Kai dragged out the word, narrowing her eyes slightly at the youthful boy sitting across from her. Startled, Jai looked immediately up from the graphic novel he'd been perusing in the moments since Kai had fallen silent. His round, brown eyes opened wide as he returned his attention to her, reaching up to brush the bangs out of his face. His brows lifted expectantly, then knit together at the expression on Kai's face. It was thoughtful, but suspicious, almost, as though she were trying to figure something out. "How long have you known Thorne?" She asked at last.

"I've been a Reaper for nearly ten years now," Jai responded, and she blinked.

"Wait, you weren't like, born—or created, or whatever—like this?" Jai laughed softly and shook his head, the light above them glinting against the delicate gold chains dangling from his earlobes.

"None of us were," he said. "Except for Thorne, all of us Reapers were ordinary humans who died with what we call *unfinished business.* Being a Reaper helps us...not always *finish* that business, per se, but to get the closure that we need to move on." Kai opened her mouth to say something, then shut it, unsure of what she could possibly say in response to that. A billion questions were already buzzing around her mind, but she couldn't figure out which one to ask first. Her forehead creased, and she squinted, trying to make sense of it all.

"You said *except* for Thorne," she said. "But Thorne said...he said that *he* used to be human, too. How did *he* become a Reaper, then?" Jai hesitated, gnawing on his lower lip as his gaze flickered briefly to Thorne, still standing with Minho in the corner of the room as they spoke in lowered tones, oblivious to the conversation happening behind them.

"It's not my story to tell," Jai said at last, shaking his head again.

"What do you mean?" Kai tilted her head, but Jai's lips were sealed.

"You'd just have to ask Thorne," was all he said, and Kai sighed in frustration, but moved on.

"Fine." She twisted her lips, taking a moment to consider her next question. "*Your* unfinished business. After ten years, you still haven't...?" A grieved expression darkened Jai's boyish features, and Kai instantly regretted asking.

"No," he responded, the corners of his lips curving upward in a tight smile that was clearly forced. Despite her guilt, Kai was itching to ask him what his 'unfinished business' was, the curious side of her battling with the more sensible part that argued that it was none of her business.

Fortunately, he seemed to sense what it was that she wanted to know.

"I have—*had*—a younger sister. Nadiya. She was six years younger than me, only fourteen when I died. She was still just a kid." His lips twisted as his eyes shone with unshed tears, and Kai's heart ached, her fingers twitching slightly, instinctively wanting to reach out in comfort. "I was always her protector," Jai said, pausing briefly to swallow the lump in his throat. "It was ingrained in me, since the moment she was born. And then I died, and I just...I don't know, couldn't let that side of me go, I guess. I still can't." He stared down at his heavy black combat boots.

"I'm sorry," Kai said, meaning it. Jai glanced up at her through his bangs, and she offered a small, sympathetic smile. "I know what it's like to...to lose a sibling like that. So abruptly." She nearly choked as her throat began to close up, and she quickly cleared it, sniffling a little as she looked away and opened her eyes wide, fighting the tears that she felt trying to make their way to the surface.

She started when she felt a cold hand cover hers, and she looked up to find Jai leaning forward, a little bit of his former brightness returning to his expression as he smiled at her.

"Thank you," he said, and when she nodded, he pulled away, his bronze cheeks flushed slightly. They sat in somewhat awkward silence once more until, hesitantly, Kai asked another of the hundreds of questions still swirling around her mind.

"What happens when you finally *do* move on?" Jai seemed to perk up at the question, glad to be moving on to a less depressing topic.

"Well," he began, rubbing his palms over his ripped black jeans, leaning forward slightly as he considered the question. "There are two options, really: you can either, as you said, *move on,* and enter the afterlife for judgment—you know, heaven or hell, perfect paradise or eternal damnation, that sort of thing—or you can choose to stay, to be a Reaper and spend eternity harvesting souls and guiding them to their afterlife."

"Who in their right mind would choose *that?*" Kai's tone and expression echoed her bewilderment, and a small smile lifted the corners of Jai's mouth.

"I did." Kai nearly jumped out of her skin as Minho suddenly appeared at their sides, having apparently finished his conversation with Thorne and approached them without a sound. There was a soft smile on his face, and a gentle expression in his eyes as he looked down at her.

"You—but—*why?*" Kai blurted, unable to help herself, and her cheeks heated again as she saw Thorne, standing just behind Minho, smother a grin. Minho himself seemed to be alight with amusement, his eyes twinkling as he took a seat on the edge of the hospital bed, taking a deep, thoughtful breath as he considered the question.

"It took...*some* time for me to move on from my unfinished business," he said slowly, and his expression grew distant, losing himself to a time long gone. "Thorne was...he was there for me during a time that I desperately needed it. He helped me through my anger and my grief, and never made me feel as if moving on was something that was *expected* of me." He smiled, his eyes shining as he looked at his friend. Kai was surprised to see the same warm, affectionate expression on Thorne's face. It was the most open she had ever seen him.

Minho continued. "By the time that I was truly *ready* to move on, he had become my closest friend. More like a brother, really; he knew me better than anyone, save for one other that I...left behind." Kai's brows knit together, and she tilted her head, struggling to understand.

"So you felt like you owed him?"

"Not at all," he waved her question aside, shaking his head. "I merely felt that it was better to stay in the In-Between with a friend than to venture into the unknown that lay ahead alone. Besides, I don't mind the work—contrary to what you may think, it's really not that bad, and the paperwork relaxes me." He grinned widely, the expression making him look years younger.

"Huh." Kai sat back in her seat, staring down at her hands as she tried to process what she had just heard. Everything about this was so different from anything that she had ever expected or imagined; she wasn't sure what to *think,* let alone what to say next.

"My family," she said suddenly, hopeful. "Does this mean—could they be...?" The trio of suddenly somber Reapers refused to meet her eyes, letting their silence speak for them. "Oh," she said softly, the disappointment far more crushing than she wanted to admit. She took a steadying breath and nodded once, firmly. "*Right.* Well, then." She rose to her feet, running her palms over her sweater to smooth an invisible wrinkle as she glanced tentatively toward the bed that Minho was still sitting on. "Explain it to me one more time, please?"

All three Reapers seemed relieved that she wasn't awaiting a verbal answer to her previous question, and they sprang into action, practically tripping over each other as they all tried to move around the small room at once.

"The basic idea is for you to be unconscious. Not *dead,* because that is exactly what we are trying to avoid, and there is pretty much a zero-point-one percent chance that we would actually be able to resuscitate you, given that there are multiple entities that are currently in active pursuit of your death," Minho explained, surprisingly upbeat in light of the subject matter. "So we are going to induce unconsciousness via hypothermia, and Thorne is going to, in his own words," he rolled his eyes a little. "*Drag your soul kicking and screaming into the Underworld.*" Thorne nodded, an almost proud smile on his face. Kai couldn't help the giggle that escaped her, though she smothered it quickly when his attention turned to her, her cheeks warming involuntarily. Minho snapped his fingers, and Thorne blinked.

"Pay attention to this," said Minho sternly. "The first couple seconds that she is under will be when she is at her most vulnerable, so you need to act fast—get her to the Underworld, and get her where she needs to be. *Do not lose her.* If you do, there is a strong chance that she won't be coming back." Everyone in the room had the good sense to look nervous, and not for the first time, Kai heard the little voice in her head whisper that this was a terrible, horrible idea that was going to end badly for all parties involved.

Minho continued. "The longer that you're there, the more at risk you are that someone will find out about all of this, so try and make it fast. I know that you will have a lot of ground to cover, and time works differently in the Underworld, but still, it is absolutely imperative that this be an in-and-out operation—do you understand?" Thorne nodded, and though he looked nervous, he appeared resolute, utterly determined to do everything in his power to bring Kai back alive. Minho nodded. "Good. Now, Kailani—do you go by Kailani?"

"Just Kai is fine," she said weakly, not bothering to ask how he knew her full name.

"Alright, *Kai*, you have the easy job: all you have to do is lie down on this bed and let us do our part. Oh, and when you get down there, try not to die." Kai nodded, a knot of anxious nerves stabbing at the lining of her stomach, and Minho rolled his shoulders back, looking around between the three of them. "Ready?"

"As we'll ever be, I suppose," said Thorne, flexing his hands as he pulled his hair back into a neat ponytail. He flashed Kai a smile of confident reassurance that, if the fingers tapping a rapid rhythm against his denim-covered thigh were any indication, he did not feel himself. Nevertheless, Kai returned the smile, taking a deep, albeit slightly shaky, breath as she perched delicately on the end of the bed.

"This is a paralytic," Minho said as he inserted a long, slender needle into her arm, slowly injecting the liquid within into her veins. "This will keep you from shivering and putting undue stress on your heart and lungs when we put you under—it is vital that your body be as relaxed as possible while you're unconscious." Kai nodded, swallowing as she tried to push down the feeling of panic that arose at the idea of being unable to move. Minho helped her lie down, and she felt another pang of anxiety in her stomach as she stared up at the tiled ceiling.

"And here's the sedative," Minho murmured as he slid another needle into her arm, just below where he had injected the paralytic. Kai flinched at the brief sting. "Feeling alright?"

"So far, so good." The words came out slightly slurred, her eyes already beginning to droop heavily as her arms and legs went limp, her blood pumping the sedative quickly through her veins. Minho let out a sharp breath and gave a quick nod to Jai and Thorne, who began piling bags of ice on and around Kai's body.

"It's a rather crude and admittedly risky method," Minho had admitted when he'd suggested it. *"But it's the only feasible option. Ideally, it will both induce the comatose state and preserve her neural function, so that she*

doesn't experience brain damage when she wakes up." Kai had appreciated his use of *when* and not *if* when referring to her return to consciousness.

She inhaled sharply through her nose as the cold began to seep in, permeating her very bones, and several pained gasps escaped her blue lips. The inability to shiver almost made it worse, forcing her to simply lay there and wait for the sedative and the cold to render her unconscious. Out of the corner of her eye, she saw Thorne stealing nervous glances at her as he continued to arrange the bags of ice around her body.

"This is a terrible idea," she heard Minho's voice, faintly distant, say from somewhere above her.

"Minho!" Thorne snapped, his voice sharp and tight with irritation. Minho snapped right back.

"Excuse me for having reservations about practically killing the very human that you are so desperate to keep alive using a medical procedure I found out how to perform from The Google all of *two hours ago!*"

"For fuck's sake, Min, it's medically-induced *hypothermia,* not *rocket science.*"

"I thought you said he had a background in medicine?" Jai's voice was high in alarm.

"My *father* was a Physician's Assistant—*in the seventeenth century!*"

"Family background in medicine," Thorne said smoothly, though even as she began to slip out of consciousness, Kai could hear the strain of stress in his voice.

"I'm about to put *you* into a state of medically-induced unconsciousness," Minho threatened, and Thorne growled something in response. The last thing that Kai heard, dimly and far in the distance as her awareness began to fade, was Jai's exclaimed,

"Guys, I think it's working!"

Chapter Twenty-Two
THE UNDERWORLD

KAI

She awoke with a gasp, her surroundings coming sharply into focus just as the stench of death slammed into her nostrils. She clamped a hand over her mouth in an attempt to keep herself from gagging.

Everything around her was painted in muted, drab shades of gray, and there was a sort of static hanging in the air, dulling any sound that might have existed. The air itself was thick and stifling, crushing her, as if she was being gradually boxed in from every angle. Something to her right moved, and not even the suffocating static around her could muffle the horrified shriek that tore from Kai's throat as she realized that she was surrounded.

The crowd slowly milling around her did not seem to notice her presence—or if they noticed, they simply didn't care. There seemed to be far too many of them for it to be comfortable, each person brushing against the next and scarcely leaving room to breathe, but Kai heard no complaints. In fact, they weren't saying *anything*.

Swallowing her fear, Kai tapped the shoulder of the woman nearest to her, hoping to find out where they all were—or at least, how she could get out. The woman, however, paid her no mind, not sparing her a glance as she trudged along, her eyes blank as they stared straight ahead, not seeming to be focused on anything or anyone in particular.

Kai's brows furrowed as she watched the woman go, trepidation building in her stomach as her skin began to crawl with the distinct feeling that something wasn't right—*this* wasn't right. She shouldn't be here. Thorne—where was Thorne?

Something dripped onto the sand beneath her feet, and she froze, daring to slowly lower her gaze to the dark stain. Was that—?

Blood, she realized, her spine locking just as she came face to face with the person that the blood must have come from. It was hard to tell whether they had been a man or a woman or perhaps neither, because what was left of their face was covered in red.

Kai screamed.

She screamed so loudly that her throat burned as she stumbled quickly back, desperate to get away from the gaping skull that was pouring crimson, realizing with a sudden cold horror the reason that everyone was so quiet, why they didn't seem to notice her. She could see the woman whose attention she had tried to catch a moment ago—there was red staining her side, as if she had been stabbed or impaled. Another woman stood nearby with her neck bent at an unnatural angle, bruises in the shape of large hands wrapped around her ivory throat. A young boy brushed Kai's hand as he walked past, water spilling from his mouth and onto his already-soaked clothes.

Some of the figures surrounding Kai *weren't* quite so gruesome, hadn't seemed to face such horrifying, bloody ends; some of them were old, men and women with wrinkled, paper-thin skin and bags under their eyes, looking as though the very oxygen had been stolen from their lungs, slipping quietly between their lips as they slept. There were sickly children with no hair and middle-aged men with yellowed skin who reeked of alcohol, and women who exhaled frost as snow fell from their eyelashes.

Nausea rolled violently in Kai's stomach as she backed away, trying in vain to put some distance between herself and the dead. She couldn't breathe; she gasped desperately for air as she felt several cold, stiff limbs brush against hers as the crowd continued to move around her, black spots beginning to cloud her vision.

A hand—ever so slightly warmer than those of the surrounding dead—latched onto her, and Kai shrieked again as she smacked at the tanned fingers wrapped tightly around her wrist. Another arm looped around her waist, and a few petrified tears slipped down her cheeks as she thrashed in the firm grip of her captor, her screams growing loud and frantic.

In the distance, she could hear someone calling her name, but it wasn't until she was set on her feet in what seemed to be a dim, secluded cave and looking into a familiar face that she realized that the voice wasn't distant at all, but right in front of her, and that her captor, who was shaking her by the shoulders and repeating her name with increasing urgency, was none other than Thorne.

The realization washed over Kai in a wave of relief and inexplicable anger, and she shoved him away from her, nostrils flaring as fury blazed in her eyes.

"*Asshole!*" She shoved him again for good measure, and under any other circumstances, the shock painted across his expression might have made her laugh. "You scared me half to death!" His lips parted softly, his bewildered expression melting into something tender and apologetic, and that was enough to make Kai's lip quiver, a couple of leftover tears spilling down her cheeks as she threw herself into his arms.

She felt his surprise in the way that he recoiled slightly, his body going stiff as his fingers wrapped around her upper arms, possibly to push her away, before he relaxed into her touch, his hands sliding around to her back as he returned the embrace, hesitant and awkward, as though it were a gesture most unfamiliar to him.

"Are you alright?" He asked, craning his neck back in an attempt to see her face, which she had buried in his shirt—black and soft, smelling of pine and leather and something that seemed tangibly familiar, but that she still couldn't quite place.

He seemed to be waiting for an answer, one of his hands rubbing comforting, absentminded circles between her shoulders.

"I'm fine," she said, her voice muffled by his shirt, and she felt his other hand begin to carefully stroke her hair. *Oh,* she thought, the furrow between her brows easing as her heartbeat began to slow. "You just caught me off guard, is all."

"This is exactly what I was afraid of," he sighed, his tone laced with disapproval. "I knew that you wouldn't be able to handle this. It's a shock to people who actually *belong* here, let alone somebody who isn't *actually* dead."

"I can handle it," Kai said automatically, defensively, and she could feel in the set of his shoulders how little he believed her. She took a deep, shuddering breath, pulling reluctantly out of his arms as she used the sleeves of her sweater to dry her tears. "I can handle it," she repeated with conviction. Thorne leaned down slightly to meet her eyes, and she tried not to cringe away from the way that they seemed to see into her very soul. *Technically, they are,* the voice in her head told her. It was an odd thought, but one that she had no time to dwell on.

Finally, Thorne straightened, sighing deeply as he shook his head in the remnants of disbelief. He rolled his eyes, not unkindly. "Come on," he said in resignation, tilting his head toward the entrance of the cave. Kai hesitated.

"Isn't there another way?" She asked, and Thorne turned back to her, his expression softening.

"Afraid not," he said, walking back over to her. She swallowed as he came close, her chest tight as she stared up at him, into the eyes that did seem to be truly *sorry* that this was the only solution. She sighed, looking down and scuffing her sneaker in the damp sand. The top of her head brushed against Thorne's chest, and she let it stay there a moment, closing her eyes and imagining that this was all just a horrendously bad dream. Minho had been right—this *was* a bad idea. What had Kai been thinking, coming here? This was no place for the living.

"Come on," Thorne said again, his voice soft and quiet, and he wrapped his hand around one of Kai's, tugging her gently toward the jagged arch of the cave's entrance. Though every shred of self-preserving instinct inside of her screamed not to follow, to turn *back*, Kai let him lead her back onto the beach from whence they had come, her stomach tightening as the gruesome crowd came back into view.

"They can't hurt you." Despite Thorne's words, Kai clung to his hand tightly as they skirted around the edge of the beach, giving the crowd a generous berth. They walked in silence for some time, and Kai took the opportunity to slowly take in her surroundings, the knot of anxiety in her stomach growing with every step that they took.

They were, as she had previously observed, on a beach, but it was nothing like any beach that she had ever seen; for one, while it was certainly long—so long that Kai could see it fading into the distance with no sign of an end—it was more akin to a narrow strip of sand than a *true* beach, which would have been open and wide and golden, with the sun shining overhead and a sky of bright blue as far as the eye could see.

There was no sun here, and what was overhead seemed to be less of a sky than it was a swirling mass of black and gray. The cave that they had just left seemed to be one of many—indeed, the beach itself backed up to what seemed to be a border of small caves and piles of large, heavy-looking boulders, and beyond that...

A wall. Kai's mouth fell softly open at the realization that they were not, as she had thought, on an open beach, but inside of a *cave.* The wall of dark adamant stretched high and far, disappearing into the darkness overhead and stretching down the beach until it disappeared into the thick fog, enclosing them in a space that seemed far smaller than Kai had first imagined.

And yet, it was bigger than she had thought, too, because on the side of the beach opposite the wall, waves lapped gently against the shoreline, and the water—dark, with what seemed to be a light layer of steam or mist dancing above the surface—seemed to go on endlessly, without a building or island in sight. The way that the veritable ocean seemed to disappear into the great blue-black beyond gave Kai a shiver, and she realized suddenly that their pace had slowed considerably.

Glancing up, she found Thorne looking directly back at her, and she flushed, ducking her head as she jogged forward a couple of steps to catch up with him, using his hand as an anchor as her sneakered feet tried to sink into the sand below.

"Sorry," she murmured, and Thorne shook his head and gave her hand a small squeeze, as if telling her not to worry about it. She sighed lightly as she took another look over her shoulder, glad to see that they seemed to be leaving the pacing mass of the deceased behind them.

Several more moments passed where the only sounds were that of their breath, coming out in soft pants as they walked farther and farther down the strip of beach and into the unknown beyond, and that of the waves softly caressing the sands of the shore.

When they had put what felt like a safe enough distance between them and the dead, Kai finally asked, at a volume barely above a whisper, "Who were those...*people?* What is this place?"

"What you see to our left is the Styx—the River of Lost Souls. you may know of it from your mortal legends as the river that the ferryman

Charon used to transport souls to the Gates of the Underworld, where they received their judgment and moved on to the afterlife." Kai nodded, the myth sounding vaguely familiar. "This, here, used to be a deceased mortal's first glimpse of the Underworld. When they died, they would make their way here, and if they had something with which to pay him, Charon would take them across the river." Kai's brows furrowed.

"But how could they pay him if they were dead?"

"A long, long time ago, people used to bury their dead with coins—traditionally an *obolus* or *danake*—over their mouths or eyes, believing that when their loved ones reached the Underworld, the coins would help them gain access to the afterlife so that they could find peace. They were correct, in that aspect; every mortal who was buried in that manner found themselves with those same coins when they arrived here, and they were able to use them to buy passage across the Styx.

"Sometime during the Middle Ages, however, people began to stop believing in the Greek deities, writing them off as mere stories or legends—myths. And so they stopped burying their dead with currency. As a result, the banks of the Styx started to grow overcrowded, as the souls that arrived here found themselves with no method of paying the ferryman, who refused to take anyone across the river without compensation.

"This created several problems—namely that, with such a large number of souls left to wander the banks of the Styx in eternal unrest, some of those souls began to make their way back *out* of the Underworld."

"That's possible?"

"It used to be."

"But not anymore?"

The corner of Thorne's mouth twitched. "I'm getting there. *Patience*, Sanchez."

"Sorry," Kai's cheeks heated, pretending to lock her lips and throw away the key. Thorne's lips twitched again, and he continued.

"The journey back to the mortal plane was often incredibly traumatic, especially to souls who had been dead and wandering the banks of the Styx for some time, as they would find themselves in a world that was not only utterly unfamiliar, but could no longer take notice of them. They would seek out whatever was familiar, like their former homes or the place of their death, which resulted, as you might have guessed, in what mortals began referring to as *ghosts*—restless spirits who could not find peace, and who simply wanted for their torment to be seen.

"That's where I come in. Ghosts had become such a problem that the Keeper herself was forced to take action. Clearly, these spirits could not be allowed to continue roaming about the mortal plane, but neither could they truly enter the Underworld; their souls had become stuck in limbo, with no place among mortals, but no way to pass into the afterlife, either.

"When I was...well, when I became what I am," said Thorne, his expression darkening slightly at the vague mention of his past. "The Fates had the perfect solution to the problem: *me.* They convinced the Keeper that I was the answer to their little spirit dilemma, and so they made me into the Grim Reaper, something not quite dead, yet not quite alive, either; a being of both worlds that could make the trip directly from the mortal plane to the Gates of the Underworld. It bypassed the need for Charon, though the souls to which he refused passage are, unfortunately, damned to wander the banks of the Styx for all eternity. The Keeper sealed all other entrances in and out of the Underworld, so that no spirit could ever find their way to the mortal world again."

"That's so sad," Kai said, her chest aching for the souls they had left on the beach behind him. *What a tragedy to never find peace.*

"It is," Thorne agreed quietly, and Kai realized that she had spoken the last sentence aloud, suddenly becoming hyper-aware of the fact that her hand was still clasped tightly in his, their shoulders brushing every time that she lost her balance on the shifting sand beneath her feet.

Neither of them spoke again until what appeared to be a small, one-room cabin came into view, lights flickering dimly in the curtained windows as someone tall and dark moved about the interior. Just in front of the cabin was a short, wooden pier to which a long rowboat was tied, and the knot that had begun to unwind in Kai's stomach snapped back into a tight coil, familiarity flickering in the back of her mind.

Their footsteps on the wooden stairs of the cabin sounded loud in what had, up until now, been relative silence, and the noise was an abrupt jar to Kai's already frazzled nerves. On the very top step, Thorne paused, turning around to face her. In the dim light of the cabin, his expression was drawn, something akin to anxious concern in his eyes. Kai hoped it was just a trick of the light, already feeling incredibly on edge in the frightening, unfamiliar landscape of the Underworld; the last thing that she wanted to know was that he was afraid, too.

"Here," Thorne said, drawing the hood of Kai's sweater over her head, pulling it forward just enough to cast a shadow over her features. Her cheeks heated as he arranged her hair around her face, his eyes averted, as if he knew how intimate the simple act felt. "It would probably be best," he said as he absentmindedly lifted a stray curl off of her shoulder and began to wind it around his pointer finger. "If you let me do the talking in here. I don't believe that he will betray our presence to...that he will tell anyone that we are here, but I would rather be on the safe side of things."

"No argument there," Kai agreed weakly, forcing a small, shaky smile. Her voice must have wavered more than she thought, because Thorne immediately looked up to meet her eyes. She swallowed.

"Are you afraid?" He said it without judgment, his gaze holding hers captive, laying her soul bare, making it hard for her to breathe. She laughed quietly, and a little nervously, as she shifted on her feet.

"Aren't you?" He didn't answer, but his eyes suddenly sharpened slightly, his expression growing more serious.

"Whatever happens, I will be there, alright? I won't let anything happen to you." *I will protect you,* seemed to be his unspoken pledge, his eyes staring almost urgently into hers, as though it were imperative that she believed him. She nodded, the motion almost imperceptible, and he seemed to relax ever so slightly, giving her a firm nod as he finally withdrew his hand from her hair, turning and knocking three times on the wooden door.

In the cabin beyond there was a quiet creak as whoever resided within seemed to be crossing the room, and then the door opened, and the light that spilled from the cabin eclipsed the figure for a split second before it shifted slightly, and Kai could barely restrain the gasp that threatened to escape her lips.

The tall, slender figure appeared to be vaguely humanoid, though precisely what manner of creature it truly was Kai could scarcely tell, for it was covered head to toe by a thick, brownish-gray cloak that was ragged to the point of looking as though it were going to fall to pieces at any moment. And though Kai squinted, she found it impossible to make out a face in the depthless black that lay beneath the cloak's hood.

"Reaper." The figure's voice was ancient—thin and low and rasping, nearly silent with the hoarseness of what must have been centuries of disuse. "To what do I owe this pleasure?"

"I have come to request passage across the Styx," said Thorne, his voice steady.

"Surely, young Reaper, you do not need my talents for this?" The figure questioned, and Kai could hear what sounded like a bitter sneer leaking into its tone.

"Not ordinarily," Thorne agreed. "But this time I do." He offered no further clarification, and the figure merely stared silently at him for a moment, before turning its head toward Kai.

"And who is your...friend?" Kai's stomach clenched, and her fingers twitched; she had to force herself to keep her hands relaxed, her expression a guarded mask of indifference.

"I have coin for the fare," said Thorne, and the creature's attention swiveled immediately back to Thorne, its interest piqued. "And extra to not ask questions." The figure stared in what appeared to be rapt reverence as Thorne pulled a small leather coin pouch from his belt, holding it out for the creature to take. A pair of skeletal hands moved from under the sleeves of the cloak, and Thorne dropped the pouch into them, the long fingers cradling it with care. Slowly, carefully, the creature plucked several of the coins—ancient, slightly lumpy, and vaguely round pieces of silver—and lifted it to the face of the cloak, breathing in deeply.

A pleased growl emanated from its chest, and in several quick, fluid motions it had dropped the coins back into the pouch, tied it shut, and deposited it somewhere safely inside the folds of the cloak.

"I will take you." The figure pulled the door of the cabin shut and brushed promptly past them, moving with purpose down the steps and across the sand to the pier. Kai fought the nausea that rolled in her stomach as the figure's cloak brushed against her, smelling of rot and decay and intensely of ocean salt.

"Come on," murmured Thorne as he moved to follow the creature, leading her onto the pier and to the rowboat, which the figure that Kai now realized must be none other than Charon was currently untying from the small dock. He swept out his bony hand in a gesture for them to board, Kai doing so after a split second of hesitation, and after Charon joined them, standing at the head of the boat with his long, spindly fingers wrapped around a long wooden pole, they were off.

They were, the three of them, utterly silent during what seemed like a timeless journey up the river. It felt, somehow, as if the trip were taking years, the boat gliding slowly and quietly through the dark, still water, and yet Kai knew that this could not be true; they were on a deadline, and surely if they had been down here for very long, Thorne would have said something. What Minho had mentioned about time moving differently in the Underworld was beginning to make sense.

There were spots in the cave where light seemed to leak in, turning the water a lighter, more translucent blue, and it was in one of these spots that Kai caught a glimpse of something moving below the surface of the water. Despite herself, Kai leaned closer to the edge of the boat for a closer look.

And promptly drew back with a sharp gasp of surprise.

With wide eyes and a racing heart, Kai looked at Thorne. His expression was impassive, but something about the way that his eyes caught hers made Kai's heartbeat slow, breath returning to her lungs as he shifted ever so slightly closer, his voice low so that Charon could not overhear.

"What you saw just now was likely one of the Lost Souls," he said, his gaze shifting briefly to where Charon was standing at the rear of the boat, still as stone save for the way that he periodically lifted his pole to push them further along the river. "Until now, I wasn't sure whether it was entirely true, but I had heard that there were many who tried to cross the river on their own when they discovered that Charon would not grant them passage without payment. The river is, unfortunately, impossible to cross without a vessel, and so the souls became trapped."

"Is there no way to get them out?" asked Kai, peering tentatively back over the side of the boat. The ghostly figure was nowhere to be seen. Thorne shook his head gravely.

"None that I am aware of. It's been said that the river used to be a favorite punishment of Hades—for some souls, living in limbo is a fate worse than anything that could be brewed up in the Fields of Punishment." Kai didn't think that she had imagined the bitter resentment that flickered across Thorne's face at the mention of Hades.

They did not speak again until they reached their destination—a rocky shore that seemed to be completely abandoned, a thick haze of gray fog coating the stones of the narrow shoreline. Thorne disembarked first, then held out his hand to assist Kai, his gaze holding steady with the infinite black of Charon's hood as Kai half-stepped, half-fell out of the boat. Letting go of her hand, Thorne pulled out another small pouch and tossed it into Charon's waiting palm.

"For your silence," he said, and Charon nodded, sniffing the coins greedily before dropping them into his cloak, lifting his heavy pole to begin the return journey.

"How will we get back?" asked Kai once the ferryman had begun to fade into the fog. She slipped on a rock as she tried to follow Thorne further inland, and he caught her by the elbow. Electricity shot down Kai's spine as their eyes met. "Thanks," she murmured as, after making sure that she was steady, Thorne released his hold on her. He nodded.

"We'll cross that bridge when we come to it," was all he said in response to her question. Kai stopped in her tracks.

"You *do* have a plan to get back, right?" Thorne didn't answer. After a beat, with a sigh of exasperation, Kai jogged to catch up with him. They walked on, and eventually the scenery around them changed from open, foggy nothingness to something of a road, gray walls of stone rising above them higher than the eye could see. In the distance, Kai could see what appeared to be a wide set of gates, and beyond that, three tall sets of doors set into the stone, one directly behind the gates, and the others facing each other on opposite sides of the road. Pairs of great stone gargoyles were carved into the walls above each set of doors, and between the gargoyles flowed glowing script written in what seemed to be Greek. She blinked, and suddenly the golden script seemed to change shape, shifting into words that she recognized: *Elysium, Tartarus, Meadows of Asphodel.*

On the road leading to and through the open set of gates was a sight that sent a shiver down Kai's spine.

It was a procession, growing longer with every passing second, of souls; these souls were not milling about aimlessly as the ones on the beach had, but waited patiently in the long, neat line. Every couple of minutes the line would move forward, and one of the sets of doors would open a crack to grant admittance to whoever had just passed through the gates.

Kai was about to ask if they were meant to pass through the gates as well, a knot of trepidation growing in her stomach as she caught side of the gigantic three-headed dog just beyond them, when she abruptly collided with Thorne's back. He looked down at her, then tilted his head toward a set of small iron gates set into the wall. Kai wondered how she hadn't noticed them before, then noticed that they were cleverly concealed behind a group of rocks standing in a formation that made the gates difficult to see if you weren't looking for them.

"Come on," said Thorne, pushing one of the creaky gates open for Kai to step through. "This is a shortcut—strictly for the non-deceased, so as to avoid the zombie parade."

"Yay," Kai pumped her fists weakly, relief flooding her. She glanced over her shoulder once more, half-expecting to find the dog behind her, breathing down her neck, then slipped through the narrow entrance. Thorne ducked into the corridor behind her and pulled the gate shut.

They were in a long, narrow hallway, the ceiling only just high enough to allow Thorne to walk without ducking his head. Torches with blue flame flickered along the walls at perfectly even intervals, dimly lighting the path ahead.

Thorne took the lead, and they walked side by side in silence for a time that Kai couldn't define. It could have been hours, it could have been mere minutes; it was hard to tell with the way that the hallway stretched on and on without changing, with no indication of how far they had traveled or how far they had yet to go.

When the quiet began to grow unbearable, weighing down on her chest as though it were something tangible, Kai broke the silence with a question that had been burning in the forefront of her mind since they'd arrived.

"When I woke up," she began slowly, carefully, struggling to suppress the nausea that rolled in her stomach at the memory. "Where were you? Why was I alone?" Her voice sounded embarrassingly small as it echoed off of the stone walls.

"Well," Thorne cleared his throat, and Kai's tense shoulders instantly relaxed at the sound of his voice, the boy walking beside her the only familiarity that she had in this cold, foreign place. "In order to bring you here, to the land of the dead, but also keep you alive up there," he pointed a finger toward the ceiling. "I essentially had to yank your soul from your physical form and haul ass through the In-Between and into the Underworld. It worked pretty well..." he trailed off, and Kai could have sworn that she saw a flush of red tinting his cheeks as he rubbed the back of his neck, looking sheepish. Her eyes narrowed suspiciously,

"Did something happen?"

"No," he said quickly, then amended, "Well, not *exactly*." He cringed slightly. "I've just never made the journey with a *living* soul before, and it's not like there's a *guidebook* for it, so I had to make an on-the-spot decision and kind of just...threw you in?" Kai blinked.

"You—excuse me?"

"Well, it worked!" Thorne's voice pitched upward defensively, his dark brows lowering into a scowl as he glowered down at her.

"You *threw* my soul into the Underworld?!" Thorne winced at the shrillness of her tone.

"Well, when you put it like *that*," he mumbled, and Kai rolled her eyes, mumbling something about her soul being little more than a sack of potatoes under her breath as they lapsed into a more comfortable silence.

As they continued down the unchanging pathway, the air around herself and Thorne seemed to thicken, tension rolling between them and pressing oppressively on her chest and into her lungs, forcing her to struggle slightly for breath. Thorne seemed to feel it too, rolling his neck and pushing his shoulders back, his spine straightening almost imperceptibly.

"I know that I warned you before," he said after a moment, speaking so suddenly that Kai nearly started out of her skin in surprise. "But I worry that I may have undersold it a bit. When I said that this would be dangerous, I didn't just mean that you could die *up there*. That's definitely a possibility, and it is absolutely something that we need to avoid, but there are dangers *down here* that I...may not be able to protect you from." He seemed loathe to admit this fact, his expression darkening momentarily as he let the information sink in. "I need you to keep your senses sharp, I need you to stay by my side, and above all, I need you to do everything that I say. Do you understand?"

By now, he had stopped walking and was standing in front of her, looking down at her with a gaze so serious that she fought not to shrink beneath its weight. She nodded, not quite trusting her voice, and he waited, his expression unchanging.

"I understand," she said quietly. Her mouth was dry.

That seemed to satisfy him, and he nodded, stepping away from her and taking the lead again down the dark corridor. She trailed behind him, noting the way that his shoulders seemed to be getting tenser by the second, the way that his jaw began to strain with the way that he was clenching it; how his fingers twitched and flexed and tapped against his thigh, curling and uncurling into fists at his sides. Kai had never seen him like this, and she couldn't help but feel that, if Thorne was this worried, then she should be absolutely terrified.

"We're close," he said. He looked over his shoulder, and Kai increased her pace just slightly until she was by his side. He didn't *sound* very afraid, but then again, he didn't sound as though he was feeling much of anything at the moment.

"Are you—" she hesitated, licking her lips. "Are you okay?" He glanced sharply down at her out of the corner of his eye, then jerked his gaze back to the hallway ahead, the muscles in his jaw tensing a little more.

"I'm fine," he said brusquely, then forced a slow exhale, flexing his fingers so hard that his knuckles turned white. "Just remember what I told you: stay close, listen to what I tell you, and if I tell you to run, you *run.*" Kai nodded and swallowed hard, fear finally beginning to spread through her limbs like the cold paralytic that Minho had given her. In the corner of her vision, she saw Thorne take notice, his expression softening.

She inhaled sharply, quietly, through her nose as she felt his fingers brush against hers, his pinky curling around the tip of her right pointer finger, brushing against it so softly that she wondered if she were only imagining it.

But when she looked down, there they were: her hand and his. Something small and warm flickered to life in her heart, and she curled her finger around his, suddenly afraid that he would pull away if she didn't.

"Hey." His voice, gentle and soft, drew her attention back up to his face. He offered her the smallest of smiles, reassurance shining in his eyes. "You'll be okay." It did not escape Kai's notice that he said *you* and not *we,* but she said nothing, forcing herself to return the smile with a short, jerky nod.

Before she had the chance to verbally respond, the hallway opened and they came upon a pair of large, black double doors so tall that Kai had to tilt her head to see the top, and so ornately carved that she wondered how many lifetimes it had taken to engrave.

But there was little time to admire the engravings, or to marvel at how lifelike the people within them appeared, because Kai's hand was cold where Thorne had released it to step forward and press his palm against one of the heavy doors, which shifted slowly open at his touch.

Thorne stepped through first, gesturing for her to follow, and as she stepped over the threshold and into the room beyond, Kai's breath left her truly and completely.

If the doors had been impressive, then the room itself was...there were no words. A high, domed ceiling blended into black walls laden with burnished frames surrounding artwork that spoke tales of death and destruction, of war and grief, of hurt and betrayal and everything that the poets wrote about in their tragedies. Torchlight bounced off polished onyx floors where Kai found her face reflected sharply back up at her, and a burgundy carpet ran the length of the room from another set of double doors, and up onto a dais that featured two large, elegant thrones.

Realization jolted to the forefront of Kai's mind at the sight, and she whirled to face Thorne, her eyes wide, lips parting to voice the question that was already fully formed on her tongue.

"I thought I smelled the damp stench of a rat." A dark, sinister voice curled around the spires of the thrones, dancing across the floor and wrapping its dark tendrils around Kai's ankles; it felt so real that she nearly gasped aloud. Thorne seemed to freeze in place, his face paling noticeably as he slowly let his gaze rise to rest on the person stepping out of the shadows to the right of the dais.

He was tall and thin, his figure swathed in velvet robes of the deepest black, his alabaster features sharp and pointed, as if centuries of cruelty and disdain had filed away anything that was deemed soft or unnecessary. From the roots of soft, black hair that curled at his shoulders rose sharp, onyx spikes—a crown, Kai realized.

As he reached the throne, one pale, black-tipped hand rose to curl around one of the many spires on the throne to the right, and even from halfway across the room Kai could see his black eyes glittering as they rested on the boy at her side. When he spoke again, it nearly paralyzed her.

"Hello, son."

Chapter Twenty-Three
MEMORIES OF A LIFE LOST

MINHO

In a secluded, mostly empty wing of the small hospital, just beyond a door marked **DO NOT DISTURB**, two young men sat on either side of a bed where a young woman lay in a seemingly peaceful slumber, her brown hair splayed around her like a halo. The men had settled themselves at the foot of the bed, where a stack of playing cards was balanced precariously on the white sheets. The rest of the bed was taken up by cards scattered in groups of four, one side arranged neatly and with care, the other in a chaotic jumble of numbers and colors.

Both men sat hunched forward with their elbows resting on the edges of the bed, and the one closest to the door wore a look of intense concentration as he shuffled through his cards, thick brows drawn low over dark, hooded eyes. His lower lip was tucked lightly between his teeth, and his narrowed gaze flicked up to his companion as his mouth curved upward in a satisfied smirk.

"Go Fish," he declared, a smug expression on his face as he leaned back in his seat, the smirk widening into a boyish grin. On the other side of the bed, Jai rolled his eyes, mumbling under his breath as he reached for the deck of cards resting on Kai's shins. His eyes widened briefly, and he gave a joyous whoop.

"Ha!" He grinned widely as he set the card, along with three others to match, on the bed. "I think I like this game."

"I'm not sure I agree," Minho said drily, casting a furtive glance toward the door.

"You're just a bitter old man," Jai goaded, beaming with uncontained glee as he examined his remaining cards to see which suit he should try to complete next.

"That overconfidence will be your downfall," Minho warned, even as he evaluated his own hand. "See if you are still making such grand statements when you lose—miserably."

"Lose? *Moi?*" Jai laid an offended hand on his chest and shook his head, his long earrings swaying. "Impossible." Minho couldn't help the small smile that lifted the corners of his mouth, and he briefly ran his eyes over Kai, double-checking that she had not stopped breathing as they played.

It was fortunate, indeed, that they had not yet been discovered by a member of the hospital staff. Despite this wing being mostly empty at the moment, there was always the chance that someone might wander in; it was just another risk to add to the list of things that were making their timeframe increasingly slim.

Barely an hour had passed, and they had already played several rounds of Slapjack and two rounds—one won by Minho, one by Jai—of Go Fish. Having finished his graphic novel, Jai had already begun to go slightly stir-crazy without something to occupy his youthful mind, and Minho, who had not thought to bring along a novel or his sketchpad, was beginning to feel the same.

"I can't take this anymore," Jai whined, tossing his cards haphazardly onto the bed as he slid further down in his chair. His lower lip jutted out in a pout. "How long do you think they're going to be gone? *Hours* have to have passed by now in Underworld time." Minho smiled sympathetically at the younger Reaper, shaking his head with a light sigh.

"Thorne didn't say how long he thought it would take, but my guess is that we'll be here for a while." Jai groaned, and Minho's smile widened slightly. "He hasn't seen his father in quite some time, and it will likely be a difficult reunion; have some patience." Jai was quiet at that. While he didn't know *much* about Thorne's father, he knew that Thorne detested the man, and that nothing short of absolute and utter desperation would have prompted him to ask his father for help.

Now silent, he occupied his idle hands by practicing some of the card tricks that he had learned when he was a mortal. Colors flashed as he flicked the cards over his knuckles, making them disappear between his deft fingers, only to reappear half a second later in his other hand.

A fond twinkle gleamed in Minho's eyes as he watched, his chest warming with affection. Jai had not been a Reaper very long—not long at all, in the grand scheme of things, not in comparison to how long Minho had been a Reaper, or Thorne, for that matter. Sometimes—often—Minho worried about the boy; with his innate need to be constantly moving, to always have his mind and his hands occupied, knees and fingers twitching relentlessly for the next thing to do, it was going to be a long, painful existence if he did not learn to be at peace with doing nothing. Minho had mastered that long ago, but then, he had always been like that—had always been able to occupy himself with a book or people-watching, or even just his own thoughts.

He had never needed much to be happy.

Even as a child, Minho had never felt that he needed or desired the toys that his friends all envied each other for. He was perfectly happy to read the medical texts, boring as they were, in his father's study, or to draw pictures in the dirt, or to sit quietly and watch as his mother—his angel mother with unending smiles and everlasting patience—cooked dinner in their open, airy kitchen.

As he'd grown older, the medical texts turned to novels that he had collected on birthdays and special occasions, and drawings in the dirt turned into beautiful sketches and paintings that made him *feel* something, emotions rendered on paper and canvas that he would scrape pennies together to buy. His mother bought him a set of paints, once—inexpensive, requiring many layers if you didn't want the canvas to show through, but the gesture meaning more than money could buy.

His father hadn't understood when, at seventeen, Minho had announced in a tone of finality during one of their increasingly heated arguments that he did not want to pursue the family profession of medicine, but instead intended to become an artist. His father had understood even less when, weeks later, he had caught Minho in the embrace of the neighbor's son.

Jiyoo had been Minho's dearest friend, but they never spoke again after that; whilst Minho was mercilessly exiled, banished without ceremony from his childhood home and told to leave before his mother returned from the market for even the briefest of goodbyes, Jiyoo had told his family that Minho was to blame. The next time Minho saw him, Jiyoo was arm-in-arm with a beautiful young woman—his wife, whom he had been swiftly married off to after Minho's banishment. The sight had cut deep, but not nearly as deeply as Jiyoo passing by without so much as a backward glance for the boy that he had once called friend.

It wasn't until Minho relocated to another town, a place where no one knew who he was or what he had done, that he was once again able to find happiness. He began selling his art in the town marketplace, and it was there that he met the love of his life, the most gorgeous man that he had ever met—a young man with soft brown eyes and a compassionate heart who introduced himself with a warm, gentle handshake, as Hyungsik.

It had been a quiet romance, shy brushes of their fingers as Hyungsik bought countless sketches and paintings from Minho whenever he found himself in town; longing glances across social functions that neither of them particularly wanted to attend, save to catch fleeting glimpses of the other; wildflowers left outside Hyungsik's window early in the morning, sometimes with a note, sometimes with a bun still steaming from the oven for Hyungsik's breakfast.

Their first kiss had been through that window, and when Hyungsik had arrived, breathless and flushed, in the marketplace the next morning and asked Minho to marry him, it hadn't taken a thought or a pause to accept. He was Hyungsik's, and Hyungsik was his.

They moved into a small, rundown house at the edge of town and, less than a year later, welcomed into it a small girl, barely two years old, whom they had found crying and abandoned in a house not far from their own. They had named her Yoona, and with the addition of a small, orange cat who eventually turned up on their doorstep, their family was complete.

It was a simple life: balmy evenings where Minho sketched Hyungsik where he sat by the fire, reading one of his philosophical novels with Yoona curled up in his lap, sleeping more often than not; warm, sunny afternoons of carrying Yoona on his shoulders on the days that he went to town to sell his paintings; and cool, endless midnights where he would pull Hyungsik into his arms after they finally settled down in bed, skin against warm skin, fingers intertwined on the pillow as they drifted into sleep together.

Such perfect happiness.

Such a swift end.

The illness had taken Minho too soon—only seven years after he had been kicked out of his family's home, a mere six years into his wonderful new life.

It had been fast, over just as suddenly as it had begun, so quickly that now, Minho could barely recall if it had lasted for weeks or mere days. But he would remember the expression on Hyungsik's face until the day that he ceased to exist: teary-eyed and full of grief, yes, but filled—spilling over the brim—with such *love*. It had made leaving a little easier, knowing that he was so cared for, that he would not have to pass into the afterlife cold and alone, as he had once thought during that heartbroken time following his banishment.

It had been a shock to find out that, alone or not, he would not be passing on to the afterlife at *all*—at least not yet.

"You carry a lot of bitterness," Thorne had told him, just after explaining who he was and why he was there in the first place. *"So you can't **truly** move on until you have let go of that—until you stop living in the present and move past it. It wouldn't be called the **after**life otherwise, I suppose."* He had rolled his eyes at that, though his expression had softened when he saw just how heartbroken, how utterly shell-shocked and lifeless, the young man standing in front of him appeared. With a sigh, he had placed a hand on Minho's shoulder, squeezing briefly as he said, *"I know this is a lot to digest, but I have a feeling you're going to fit right in. Come, I will introduce you to the others."*

And there *had* been others. Over the years, so many souls had come and gone that Minho could no longer remember most of their names, could no longer be certain that he would recognize half of them if he ever saw them again. Some had stayed longer than others, had taken longer to resolve their *unfinished business,* as it was referred to, but in the end, everyone left. Everyone moved on, and most of them had elected to pass into the afterlife to find whatever might await them there.

Some, like Minho, had chosen to remain Reapers, but did not stick around as he had; there was much of the world to see, and there were pockets of In-Between all over the globe—plenty of room for other

Reapers. Only Minho had stayed, even after resolving his unfinished business.

It had been painful, moving on; Minho had spent much of the first year that followed his death merely watching his family from afar. They couldn't see him—he had discovered that quickly enough, after a heartbreaking attempt to catch their attention that resulted in Yoona walking straight through him as though he were nothing, little more than a ghost.

So he watched them. He watched Hyungsik grieve, watched him water the plants that they had so lovingly planted together; watched as, eventually, he mournfully packed away Minho's clothes. He watched as Yoona grew, saw her make friends—some that broke her heart, and some who never failed to make her smile and laugh with joy. His heart broke as he watched her cry for him, for the lost father whose voice that she had begun to forget, and whose face she could now only faintly remember.

He watched as, one day several years after his passing, Hyungsik removed the ring—the promise of a life together that had been cut all too short. He watched him learn to smile at someone else, watched him hold his hand, watched them curl up by the fireplace together and read aloud to Yoona, who almost always chose to sit in the armchair that had been Minho's. He watched as Hyungsik eventually married the man who smiled at him the way that Minho once had—as if Hyungsik held the sun, the moon, and all the stars in his beautiful hands.

Minho couldn't count all the times that he had cried—had screamed, had *raged* in Thorne's office, how many times he had fallen breathlessly to the ground with tears streaming down his face. How many times Thorne had pulled him into a fierce embrace, promising him that he would survive this, that he would make it past it, that he would move on.

Thorne had been right, in the end; it had hurt, and it had taken a long, *long* time, but eventually, Minho *had* moved on. He stopped watching, choosing instead to throw himself into his work, deciding that if this was to be his eternity, then he was going to make the best of it. He became an expert at guiding souls to their afterlife, at gently explaining what was happening and that it was going to be okay, even if he wasn't sure that it would be. He grew skilled at explaining, to those souls who found that they couldn't move on, that they had to find a way to let the past go, even though he himself had not quite managed to accomplish that particular feat.

And then, one spring day when the cherry blossoms were in full bloom, he saw them: Hyungsik and the man that he now called husband, Yoona skipping along in between, clasping their hands tightly in each of hers as she looked up at them both in adoration.

The sight had initially knocked the air out of Minho's lungs—the glimpse of the life that he could have had, the reminder of the life he had lost. But, while he waited for the bitterness and the resentment and the unrelenting *despair,* it didn't come. He realized, with a start, that he had made his peace with it—had made his peace with Hyungsik finding happiness in the arms of another, had found joy in the fact that, whilst Yoona still wore the bracelet that Minho had gifted her on one of the few birthdays they had spent together, she no longer cried herself to sleep every night.

And in his heart, Minho knew that *this* was moving on—not *forgetting,* but letting go.

He could move on.

But when Thorne, at long last, presented him with the option—to stay and spend eternity as a Reaper alongside him, or to pass on into an afterlife of his own...Minho chose to stay. He had found a true friend in Thorne, and as he had told Kai, he simply imagined that it was better to stay in the In-Between with someone that he knew and loved and trusted, than to pass on to an afterlife that he was no longer certain he would be sharing with someone else.

So he stayed, and he explained, as gently as he could, to newly dead souls that their time had come to pass on, and if they couldn't, he told them why, and he did his best to help them move past their bitterness and their resentment and their grief, so that they could find peace as he had. And when they left, sometimes he missed them.

Jai would probably leave too, eventually, Minho thought, and he knew that he would mourn for him when he did; Jai was one of his favorites.

Even if he was, at present, making snow angels on the floor of Kai's hospital room, all six-foot-two-inches of him sprawled across the probably somewhat dirty tiled floors, a ridiculously proud smile on his face.

Yes, Minho thought as he rolled his eyes in feigned exasperation, unable to bite back the smile of amusement that, unbidden, curved the corners of his mouth upward. Yes, he would miss Jai.

Chapter Twenty-Four
BEAUTY AND CRUELTY

KAI

It was so quiet one could have heard a pin drop.

The man moved around the throne, his movements effortless and fluid, as though he himself was made of the shadows that followed him as he dropped gracefully into the seat. His gaze was focused intently on Thorne, waiting—a snake poised to strike.

"Well, I'm not going to call you *dad,* if that's what you're waiting for," Thorne said, at last breaking the tense silence that had wound its way through the room, thickening the air between them until it was stifling. The man hummed lightly—in amusement? Kai wasn't sure, but the way one corner of his thin, cruel mouth curved subtly upward made a black pit form in the depths of her stomach.

The man's sharp, elongated nails stroked the arm of the throne slowly, lazily, as he asked, "And what *does* bring you here, Reaper?" Several feet away from her, Kai noticed Thorne stiffen at the title. "I can hardly *imagine* what dark, desperate business could drag you to my doorstep." His voice was low, as smooth and soft as silk, a gleam in his coal-black eyes as he noted the way that Thorne shifted his weight subtly from one foot to the other.

"I have—" The words were little more than a hoarse whisper, and Thorne cleared his throat, spine straightening as he tipped his chin upward, looking the man—his father—in the eye, meeting his gaze with an edge of defiance in his own. "I have come to ask a favor."

For a moment, the man merely stared, blinking once, twice, his expression carefully blank, as though he could not quite believe the words that had been said. Thorne's gaze was unflinching, and Kai felt something akin to pride flare up inside of her.

As the man's mouth began to curve further upward, a low, dark laugh began to rise from his chest, gradually increasing in volume as he tipped his head back, until he was laughing outright in their faces. The sound filled the large, cavernous space, mocking them from every angle and height. Kai saw Thorne's fingers twitch, hands flexing as though he were trying to stop his fists from clenching.

The man did not stop laughing, even as the double doors to the left of the dais abruptly opened, widening slowly to allow one of the most beautiful women that Kai had ever seen into the throne room.

The train of her dress, made of the deepest black and covered with stars that shone so brightly that Kai wondered, distantly, if they were perhaps real, flowed easily behind her as she breezed onto the dais. Her cape—sheer, but that same impenetrable black that glittered with stardust—was clasped with rubies at her narrow shoulders, dipping in the middle to show off the low back of her dress.

From the roots of her hair, dark and tumbling in loose curls to the center of her back, rose a tall, spired diadem to match that of the man that she was softly approaching. Small, shining ivory pearls and flowers of every color and shape were arranged amongst her hair, and golden vines wound their way up her arms, long and slender and tinted the soft brown of warm desert sand. A distinct floral aroma floated through the room, filling Kai's nostrils and ensnaring her senses, hypnotizing her.

She was a perfect portrait of light and darkness.

As she laid a delicate hand on the still-laughing man's shoulder and surveyed the other occupants of the room, her brows lifted slightly.

"What amuses you so, my love?" She smiled softly as she asked it, not looking away from Thorne, who refused to meet her eyes. The man covered her hand in his significantly larger one, using the others to wipe mock tears from his eyes.

"You may recall, dearest, that I have a son?" Faint recognition lit in those honey-brown eyes, and she nodded. The man, with a sardonic smile, swept a hand toward Thorne. "My son."

"Thorne, my lady." To Kai's surprise, Thorne bowed low before the woman, his tone respectful, if a bit stiff.

"It is wonderful to meet you, Thorne—at last," the woman added, cutting her eyes narrowly to the man at her side. He rolled his own, and she smiled, love clear in her gaze as she looked down at him.

Before Kai had time to fully wonder how—or *why*—such a lovely creature could be with someone so utterly abhorrent, both of their gazes shifted quite suddenly to her, and her eyes widened, lips parting slightly as she faltered for something to say.

Fortunately, she didn't have to.

"This is my..." *Associate? Companion?* "Friend, Kailani Sanchez." Kai waved awkwardly from where she was practically rooted to the floor, and she forced a small, polite smile. Her eyes nearly bulged out of her head as Thorne continued. "Kai, meet the Lord of the Underworld, Hades, and his wife, Queen of the Underworld and Lady of Spring, Persephone." Kai's mouth went dry.

"Hades and Persephone—like, *Hades and Persephone?*"

"Our reputations precede us, I see," said Hades, a sharp glint in his eye, like that of a predator whose gaze had just locked onto easy prey. "How very..." He inhaled deeply through his narrow, straight nose, his eyes fluttering briefly shut, and Kai suddenly felt the full weight of his gaze as his eyes snapped back open and his smirk widened, wolfish canines on display as he said, "*Mortal,* if I am not mistaken." Kai's skin crawled under his penetrating gaze, and almost imperceptibly, Thorne moved closer, positioning himself warily between her and Hades.

After a moment, Hades waved his hand, as if Kai were no more than a fly on the wall to him, and at last, he looked away from her. Kai's shoulders sagged in relief and, though Thorne seemed to be refusing to look at her, she sent him a quiet, mental *thank you.*

Hades was once again watching Thorne, his eyes half-lidded as his finger stroked up and down the back of Persephone's hand. "Persephone, dearest, the boy comes to ask us for a *favor.*" One of those delicate, perfect brows arched upward again, and Persephone's gaze held no judgment as she looked at Thorne for confirmation.

"Oh?" Unlike her husband, she seemed genuinely interested—perhaps even eager—to hear them out. Again, Kai wondered how these two could *possibly* be married. "Go on, then—surely we can find some way to help." Hades said nothing, but from the look in his eyes, Kai felt that he had no intention whatsoever of helping them. He gave his wife's hand a light, affectionate squeeze, and somehow the shadows fled from his face as he looked, briefly, up at her with an affectionate smile.

"Of course, my darling. But I would very much like a moment alone with my son before we hear him out—it has been a long time." Darkness trembled beneath their feet at those last words, and Kai swallowed. "Perhaps you can show his *friend* your garden; I do not imagine that our discussion will take very long." Persephone paused, tearing her eyes from Thorne to fully meet the gaze of her husband, and Kai felt awkward, almost intrusive, at witnessing the silent conversation that they seemed to be having.

Finally, Persephone nodded, a smile warming her face as she held a bejeweled hand out to Kai. "Come, dear, I have a feeling that this conversation is going to be very dull, anyway." Hades narrowed his eyes playfully at her, and she laughed, the sound echoing off of the high ceilings like music.

Despite her reluctance to offend Persephone, Kai hesitated, opening her mouth to protest as she looked to Thorne, who was already by her side. She didn't know when he had moved, and she started in surprise to find him so close. He touched a hand to her elbow lightly, and she resisted the urge to shiver as he leaned closer, placing his lips by her ear to murmur,

"Go with Persephone. You'll be safe with her, and I will find you as soon as I can. *I promise.*" He pulled away just enough to search her eyes, honesty shining in his own, and despite the queasy feeling already beginning to build in her stomach, Kai nodded.

She met Persephone by the doors through which the Queen had entered, and allowed the Lady of Spring to loop her arm through one of Kai's own, tugging her eagerly toward the doors and quietly murmuring something about how she thought that Kai would thoroughly enjoy what they were about to see.

But Kai could hardly focus on Persephone's words as she glanced over her shoulder to find Thorne staring, jaw tight and fists clenched, up at Hades, whose loving smile had already morphed back into that sharp cruelty, one leg crossed over his knee as he leaned back in his seat.

"Now," Kai heard him say as the doors closed behind them, Persephone tugging her ever-farther down the foreign hallway. "The fun can begin."

Chapter Twenty-Five
SCORES AND SHADOWS

THORNE

Alone at last in the throne room, Thorne and Hades observed each other silently for several long moments, neither willing to be the first to break the tense silence hanging thickly between them. Thorne wanted desperately to avoid his father's eyes, as he had the last time that he had seen him—so long ago it seemed another lifetime—but he knew that he couldn't let his gaze drop, even if only for a second. It would show weakness, and if there was anything that Thorne knew of his father, it was that he would take advantage of the first weakness he could find. It was why Thorne had so stoically refused to look at Kai after Hades had made his presence known, save to assure her that she would be safe with Persephone.

No, he could not show weakness. Not when he had come to beg for assistance; not when he needed to show that he was no longer...intimidated? Terrified? *Paralyzed* with fear so tangible that it used to keep him up at night.

I will live in fear of your shadows no longer, Thorne silently promised as he unflinchingly held his father's gaze, smothering the shame that attempted to flicker to life in his stomach under the intensity of Hades' glittering black eyes.

If Hades was impressed by his son, he did not show it. He visually examined Thorne, piercing eyes sweeping over the all-black attire—the shirt with the long, sheer sleeves and the top couple of buttons left undone; the hair, several shades lighter than his own, pulled neatly into a ponytail, save for a few strands that framed Thorne's angled cheekbones; down to the steel-toed combat boots, sharp gaze catching the outline of a knife sheathed in the right. He snorted lightly.

"Do I amuse you?" Thorne asked, his tone cutting. He took a slow, steadying breath, caught off guard by how strongly his hatred for his father bled into his tone. If he wanted to succeed, he needed to reign it in, as impossible as that task seemed.

"Oh, it's nothing," Hades hummed noncommittally, mouth lifting at the corners as if he knew something Thorne didn't. Thorne clenched his jaw, teeth grinding together as he measured his breaths carefully, forcing his fingers to flex outward from the fists that they were beginning to curl into. Less than five minutes in the presence of his father and here he was, practically steaming, ready to blow at the slightest provocation.

"Well, then," said Thorne, pushing his shoulders back and tipping his chin slightly upward, chest falling as he slowly exhaled. "We should probably get down to business."

"Yes." Hades' smile was predatory. "You want to ask me for a *favor*." He relaxed further into his seat, flicking several heavily-ringed fingers outward—a gesture for Thorne to speak.

Thorne hesitated. What he was going to ask...he had no idea what Hades would ask for in return. For this would not be a favor—not *truly*, not in the sense that it would be given freely, unrequited. Never in his long life had he ever asked his father for anything, be it for himself or someone else; was it truly worth whatever price that Hades might exact?

He knew the answer before the question had finished passing through his mind. *Yes.* **Yes,** of course it was. It was their best chance. It was their *only* chance.

He took a breath.

"I know what you think of me," he began, and then, "I know that you hate me, and wish that I had never been born." Aside from arching one singular, pitch-black brow, Hades' expression was unchanging. And of course it was—what Thorne had said came as no surprise to either of them. It was a fact, stated as coldly as whether the sky outside appeared gray or blue. "And I know that you are likely little inclined to help me with anything, regardless of what I could possibly offer in exchange." He paused, swallowing, his mouth going dry. He licked his lips. He *had* to push on—for Kai. "But I have never asked you for anything, and what I ask of you now is not a favor that I ask for myself, but on behalf of another."

"The mortal," Hades surmised in a tone laced with amusement. Thorne nodded.

"Yes. I—" he hesitated, wondering just how much of the situation he should reveal. Too little, and he risked Hades not thinking it worth his time to extend assistance; too much, and it could just as easily be used against him. He decided on something in-between—Hades could read between the lines if he liked, but Thorne need not explain every detail down to the letter.

"Something happened," he continued. "She was supposed to die—was *fated* to die, but..." he realized suddenly the futility of his mission. For how could he explain to his father, who hated him perhaps more than he hated anyone or anything else, why he wanted to keep a single, seemingly unimportant mortal alive?

When he spoke again, his voice was weaker than it had been before, barely making it the short distance from him to Hades, who was waiting with a bored expression. "Well, as you can see, she remains alive. I have—I've pledged to help her remain that way. But there are other factors at play—the Keeper, for one." Thorne watched his father carefully as he added that last bit, waiting to gauge his reaction.

It worked; the mention of the Keeper caught Hades' interest, and he sat a little straighter in his seat, even leaning forward slightly, fingers curling around the arms of the throne so tightly that his knuckles whitened. His gaze sharpened, and he seemed to listen more intently as Thorne continued.

"She is adamant that the balance of Fate be restored—that Kai dies, and that I be the one to reap her soul, as it should have been in the first place. But it—" *It doesn't seem fair,* he wanted to say. "I promised Kai that I would not let that happen, that I would find a way to keep her alive. Not forever, obviously, just...until it is truly her time to go. After she's had...a *chance.*" *A chance to live,* Kai had said last night, eyes shining with passion and determination, with the fear that she had wasted what little time she'd had thus far, that she wouldn't get the chance to make it up.

"And you want me to go against that...*Keeper,*" Hades sneered, nails digging into the arms of the throne just a little more at that, the words sounding bitter on his tongue. "Why?" He demanded, and Thorne's heart faltered. "Why should I help you keep one silly, insignificant, *meaningless* little mortal alive?" He chuckled lowly, dark amusement glittering in his eyes as he shook his head. "You are *stupider* than I remembered."

"Please." Before he could stop himself, he was pleading—*begging,* knees trembling as he took an involuntary step forward, ready to drop onto them if that's what it took, ready to kiss the floor at his father's feet and swear to do anything that he asked. *I will do **anything,*** he thought, knowing that it was written all over his face, unable to care. "Father, *please.* Whatever you want in return, *anything* that you ask, I—"

"And what could you *possibly* offer *me?*" Hades hissed, rising suddenly from his throne. Even the shadows at his feet seemed to skitter back at the utter disdain dripping from his words, his tone, flames flickering to life in his black, bottomless eyes. His voice echoed throughout the cavernous space, reaching Thorne from every angle, making him visibly flinch. "You are *nothing*—you always have been. Just an ant beneath my boot. An eternal *thorn in my side.*" His upper lip curled as he looked down his long, thin nose at Thorne. "I suppose it is only to be expected; after all, *you* cheated a deserved death, so why not help others do the same?"

"*I cheated **nothing!***" The words tore from Thorne's throat, eyes blazing as his fists clenched so tightly at his sides that he could feel his nails biting into his skin, drawing thick beads of crimson. He could feel the darkness hovering at his shoulders, and his chest heaved. Hades seemed to shrink back slightly at the sigh, unchecked hatred mixed with surprise clear on his face and in his eyes. "*You are the reason I **exist.*** It is because of your *weakness* and *stupidity* that I am even *here!* Do you think that I wanted this?" His voice broke, and he hated himself for it. He paused for a moment, biting back the tears that pressed insistently against the backs of his eyes, the bile threatening to rise in his throat at the utter vulnerability that he was showing in front of his greatest enemy.

He took a deep breath through his nose, forcing his shoulders back and his spine to straighten, his shadows slipping away. He would *not* show weakness; he would not give his father the satisfaction of watching him crumble.

"And for that," he said, his voice and eyes hard, unrelenting. "You *owe* me." He knew that he sounded like a petulant child begging for scraps, but he didn't care. Hades had clearly had no intention of helping him from the start—Thorne had nothing to lose.

When he spoke, Hades' voice was low and dark, creeping with freshly emboldened shadows across the floor, dancing across the gleaming onyx tiles toward Thorne's feet. Hades' eyes were as cold as ice as he took several slow, measured steps forward and down the dais, pausing on the middle step.

"I owe you *nothing*," he hissed, and the shadows hovering over the floor began to take shape, rising upward and forming vaguely humanoid outlines, the edges continuing to dance this way and that, as if holding a solid form was difficult. "It is high time that someone taught you your place, *boy*," he spat, and then, over his shoulder as he turned away, "Take him."

The shadows sprang forward and swallowed him whole, and even if he had wanted to resist—had tried to fight his way out of the darkness that enveloped him, obscuring his senses and leaving him with nothing more than a vague, instinctive knowledge that they were *moving*, even if he thought that he had the slightest *chance* of escaping their grasp and somehow finding Kai in this infernal place—the strong, sharp tang that hit his nostrils and rendered him instantly unconscious made such a thing completely impossible.

***

When he awoke, he was in a damp, dimly lit cell with no windows, the only light supplied by a flickering lantern creaking on its hinge somewhere further down the stone hallway beyond the bars that caged him. There was nothing in the cell, no blanket or bucket to sit on, not even a speck of dust to litter the cold stone floor that Thorne had woken to find himself unceremoniously sprawled across. There was nothing, only himself and his thoughts and a raging headache.

And the knowledge that, somewhere in this endless, impenetrable fortress, Kai was alone, probably terrified, without a clue as to what had become of him.

In his lap, Thorne's hands began to shake with rage, his entire body trembling with the wild anger that Hades had lit within him. All of this—everything that he was, everything he had ever done or thought or had *been*...

It had all started with *him*.

Chapter Twenty-Six
A Light in the Dark

KAI

Kai couldn't ignore the worry eating away at her as she walked alongside Persephone through the seemingly endless hallways of the palace. In truth, it more resembled a *fortress* than a palace—the windows that they passed, though spanning from ceiling to floor, had barred shutters on the outside, and Kai wondered with a shiver what it was that they were trying to keep out.

They had not encountered anyone else, but Kai could almost swear that she could see movement in the gleaming, ruby-red eyes of the stone gargoyles that they passed, feeling as though their gazes followed her as she walked down the hallway.

Kai felt positively infinitesimal as she walked alongside the Lady of Spring. Persephone was the stuff of actual myth and legend, and here she was, as real as Kai herself; it was hard to wrap her mortal mind around. If Persephone was feeling the same tense, nervous awkwardness, however, she certainly didn't show it, keeping up a steady stream of light conversation, pointing out various mythical objects or pieces of artwork as they passed by on their way to wherever it was that they were going.

At long last, they arrived at a set of double doors, solid black save for the gold inlay swirling across them, and the instant that Persephone laid one of her finely manicured hands against the doors they opened of their own accord, allowing the Queen and her companion to enter.

The light in the large, open space into which they emerged was blinding, so bright that Kai had to shield her eyes with her hands for a moment, retinas burning from the sudden glare. When at last, she was able to lower her hands without squinting, she couldn't help the gasp that escaped her, mouth falling unabashedly open at the sight before her.

It was a garden, larger than Kai could have possibly imagined even in her wildest dreams, spanning such a distance that she could not tell where it ended. It was bursting with color, the first sign of true *life* that she had seen since entering this place, and thirstily, she drank it in, the air that enveloped her senses clean and sweet, and exuding the same pleasant aroma that seemed to hang over Persephone like a delicate veil.

The garden was in full bloom, flowers of every shape and color and size and species spread throughout the space in wooden boxes and clay pots, some of them hanging alongside lanterns that glowed with all the pastel colors of a sunrise. Oddly enough, the garden didn't seem to *need* the lights—the source of brightness that had first blinded Kai upon their arrival seemed to come from above, bathing every inch of the garden in light. There did not, Kai discovered, seem to be a sun, and her brows furrowed slightly as she wondered where exactly the light was coming from.

Persephone smiled softly at the look of wonderment that painted Kai's expression, and she said nothing as she let the mortal girl take it in, merely stooping to tenderly caress the wilting bud of a red rose. The plant curled into her touch, and before Kai's eyes, began to perk up, the thorny stems straightening and regaining their color, more buds sprouting out of thin air and blooming instantly.

"This garden is my happy place," Persephone explained as her hand lovingly parted from the rose. She continued slowly down the path, fingertips trailing along various plants and flowers, leaving fresh sprouts and blooms in her wake. "Though I have found great happiness here with my husband, I do not think that I could stay here nearly as long as I do each year without my garden. It is a true privilege, watching life bloom in this way; to see that in a place of such darkness, you can still find light." She smiled. Her eyes were bright, brown skin flushed, as if the plants somehow breathed life into her, also.

Though Kai said nothing, Persephone seemed to sense her confusion, for she laughed lightly, the pearls in her hair catching the light as she shook her head.

"I see you doubt that I could be happy with such a man as my husband, but you have seen him only for a moment; I have had millennia to know and love and understand him." Her expression clouded slightly, her bright tone sobering a little as she continued. "Nobody is perfect, Kailani, and my husband is no different. Though it is a subject we disagree on—vehemently so—his son is a topic that...well, you saw it for yourself. They are not on what you might call *good terms,* and I am not sure that it is my place to interfere." Kai hesitated, not sure if it was *her* place to ask the questions burning on her tongue, curiosity warring with the fear that, perhaps, she did not want to know.

Curiosity won.

"What *happened,* exactly? With Thorne and his...father." Persephone smiled that sad smile again, shaking her head gently as she released a yellow rose blossom from her life-giving grasp.

"That is not my story to tell, I am afraid," she said softly, though empathy shone earnestly in her eyes. "But I *can* say that, whatever his faults—however bitter he may be about his father, about the world—from what little I know of him, Thorne is a *good* boy. A good *man.* Him trying to help you like this..." There was a knowing gleam in her eye as she smiled a little wider. "It says a lot, for someone who is immortal to go to such lengths to assist someone who is not."

Kai blinked. "How did you know that he wants to help me?" Persephone arched one of those perfect brows.

"Why else would he have brought you to this place—to ask a favor from his father, whom he hates?" Kai flushed, supposing that it *was* rather obvious.

She sighed and plopped heavily down on a stone bench nearby. Persephone joined her, waiting patiently for Kai to speak the words so clearly weighing on her mind.

"I still don't get it," Kai said with a soft laugh of disbelief. Her voice was thick. "There have to be hundreds—*thousands*—of people who he's...reaped." She swallowed. "Thousands of people who didn't deserve to die, who deserved the chance to live just as much as any-one else." She looked at Persephone. "Why me?" Persephone's gaze searched her own for a long moment, and for once, Kai did not fear that her soul was being put on display for all to see.

"Maybe it's not about *deserve.*" Persephone's voice was soft, easing into the quiet that had fallen over them. "Maybe it was just time." Kai's brows pushed together, and she turned again to face the Queen, pulling her gaze from where it had lowered to her hands, clasped in her lap.

"What do you mean?"

"It could be that this was just something that was bound to happen, at one point in time or another; perhaps he saw something in you that resonated somewhere inside of him—a connection—and maybe he decided that he'd had enough."

"So I was just...what, convenient?" As stupid as it was, Kai couldn't help but feel a stab of hurt at that. Persephone laughed, crescent moons swinging on delicate chains from her earlobes as she shook her head.

"You mortals, always twisting things this way and that to find *something* that is amiss." She did not say it with malice, and she placed a hand gently on Kai's shoulder, lifting her brows. "But better convenient than dead, yes?"

"Well, when you put it like *that*," Kai mumbled, and Persephone laughed again. Something struck Kai suddenly, and without thinking about it, she blurted, "He can see me." Persephone cocked her head.

"What?"

"Thorne—he said once that he could *see* me. He said that usually people—mortals—who are alive look blurry to him, but I'm not." She didn't know why her cheeks heated, but she didn't take the time to analyze it as a smile played at the corners of Persephone's mouth. "What is it?"

"I'm sure it is nothing," Persephone said, though the twinkle in her eye seemed to contradict that statement. Kai wanted to press further, and was about to beg Persephone to elaborate when they were interrupted.

Her eyes nearly bulged out of her head when he bounced up to them—a small, gray-skinned man with a large, bulbous nose and ruby-red eyes, clothed only in a small tunic that was tied with a wide sash around his waist, two tiny wings protruding from his back.

"My lady," the small man said, tipping forward slightly in respect for Persephone. As he spoke, Kai noticed his teeth, charred with black, and as sharp as the talons extending from his stubby fingers and bare toes. She swallowed, fear washing over her and blood running cold as his gaze shifted nervously to her, then quickly back to Persephone as he said, "His Majesty requests your immediate return to the throne room." Though Persephone's expression remained smooth and unbothered, Kai noticed that she sat a little straighter, her left brow ticking upward, so fast and slight that Kai wondered if she had merely imagined it.

"Did he say *why?*" The man—gargoyle, Kai realized—hesitated.

"He requests your presence, my lady," he repeated, and Kai could scarcely breathe, the dread pulsing through her with every stuttering beat of her heart so intense she found that she could not move.

After a beat, Persephone smiled serenely.

"I understand," she said in that angelic voice of hers. "We will be on our way in a moment—the lady and I were just finishing our conversation." The gargoyle stood as still as stone, making no move to leave. Persephone arched a brow. "Is there something else that you need?"

"I am supposed to escort you, my lady." Persephone laughed musically, shaking her head.

"That will not be necessary, but I thank you." He did not move a muscle, and did not return her smile. Kai wondered if he *could* smile. Persephone's eyes flashed a deep red as her own smile dropped, and she leaned forward to meet the creature's eyes. She spoke, her voice as smooth as silk, so enchanting that Kai found her eyes beginning to droop. "I said, ***that will not be necessary. Return to your master and tell him that we will be along presently.***" The gargoyle's ruby eyes glazed over as the scent of flowers sharpened slightly in the air, and he nodded, turning to leave.

He was scarcely gone before Persephone straightened, turning to Kai with urgency in her eyes, which had returned to their bright honey brown. Kai had a multitude of questions, but the Queen was already moving, snatching Kai's hand and pulling her up and off of the bench, practically dragging her along with quickening footsteps down the gravel path that wound through the garden. Kai couldn't help but notice that they were going in the opposite direction of the garden's entrance.

"I sense that something is not quite right," Persephone said as they went, eyes darting anxiously this way and that, as though she were waiting for the gargoyle to jump back out, possibly with Hades in tow. "I fear that if we return to the throne room, you may not make it back to the mortal world. I fear that Thorne's conversation with my husband did not go to plan, and I fear that something may have already befallen him for his efforts—the same thing that may be in store for you, should we return as my husband requested."

"What do you mean?" Kai asked, her voice shaking, knees unsteady as they continued at an unrelenting pace down the path. Persephone sighed, shaking her head.

"I know my husband. The son that he loathes coming to ask him for a favor after all this time...it could only end badly. And if my suspicions regarding your purpose here are correct...to be truthful, my husband could stand to be on the Fates' *good* side, for a change." Kai wanted to ask what that meant—what *all* of this meant, but Persephone carried quickly on as they came to a sudden stop, the wall in front of them preventing them from progressing further.

Persephone turned to Kai, her expression calm, but deadly serious. "Through this door, you will find yourself in a small room just across from a staircase. Before you exit, be *absolutely certain* that you are not seen. Go down the stairs. Once you reach the bottom, there will be a door." She pressed a key into Kai's palm, her hands warm. "Through this door will be a corridor—no one should be down there, but *be careful,* and *do not stop.* Do you understand?"

Kai's eyes were wide and panicked, chest rising and falling like that of a petrified hummingbird, and she wanted to ask *why*—why was Persephone helping her? The Queen offered a sympathetic smile and reached out to tuck a strand of hair behind Kai's ear, knuckles brushing softly against her cheek. Something flipped in Kai's stomach, the bittersweet taste of nostalgia on her tongue.

"I am sorry that it has to be this way," Persephone said quietly. "My husband is a stubborn man, and I fear that his son is someone he will never be able to make his peace with."

"Thorne!" Kai exclaimed, the panic that had barely begun to subside crashing back in like a tidal wave. "I can't leave without him—I don't know *how*, what if I—"

"Thorne will be fine," Persephone said soothingly, reassuringly, palms on either side of Kai's face as she held her gaze firmly, waiting until she calmed again. With a small, encouraging smile, Persephone nodded. "He will be fine, I *promise*. Now go. Run. *Do not stop.*"

As Persephone's palm made contact, the wall in front of them melted into a door, and before Kai could hesitate or protest, Persephone shoved her through. "*Run,*" she reminded her as the wall closed between them.

In the dim light of the room, Kai realized that she hadn't gotten the chance to thank her.

Thank you, she thought, hoping that, somehow, the words made their way to Persephone.

Chapter Twenty-Seven
FEEL ALIVE

THORNE

"*D**amn it!*" Giving one last violent shake to the bars that kept him caged, Thorne staggered back, tugging at the roots of his hair in frustration as he hit the wall, sliding down it until he landed in an ungraceful heap on the hard floor. He tugged loose his hair tie, wavy strands spilling over his shoulders and falling into his eyes. He didn't bother pushing it aside. His jaw clenched, chest heaving as he took long, ragged breaths, trying to quell the waves of rage crashing into each other inside of him.

He had known that something like this would happen. He had *known*, and he'd come anyway, even dragging Kai along with him, both of them knowing that this was their last chance to save her.

He drew his knees up to his chest, crossing his arms atop them and using them as a rest for his chin as he stared bleakly ahead at the bars holding him captive, the wall beyond staring back unforgivingly. Alone with his own thoughts, bitter as they were, it seemed that not much had changed; he had the other Reapers, sure—had Minho, the only constant, as the others came and went so often now that Thorne barely bothered to learn their names anymore, but truly, it had always been him, *alone*. He was the only one truly *doomed*—cursed—to this existence, never to escape, forced to watch others move on whilst he remained, stuck.

He wondered what had become of Kai. Had Hades already sent for the Keeper? Was Kai dead already, some other Reaper given the task of collecting her soul and sending it down to that endless line of hopeless deceased awaiting judgment? He hoped, morbidly, that if she *was* dead, that it had been quick, painless; he hoped that she hadn't been afraid.

A month ago, he couldn't have imagined himself caring for *anyone* the way that he now found himself caring for Kai. In the damp darkness of the cell, he could admit it—he cared for her. Deeply.

He had never felt this way for anyone before—had never gotten the chance before he had been cursed, turned into this...*thing*. And after that, what was the point? Everyone was going to leave him in the end, anyway.

Yet here he was now, with a heavy ache in his chest at the thought of Kai. At the thought of her being dead, after everything they had gone through to keep her alive. He felt pressure at the backs of his eyes, and he didn't try to hold back the tear that slipped down his cheek, clinging briefly to his jaw before it dropped onto the stone floor by his boot.

How was it possible, after all this time, that he could feel so...*human?* He had felt hopeless for a lifetime—had felt rage and bitterness and hate, had felt loss for the life that had been stolen from him, the life that he had never gotten the opportunity to live. But this felt *different,* somehow; he felt this way for someone *else,* felt anger and sadness for another, and grief that he had not felt since—

He shook his head, banishing the thought. He could not—*would not*—relive that day.

Utterly defeated, he tipped his head back against the wall and let his eyes flutter shut. Idly, he wondered what Hades planned to do with him. He couldn't keep him locked up here forever, nor could he kill him—Thorne was fairly certain that the Fates would not take kindly to that.

In light of that, keeping him caged in here seemed rather petty. But then, Hades had always been like that, Thorne supposed; petty and childish, always placing blame on the wrong person's head.

Maybe it didn't matter what happened to him now, though. Kai was most likely dead, and while he had only known her for a short while, she had made Thorne feel things that he had not felt in...*ever*. Or at least, not in a very, very long time. Alive, for one—she made him feel *alive*. He had not thought such a thing was possible, anymore. Not until her.

And he was tired. So, *so* tired, deep in his immortal bones, of this cursed existence. He had been tired for so long, and so *lonely*. He didn't want to feel alone again. Perhaps this was his way out; perhaps, at last, he would be free.

And maybe, just *maybe,* he would see Kai again, if he was good enough to make it to that blessed afterlife where she was surely headed. Just as he began to chide himself for the absurdity of that thought—for it would be a cold day in hell when Hades allowed Thorne's soul into paradise—there came a rattling at the door.

"I don't understand," Aristides said as he paced restlessly back and forth, hands wringing anxiously, his hair thoroughly mussed from the multiple times he'd reached up to run a hand through it, tugging at the roots in an attempt to alleviate the headache pounding at his temples. Cyrus, standing in front of his wall of mirrors, hummed idly in response, fingers steepled below his chin, his generous lower lip resting on his fingertips as he studied the images.

Aristides carried on. "Where could they possibly have gone where you cannot see them? Thorne, I can understand easily enough, but the girl is mortal—*human*. She cannot travel between worlds as we can. And yet, she isn't dead; we would know, by now, if she was."

"It *is* interesting," Cyrus mused, not tearing his trio of eyes from the mirrors.

"What is?" Aristides asked, exasperation leaking into his tone. He had been pacing like this for nearly forty minutes, and Cyrus had yet to say anything aside from murmured *yeses, hm's,* and *I see's* here and there to make it seem as though he were paying attention.

"Mm," Cyrus hummed noncommittally, tilting his head. "We shall see." Aristides huffed and rolled his eyes, resuming his pacing. Cyrus could be so infuriatingly mysterious at times, and for no reason other than self-important secrecy, always keeping things to himself until he felt that they truly *needed* to be shared with the class. "Where are you?" He murmured to his mirrors, leaning closer. Aristides ignored him, losing himself in his own thoughts.

In all his years—*centuries*—of knowing Thorne, he had never seen him behave in such a fashion. Of course, he knew that Thorne hated the hand that he had been dealt—how could he not?—but Aristides had never dreamed that the boy would defy the *Keeper,* of all people. And by saving the life of a *mortal,* no less.

What was it about this girl, this *mortal,* that had Thorne under such a thrall? Aristides had been alive long enough to know that 'love at first sight' was a complete and utter lie that the mortals had romanticized amongst themselves to explain attraction; you couldn't love someone at first sight, not *truly.* You had to know their *soul,* first.

But perhaps Thorne *did* know this girl's soul, in a manner of speaking; perhaps he had seen something inside of her that he felt within his own heart, something that connected them. Perhaps, then, he felt as if he *did* know her—as if he *understood* her. Perhaps he felt that she could understand *him*—a kindred spirit. Thorne had always felt misunderstood, Aristides knew this. It was no wonder, then, that he had taken this hard-headed stand, this hopeless mission. He had lived lifetimes of feeling alone and misunderstood, so of course, *of course,* the moment he found a soul that he identified with, *of course* he would not want to give that up.

"Interesting," Cyrus murmured, his tone changed slightly from the last time he had said this, as though what he had found now truly *was* interesting, and in a heartbeat, Aristides was at his side, peering over his shoulders into the mirrors.

"Did you find them?"

"Not quite," Cyrus shook his head, and Aristides' hands curled into fists, ready to throttle his brother if this was merely another idle musing. Cyrus flicked a finger toward one of the mirrors, and in the small, liquid surface, Aristides saw the girl—*Kai*—lying unconscious in a hospital bed, the two figures seated on either side of her appearing blurred and unfocused, as though the mirror could not get a solid grasp on their forms. *Reapers,* Aristides realized. No wonder Cyrus had been unable to locate the girl; his mirrors were meant for *living* things, and whilst he could still see the Reapers when they walked the mortal plane, the mirrors seemed to have difficulty focusing on more than a single Reaper at a time. The girl had been surrounded by *three* of them, and Aristides had little doubt that they'd acted quickly to make this happen for this very reason: to slip through a gap in Cyrus' vision. Like his father, it seemed as though Thorne was skilled at finding loopholes.

His forehead creased. "But then…how is it that she is not dead? Surely if the Keeper knew of this, the girl would no longer be breathing."

Linus swept suddenly into the room, moving soundlessly across the floor, his long robe trailing behind him. ***They are in the Underworld,*** his voice announced into their minds, and realization washed over Aristides. Beside him, Cyrus' face lit up in understanding.

"Of *course*," he whispered, turning back to the mirror. "That is how she still lives, yet it took me so long to find her—she is not dead, but neither is her soul quite *here*. It is *there*, with him, in the Underworld."

The Underworld—one of the few places that even Cyrus' near-infinite gaze could not penetrate.

"But why the Underworld?" Aristides was still struggling to understand. "What possible purpose could that serve?"

"His father," Cyrus responded, and Aristides blinked. "It is possible, despite the malice between them, that Thorne is so desperate as to ask Hades for help." Aristides' heart dropped as, at last, he understood. *Thorne, what have you done?*

"I must inform the Keeper." Cyrus turned to leave and, weakly, Aristides spoke up in protest.

"Are we not supposed to keep out of these sorts of affairs? Is it not our duty to remain neutral?"

"That is true enough," Cyrus nodded, his expression grave. "But I fear that this is one instance where we must choose a side. This situation needs to be put to rest—it should have been long before now. The longer that this continues, the more complicated and dangerous things will get—for all of us." With that, he swiftly exited the room, Linus following closely behind.

Aristides sighed, fists clenching in frustration. He knew his duty, but Thorne was his *friend.* The conscience that he had long forgotten was pricking at him, needling his neutral heart, some small voice in his head telling him that he could not allow Thorne to be blindsided by this.

We must choose a side.

"Damn you, Reaper," he grumbled as he raised his hood, rolling his eyes in exasperation as he straightened the clasps at his shoulders. "Damn you."

Chapter Twenty-Eight

STAIRWAY TO NOWHERE

Kai's heart pounded wildly in her chest as the wall sealed back into place behind her, cutting her off from Persephone. As her eyes adjusted to the light, she realized that she was in a storage closet of sorts, barrels and chests and cabinets made of ebony lining the walls, their handles crafted from something that eerily resembled bone. The room was dimly lit, and directly across from where she stood, Kai saw a small door.

Run. She lurched forward, Persephone's warning ringing loud as a bell in her mind as, quietly, she raised the iron handle of the door and pulled. Mercifully, it didn't make a sound as it swung open, and Kai couldn't help but hold her breath as she cautiously poked her head into the hallway, surveying both ends carefully to ensure that no one was lurking about to catch her as she finally stepped out of the room.

In the open like this, where anyone could stumble upon her and raise the alarm, panic settled heavily in Kai's chest, seeping into her lungs and her throat, making breathing difficult. Her palms began to sweat.

Her eyes widened in alarm when she heard voices floating around the corner, growing closer with every passing second. Quickly, she lunged across the hallway to the staircase that Persephone had said would be

"

there, practically throwing herself down the steps as she hurried to get out of sight.

She reached the first landing and, thanking her lucky stars that the following row of steps turned the corner, she swung herself around the wall and pressed herself against it, chest heaving with exertion as she fought quietly to catch her breath.

Above her, she heard the voices again; they must have been just at the top of the steps, because she could hear them clearly now, their words sending shivers down her spine.

"Lord Hades wants the girl found as quickly as possible," said a low, nasally voice. "Alive, he said—she is useless to him dead. But," the voice added, and Kai could have sworn she heard a grin in his tone as he continued, "He said nothing of bringing her back unscathed." The blood in her veins ran cold, and she didn't wait to hear the voices disappear down the hallway as she continued down the stairs, moving as quickly as she dared, making an effort to avoid making excessive noise.

By the time she reached the next landing and rounded the following corner, her hands were shaking. Where was Thorne? Even if by some miracle she did make it back to some place of relative safety here, there was no way that she would be able to return to her body in the mortal realm without him. And even if she could...

She didn't want to leave him. Not here, not after everything that he had done for her—was *still* doing for her.

Please find me, she thought quietly, desperately.

She continued down the stairs, pausing every time she thought she heard a sound from above, holding her breath until all was eerily quiet again before resuming her breakneck pace.

The farther down she went, the darker it got, and soon, only the very occasional torch flickered to dimly light her path. If she wanted to see anything, she had to squint. Not that there was anything to see down here, in what had to be at least a dozen levels below the spired fortress from which she had fled. Still, it was a rather unsettling experience to travel down an endless flight of stairs in the dark.

Again, she found herself wishing that Thorne was here. She wasn't sure when he had become someone that she trusted, that she wished to be around—she could wish for *anyone* to be here to comfort her in this situation, to protect her, to hold her hand as she made her way down the ever-winding stairwell, but for whatever reason, she found herself wanting *him*.

Alone in the dark, she finally allowed herself to think about him at length. *Thorne.* Things with him were so *complicated.* Not only was he the actual, completely non-mythical *Grim Reaper,* live and in the flesh, but he was also the Reaper who had taken her family. To be fair, he hadn't exactly *made the decision* that it was time for them to die, but...

She huffed in frustration. There shouldn't be a 'but.' *He had not killed them*—he was just doing his job. Period. Full stop.

*But...*she couldn't help but feel conflicted about it. *He had been there when they died.* He had taken their souls, probably confused and terrified, into his arms, and taken them from her.

And what would you have had him do? Her inner voice nagged at her, guilt tugging painfully at her heartstrings. Deep down, she knew that he wasn't to blame; she just wanted someone—had *needed* someone, for nearly as long as she could remember—to place the blame on. Needed something tangible to rage against so that she could just stop wondering *why.* Why *them,* why *then,* why *her?* **Why was I left alone?**

Maybe there wasn't a *why.* Maybe there was no cosmic reason that her family's deaths had to happen. There *couldn't* be, because what could possibly justify that?

Just like maybe there wasn't a 'why' as to *why* Thorne had chosen *her,* out of everyone that he'd ever reaped, to spare. To save. To *protect.*

But all the same, she still wondered. The question had been playing on a loop in her mind ever since that fateful day at the tracks, and the night that he had promised to do everything in his power to save her life—a promise that was perhaps not his to make, but one that he had made anyway, despite having known her for all of three days at the time.

Whatever the reason, she was grateful. She was grateful for the chance to make things right, to live the life that she should have been living in the first place. To get the chance to make herself and her family, wherever they were, proud. To make *Thorne* proud—to make him glad that he had saved her, to never cause him to question whether he had perhaps made a mistake in doing so.

Kai's feet had long passed the point of merely aching, and were now beginning to go fully numb. She was starting to wonder if this staircase was *ever* going to end, or if she would be forced to walk it with callused, bleeding feet for eternity.

By the time she reached the bottom, she was half-inclined to weep with joy, but settled instead for pulling from her pocket the key that Persephone had given her and fitting it into the lock of the small wooden door. She didn't breathe, didn't *blink* as she turned it, a wave of relief washing over her when she heard a small *click*.

Her hand hovering over the handle, she allowed herself a brief three seconds of hesitation, then opened the door.

Chapter Twenty-Nine

A Daring Rescue from a Friend

There was nothing with which to defend himself save for his fists as Thorne leaped to his feet, his body tensing warily as he narrowed his eyes, trying to catch a glimpse of the intruder. They were tall, but hooded, their worn black cloak brushing the floor. Tanned, smooth hands reached from the sleeves, long fingers curling around the bars of the cell door to give it another firm shake, flecks of rust dropping to the floor with the violence of the motion.

The intruder sighed. "Step back." The voice was masculine—familiar. Thorne hesitated, but upon seeing the intruder pull their right arm back in preparation, his eyes widened, and he scrambled aside just in time for the figure to send their palm slamming into the cell door, blowing it halfway off its hinges.

The intruder straightened, brushing miniscule particles of rust off of his shoulder and straightening his cloak. He turned to go, then paused, tilting his head.

"Well? Are you coming?" Thorne's eyes narrowed further. What was this, some sort of trick? He didn't think that Hades' shadows would need to blow the cell door clean off, but then again, he couldn't think of anyone who would be mounting a rescue mission for him. The only people who knew that he was here were Minho and Jai, and they were supposed to be guarding Kai's body in the mortal world.

With a sigh that echoed irritation and impatience, the intruder snapped his fingers, sending the dim torch down the hallway blazing to life and, stepping into the light, he pushed back his hood.

"*Ris?*" Thorne's voice conveyed his complete and utter shock. "What—what are you *doing* here?"

"Rescuing *you*, obviously," Aristides rolled his eyes, as though the answer were clear. "Now come, we don't have much time." Too surprised to object, or to ask one of the myriad of questions hovering on the tip of his tongue, Thorne mutely obeyed, stepping over the mangled cell door and following Aristides down the hallway. They passed dozens of cells—most empty, some occupied by dark shapes huddled in corners, but none of them holding the one person that Thorne was searching for, his desperation steadily growing. If Hades had her—

Aristides interrupted his panicked train of thought. "Cyrus knows that you're here—he is sending a message to the Keeper as we speak. I can get you to the entrance of the dungeon, but after that you're on your own; I risked a great deal to come here, and I need to get back before the others notice, assuming they haven't already."

"Why *did* you come?" Thorne asked, boots scuffing against the stone floor as he hastened to catch up, working with slight difficulty to match Aristides' long, swift strides. Something unreadable simmered in Aristides' hooded brown eyes at the question, and he jerked his gaze sharply away.

"I don't know," he said stiffly. "I...I suppose that I could not let you face the Keeper without a warning. And I...consider you to be something of a friend, if you *must* know." His eyes roved the unguarded hallway ahead of them, refusing to meet Thorne's wide-eyed gaze.

"Ris..." Thorne swallowed, his mouth suddenly dry. Aristides sniffed.

"There, there, no need to make a *scene,* Reaper. Get out of here without ever letting anyone know how it was done, and that will be thanks enough." A little huff of laughter escaped Thorne as he grinned crookedly, giving a quick nod of assent, and meeting his eyes briefly, Aristides smiled a little, too.

They soon reached a set of large, arched double doors, and Aristides slowed to a halt, turning to face Thorne fully. "The entrance, as promised. I know that this has been relatively easy so far, but out there...be safe, Thorne. Escape from whatever hole you dove down to get here, and do not look back." Thorne nodded once, jerkily, and as Aristides turned to go, he reached out suddenly, grabbing a firm hold of his sleeve.

"Wait! Do—"

"I do not know where the girl is," Aristides interrupted, shaking his head somberly. Several messy strands of hair framed his face, and it struck Thorne that he didn't think he had ever seen his friend looking so untidy. "No one does, beyond the fact that she is here in the Underworld with you."

"I have to find her."

"There isn't *time,* you have to *leave* before—"

"I *have* to find her," Thorne repeated, a note of urgency in his tone that had not been there a moment before, determination blazing fiercely in his eyes. He *would* find Kai, or he would die trying. Aristides seemed to realize this and sighed deeply, his broad shoulders sagging.

"Find her quickly, then; I cannot imagine you have much time." He raised his hood, and Thorne reached out again, hesitating briefly before setting his hand on Aristides' shoulder.

"For the record...I consider you to be something of a friend, too." Aristides laughed, rolling his eyes.

"Go on then, young Reaper—your damsel awaits." With a flick of his wrist, the double doors swung open, and when Thorne looked back at the spot where Aristides had been, it was empty.

Kai had no way of knowing how long it had been since she'd entered the long, gray corridor. Much like the first hallway that she had traversed upon her arrival to this cursed place—that endless obsidian hallway where she had walked practically hand-in-hand with Thorne to meet his father—this hallway was also dimly lit and seemingly infinite. She had thought, a good while ago it seemed, that at some point, the hallway *had* to come to an end. It couldn't *possibly* go on forever. Persephone had made it sound as though there *would* be an end, that she *would* eventually escape the Underworld, as impossible as it currently seemed.

She was now inclined to believe that this might indeed be some sort of elaborate, humiliating trick. It was impossible to tell whether or not she was making any sort of progress—the faintly flickering lamps on the wall were all mounted the same distance apart, and she kept noticing the same cracks in the wall, and in the midnight-tinted stone beneath her feet.

Kai paused, eyelids drooping heavily with the urge to sleep, and tilted her head. Perhaps this was some sort of optical illusion, something to play tricks on her mortal eyes. To make her believe that she was walking in an infinite corridor when, in fact, the end was well within her reach. Some sort of magical *loop*, dooming her to walk in circles for eternity unless she cracked the code. The logical part of her brain shouted dimly at her that it was impossible, an absurd idea, but this was the *Underworld*—surely very little was impossible here.

Taking a deep, steadying breath, she let her eyes flutter shut and focused. She wasn't exactly sure what she was supposed to do here, so she let her instincts guide her, following the first impulse that came to mind. She focused closely on her breathing, concentrating on the sound of her lungs inhaling and exhaling long, slow breaths. She let herself *feel* her surroundings, awareness prickling beneath her skin, and she turned that focus outward.

"Hey!" What was supposed to be a shout came out incredibly under-whelming, her voice wavering as it failed her utterly in her moment of need, and she cringed. *What am I **doing?*** Feeling stupid, she let her shoulders sag, chewing the inside of her lower lip as she wondered if she should just give up.

No. A voice roared fiercely to life inside of her, the flame that she had felt when she'd first realized that she was fated to die blazing back in full force, chanting, *don't give up, I want to live. **Don't** give up. **I want to live.***

Reminding herself that no one was here to see her shouting blindly into the great abyss, Kai screwed her eyes tightly shut once more and shook out her hands, trying to relax. She took a breath.

"HEY!" The word tore almost painfully from her throat, and this time she heard it echoing down the hallway that, a moment before, had seemed so vast, but now sounded strangely as if an end were in sight. But that was impossible—with how quickly her voice traveled back to her, the end *had* to be near, but she hadn't seen so much as a glimpse of a door. She cracked one eye open.

Nothing. Just the same endless obsidian corridor that had been there a moment before. She tried not to let the disappointment crush her.

But she had *heard* it. There *had* to be an end—and a close one.

Taking one more long, deep breath, she closed her eyes again and shouted. Again, it sounded as though the exit must be very close. Her brows pushed together. *I wonder...* Hesitantly, she put her hands out in front of her, making sure to keep her eyes firmly shut, and slowly, barely lifting her foot from the floor as she slid it forward, she took a step. And then another, and another. And then several more.

"HELLO!" She still felt incredibly sheepish as she shouted and walked about with her eyes closed, but the embarrassment was quickly drowned out by the hope that soared in her chest as she heard her shout echo back to her, this time sounding significantly closer than it had before. *I'm coming,* she thought, willing the message to find its way to Thorne, her feet taking her faster and faster as she continued to advance, eyes shut and heart pounding, down the hallway that was beginning to sound as though it might soon come to an end. *I'm coming. I'm coming. I'm coming. Wait for me. I'm coming.*

She continued to shout every couple of steps, a giddy feeling of victory beginning to build each time that she heard her shout echoed more and more briefly back to her. A breathless laugh escaped the relaxed confines of her chest as she increased her pace, almost running down the hallway with her eyes shut and her hands still extended in front of her. She was close now—she could feel it in the very framework of her being. She took three more steps forward, and then—

She was falling.

Tumbling would be a more accurate description, truth be told. A slew of curses fell from her lips as she rolled wildly down the stone steps, the sharp, chipped corners bruising every part of her. She landed with a pained grunt at the bottom, feeling thoroughly beaten, her head splitting so badly that it took several moments for her vision to clear enough to properly see, the dark ceiling above coming slowly into focus, those same dimly flickering torches on the wall illuminating the long staircase that she had just plummeted down.

Slowly, painfully, she pushed herself into a seated position, gasping at the sudden twinge that she felt in her ribs, so sharp that she had to scoot back and rest her head against the wall, taking slow, shallow breaths as she waited for the throbbing pain in her sides to ease.

She wondered again where Thorne was. Was he coming for her? Or had Hades done something to him—caught or imprisoned him or...something worse?

No. She couldn't allow herself to think like that; couldn't let herself dwell, however briefly, on the possibility that, wherever she was headed, Thorne might not be waiting for her. Because if he wasn't...

She would be stuck here.

Inhaling carefully through her nose, Kai placed a hand on the stairs beside her, using them as an aid to push herself off of the floor. She had barely gotten to her feet when her right knee buckled abruptly, and a surprised cry escaped her lips, tears springing to her eyes as she slammed back against the wall for support, electrifying pain shooting up her ribs and through her skull. Black spots quickly clouded her vision, and she took desperate, gasping breaths as she fought to remain conscious.

When her eyes had cleared enough to see—albeit dizzily—the hallway in front of her, she steeled herself, setting her teeth in determination before pushing away from the wall. Nausea rolled in her stomach at the pain radiating from every corner of her body, but she pushed forward, unable to think past putting one foot in front of the other.

This hallway was wider than the last, but visibly shorter, and just ahead Kai could see a pair of massive double doors, heavy and black as the midnight sky, with two rusted handles that might have once been gold.

Kai couldn't explain it, but with a sudden clarity, she *knew,* somewhere deep within herself, that home was on the other side of those doors. All she had to do was push through them, and she would escape this cursed place once and for all.

Pushing past the pain, she began to hobble forward at a considerably faster pace, the giddy joy of escape numbing the pain somewhat. She quickened her steps, the doors mere feet away now. She was so close—!

From hidden, narrow hallways on either side of her, three short, gray
figures leaped suddenly out into the open. Kai stopped short, skidding
to a halt less than a yard away from the three pairs of glowing red eyes
that obstructed her path.

CHAPTER THIRTY
RED AS RUBIES

THORNE

*W*here the hell is she? Thorne had been down countless corridors, cautiously and thoroughly checking every room, nook, closet, and cranny that he came across for any sign of her, to no avail. Kai was nowhere to be found.

He couldn't go on like this much longer, he knew; never mind what could be happening in the mortal world, where Kai's unconscious body lay in an abandoned wing of the Briar Glen hospital, Thorne had very nearly run into several gargoyles—his father's henchmen of choice. If he was to be discovered, he knew beyond the shadow of a doubt that he would not have the opportunity to escape again.

He needed to find Kai, and he needed to do it *fast*.

The gargoyles were slight, only coming up to Kai's hips, but one look at the bone-white talons by their sides had Kai second-guessing any chances at escape.

She tried to swallow her fear, her mouth suddenly dry as sand as she fought the urge to turn and run. Every part of her was screaming to get out of there, to start running like hell and not look back, to put as much distance between herself and those *things* as humanly possible. The dark hairs on the backs of her arms and neck stood on end in warning even as she rolled her shoulders back, spine straightening and hands curling into fists by her sides as she tipped her chin up stubbornly. Her mind raced, scrambling to come up with some semblance of a strategy, some way to fight herself out of this.

She didn't get the chance.

With a snarling screech, one of the gargoyles lunged forward in a flash of razor-sharp claws and black teeth, and with a startled yelp, Kai took a little half-skip, half-step like she used to when she played soccer as a kid, her foot making painful contact with the gargoyle's side. A piercing shriek echoed throughout the chamber as he flew backward, colliding with the wall beyond and falling limply to the floor. Her knee throbbing in red-hot pain, Kai didn't have time to wonder or wait to see if he was dead or merely unconscious, because his comrades were on her.

Literally.

An agonized scream ripped from Kai's throat as two pairs of talons sunk into her skin, ripping easily through her shirt and her flesh and leaving long, painful streaks of red in their wake. It burned like nothing Kai had ever felt before, and tears sprang to her eyes at the blinding pain.

She stumbled back, twisting and flailing in a desperate attempt to loosen their hold. She managed to wrap her hands around a scaled, spindly leg, and she gave a sharp yank, tearing him off of herself and throwing him blindly as far as she could manage. She only barely heard him let out an angered screech as he went, too focused on the remaining gargoyle, who had attached himself firmly to her shoulders and was determinedly trying to make his way up to her head. He lashed out, talons swiping swiftly across Kai's cheek as he scrambled for higher purchase, and another scream tore from her throat at the hot flash of pain. She tasted blood.

This gargoyle was more clever than the previous two, and he had learned from their mistakes, dodging Kai's hands as she made weakening grabs in his direction. This wasn't working; if they continued like this, her back would end up in shreds. ***Think,*** *Kai!* Her thoughts raced.

She'd only seen stuff like this in movies, so there was a strong chance that it wouldn't work, but it was the only idea she had. Acting off instinct and what little she could remember, Kai stumbled hastily backward, acting too quickly for the gargoyle to shift out of the way, and she heard a satisfying *crunch* as she collided with the wall behind her, crushing the gargoyle between it and her body. The gargoyle shrieked loudly in anger and pain, but his grip slipped a bit, talons dragging down Kai's arms. Ears ringing and flesh screaming in agony, Kai clenched her teeth and slammed herself backward again, and again and again and again, until she felt the gargoyle's hold release.

Spinning on her heel, she found the creature curled in a mangled heap on the ground, struggling and gasping for breath, ruby eyes glowing brightly at her in unfettered hatred. With a hoarse scream, Kai reared back and kicked him solidly once, then twice. She was readying herself for a third when one of the gargoyles she'd forgotten about suddenly sank his claws deeply into her shoulders, pulling a visceral cry from somewhere deep within the caverns of Kai's chest, the sound echoing through the chamber so loudly that she wondered if Hades could hear it from his throne room.

Kai fell hard to her knees, chest heaving as she gasped painfully for breath, vision clouded by tears and sweat, her mouth tasting distinctly metallic, and she wondered if this was how she died—in a haze of blood and pain.

Please, she thought weakly.

Cyrus did not wait for Alastair to guide him as he swept through the halls of the Keeper's palace, his hurried footsteps echoing off of the high ceilings like a ticking clock, urging him ever faster. Not for the first time, he found himself cursing whatever instinct had led him to save Thorne on that long-ago day, when a mortal boy had been turned into a solution.

Because whilst Thorne's creation had solved one problem, his rebellion had now created one much worse, with far deadlier consequences. His actions impacted more than the life of a single mortal. What he had done would affect everyone who crossed paths with the girl, and worse, rip a hole in the fabric of reality as mortals knew it. By saving a single mortal, Thorne had created a crack in Fate itself, and a cracked door opens far more easily than a locked one.

He found the Keeper, as usual, in her garden, lovingly tending to a youthful fruit tree, a pair of old shears in hand to prune back some of the slender branches.

"My lady," Cyrus bowed, not mincing words as he straightened and said, "Thorne and the mortal—they are in the Underworld. I believe they are seeking aid from Hades."

The Keeper smiled, tilting her head, eyes narrowed as she snipped off a dying leaf. "I know."

"You...know?" Cyrus blinked. "Forgive me, my lady, but then why—"

"—am I allowing it?" She finished, setting the shears down and turning to face him fully. "You know as well as I do that Hades despises that boy; he will find no help in the Underworld. In the meantime, the girl is vulnerable, and practically alone. Alastair is on his way to find her as we speak."

"Oh." Cyrus was unsure how to proceed, caught off guard by how calmly she had received the information, given how frantically he had searched to procure it. "Good. I will return to my duties, then." The Keeper merely hummed as she turned back to her pruning, and Cyrus left the way he came, feeling oddly stung by the experience.

Chapter Thirty-One
THE ECHOES THAT HAUNT US

MINHO

"So how long are we supposed to wait before we get worried?" Jai was back in the chair, but was now positioned precariously upside down, heavy combat boot-clad feet swinging boredly above him, his wavy hair just brushing the floor. Minho had already cautioned him that this position could *not* be good for his spine, to which Jai had quipped, ***"Death*** *is not good for my spine, yet here I am."* Minho had only rolled his eyes, and Jai had grinned impishly at his exasperation.

Minho sighed heavily and shook his head—in response to the question or continued vexation at Jai's current position, it was unclear. "We knew this could take a while," Minho said. "It's not as though they ran out for a quick errand—they are in the *Underworld*. Getting them *in* was the easy part; knowing what little I do of Hades, it is unlikely that he will allow them to leave without a fight." The gravity of his tone made Jai uneasy—or maybe that was just nausea from being upside down for so long.

Cheeks flushed, he twisted until he was right-side-up in the chair, gnawing at his lip as he picked anxiously at the sleeves of his black hoodie. He glanced over at Kai, still unconscious and lifelessly pale.

"Do you think they'll make it out?" He asked quietly, and then, quieter still, "What happens to us if they don't?" Sympathy bloomed in Minho's chest, his heart aching for the boy. He knew that Jai did not want to be a Reaper forever—after all, who would? Minho was the *exception,* not the rule.

With a gentle smile that he hoped came off as comforting, Minho replied, "I am sure that they will be fine; Thorne will likely return any minute now, and all will be well."

"You think so?" Jai perked up hopefully, and Minho gave a single nod, feeling warm as Jai cracked a small grin. He sometimes forgot how very *young* Jai was; he admired that easy optimism, the kind that only came with youth. That kind of thing seemed to grow harder as you got older—started to become more of a choice than an instinct. Minho missed it.

Just as quickly as Jai had cheered up, his expression quickly dimmed again, trepidation in his eyes as he tilted his head, indicating something beyond the door. "It may be too late for that," he said, and, brows pushing together, Minho turned to look.

"Shit." He couldn't help the expletive that escaped his lips, for through the barely-parted blinds, lurking ominously by the abandoned nurse's station, was Alastair.

He didn't seem to know they were here, but his hawk-eyed gaze was carefully scanning the area, so Minho had no doubt that this would soon change.

He swore again, this time lapsing into the familiarity of his native language as he wracked his brain for a solution. They had known it was a strong possibility that something like this could happen, but he had hoped—well, it mattered little now what he had hoped. *Thorne, where are you?* With a shake of his head, he leaned quickly forward in his seat, turning authoritatively to Jai.

"Listen to me carefully," he began, and with wide eyes, Jai nodded hastily, leaning forward as he shifted his full focus to Minho. "I am going to try and lead him toward the East Wing of the hospital. You stay here with Kai and try to stay hidden—cover her with a sheet and turn off the machines if you have to, but *protect her.* **Do not be seen.** Do you understand?" Again, Jai nodded, and Minho disappeared.

He reappeared less than a second later in a hallway on the opposite side of the nurses' station and, taking care not to so much as glance in Alastair's direction, he set off at a brisk pace, his chest tightening as he wondered if Alastair would follow.

He didn't allow himself to check as he turned the corner to continue down another corridor, but as he passed a curtained window, the reflection within showed a silhouette trailing suspiciously behind. The Guardian had taken the bait.

Allwas quiet when Aristides returned to the stone sanctuary that he and his brothers called home. This was not unusual—it was always quiet. Still, he felt a foreboding sense of unease as he walked silently through the dim corridors in search of his brothers, wondering if Cyrus had already relayed the news of Thorne's location to the Keeper. Though he felt undeniably uncomfortable deceiving his brother in this manner, Aristides could not find it within himself to regret helping Thorne, and he only hoped that what little assistance he had managed to provide had been enough, that he had not been too late.

Still, he had his fingers crossed that his brothers did not find out what he had done.

Cyrus was not in his room of mirrors. While this, too, was not entirely out of the ordinary, it did little to ease the feeling of discomfort spreading across Aristides' skin like a plague. He did not believe his brother had been long away from his mirrors since Thorne had rescued the mortal, determined to monitor the situation as closely as possible until the matter had been resolved.

The silver-haired Fate was nowhere to be found as Aristides continued on in search of him, and neither to be seen was Linus, though this was far less unusual. Though Aristides didn't bother checking to confirm, he had little doubt that his other brother was back at his wheel, forever spinning the golden life threads of mortals, as had been his task since their creation. It was a task that Linus took incredibly seriously—so much so that he had sewn his own mouth shut to avoid the temptation that came with his gift of Sight. For while Cyrus could see the present, and Aristides the past, Linus' ability was of the future. It was that ability that allowed him to breathe life into those delicate golden threads.

Personally, Aristides thought that Linus' whole 'sewing his mouth shut' gesture was a tad melodramatic, and more symbolic than anything; after all, Linus still possessed the ability to speak into his brothers' minds when he so chose, so what did it matter whether he spoke through his mind or his mouth? Aristides had long suspected that the real reason Linus had rendered himself mute was for a bit of peace and quiet.

Since Aristides' task was to *cut* the life threads of mortals—something that he had never shared with Thorne, nor would he for the foreseeable future—he worked closely with Linus, and indeed, had spent decades at a time pestering the reclusive Fate for some semblance of a conversation, largely to no avail. Cyrus was nearly the same—he did not seem to possess the same aversion to companionship as Linus, but between his task of measuring the life threads of mortals and his ability to watch over the present, he was often so utterly consumed in work that Aristides would have had better luck drawing a response from a stone.

This left Aristides, ever talkative and outgoing, the odd man out. Perhaps this was the reason that he and Thorne had become friends—that, after millennia of silence, Aristides had merely wanted someone to talk to.

"Aristides." He stopped short, caught off guard by his brother's sudden, silent appearance, and his chest tightened at Cyrus' expression—stony and controlled as ever, but something dark simmering in the endless silver pools of his eyes.

"Brother." Aristides forced an uneasy laugh, forcing his feet to begin moving forward again. "You startled me."

"I can see that." A pause. "Where have you been?" The question, phrased simply, was clearly a trap; Aristides had learned long ago that when someone asked a question like that, the odds were that they knew the answer already. Cyrus wasn't stupid—the only reason that Aristides ever left the sanctuary at this point was to visit Thorne, who was currently in the Underworld, which Cyrus knew.

But Aristides was no fool, either; even if Cyrus suspected, Aristides did not have to confirm those suspicions.

"I was out," he responded lightly, eyes narrowing slightly as he sauntered slowly, carefully, toward his brother.

"Yes," Cyrus mused, and as Aristides grew closer, he saw anger and disapproval brewing in Cyrus' eyes. His mouth went dry. "I have a guess as to where you may have been, but I was hopeful that you would have the strength of character to tell me yourself, rather than force me to draw my own conclusions."

"Oh, Cy," Aristides forced a grin that he did not feel and clapped his brother firmly on the shoulder. "Always the honest one. I admire that about you." Like lightning, Cyrus' hand closed around Aristides' wrist like a vise, his grip bruising. Aristides attempted to pull his hand back, but Cyrus yanked him closer, the fury in his eyes no longer veiled as he hissed,

"*What have you done?*" His voice was low, dangerous, and for the first time in his long life, Aristides feared his brother. With a sharp tug that left his wrist red and stinging, Aristides managed at last to free himself. He straightened, smoothing his robes as he took a quietly shuddering breath, trying not to let Cyrus see the effect that he had rendered.

"I do not know what to tell you, brother," he said with a shake of his head, finally daring to meet Cyrus' eyes. Aristides opened his mouth, faltered, ran a hand through his hair, and finally lifted his shoulders in defeat, helpless to explain to his furious brother something that he did not know how to explain to himself. "He is my *friend.*"

"We **cannot** work against Fate, Aristides—you **know** this." Though he was not quite shouting, Cyrus' voice echoed powerfully down the long corridor, and Aristides had little doubt that Linus, wherever he was, had heard the *accusation*, the bitter disappointment, in their eldest brother's tone. Aristides swallowed, but refused to avert his eyes. What he had done...he felt somewhere deep and vital within that he had *not* been wrong. Cyrus sighed. "The rules—"

"The rules don't exist anymore!" Aristides' vehement exclamation chased the echoes of Cyrus' words, and the other Fate looked taken aback by the force with which Aristides spoke. Aristides inhaled sharply, then let it go. "We have never experienced a situation like this before, brother, and since this is rather partially our fault—"

"Thorne's actions are entirely his own; I will not allow you to stand here and blame *me* for the choices that he alone has made."

"But *we* are the ones that turned him into this!" Aristides' chest was heaving, his fingers twitching as he stared into Cyrus' eyes, so close that he could see his own reflection staring back at him three times over. He barely recognized himself: messy-haired and passionate with wide, desperate eyes—a far cry from the kempt rule-follower he had been only days ago.

Cyrus seemed to realize it, too.

"We were doing our job," he said slowly. He seemed calmer now, but more disappointed than Aristides had ever seen him. "What that boy became is a direct result of Hades' disobedience. *He* tipped the scales, and it was our *duty* to right that mistake, to maintain the Balance."

"I am not saying that we should not have done it." Aristides was desperate to make his brother understand, to make him *see*. "But can you truly blame him for wanting to save *one* mortal, after all this time? To carry out what he must perceive as justice?" Cyrus was silent for a long moment, then he turned away, shaking his head.

"Such things are not for us to decide." Without another word, he walked away, leaving an emotionally fractured Aristides behind.

Chapter Thirty-Two
CONFRONTATION

The hairs on the nape of Minho's neck stood on end as he moved in and out of various hallways, surreptitiously leading Alastair through the maze of a hospital to draw him farther away from the abandoned wing where Jai and Kai were hiding. He wasn't exactly certain what Alastair might do if he found them, but he had little doubt that it would end in Kai's death.

He could not let that happen.

He tried to stall as long as he could, weaving artfully through various wings and corridors until at last, there was nowhere left on this floor to go. If he re-traced his footsteps, Alastair would grow suspicious; so, taking a breath, Minho pushed open the door to the East Stairwell.

It was empty, confirming what he already knew—this was where Alastair was most likely going to confront him, and where Minho would have to make a stand. At any cost, Alastair must *not* find Kai. Minho might go down, but certainly not without a fight.

He had scarcely made it to the first landing when he heard the door above him swing open, and slowly, he turned to face the Guardian, who was standing on the landing above with one thick, angular brow arched slightly.

"

"I don't suppose you could point me to the nearest washroom?" Minho inquired, lifting one corner of his mouth in a crooked grin. Stone-faced, Alastair didn't deign to acknowledge the lame joke, beginning a slow, steady descent.

"Where is the mortal?" His voice wasn't loud, but it carried, the low, silky tone sending a shiver down Minho's spine. *Guardians,* he thought with distaste. He resisted the urge to step back as Alastair grew closer. "Surely you must realize how futile this all is," Alastair continued, his eyes dark. "Cease this pointless stalling and tell me where she is. I will make it painless, I promise."

"Well, when you put it like *that.*" Minho cocked his head, as though he were taking the time to consider all of his options, and then shrugged a shoulder, his smile dissipating. "I'm afraid I must refuse."

"Your mistake," Alastair said. He was close now. "I will defeat you here, and then I will find her myself."

"Perhaps," Minho agreed. "But you'll have to put up a hell of a fight before you do." Alastair stepped onto the landing, and Minho braced himself.

Thorne was becoming desperate. He didn't know how long it had been since he'd parted ways with Aristides, but he knew with cold certainty that his time was quickly running out. But he still hadn't been able to find Kai, and there wasn't a chance in hell that he was going to leave this infernal place without her.

Think, Thorne. **Think.**

Until today, he had only been to Hades' fortress once, and even then, he'd never seen anything beyond the throne room. But he recalled hearing stories of tunnels that were said to run underneath the obsidian fortress—tunnels that led *up,* that led *out,* into the mortal realm and all that lay beyond. It was how Persephone had wandered into the Underworld in the first place, or so the stories went; they were only rumors, gossip, *myths,* but perhaps there was some truth to them.

Only one way to find out.

After a glance around the corner to confirm that the path ahead was clear, Thorne paused to consider. Where would one even go about *looking* for the entrance to a secret tunnel?

Down.

He faintly remembered seeing a set of stairs two corridors back. Was it possible...?

Backtracking quickly, he barely took the time to pause and scan for danger as he plunged back down the hallway, barely able to form a coherent thought over the roaring possibility.

And there it was: a staircase, wholly unguarded, positioned across from a storeroom that had been empty when he had checked it just moments before. He stepped forward, brows furrowing as he caught sight of something lying on the floor just in front of the steps. *Yellow hibiscus?* It was a fresh bloom, its petals soft and vibrant, the edges only slightly curled. Did he dare hope that it was a sign? Some signal that he was on the right path?

Again, there was only one way to find out.

Taking a deep breath, Thorne began to descend the stairs.

CHAPTER THIRTY-THREE

MISSION ACCOMPLISHED

JAI

It's been too long, Jai thought as he anxiously paced the floors of Kai's hospital room, pausing periodically to peek through the now-closed blinds, his hopes that Minho would be returning anytime soon—or at all—dwindling by the minute. What would happen if Minho did not return?

Unconsciously, Jai began to chew his nails, which were already reduced to stubs. He reached the other side of the room, turned, and continued his pacing as he silently worried. He didn't think that Reapers could really *die*—they were already dead, after all, but who was he to say what a Guardian was capable of? He didn't even truly know what Guardians *were.* Whoever this Alastair guy was, maybe the Keeper had given him permission to blot Minho, Thorne, Jai, and anyone else who stood in his way, off the face of the planet.

Jai turned again, fully prepared to continue wearing a hole in the tiled floor, when something caught his eye. *What on earth—?* He crossed the room in a blink to reach Kai's side and leaned over her, brows pushing together. Hastily, he swept the bags of ice off of her body and dropped them to the floor before turning back to the bed, his eyes widening in panic as, like something out of a horror film, Kai's skin began to split of its own accord. First it was her shoulders—long, terrible gashes that had blood spilling onto the white sheets of the bed. Then it was her arms, her hands, the side of her neck. *There's too much blood.* Jai felt nauseous—and dizzy, and *sick,* the nausea rolling like a tidal wave in his stomach and threatening to rise up his throat.

The machine displaying Kai's vitals began to alarm rapidly, drawing Jai's attention away from the crimson-soaked bedding. Kai's heart rate was all over the place, first beating so quickly that he wondered if it was going to explode out of her chest, then plummeting, going almost completely flat. Fear pooled in his stomach at the thought of her dying here—alone in this room and right in front of him, when there wasn't a damned thing he could do to stop it.

"No, no, no," he murmured frantically, fingers trembling as he searched for something—*anything*—that would help, hands hovering helplessly over Kai's unconscious, bleeding form as he tried to think. *Think!* He tried holding the wounds shut with his hands, hoping to staunch the bleeding, but the warm red liquid continued to pour through his fingers, and new wounds were opening every second. All Jai could see was blood, trickling down her face and streaming out from beneath her, spilling onto the floor in a pool of red.

"Kai, please, *please,* don't die," Jai pleaded as he tried to close a new wound on her arm, his hands slipping, blood coating his trembling fingers. Never before had he felt so utterly *helpless.* He wished Minho were here. Minho would know what to do.

Minho would know what to do.

Jai glanced toward the door, conflicted. He didn't want to leave Kai by herself, but whatever was happening to her, he could not stop it by himself. He *needed* help.

Grabbing a thick blue quilt from the cabinet on the opposite wall, he laid it carefully over Kai, pulling it up to cover her face in case anyone happened to walk by. He hesitated, drawing a sharp breath through his teeth as a vicious cut opened on her right cheek.

"I'll be back," he said, his hand hovering briefly over her face as if to wipe away the blood, then thinking better of it. Tearing his gaze from the gruesome wound that covered half of Kai's face, which had drained almost completely of color, Jai finished covering her with the blanket and sprinted out of the room, running through the hallways as fast as his feet would take him.

"I am going to try and lead him toward the East Wing of the hospital," Minho had said. Jai had never been good with directions, but fortunately for him there were signs to point out the path that Minho had said he would take.

He ran like hell until he reached the East Wing, and skidded to an abrupt stop between the stairs and the elevator. His mind raced, struggling to come to a decision. The elevator would take too long, and he didn't have time to scour every floor of this wing; if Alastair was as powerful as Jai had been led to believe, Minho's best chance would have been to isolate the Guardian. *The stairs.*

Jai burst through the door to the stairwell and plunged downward at a breakneck pace, skipping steps and even tripping over them as he used the metal railing to swing himself around the corners of the winding staircase. He must have descended two or three floors when at last, he heard voices.

Minho's, he recognized immediately; then, after the distinct sound of a fist connecting with flesh and bone, another voice, this one deep and powerful and unfamiliar. *Alastair.*

Jai rounded the corner, nearly throwing himself over the railing as he slammed to a halt. On the landing below, he saw them: the tall, brutal Guardian towering over a bruised and bloody Minho, who was struggling to push himself off of the floor. His hair was messy and his swollen bottom lip was split, but there was fire in his eyes as he looked up at Alastair, determination burning bright in his gaze even as he turned his head to spit out blood.

"Give it up, Reaper," Alastair advised, tilting his head as he watched Minho slip in a puddle of his own blood, leaving a crimson handprint in his wake as he managed to rise to one knee. "This hopeless endeavor is not worth your effort, and in the end it will amount to nothing, I assure you."

"That is where we disagree," Minho said with a stifled groan of pain as he finally managed to pull himself to his feet. "Besides," he said with a faint grin, his breathing ragged as his eyes rose to rest on Jai, still standing frozen on the landing above. "You're outnumbered."

Alastair turned instantly to follow Minho's gaze, but Jai was quicker, having gotten a running start before Minho had finished speaking. By the time that Alastair had turned to fully face him, Jai was leaping through the air, leaving Alastair with no time to brace himself as both of Jai's feet connected solidly with the Guardian's chest, sending him tumbling down the stairs.

Having overestimated the amount of force that it would take to reach Alastair, Jai nearly followed, but was saved by Minho's hands wrapping solidly around his biceps and yanking him backward.

"You're supposed to be with Kai," Minho said as he helped Jai regain his balance. His eyes searched those of the younger Reaper, his hand resting briefly, almost absentmindedly, on the side of Jai's neck as he quickly scanned the boy's body, as though to confirm he was uninjured.

"Something's happening—she's bleeding a lot and I didn't know what to do and I thought that you might, and—"

"Okay," Minho interrupted with a nod, his expression concerned, but calm, and Jai took a shuddering breath of air. "But one situation at a time, alright? You okay?" He had caught sight of Jai's hands.

"It's hers," Jai said, and Minho's jaw tightened. But there was no time to say anything more as they turned to face Alastair as one. The Guardian was already back on his feet and was staring up at them from the landing below, the dark brows drawn low over his eyes the only betrayal of his frustration.

Minho and Jai descended the steps together, exchanging grim glances as Alastair drew himself to his full height and planted his feet, preparing to meet the impending onslaught. A red haze covered his body, his eyes a determined flash of gold.

The two Reapers attacked as a team, Jai going high as Minho went low, instinctively coordinating their attacks in an attempt to knock Alastair off-balance. The Guardian dodged Jai's first attack with ease, seeming unbothered by the solid blow that Minho landed on his ribs; Jai recovered quickly, closed fist already swinging as he turned to face Alastair again.

Alastair met the attack effortlessly, his large hand snapping shut around Jai's fist and twisting, eliciting a cry of pain and surprise from the young Reaper as a *crack!* echoed like a gunshot in the empty stairwell. Alastair swatted him aside as easily as he would a fly, sending Jai rolling painfully down to the next landing.

The Guardian turned his attention back to Minho. The Reaper was already balanced on one leg as the other sliced through the air, boot aiming for Alastair's head, so close to making contact—

Alastair closed both of his strong hands around Minho's ankle and yanked sharply, bringing Minho crashing to the floor, his head colliding hard with the tiled floor beneath him. In a fluid motion, Alastair had closed a hand around Minho's throat and lifted him easily off the ground, slamming him hard against the wall. Minho's feet dangled helplessly several inches above the floor, his eyes widening as his windpipe was slowly crushed beneath Alastair's powerful fingers.

Jai had nearly made his way back up to the pair when Alastair's demeanor suddenly changed, his spine going ramrod straight as he abruptly released his hold on Minho. The Reaper crumpled, gasping for air, to the floor as Alastair stepped back, his icy features morphing back into something stoic and unreadable.

"I am finished here," was all that he said before he disappeared abruptly, a faint flutter of wings echoing in his wake. Jai blinked, faltering for something to say as he shook his head in utter confusion.

"What...what does that mean?" Minho, still slumped against the wall as he tried to recover enough energy to drag himself back to his feet, seemed just as bewildered. "The only way he would just give up like that is if—" Jai's eyes widened, and realization seemed to hit Minho at the same time as they exclaimed in unison,

"KAI!"

Chapter Thirty-Four
FOUND

The fear was paralyzing, clutching her heart in a grip almost as painful as the talons digging cruelly into her flesh. She couldn't even turn to fight, the gargoyle positioned in such a way that rendered her arms useless.

Kai screwed her eyes shut, praying that it would be quick, mentally pleading for it to just be over. She couldn't take any more of the red-hot pain, the fire searing into her very bones and setting her blood to a boil.

Mom, Dad, I tried.

Abruptly, the talons were torn away, and Kai let out an inhuman shriek as the claws ripped out of her, black spots swarming her vision at the overwhelming wave of pain. As she doubled over, her back and shoulders screaming in agony, she heard the wet, crunching sound of a knife being plunged into hard, cracked flesh.

It all happened so fast, and she was so lost in the haze of pain that was threatening to pull her under completely, that Kai didn't get the chance to turn and look at her rescuer. She didn't need to, because in seconds, Thorne was falling to his knees in front of her, his warm hands encasing her cheeks, brushing her hair away from her face, his terrified eyes frantically scanning her face, her body, cataloging the wounds, the tangled hair wet with blood, the dusty tears mingled with crimson already beginning to dry on her skin.

She realized abruptly that he was talking, but she couldn't concentrate, the words leaving his lips muted, like he was behind a thick layer of glass. Kai blinked hard, shaking her head, and everything snapped suddenly back into focus.

"KAI!" He was shaking her, his eyes and voice filled with such panic that it scared her, freezing her to the core. Somehow her hands had wrapped themselves in his shirt, and her wide eyes snapped up to meet his.

"What?" Her voice was small, hoarse and cracked from her screams of anger and pain. A garbled sound somewhere between a sob and a laugh of relief tumbled from Thorne's lips, and sharply, so suddenly it was as if it were an innate instinct rather than something he had actively decided to do, he yanked her close, wrapping his arms tightly around her as one hand carefully cupped the back of her head, pressing her face to his shoulder. The way that he held her snugly against him, as though he had been terrified out of his mind that he would never see her again, tugged something loose from the confines of Kai's chest, and a sob ripped raggedly from her aching throat.

Thorne instantly pulled back, lips already parting to ask what was wrong, but she didn't give him the chance, throwing her arms around his neck and pulling herself up against him, burrowing into the warmth of his body until she could feel the ridges of his chest pressed against hers. She buried her face in his shoulder, her hot tears melting through the fabric of his shirt and into his skin.

His response was instant, arms wrapping around her waist so tightly that she could barely breathe. His forearms pressed against her wounds, but she didn't care; Thorne was here. He had come for her.

He struggled slightly to pull the both of them off of the floor, his movements clumsy, but he refused to let Kai go. The second her feet hit solid ground, her knees buckled, and Thorne was quick to slip one arm under her knees and sweep her off her feet, sliding his other arm down to the middle of her back in an attempt to avoid the painful gashes on her shoulders.

He shifted her in his arms for a better grip, and their eyes met. His expression…Kai swallowed, a fresh burst of tears pressing insistently against the backs of her eyes. It was like a wound, open and raw, putting on display everything that he was feeling—everything that he *had* felt, every fear and hope and paralyzing jolt of terror that he had experienced as he had tried to find her.

Something in his gaze shifted a little at her expression and, so unexpectedly that it caused Kai to draw in a sharp breath of surprise, Thorne pressed his lips firmly to her temple. He didn't linger long, and when he pulled away, he just looked tired, the crooked smile he offered her nearly as weak as she felt.

"Let's get you home, sunshine," he murmured, and turned to walk toward the doors. Kai tilted her head to rest comfortably on his shoulder as she let her eyes flutter shut, the fading adrenaline leaving her with no energy to keep the heavy lids open another second.

Funny, she thought as she began to drift to sleep in his arms, the steady rise and fall of his chest lulling her into a contented slumber. *I feel like I **am** home.*

CHAPTER THIRTY-FIVE
NOT TODAY

THORNE

When Thorne reappeared in Kai's hospital room, Jai and Minho were nowhere to be seen. *Shit.* Alastair must have found them; Thorne could only hope that his Reapers were holding their own against the Guardian. They just needed to keep him distracted until Thorne managed to bring Kai back.

Turning, his brows furrowed as he noticed Kai's body, covered from head to toe with a thick blue blanket. The bags of ice that had been covering her were sprawled across the floor like they'd been swept off of her in one fell swoop. Thorne pulled the blanket back slowly, dread pitting in his stomach as he caught sight of a gruesome cut, one that he had seen only moments ago, etched in the soft flesh of Kai's cheek. With trembling fingers, he inhaled sharply as he dared to pull the blanket further back, physically recoiling at the sight that met him.

Every bit as bruised and battered and bloody as she had been when he'd seen her only moments ago, Kai's entire body reflected the wounds that she had received in the Underworld. It hadn't occurred to Thorne that those wounds might also be sustained on her physical form; he felt nauseous, horror flowing like ice through his veins.

Her vitals were still stable, though, and it appeared that the blood had stopped flowing, the wounds likely beginning to clot, so that was something; if Minho's estimations were correct, once she was warmed back up, Kai could awaken at any moment. Thorne plugged in the heated blanket that they had scavenged prior to beginning this endeavor and spread it over Kai's body, pulling a fresh blanket from the cabinet and layering it on top to seal in the heat. The stained blanket he deposited in the corner, trying not to think about how much blood it seemed Kai had lost.

All that was left to do now was wait.

Exhaling slowly, Thorne lowered himself into Minho's vacated seat, his gaze glued to Kai's face as he waited for any sign of her returning to consciousness. The minutes ticked by agonizingly slow, and though it didn't take long for the color to begin bleeding back into Kai's skin, she did not wake, and the more time that passed, the more anxious Thorne became. His knee bounced at a breakneck pace, and he began to absentmindedly chew on his nails, an unfortunate habit he'd picked up from Jai—a habit that annoyed him to no end, and that he had, with little success, tried to break Jai of. But he didn't know what else to do, and the trepidation that was growing inside of him with every passing second threatened to burst out of his body if he didn't do *something*.

Slowly, hesitantly, he took Kai's hand in his. For once, their temperatures matched, her skin no longer burning hot to touch; he pressed her hand between both of his, willing warmth that did not exist into them, willing her to wake, for her eyes to open and meet his.

"Please wake up," he said softly. "*Please.*" He waited, and he waited, and he pressed his forehead against their joined hands, praying fervently to anyone who would listen. *Please wake up. I will do anything. I will **be** anything. Spare her. Please. **Please.***

It seemed an eternity before the machine displaying Kai's vitals began to alarm urgently, signaling the rapid rise of her heart rate. Thorne's head snapped up, eyes wide as he watched Kai's face, not daring to *breathe* as he waited. He barely registered the fact that he was squeezing her hand so tightly he was likely cutting off her circulation. He could only watch, and wait, and *hope* that, finally, she was coming back to him.

And then—

Flatline.

Her heart rate plummeted to zero, the machine letting out a flat, droning signal as Kai stopped breathing. Thorne's own heart fell in his chest, and he was suffocating. *No.* This couldn't be happening—this *wasn't* happening.

Thorne sprang into action, acting on pure instinct as he stacked his hands, one over the other, on top of her chest. He gazed fiercely at the pale, still face beneath him, and ground out through clenched teeth,

"You are *not* dying today, do you hear me? *Not. Today.*" He began to press rhythmically down on her chest, putting all of his strength into it, letting hope run through his veins and into his touch, as though his will alone could bring her back to life. He continued his efforts to restart her heart, broken pleas for her to wake up and desperate demands for her to *come back* spilling from his trembling lips.

The droning sound continued.

"Damn it!" He choked as his hands slipped, and he pounded a fist into the bed. *"Damn it!"* A familiar dampness pressed against his eyes, his vision blurring as he hung his head, eyes squeezing shut as he tried not to drown in the vast ocean of grief. "I'm sorry. *I'm so sorry.*"

"For what?" A familiar voice beneath him croaked hoarsely. Thorne's eyes snapped open and, hardly daring to believe his eyes, he slowly looked up to meet Kai's faintly amused gaze, a tired smile on her lips as she weakly lifted a brow. "Aww, did the Grim Reaper miss his human?" A relieved huff of air expelled itself from Thorne's lungs, and without stopping to think, he pulled her into his arms, one hand burying itself in her hair as he breathed in her faintly floral scent, not entirely sure that this was real—that this was truly happening.

"I thought you were dead," he whispered, his voice muffled by Kai's shoulder as she weakly shifted her arms to return his embrace. "I thought—"

"Don't worry." He could hear the smile in her voice. "You're not gonna get rid of me that easily—not after everything we've done to keep me alive." Thorne laughed, hugging her a little tighter before reluctantly releasing her, watching as she lowered her head back onto the pillows with a wince. Their eyes met, and Thorne's lips parted—to say what, he didn't know, but he didn't get the chance to find out. The door suddenly flew open, slamming loudly against the wall as Minho and Jai skidded to a halt.

"Oh, thank God." Minho's eyes fluttered shut in relief as he sagged against the doorframe, and an elated Jai blurted,

"You're alive!" Kai laughed, then winced again. Everyone seemed to notice her wounds all at once, and Kai's face paled, a nauseated expression passing over her features as she seemed to struggle against losing consciousness.

"Well," she said. "This isn't ideal."

Thorne wasn't sure if he was allowed to laugh.

inho offered to clean and bandage Kai's wounds and, as she would need to undress from the waist up for him to do so, Thorne and Jai stepped outside of the room to wait, Jai plunging into a rapid recount of what had transpired here whilst Thorne and Kai had been in the Underworld.

Kai felt less awkward than she would have expected having to undress herself in front of a complete stranger, his eyes focused steadily on the opposite wall as he offered her a pillow.

"To cover yourself," he said without inflection, and Kai flushed slightly, accepting the pillow with a murmured *thank you.* She shifted the pillow to cover her bare chest, and at last, Minho turned to look at her fully, inhaling softly through his nose as he took in the mangled mess of her back.

"That bad, huh?" Kai cracked a weak grin, anxiety pooling in her stomach as she tried not to twist around in an attempt to see what Minho was seeing, knowing that it would only hurt more if she tried to move.

"Not at all," he said smoothly, reassurance and faint amusement shining in his eyes as he smiled back at her, clearly seeing through her nervous facade. He had collected from a nearby supply closet everything that he thought he might need and laid it out neatly on a small cart beside the bed, plucking from it a bottle of liquid that Kai recognized well from her childhood. "This may sting a bit, and I think it may be most effective if I just pour it straight over everything," he said, and Kai nodded, setting her teeth and clenching the pillow in her fists as she braced herself. She tried to hold back the grunt of pain as he poured the cool, bubbling cleanser over the cuts in her shoulders and back, sagging in relief when it was over.

"There, that wasn't so bad, right?" Minho capped the bottle and put it back on the cart, frowning as he glanced between it and her wounds.

"This part will be far more unpleasant, I am afraid; some of these cuts look like they will heal just fine on their own, but…"

"Just say it," mumbled Kai, her face buried in the pillow as she waited anxiously to hear the words she knew were coming.

"You're going to need stitches," Minho said, not without sympathy. "I found some gel that looks as if it may numb the area slightly, but if you'd like, I can get Thorne or Jai to come back in so that you may hold their hand during the process." Kai shook her head, swallowing hard as she tried to keep her breathing even.

"No, thank you," she said, her voice small. She liked Jai well enough, but she didn't particularly care for another stranger to see her shirtless just now, and Thorne…

She swallowed, shaking her head again. "Just do it." Minho nodded.

"Very well. Lie down on your stomach." Kai did, wincing at the pain of moving, and hissed as Minho spread the gel gently across her wounds, the cold of it seeping into her bones and making her teeth chatter. "I am going to begin now," he said, and Kai inhaled shakily as she nodded in acknowledgment, gripping the pillow beneath her so tightly that her knuckles whitened. "I will try to be quick."

***

When Kai awoke, it was inches away from a wide-eyed Minho, concern painting his expression as he crouched at her bedside.

"Welcome back," he said with a small, gentle smile, reaching up to brush her hair out of her face. Kai's brows furrowed as she glanced toward the window, expecting to see darkness, but instead finding the soft colors of twilight greeting her, the sky only slightly changed from when she had seen it last.

"What happened?" Her voice was hoarse, and her mouth was dry, her tongue feeling heavy and numb.

"You passed out," Minho said, then she remembered: the Underworld, the gargoyles, the very real effects of the attack on her body. She groaned, burying her face back in the pillow, and Minho laughed softly. "If it helps, I'm finished with your back; you're all bandaged up and everything. All that's left now is that nasty cut on your face."

"Okay," Kai mumbled, too tired to protest as he helped her move into a seated position. As he carefully cleansed the cut with that same stinging solution and a sterile towel, she occupied herself with admiring his features—the symmetry of his facial structure, and the way his eyes, brown and monolid, focused intently on gently cleansing her face. The constellation of small brown moles scattered across the flawless golden skin of his face and neck. The dark, serious brows that drew low over his eyes as his tongue poked briefly out to dampen his plump lips, pursed in concentration.

Normally, Kai would feel awkward being in such close quarters with a man she hardly knew, especially one with such intimidating beauty, but somehow, it didn't feel awkward with Minho. It wasn't the same as it was with Thorne, who made her heart pound so loudly in her chest that she wondered if he could hear it, too; who made her palms sweat and her cheeks heat like furnaces, and who made her mind go blank.

It wasn't like that with Minho. This was something else—something quiet and comfortable and familiar, as though they were old friends, kindred spirits from another lifetime. He met her eyes and smiled, and her lips curved upward to return the gesture, lapsing into a comfortable silence as he reached for a bandage.

The anxiety was going to drive him insane.

First it had been the cries of pain—terrible, agonized sounds reminiscent of her screams in the Underworld when she was being attacked by those gargoyles; and then it had been the silence, sudden and abrupt, and the concerned murmur of Minho's voice in the room beyond, the thick door between them preventing Thorne from being able to clearly hear what was going on.

Jai had had to hold him back from bursting into the room, his arms wrapped around Thorne's chest and his boots squeaking as he dug his heels into the tile to prevent Thorne from breaking the door down in a blaze of worry and panic so staggering it felt as though his heart was going to burst from his chest.

He had been too tired to put up much of a fight, and eventually, Jai had let go of him, patting him on the shoulder and trying to comfort him with reassurances that, if something were truly wrong, Minho would call for them. Numbly, Thorne had nodded, slumping against the wall and letting himself tune out, unable to focus on the steady stream of chatter that Jai kept going in an attempt to distract him.

The youngest Reaper had just finished an animated retelling of the fight with Alastair when Minho finally stepped out of the room, running a hand faintly stained with red through his dark, messy hair as he clicked the door shut behind him.

"She's just getting dressed, and then she'll be ready to go." Thorne nodded, letting his eyes fall shut for a moment as he rested his head back against the wall, the tension easing out of his muscles as relief washed over him, letting the exhaustion seep into his bones. With a deep sigh, he straightened, turning first to look at Minho, and then Jai.

"Thank you," he said earnestly, trying to push past the lump in his throat. "I tru—I truly appreciate everything that you two have done to help me—*and* her."

"Anytime, dude," Jai grinned, holding up his fist, which Thorne bumped with his own after only a second of confused hesitation. Minho laughed.

"What the kid said," he agreed, then tilted his head toward the room. "Are you taking her home?"

"Yeah," Thorne nodded in assent, rubbing the back of his neck as his gaze shifted toward the closed door. "With everything that happened today, I'm not taking any chances."

"Speaking of what happened today," Minho's voice lowered, and his brows lifted slightly. "How *was* your trip to the Underworld?" Thorne shook his head, and Minho's lips flattened into a thin line as he watched Thorne tie back his messy hair, a few stubborn strands slipping out to frame his grim features.

"We won't be receiving any assistance there," he said, in a tone of finality that indicated he did not feel like elaborating on that point just now. Minho nodded. It was a long, tense silence that followed, none of them wanting to say aloud what they were all thinking: they were now, officially, out of options. Not that they'd had many to begin with.

They were rescued from attempting further conversation when the door behind them swung open, a freshly-bandaged Kai stepping through it, looking exhausted and bruised, but smiling. She was wearing a familiar long-sleeved patterned button-up, the shirt clearly several sizes too large for her, and Thorne's eyes shifted to Minho, whose arms were notably bare. Minho slipped his hands into his pockets, cocking a brow in amusement as he grinned crookedly at Thorne, who rolled his eyes in response, eliciting a quiet laugh from Minho.

"Thank you," Kai said. "*All* of you. I—I know I don't deserve any of this, but I appreciate it more than you could imagine. Thank you." After a split second of stilted, awkward hesitation, she stepped forward with open arms. She embraced Jai first—inhaling sharply in pain as the tall, eager puppy of a boy returned her hug a little too enthusiastically—and then Minho, who took care to be gentle, avoiding the bandaged wounds on her shoulders as he gave her a gentle squeeze. He handed her a small bottle of pain medication he'd nicked from the hospital pharmacy, murmuring for her to take it when she felt the current medicine start to wear off. Kai nodded as she stepped back.

"I'll see you guys...sometime, I guess," Kai forced a small laugh, shaking her head as if to physically shake away her awkwardness.

She turned to find Thorne standing just behind her, and swallowed, a flush of pink dusting her cheeks as she allowed him to lift her gently off her feet, his arms carefully positioned to cause her the least amount of pain possible. Kai sighed in relief as the pressure was taken off of her bruised knees, dropping her head onto his shoulder and letting her aching eyes fall shut. Thorne's mouth brushed against her temple, not quite a kiss, and he smiled over her head at Minho and Jai, who lifted their hands—one in a wave, the other in a reflexive peace sign—in farewell.

Chapter Thirty-Six
NOT SUCH A HARD THING

Kai's shoulders sagged in relief as they finally entered her apartment, and she tossed her keys onto the coffee table as Thorne, still holding her in the warm cocoon of his arms, kicked the door shut with his boot. Kai turned the lock, and Thorne carried her over to the couch, a deep sigh of contentment releasing from the confines of her chest as he bent to lay her down on the sofa that seemed suddenly so much softer and deeper than it had ever felt before.

As he slid his hands out from beneath her, one of his rings caught abruptly in the fabric of her borrowed shirt, and Thorne, who had already been straightening back up, was pulled back down by the sudden halt. Kai's eyes flew wide as he fell onto her, her breath catching in her throat. By the time Thorne's free hand slammed against the back of the couch, effectively stopping his fall, his mouth hovered only inches from her own. Kai's gaze locked with his, and in the reflection of his wide, startled eyes, she was unsurprised to find a similar expression in her own.

Her skin felt as though it were burning up, every nerve on end and buzzing with anticipation, the air in the small space between them thick, making it difficult for Kai to breathe. Her mouth was dry; reflexively, her tongue poked out to dampen her lips, her stomach tightening as she saw Thorne's eyes track the movement. She saw the sharp outline of his Adam's apple move as he swallowed. Her mind was a complete blank, and in her moment of need, the etiquette her mother had drilled into her as a child shifted to the forefront of her mind, causing her to say, completely without consciously deciding to,

"Thank you." Thorne blinked rapidly as if coming out of a haze, and nodded, clearing his throat softly.

"Of course." She felt his hand shift beneath her, and he rose to his feet, twisting the silver culprit of the incident around his finger as he shook his head.

"I should..." he glanced over his shoulder at the door, and hesitated.

"Do you want to sit?" The words were out before Kai could over-think them. Thorne started, surprised by the question, and Kai cleared her throat, gesturing loosely to the armchair. "You can sit down if you want." He nodded, a single jerk of his chin, before stepping back and easing down into the chair. He nervously twiddled his thumbs before asking,

"How are you feeling?" Kai couldn't help a laugh, and winced as the vibration sent a stab of pain shooting through her sore ribs. She sighed.

"Tired. Bruised. Like a rotten banana." She snorted, wincing again. "Ow." Thorne couldn't contain a grimace, hating to see her in such pain—pain that he had caused. Not directly, not on purpose, but he had caused it, nonetheless. And sure, Kai was alive for now, but for how long? And at what cost? Already this endeavor had claimed the consciousness of Kai's best friend.

Maybe he was just delaying the inevitable. Maybe there truly was no way out of this mess they were in, and he was just making it harder on the both of them by holding on. But the idea of losing her, however brief their acquaintance had been...it was an idea he could hardly bear to think of.

"I'm sorry." Kai opened her eyes, which had fallen shut during Thorne's silent musings. Her forehead creased in confusion as she lifted her head to look at him.

"This isn't your fault," she said, sounding surprisingly as though she meant it. Thorne smiled sadly.

"It is, though—I'm the reason that this is even happening in the first place. I'm the one that set this whole thing in motion, and I have done nothing but make one mistake after another ever since."

"Was saving me a mistake?" Kai's voice was soft, and when Thorne looked sharply up, his eyes incredulous at the question, she avoided his gaze, eyes rising only briefly to meet his before darting away, picking anxiously at a stray thread on the couch cushion.

"Absolutely not," he said firmly. He waited for her to meet his eyes again before he repeated the words—a little softer this time, but no less resolute. "Absolutely *not*." He paused, sighing deeply. "But taking you to the Underworld was." Kai's lips parted in protest, but Thorne shook his head, rising so suddenly to his feet that it nearly made Kai jump. "That could've been *it,* Kai—everything that we've done to keep you alive, it could've been over like *that*." He snapped his fingers for emphasis.

"But it *wasn't*. We *all* make mistakes, Thorne." He liked the way that she said his name, and felt instantly guilty for it; he didn't deserve for her to look at him like that, with no more animosity in her gaze, no judgment or resentment, not the faintest suggestion in her earnest gaze to suggest that he was any longer someone deserving of her hatred.

She continued. "But taking me with you *wasn't* a mistake. I asked to go so that I could have some *tiny* portion of control over my own Fate. I knew that it would be dangerous, but it was *my* choice. It was worth the risk for me."

"I should have known better," Thorne shook his head stubbornly. "Nothing with Hades ever ends well; I knew that, and I should have known better than to involve you with him." Unsure of how to respond to that, Kai was quiet, silence hanging tensely between them for several long, painful minutes. Thorne stared intently at the set of coasters stacked in the center of the coffee table, his expression clouded.

After what felt like forever, Kai finally broke the silence.

"So...Hades, huh?" Thorne's gaze snapped back up to meet hers, and she offered a hesitant half-grin, lifting a shoulder. "He seems like a shitty dad—no offense." Thorne laughed, then sighed as he shook his head, a bitter smile playing on his lips.

"Yeah, he's never really been into the whole 'father' thing, to be honest." He paused, chewing on his lower lip for a moment before adding, "He hates me."

"How come?" Thorne's smile widened just a little at that, his unfocused gaze resting on the rug beneath his feet. He appreciated that she didn't try to console him with lies as mortals so often did; that she hadn't tried to reassure him with phrases like, *I'm sure that's not true,* or *he's your father, of course he doesn't hate you,* when she had no way of knowing whether or not her words actually rang true. Thorne didn't want pity. Hades hated him; it was a simple fact.

Thorne sighed deeply, contemplating her question. He knew the answer, of course—he had been brooding over the reason for his father's hatred for the past half-millennium. But he had never told anyone aside from Minho the true nature of his creation. Even Jai knew very little, and Aristides only knew because he had been there to witness it. It was something Thorne preferred not to talk about—to even *think* about, lest he drown in the bitter resentment that threatened constantly to consume him.

And yet he found himself *wanting* to tell Kai—found himself wanting to let her know everything about him, the good *and* the bad. Found himself wanting to find out if, somehow, even just a little, she would understand him.

So, he told her.

He seated himself in the armchair, crossing his legs at the ankle as he lifted them to rest on the end of the couch alongside Kai's sock-covered feet. He leaned back in his seat, and Kai sensed that he was settling in for a story, so she did the same, pulling a blanket over herself and shifting around until she was completely comfortable, ready to give Thorne her undivided attention, her eyes wide and expectant.

Thorne inhaled slowly.

"To provide a bit of background," he began, pausing briefly to clear his throat. Kai tried not to be obvious about the way her eyes tracked the movement of his Adam's apple, lingering briefly on his lips, before she jerked her gaze resolutely back up to focus on the upper half of his face. "Hades and the other Olympians—yes, they're *all* real," he said as Kai opened her mouth to interject. She flushed, sinking guiltily back into the couch cushions, and Thorne laughed softly. "They are all strictly prohibited from—to put it delicately—*procreating* with mortals. Oh, they've all had their share of love affairs, as I'm sure you've read about in your mortal mythology, but the *offspring* of such unions was strictly forbidden sometime after the fall of Ancient Greece.

"The other Olympians have gotten lucky—most half-mortal children are miscarried, or, in the rare event they do make it to birth, are stillborn. Most mortals just can't contain that kind of power in their bodies, even if it *is* diluted by their mortal DNA, and those stillbirths have often resulted in the death of the mortal mother, as well. When it comes to Olympian women procreating with mortal men, most don't, and the ones that do have never produced a child from it.

"*Most* Olympians, at this point, tend to steer clear of romantic entanglements with mortals altogether, given that the human lifespan is little more than the blink of an eye for a deity. They still *entangle* themselves in other ways, but they don't generally allow themselves to get involved beyond the pleasure of a single night; the risk is too great, both for the potential of offspring, and for the possibility of heartbreak.

"Hades never did like being told what to do. Nearing the end of the fifteenth century, just after the height of the Renaissance, he and Persephone were having what you mortals would refer to as *marital problems.* At one point, it got bad enough that Persephone went to be with her mother in the mortal realm two months ahead of schedule, and swore that she would not be back until Hades realized what he had to lose.

"Missing her, but too stubborn to apologize, Hades began to wander the mortal realm. He visited many countries, his travels taking him to every corner of the globe, and eventually he found himself in South Korea. It was there that he met my mother. He was instantly taken with her, and she with him, and so Hades remained in the mortal realm for quite some time, neglecting his duties in the Underworld and putting his troubles with Persephone far out of his mind.

"Their love affair lasted for the better part of a decade before my mother got pregnant. To protect his love, Hades struck a deal with the Fates: if my mother survived childbirth—which the child, being the offspring of such a powerful Olympian, surely would not—my mother would forget everything about him. The two were so confident in the power of their love, so sure that they were *destined* to be together, that they believed Hades would be able to make her fall in love with him again, despite the loss of her memories.

"My mother was, of course, devastated—both at the premature death of her coming child, and at the impending loss of her treasured memories, but she knew that the powerful love she shared with Hades would get her through it." Thorne sighed deeply, his eyes distant, as though he was reliving a time long gone. Kai was sitting on the edge of her seat (metaphorically—literally, she was still burrowed in the couch cushions), her eyes as wide and round as saucers. The blanket that had been covering her was now draped over Thorne's legs as well, though neither of them had seemed to notice how or when it had shifted over.

Thorne continued.

"The child, against all odds, survived the long and difficult birth, but tragically, his mother did not. She didn't even get to say her goodbyes before death claimed her, and in her last moments, the Fates saw to it that their deal was kept—as my mother drew her last breath, her memories of Hades and her child floated into nothing, so that even in the afterlife, they would find no goodbye, no happy ending.

"Devastated by the loss of his love, and enraged by the sight of the child who had survived, Hades returned to the Underworld, swearing that he would have nothing to do with his son, who was left to grow up in an orphanage.

"To everyone's surprise, the boy survived his entire childhood, though not without incident; the boy had been strong even in infancy, and never got sick, but it was not until his teenage years that he began to exhibit other unusual traits—strange powers and abilities that seemed to frighten everyone around him, though he knew not why. In his eighteenth year, it was decided that something must be done. This...abomination could not be allowed to simply *exist*." Thorne's jaw clenched, his upper lip curling slightly as bitterness seeped into his tone, flames beginning to dance behind his eyes.

"The Fates themselves are not permitted to take a life, so after much deliberation, they came up with another solution." Thorne chuckled mirthlessly, his expression grim. Kai waited patiently, letting him take his time. This was *his* story, *his* history; she could only count herself lucky that he found her worthy of enough trust to share it.

"They found the boy, homeless and friendless, and it was then that they told him of his heritage, revealed the *truth* of his existence: that he was an accident, unloved and unwanted by his father, the mistakes of whom the boy was now expected to pay for. Hades did not entirely escape punishment—he was now forbidden to ever step foot in the mortal realm again. Of course, now that his mortal lover was dead, he had no reason to ever wish for such a thing, as it would only serve to remind him of his loss, so it was the boy who was left to truly pay for Hades' indiscretion.

"The Fates cursed him with immortality, and gave him a task: for the rest of eternity, he was to collect souls. He would be the friendly face that greeted them in death, the helpful guide that would assist them to the afterlife. And while the souls that left behind something unfinished in life would join him as Reapers until that business was resolved, no one—or," he corrected, thinking of Minho. "*Hardly anyone* would want to do that for eternity. They would all eventually move on, leaving him, always and forever, alone, doomed to continue his existence the same way that it had begun." Thorne's eyes began to ache, brimming with something wet and familiar, and he blinked rapidly, quick to banish the oncoming tears with a short, firm shake of his head. This was a story that he had not had to relive aloud in well over a century, and he was surprised at how greatly it still affected him, reopening a pit in his stomach that was filled with the worst kind of loneliness.

He flinched as a hand suddenly covered his own, and with a start, he realized that Kai had risen from the couch and was now kneeling beside his chair, her other hand moving to rest on his arm, her soft brown eyes shining earnestly as she gazed up at him.

"You didn't deserve that," she said, and Thorne's heart constricted painfully. "You didn't—you *don't*—deserve to pay for a mistake that was not your own. Nobody does. I'm sorry that you had to go through that."

Her voice was thick, but it did not waver, and it was all that Thorne could do to manage a small nod, fearing that if he tried to speak, his voice would shatter utterly under the weight of what he was feeling.

Kai swallowed, taking a deep, shuddering breath before saying, her voice quiet and ashamed, "And I'm sorry for the part that I've played in it." Thorne opened his mouth, brows already pushing together in confusion, but Kai threw up a hand, silencing him instantly.

"I know—" her voice broke a little, and she paused for a moment, fighting a silent battle within herself for control before she continued. "I know that you aren't to blame for the deaths of my family. You told me that it was just a job, that it wasn't your choice, and I didn't understand it then—I'm not sure I do now, really, not entirely, but...I don't blame you anymore. And I am *so sorry* that I ever did." Her eyes were downcast, and Thorne found himself at a loss for words.

Not knowing what else to do, he flipped his hand over and gave hers a brief squeeze. Hesitantly, her eyes rose to meet his, and he smiled—a small, sad, exhausted smile, but one that had Kai smiling in return.

"Thank you," he said, and with a damp sniffle, Kai nodded. Inhaling sharply, she pushed herself to her feet with a grimace, cheeks flushed as she laughed in awkward embarrassment, seeming to avoid Thorne's eyes as she smoothed her palms down her pants.

"I'm just gonna...make myself some tea before bed." She swallowed, seeming to hold her breath as she glanced briefly back toward Thorne and asked, "Would you like some?" Thorne's lips parted as he faltered for a response, and his Adam's apple bobbed as he gave a sharp, jerky nod.

"Sure, why not?" He rose to his feet and followed her to the kitchen, eyes sweeping briefly over the small, cramped space and the overflowing sink before turning to lean against the counter, watching Kai fill a small, white kettle with water.

"Sorry about the mess," Kai said, her cheeks flaming as she set the kettle on the stove and turned the heat to high. "It's just been...difficult lately, doing things. Believe it or not, this is actually relatively clean for me."

"I couldn't care less about the mess," Thorne said gently, and crossing her arms across her stomach to try and calm the nerves buzzing beneath her skin, Kai nodded. Thorne changed the subject. "I've never had hot tea, you know," he remarked casually, and Kai's jaw dropped.

"You're lying." Thorne couldn't help but laugh, mimicking her stance as he crossed his arms over his chest and lifted a shoulder.

"At the time, such things were considered a luxury in the orphanage, and while I'll admit to trying a few foods here and there, I don't technically *need* to consume anything to survive, and most of the time I stay pretty busy collecting souls, so...I don't know, I guess I've just never really felt the *need* to try it. I've tried iced tea."

"That is *not* the same thing." Kai shook her head, but a smile played on her lips as she looked at him from the other side of the small kitchen. "Herbal tea was...it was kind of my mom's *thing*. When I was growing up, she always had it waiting in the afternoon when we got home from school—tea and fruit and little sandwiches with the crusts cut off because my brother was picky." She laughed, her eyes glistening as she reminisced.

"We'd have another cup before bed—non-caffeinated, of course, with herbs that were supposed to help us sleep. My mom would tuck us in and kiss us all on our foreheads, and then my dad would read us all a bedtime story. More often than not he'd end up falling asleep right alongside us, snoring loud enough to bring the roof down. It kind of drove my mom nuts, actually—she couldn't sleep unless he was in bed beside her."

"They sound like they were really good parents," Thorne said softly, and Kai smiled, nodding as she used her sleeve to press below her eyes.

"They were," she said, and silence fell over them once more. She glanced at the kettle, which was beginning to steam, and with a light sigh, she turned to pull open a cabinet door. She pulled out a floral-patterned mug and set it on the counter before reaching for another, this time straining for a pale green mug that sat on a higher shelf.

Her fingers faltered for purchase, a hiss slipping from her lips at the pain radiating from her back as she reached higher, and the smooth handle slipped from her fingers. She gasped sharply as the fragile object plummeted for the counter.

Thorne surged forward to catch the mug easily in his hand, and it wasn't until he had set the mug down alongside the other that he realized his proximity to Kai, his chest pressed against her back, the faint scent of her floral perfume greeting his nostrils as her hair tickled his chin. His nerves were alight as he swallowed, and he shifted his weight backward as Kai spun around, her lips parted in surprise, wide eyes staring up into his through dark, thick lashes. Thorne's hand seemed welded to the counter, and he found himself glued to the spot, unable to make himself move, unable to force himself to try.

"Thanks," Kai breathed softly, flushing as she remembered saying that same thing only a little while before, and he couldn't help but notice the way her throat moved as she swallowed, her chest rising slightly as she inhaled.

"No problem," he replied, his voice just as hushed, just loud enough to be heard in the small, shared space between them. His gaze dropped briefly to her full lips, his chest constricting, and when he finally tore his eyes away to meet hers, he found them focused on his mouth. *It wouldn't be such a hard thing to kiss her,* he thought, barely able to hear his own thoughts over the sound of his heart pounding in his chest. It wouldn't be so hard to lean in and close that infinitesimal space between them. It wouldn't be such a hard thing to feel her soft, pink lips against his, to pull her body close and feel his own warm to her touch, to feel her hands on his skin as he buried his fingers in the thick waves of her hair.

It wouldn't be such a hard thing to kiss her.

But it would be hard to let her go.

With difficulty, he lifted his hand from the counter, fingers trembling with the effort to not brush his knuckles to her cheek, her chin. To not press the pad of his thumb to her plump lower lip, to not run his fingers along the soft curve of her jaw and down her shoulder, slipping them beneath the hem of her borrowed shirt to feel her smooth skin.

He stepped back, shoving his hands in his pockets to avoid the temptation as he minutely shook his head, licking his dry lips as he avoided her gaze.

"We shouldn't," he said, his voice rasping, an ache in his chest as he voiced the words. Kai nodded, lower lip catching between her teeth and cheeks flushed—from embarrassment or the heat of the moment, Thorne couldn't tell.

The kettle began to whistle, and Kai cleared her throat, turning swiftly to move it off the stove.

"So," she said, her own voice slightly hoarse as she dropped two teabags into the mugs, pouring the steaming water from the kettle over them. "I guess we give up now, huh?" She smiled sadly, setting the empty kettle back on the stove. "I mean, unless you have some sort of last-minute trick up your sleeve, this was it, right?" Thorne was silent, unsure of how to respond—not *wanting* to, knowing that she already knew the answer.

Kai was quiet as she stirred a spoonful of honey into each mug before turning to hand one to Thorne, her eyes not quite meeting his as she did so, disappointment pitted in her stomach.

"It's peppermint," she murmured, her voice thick, like there was a lump in her throat. "It's my favorite flavor—I hope you like it."

"Thank you." He paused, swallowing. "Is it...is it alright if I sleep out here? Just to make sure that nothing happens, with the deadline being so close and everything," he added hastily. Kai nodded, brushing lightly past him as she limped out of the kitchen with her own mug in hand. When she reached the door of her bedroom, she hesitated, her hand on the doorframe as she turned to look over her shoulder.

"Hey, Thorne?" He looked up, and she chewed her lip thoughtfully, hesitating. "Just so you know, if by some wild chance I do make it out of this...I promise to do my best to help you break your curse. I know that I probably *won't* make it out of this, and that's okay, I know you've done your best—*more* than your best—but if I do...I just want you to know that I won't forget it, okay?"

"Okay," Thorne managed to say, feeling once again at an utter loss for words. Kai nodded, cracking a small grin as she laughed under her breath.

"Hell, you've done so much for me that even if I *don't* make it out of this, I'll escape the Underworld to help you, anyway. I've done it once already, right? How hard can it be to do it again?" Thorne snorted, and Kai's expression softened as she watched him shake his head, unable to keep the smile from his face. "Goodnight, Thorne," she said quietly.

"Goodnight, Kai."

***

Another white-hot flash of pain shot up Kai's spine as she tried once again to lift her arms above her head, and it was all she could do to hold in the scream of pain as she caught herself on the iron footboard of her bed. Her teeth ground painfully against each other as tears burned her eyes, both from the pain and from the surge of helpless anger that came with it. Could not this last shred of her dignity be preserved?

Apparently not, because while she had been able to remove the plaid shirt that Minho had lent her so that she could wipe away the dirt and sweat and dried blood crusted across her body, she had been frustratingly unsuccessful in trying to put a clean shirt *on*.

Taking a slow, shaky breath as she forced herself to straighten, she cleared her throat and tentatively called, "Thorne?" For a moment, she wasn't sure that he had heard her, then the door cracked open.

"Are you alright?" Kai swallowed, lifting her gaze heavenward as she responded, only just loud enough for him to hear,

"I can't get this stupid shirt on."

A long, horrible pause during which Kai seriously began to debate sleeping shirtless—getting dressed could be Tomorrow Kai's problem—and then,

"Do you want some help?"

"Yes, please," she breathed gratefully. For a split second, she had wondered if he was going to say something along the lines of, *that sucks,* before leaving her to fend for herself.

The door opened further, and Thorne stepped through it, flushing slightly as he saw her standing there, wearing nothing above her waist save for the oversized white t-shirt she was holding over her chest like a shield. She was sure her own cheeks were aflame, but there was nothing to be done. She didn't like to sleep shirtless on a *normal* night, and she was sure trying to do so with bandages that could come off if she tossed and turned enough would be a nightmare.

As Thorne crossed the room with painfully slow steps, Kai turned back around to face the bed, her stomach clenching as she handed him the shirt, using her hands to cover her chest as best as she could.

From Thorne's position behind her, one glance down would have had his resolve shattering into nothing, but he kept his gaze resolutely ahead at the wall above Kai's bed. If he inhaled too deeply, his chest would brush against Kai's back. He swallowed, his hands trembling.

As gently as he could, he slipped the shirt over Kai's head, clenching his jaw at her stifled whimpers of pain when he had to lift her arms through the sleeves. When he pulled the hem of the shirt down to rest on the waistband of her boxer shorts—she had evidently managed to kick her jeans off already—his fingertips felt as though they'd been electrified. When he lifted her hair out of the shirt and caught a glimpse of the bare nape of her neck, his breath caught in his throat, a fleeting image of him pressing his lips to that spot passing through his mind.

"There," he said, forcing himself to take a step back. "All good."

"Thank you," Kai said softly, turning around to face him, their gazes connecting. Moonlight shone through the window, a halo of celestial light surrounding Kai, nearly bringing Thorne to his knees. He needed to get out of this room before he did something that they would both regret.

"Unless you need anything else..." he trailed off, moving toward the door.

"Wait," Kai said suddenly, her feet moving forward of their own accord until she stood with her hand on his arm. He stilled. "Will you stay with me? You don't have to or anything, I just—" *I don't think I can sleep alone after what I just went through.*

"Yes," Thorne blurted before she could finish speaking. "Yes, I can stay." Kai nodded.

Thorne helped her pull down the blankets and slip beneath them, a hiss of pain escaping her lips as he lifted her legs into the bed, and then he walked to the other side, slipping in beside her with as much caution as one would use when trying to sneak past a sleeping bear, his movements stiff.

At first, they tried to keep to their respective sides of the bed, but the small dip in the center where Kai usually slept caused them both to slide into each other, her back snugly against his front. He inhaled sharply, which only made matters worse as he caught a fresh whiff of her trademark floral scent, his hand shooting reflexively to her hip to try and create some distance.

He heard her quiet gasp of surprise, and his fingers clenched the soft material of her shirt in his fist. She made no move to move away herself, so, slowly, hardly daring to breathe as he did it, Thorne slid his arm around her waist and pulled her closer, tucking her head securely beneath his chin. With a whispered sigh of contentment, Kai burrowed into the warmth of his comfort, and he couldn't help pressing a soft, brief kiss to the top of her head.

Several moments passed, and Thorne was sure Kai was asleep, her breathing slow and even, her eyes peacefully shut. He didn't feel as though he would be sleeping any time soon, but that was alright; he was more than content to lay here and listen to the sound of her breathing, to the sound of her living another night.

When she mumbled something on a quiet, blissful breath, he wondered at first if she was talking in her sleep, but just in case, he whispered, "Hm?"

"I said," murmured Kai sleepily, only just coherently enough for Thorne to understand. "I wish I'd met you sooner. Before all of...this." She gestured loosely with a finger, too exhausted to lift her entire hand. "I know it's impossible, but if it *wasn't*. I wish I could've met you when there was..." *A chance,* she thought, but didn't say, letting the end of her sentence hang there in the quiet of the bedroom.

When the quiet grew to be too much, the over-thoughtful gears in Kai's head beginning to rapidly turn, she gave the arm draped across her waist a poke.

"Tell *me* something, now," she said, glad that he could not see her face, flushed from embarrassment. "I'm feeling vulnerable." Thorne laughed softly, his chest rumbling against her back. It was a nice feeling.

"Okay," he said. There was a brief pause as he dampened his lips, swallowing sharply. "I lied to you." Slowly, her movements sluggish with sleep, Kai's brows furrowed.

"Hm?"

"About your name—the mail, how I knew it. I lied to you."

"Yeah?" Thorne pushed himself up on his elbow, and Kai turned her head slightly to peer at him out of the corner of her eye.

"Yeah," he said with a smile, reaching out to brush her hair away from her face. "I never needed to learn your name. From the moment I saw you, I knew you." He let the words sit there for a moment, letting them sink in. "Just before I'm about to reap a soul, their name comes into my head; I think it's Fate's way of helping me make them comfortable with me. It's hard to deny the Grim Reaper if he knows your name, you know?

"The moment I saw you on those tracks, with your hair blowing in the wind and the sun on your smiling face, I knew you." He grinned a little as he thought back. "But when you asked me how I knew your name...I don't know, I panicked. I knew that there was no way I was going to be able to explain it to your satisfaction—you thought I was a creepy stalker anyway, and knowing your name when I had no reason to definitely wouldn't have helped my case. So, I lied." When she said nothing for a long time, he wondered if she had fallen asleep.

Half-delirious, Kai voiced the only response that felt right. "I think I knew you, too." She didn't know what it meant—she hadn't known his name until later. But it didn't feel like a lie.

Thorne smiled again, pressing another soft kiss to her temple. "Get some sleep, sunshine."

Chapter Thirty-Seven
SLEEPLESS

THORNE

The hours passed painfully slow as he resisted the urge to toss and turn, trying to let the sound of Kai's soft, steady breathing lull him into sleep. While, as an immortal, he could *survive* without ever sleeping, it certainly helped to replenish his energy after a day like today.

But sleep wouldn't come.

Around two in the morning, he slipped carefully out of bed and into the living room, clicking the door to Kai's bedroom quietly shut as he began to pace the hardwood floor in his sock-clad feet, doing his utmost to avoid the creaky sections so that he wouldn't wake Kai.

Desperately, he wracked his brain for a solution. Bargaining, he knew, would not work; he had tried Hades, and the Fates, ever the neutral party, would not intervene. He had tried protecting Kai himself, and he knew that even if he tried to hide her, they would not be able to outrun the Keeper and her Guardians forever.

He wished Minho were here. Minho was always good to bounce ideas off of, and he offered sage counsel, even if Thorne didn't always take it to heart. At the very least, he would be good company.

The hands on the clock ticked by so slowly that Thorne's head began to ache, his fingers flexing as he clenched and unclenched his fists, resisting the urge to snatch the small clock off of the mantle and silence it by throwing it to the floor. It wouldn't do any good. It wouldn't save Kai's life.

And neither would just sitting here.

No, he decided as he stopped his pacing. No, he would not just sit here and agonize over what *wouldn't* work—he would get out there and find something that *would.* He would find a way out of this mess if it killed him.

***

It was even brighter than he remembered.

Chapter Thirty-Eight
A Promise So Deadly

Thorne's eyes were beginning to ache as he made his way through the long, stark-white hallways of the palace, his footsteps echoing on tiles so shiny he could see his own reflection staring back up at him.

Alastair was not here to guide him this time, so Thorne found his own way, only hesitating briefly before stepping through the golden arch into the garden, where *she* was waiting.

Despite the fact that she was sitting with her back turned to him, she seemed to sense his presence instantly.

"The stars are beautiful here, are they not, little prince?" Her eyes fluttered shut as she tipped her head back, her crown glittering in the light of the full, silver moon. When her eyes snapped open and turned suddenly to Thorne, he resisted a shiver; in the darkness, illuminated by the reflection of the fountain and the light of the heavens above, her foggy eyes seemed to *glow*.

She sighed lightly and laid her hands in her lap, not moving from her seat on the side of the fountain. "I suppose it is too much to hope that you have come to your senses?"

"Astute as ever, my lady," Thorne responded simply, hands clasped behind his back, fists flexing as he struggled to stand still. The Keeper nodded as if she had expected as much, and turned her gaze back to the sky.

"Then why is it that you have come? Surely you have not chosen to waste what little time you have left with your mortal merely to stand here and gaze at the stars with me."

"No," Thorne said, jaw clenching as he forced his locked legs to buckle, first one, and then the other, until he was on his knees in front of her. He tried not to let the resentment show as he placed his palms on the ground, bending forward until his forehead was touching the grass, prostrate at the Keeper's feet. He felt, rather than saw, her surprise, his voice tinged with amusement as she asked,

"What is *this?*"

"I have come—" his voice shook, and he swallowed. "I have come to bargain. My life...for hers." He didn't dare look up to gauge her reaction, his stomach clenching when he heard her bare feet sink into the grass as she rose from her seat, advancing slowly until she towered above him.

"How noble of you," she whispered, the soft caress of her voice sending shivers down Thorne's spine. "Offering your eternal life in exchange for that of a mortal's. All so that she can live, what, another five or six decades? Is she truly worth *so* much?"

"She is." His answer was swift, unhesitating. *She is worth all that and more.*

"Why?" It was a demand. Thorne froze, his breathing echoing loudly in his ears as he swallowed again. *"Why?"*

"She makes me feel alive," he said quietly. The Keeper was silent for a moment, and then she sighed deeply.

"That is a lovely sentiment, Thorne," she said, a note of mourning lacing her silky tone. "It is almost a pity that I cannot grant your request." Of their own volition, Thorne's hands snapped shut, ripping out strands of grass as his nails bit viciously into his palms.

Before he could think it through, his body acting almost of its own accord, he was on his feet and lunging forward, hands wrapping around her delicate throat as he pushed her back against the fountain. In the faint reflection of her frosted eyes, he saw flames leaping within his own.

"Have you not taken enough from me?" He could feel the blood pumping through her veins, and his hands squeezed infinitesimally tighter as she struggled for breath. "Let her live," he demanded. "Let her live and leave us the hell *alone,* or I swear by everything that is true that I will *destroy* you and everything you uphold. I will burn this place to ashes, and you with it."

As he was speaking, the Keeper's expression had begun to harden, and when he had finished, there was a split second of pause, and then she raised her hand, clasping it around his wrist so tightly that he expelled a jagged breath of surprise, nearly crying out as she began to twist his arm, the pain building until he was forced to release his hold on her.

A blinding light suddenly filled the courtyard, throwing him back, a pained grunt escaping him as he landed roughly on the ground a short distance from the fountain. The light emitting from the Keeper's figure dimmed as she approached him, fury painted across her beautiful, terrifying features like a declaration of war.

"I have been patient, *Reaper,* far more than you deserve, and I have even granted you time enough to say your goodbyes. But I will *not* be threatened in my own home—not by *anyone,* least of all *you.* Do I make myself clear?" Painfully, Thorne raised his head, lips curling in a snarl as he growled,

"Go to hell."

"After you," said the Keeper, and she flung one hand outward.

Screaming. All he could hear was the screaming.

From every direction, surrounding him and pressing oppressively into his eardrums, screams and shrieks of such unbearable pain, so raw and

untamed it felt as though a dagger had been driven into his own heart. He stumbled, hands clasped over his stomach that felt as if it was being torn apart from the inside out as he tried to find a way through the haze of darkness that enveloped him, blindly following the echoes of the wild cries of torment.

Suddenly, he could see them, and he had to clamp a hand over his mouth at the sight, bile rising in his throat as his heart stopped beating. They were all there—Minho and Jai and even Aristides, all who had risked themselves to help him, even despite their better judgments.

*Minho and Jai had been impaled by spears of the darkest night, black smoke swirling around the blades of the weapons. Jai, who was so **young,** still with unfinished business left to resolve, terror painted across every feature of his innocent, youthful face as he lay in a dark pool of his own blood, the stench filling Thorne's nostrils and making him audibly gag.*

And Minho, who had been such a faithful friend, pinned now to a wall of adamant, the corners of his mouth smeared with crimson as his lifeless eyes stared back at Thorne, showing him a reflection wracked with grief and guilt.

*And Ris...Ris, who Thorne had never been able to admit was a friend Ris, who had risked **everything** to help him. Ris, who had stood by him despite Thorne's endless supply of insults.*

Ris had been secured to a post with chains of that same smoking adamant, mouth sewn shut and golden scissors stitched to one outstretched hand, so that all he could do for the rest of eternity was fulfill the task that he had been created to do. Though his eyes were glassy with unshed tears, they were filled with poisonous hatred as he stared silently at Thorne, condemning him.

A black mist carried the images away, and when it cleared, Thorne found the only other person that he cared for lying at his feet. The sight before him made him crumble, a disbelieving cry of anguish wrenching from the depths of his being as he fell to his knees, raising trembling hands toward the broken body that lay in front of him.

Kai's limbs and neck were twisted at odd angles, a bloody crevice in her chest where her heart should be. Thorne's fingers felt warm and sticky, and he realized suddenly that the missing organ was in his hands. Gasping sharply, he dropped it, scrambling back as though he'd been burned, his breath coming in short, shallow pants. From where she lay with her neck unnaturally twisted, Kai's eyes, lifeless and frozen in fear, haunted Thorne's very soul, staring up at him as if to ask, **why did you not save me?**

"I'm sorry," Thorne whispered, hot tears slipping down his cheeks, clinging to his jaw. He raised one bloodied, shaking hand to Kai's face, and a sob tore from his throat as a tear fell onto her lip, mixing with dust and blood. "I'm so sorry."

Thorne's entire body was shaking when he appeared back in the courtyard, still gasping for air as sobs wracked his frame. His face was wet, but there was no blood on his trembling hands. It hadn't been real. Or had it? He wasn't sure.

The Keeper's bare feet appeared in his line of sight, and she crouched, one hand tenderly lifting his chin to make him meet her eyes. Despite the gentleness of her gesture, her expression remained as hard as stone and sharp as broken glass, her tone unyielding as she said, softly,

"This is only a *glimpse* of what will happen should you miss the deadline, Thorne. If you attempt to thwart me, if you try any tricks, I will begin taking those you love, and I will start with the mortal. And if you can believe me about anything, *believe* me when I say that I will not make it a death free of pain." She released his chin abruptly and stood, flicking her fingers outward, as if she could bear to look at him no longer. "Now go—spend what little time you have left with your precious mortal. Say your goodbyes, and then let it be finished."

Chapter Thirty-Nine
WHATEVER THE COST

Thorne was still trembling when he appeared in his office, papers flying everywhere at thc abrupt, chaotic entrance. He paid them no mind as he collapsed into his chair, lowering his head into his hands as he tried to push the images of his broken and bloodied friends from his memory, to no avail.

He yanked the bottom right drawer of his desk open and pulled out a large bottle, the label long since faded, and after plucking the cork out with trembling fingers, he took a long, deep sip straight from the bottle. He inadvertently slammed, more than set, the bottle on the desk, before digging his palms into his eyes. The images were seared into his brain, playing on a constant loop, showing him every tiny detail, forcing him to recall the nauseating scents of blood and burnt flesh, and with a frustrated cry, Thorne snatched up a decorative globe from the desk and hurled it at the wall, the glass shattering as it made contact with the wall just to the left of *The Swing.*

Thorne tilted his head, his eyes narrowing as, still shaky, he rose to his feet. Crossing the room in a single step, he lifted the painting carefully from the wall and set it on the floor, revealing a built-in lockbox. Thorne pulled open a tiny door, behind which was a faded dial lock; he entered the combination by memory and, after the briefest second of hesitation, pulled open the door to the safe.

It was empty, save for a small, dusty black box in the center, tied shut with a crimson ribbon. Thorne reached out, fingers hovering over the box for a long moment before finally closing around it and lifting it from its resting place. Carefully, he brought it to the desk and set it down, sinking back into his chair and resting his elbows on the edge of the desk, steepling his fingers as he stared thoughtfully down at the small object.

He was still staring at the box, lost completely to his thoughts, when Minho appeared at the door, arms crossed over his broad chest as he leaned against the doorframe.

"Do you have a plan?" He seemed then to notice the object of Thorne's attention, and his face paled slightly. "Thorne, tell me you're not going to—"

"It's the only way," Thorne interrupted sharply, his voice rasping. His shoulders sagged, and he pressed his fingers to his temples, his head splitting. "I'm out of options, Min," he said, utterly defeated. Minho's chest clenched at the sight, and silently, he took a seat in the armchair on the opposite side of the desk. "And I am *tired*. I am tired of all the death, of carrying out a never-ending mission that I never asked to be tasked with. I'm tired of this...*loneliness.*" His voice broke, and he looked away, his eyes glassy. His nostrils flared. "And if this will save her—if it will save *all* of you—I will do *anything*. I will pay *any* price."

"I understand," Minho said softly, reaching across the desk to place his hand on top of Thorne's. "I cannot say if it will work, but I understand—and I believe in you. I am behind you, Thorne," he said, his brown eyes shining earnestly. "Every step of the way." Thorne met his gaze and gave a grateful nod, turning his hand to clasp Minho's, giving it a brief, meaningful squeeze. The gesture said what Thorne's shaky voice could not. *Thank you.*

"You're my brother, Thorne," Minho smiled, though there was more than a little sadness to the gesture. "I will do anything that you ask of me."

"Just—" Thorne paused, struggling for words, unsure of what there was that he could say. "When this is all over...make sure that she's happy, okay? Make sure that she...that she lives her life, and that she lives it well. Please." Minho hesitated, then nodded.

"Do you love her?" He asked quietly, and Thorne swallowed. It was not a question that he hadn't asked himself already, but he still wasn't sure of the answer. It wasn't as if he had anything to compare it to, these feelings. He had never been in love—had never gotten the *chance*—so how was he to know what it felt like, after all this time? He had *loved*, of course—he loved Minho, and Jai, and even Ris, he realized, but he had never been *in* love.

"I don't know," he admitted. "This has all happened so fast, and I hardly...I hardly know *what* I feel. *Especially* now." He paused to dampen his dry lips, considering his words carefully. "I think...I think that I *could* love her, and even that I might, but what would be the point of admitting it to myself if that were the case?"

"You could tell her," Minho suggested, and Thorne smiled sadly, shaking his head.

"No, I couldn't. I don't want to leave her with words that she can do nothing with. Even if I knew, for *sure*, that I *did* love her...I wouldn't tell her. I wouldn't—I would not do that to her." Minho nodded in understanding, and sighed deeply.

"So...when?"

"In the morning, just after sunrise. I have already relayed a message to Alastair, agreeing to reap Kai's soul without protest, so long as the Keeper is there to witness it."

"What makes you think that she'll show up?" Minho questioned, his thick brows pushing together in confusion.

"What I hope is that she will see it as me making this personal, to make her see in person the innocent life that she is forcing me to take in an attempt to try and guilt her into showing mercy. I know that it would never actually work, obviously, but it isn't my *intention* for it to work—as long as she's present, that's all that matters."

"Thorne," Minho swallowed, gnawing at the inside of his cheek as he paused, shaking his head. "Are you absolutely sure about this?"

"I am more sure than I have ever been of anything in my life," Thorne said with a determined nod. "It's time to end this, once and for all. Whatever the cost."

Chapter Forty
GOODNIGHT

THORNE

When Thorne returned to Kai's apartment, he was surprised to find her waiting on the couch, wrapped comfortably in the bedsheets she must have brought with her, but wide awake, only jumping slightly when he appeared abruptly out of thin air.

"Why are you awake?" Thorne asked, quickly surveying the apartment, just as dark and quiet as still as he had left it. "Did something happen?"

"You left." Her voice was small. She must have been awake for quite a while, if she'd slept at all after his departure, because while her voice was quiet, it was clear, and her face carried none of the telltale puffiness of sleep. She swallowed, her cheeks heating as she noticed his perusal of her features. "Where did you go?"

Thorne sighed, setting the box gently on the mantlepiece before seating himself beside Kai, who scooted over to make room, lifting the blankets and draping them over his lap once he was seated. She waited patiently, expectantly, for his answer.

"I was trying to find a way out of this," he said, avoiding her gaze as she turned a little more to face him. Out of the corner of his eye, he noticed her hopeful expression, the way that she seemed to be holding her breath as she asked,

"Did—were you able to?" Thorne swallowed, and there was a long pause before he finally nodded.

"Yes," he responded simply, and Kai blinked. He could see the gears turning in her mind, likely wondering why, if he had truly found a way to save her, he seemed so dispirited, even mournful. He forced a small smile. "*Yes,*" he said again. "I found a way. But…"

"But…?" She prompted, and his heart stuttered, stomach clenching at her closeness, the way her *scent*—distinctly floral, with some faint trace of fresh citrus—permeated his senses, drowning out any attempt at coherent thought.

He cleared his throat and stood abruptly, walking quickly to the kitchen. He pulled a cup—the last clean one remaining—from the cabinet and filled it with water, downing it swiftly. He sighed, flexing his fingers, trying to will away the faint tremor.

"Thorne?" Kai had followed him, and stood waiting where the tiled floor of the kitchen met the hardwood of the living room, hands twisting in the hem of her oversized t-shirt. Her golden legs were bare, still clad in just that pair of boxer shorts. "What's going on?" She asked, and he jerked his gaze back up. "Is everything okay?"

"I'm fine," Thorne smiled, though it didn't quite reach his eyes, and he set the cup near the sink. "I found a way to save you," he said as he approached her slowly, trying not to notice the way her chest rose sharply when he drew closer. He smiled again, this time meaning it, and his fingers twitched as he noticed the stray strands of hair that had fallen over Kai's face, longing to lift his hand to tuck them back, knowing that if he did, he wouldn't be able to tear himself away. "You're going to make it through this, Kai." *Kailani Sofia Sanchez.* He turned her name over in his mind, caressing it, tasting it silently on his tongue. He swallowed, the air suddenly thick and heavy in his lungs, weighing him down.

He moved to walk past her into the living room, but had only made it a couple of steps when she spoke again.

"And you?" He stopped short, fingers reflexively twitching.

"I'll be fine," he said. He heard her soft footsteps, and his knees nearly buckled as he felt her stop just behind him, so close they were nearly touching. He could feel her breath on his shoulder, the warmth penetrating the loose, thin material of the long-sleeved shirt he was wearing.

"Thorne." He liked the way she said his name. "Thorne, will you look at me?" Slowly, he turned around, forcing himself to meet her gaze. There was a wrinkle between her brows, a concerned frown on her lips. *Don't look at me like that,* he thought, fighting the urge to yank her into his arms and kiss her senseless. This girl was going to be his undoing. "Why do I feel like you're not telling me everything?" *Because I'm not.*

"We are both going to be fine," Thorne said, wishing that it didn't feel like a lie. Her eyes, big and brown and looking up at him through those long, dark lashes, searched his carefully, that same worried furrow between her thick brows, and suddenly he couldn't fight it anymore. "But—" he took a half-step forward, and now she was *so* close—close enough that if either of them took the slightest breath, their chests would brush against each other. His mouth seemed suddenly dry, and his voice dropped to a near-whisper. "Just in case..." His gaze dropped to her mouth, the pull to feel her lips against his almost unbearable now.

"Just in case...?" Kai repeated just as quietly, and he leaned in, painfully slow, his gaze shifting between her mouth and her eyes, searching them, waiting—giving her a chance to stop this, if this wasn't what she wanted. Her eyes widened a little at his nearness, and she took a sharp breath. "Oh," she whispered, swallowing thickly, her tongue poking out to wet her lips. Thorne shot up a silent prayer—for what, he did not know. All he knew was that if he did not feel her mouth on his, just *once,* he thought he might die.

When he was close enough that their noses could nearly touch, Thorne paused again, waiting for a sign, however small, either that she did not want this, or...or a sign that she did. Seconds passed, feeling like hours, and he steeled himself, preparing mentally to pull away.

And then Kai tilted her chin ever so slightly upward, her eyes briefly meeting his before dropping lower.

And that was all he needed.

He inhaled sharply through his nose as he finally—*finally*—closed the distance, and for a moment, he could hardly move—could hardly *think* over the feeling of her soft, warm mouth against his. It was as though the word had suddenly burst into a riot of color and sound, and everything felt *right*.

Move, you idiot, his brain reminded him, and he did, their lips sliding into perfect place against each other as he pulled her closer. His hands had risen instinctively to cup either side of her face, and one slipped down now to rest against the small of her back, pulling her close as he moved his other hand, burying his fingers in the soft depths of her hair. He felt her shiver, and his brain nearly short-circuited at the pleased hum that rose from the back of her throat as he tugged, gently, at the silky strands, tilting her chin further upward to grant him better access to her mouth as he brushed his tongue against her lower lip, plump and so soft.

Her own hands were resting against his chest, fisting the soft material of his shirt, clutching it like a lifeline. He could feel her breasts, bare beneath the all-too-thin material of the shirt she was wearing, pressed against his chest, and he pulled her closer.

They would need to come up for air soon, he knew, but he could not bring himself to pull away, and neither, it seemed, could she. Every time one of them tried, the other chased their lips with an edge of desperation, like an addict in pursuit of the most alluring drug. Kai's fingers danced against his neck, digging into his shoulders, nails scratching at his skin as though begging to be pulled *closer*, though there was no room left to spare.

The hand on Kai's back had begun to creep lower, and Thorne realized suddenly that if they continued, she might never forgive him for what he was about to do, and that he might be too selfish to go through with it if that was the case. So, though it was the hardest thing he had ever had to do thus far, he pulled away first, tightening his hold slightly on Kai's hair when she tried to pursue him, his resolve slipping when a breathy whimper escaped her lips.

Their breathing was quiet and uneven as they panted softly into that small, shared space between them, foreheads resting against each other and hearts pounding.

Unable to stop himself, Thorne pressed his lips to hers once more, softly and too briefly, committing the heavenly feeling to memory, then brushed them against her forehead before he pulled away fully, hands reluctantly parting from her as he stepped back. He swallowed, feeling shaky and disoriented, as if he had emerged into a world that no longer made sense if he was not touching her, kissing her, holding her close.

Neither of them seemed to know what to say, and at last, it was Kai who broke the silence, her cheeks still warm and flushed, lips slightly swollen and hair notably messy from Thorne's hands.

"Well, um...goodnight." Thorne watched her go into the bedroom, eyes rising almost shyly to meet his as she carefully shut the door, a soft smile playing on her lovely mouth.

"Goodnight," he said to the closed door, forcing himself not to fling it open and pull her back into the warm, safe circle of his arms, knowing that if he did, he would never, ever be able to summon the strength to let her go.

CHAPTER FORTY-ONE
TRUST

THORNE

The waiting was going to kill him.

Anxiety rolled off of him in waves as he paced the floor, fingers tapping a rapid rhythm against his thigh, the soft fabric hugging his chest and arms making him feel itchy and claustrophobic. He tugged at the deep v of his shirt, wondering when he'd started sweating.

It's going to be fine, he told himself, turning again as he reached the fireplace. He avoided looking at the small black box still sitting atop the mantlepiece. *It's all going to be just fine.*

"Thorne?" He nearly jumped out of his skin at the soft mention of his name and looked up to find Kai lingering hesitantly in the doorway of her bedroom. She still wore that same t-shirt, but had put on a pair of shorts, her hair falling loosely around her face and her eyes glowing, despite the dark circles beneath them. *You're an angel.* He barely caught himself from saying it aloud, feeling as though the breath had been knocked out of his lungs. She flushed under his gaze, wrapping her arms around herself self-consciously as she approached, a slight limp in her step.

"How did you sleep?" The mundane question made Thorne's heart ache. "You never came back to bed."

"I didn't realize I was invited," he teased with a smile that grew as he watched her cheeks color, unable to stop himself from reaching up to tuck a stray hair behind her ear, letting his hand linger there, thumb brushing lightly against her soft cheek, tracing the edge of the small bandage that concealed the gruesome, jagged cut he knew was hiding beneath.

He lifted a shoulder. "I didn't, really," he said in answer to her question, and she smiled ruefully.

"Neither did I." As their eyes connected, it was like everything was laid bare before them—what had transpired between them last night, the pull to each other that they both so clearly felt, the anxiety and anticipation of what they were about to face. Thorne swallowed, finding it suddenly to be too much, and he let his own gaze drop, choosing instead to study the faint freckles dusted across Kai's cheeks and nose, the moles that dotted her neck and shoulders like pieces of some constellation. He drew mental lines between them, connecting them, committing them to memory.

"Thorne?" There was a note of concern in Kai's voice as she tilted her head to get a better look at his face. "Is everything alright?"

"Everything's fine." Thorne's tone sounded hollow to his own ears, and absently, he reached up to smooth the wrinkle between Kai's brows with his thumb.

"How can I believe that when you won't even look at me?" Thorne's fingers froze, his heartbeat echoing in his ears as he tried to force his gaze lower. *Look at her, you idiot—it could be the last time you get the chance. Simply look down and meet her eyes. Look at her. Look at her.* **Look at her.**

Fingers tentatively brushed against his cheek, and whatever air remained in his lungs left him fully at the soft touch, a thing that had become so unfamiliar. He let his eyes flutter shut as he leaned into Kai's palm, willing with everything that was inside of him that they could just stay here in this brief pocket of time and never leave.

"Whatever it is, you can tell me," Kai murmured, and Thorne nodded against her hand, which he had at some point covered with his own. He turned to press his lips to her palm, and he heard her inhale. He opened his eyes.

"Everything will be fine," he repeated, and forced a faint smile. "I promise." The lie—the first he had deliberately told her—tasted bitter and metallic on his tongue. "Whatever happens, I just need you to trust me, okay?" Kai opened her mouth, the words dying on her lips as Thorne suddenly seized her other hand, pulling it up to rest solidly against his chest and holding it there, letting her feel his heart, steadily beating beneath his chest. "*Trust me*—I will not let anything happen to you."

hatever reservations she had about believing him—believing his promise that everything would be fine, despite not even being able to meet her eyes—Kai found that she *did* believe him in this, that he would keep her safe, that he would not allow anything bad to happen to her. The look in his eyes told her everything that she needed to know. Told her that he would raze this building and reduce it to ashes if needed, but would not let a single flame near her, would let nothing touch or harm her.

Trust me. Flames had danced faintly to life in his eyes as he'd said it, his hands gripping hers so tightly it was almost painful. Kai found it suddenly hard to breathe under the intensity of his gaze, the utter vehemence with which he insisted that he would protect her, and she nodded.

"I trust you," she said softly, and nodded again. "I trust you, Thorne."

"*I trust you.*" Thorne nearly collapsed in relief, his tense shoulders dropping as his hold—unconsciously tight—relaxed on Kai's hands. He let his forehead rest against hers as she said it again. "*I trust you, Thorne.*" He could only manage a simple nod in response, lifting his chin to press his lips to her forehead.

There was a knock at the door.

His spine stiffened, his body feeling frozen in place, even as Kai lifted her head to look over his shoulder.

"Are you expecting someone?" The line between her brows was back. Forcing himself to straighten, Thorne took one last lingering look at her face, wishing more desperately than he had ever had cause to wish for anything before that they had more time. He wanted to kiss her again, he thought, but not like this—not with what awaited them on the other side of that door, with the lie that he had told her still fresh on his tongue.

He settled for brushing her hair behind her ears and pressing his lips briefly to her temple before he pulled away, squaring his shoulders and setting his jaw in determination. His footsteps were heavy as he approached the door, and with his hand on the cold metal knob, he turned back.

"*Trust me,*" he said again.

He opened the door.

CHAPTER FORTY-TWO

BROKEN

KAI

K ai didn't know what she had been expecting, but she could say with certainty that this was *not* it.

"May I come in?" The woman's voice was as soft and smooth as silk, as soothing and entrancing as a siren's call, and Thorne, his entire frame screaming reluctance, slowly stepped aside to allow what was possibly the most ethereal being that Kai had ever laid eyes on into the apartment. The woman's eyes, white and misty like a lake thickly frozen over with ice, passed over Kai very briefly, as though a mere mortal was hardly worth her time, and she was followed by a man that made Kai's blood run cold with horror. Bile rose in her throat as she met the cold, detached eyes of Alastair, and she stumbled back a step, her mouth dry.

"Whilst I certainly do not know what all the fuss was about," said the woman, who Kai realized with sudden clarity must be the Keeper. "I am glad to see that you have come to your senses, Thorne." She was, simply put, utterly stunning—her dark hair spilled over her shoulders and down her back a multitude of long, slender braids, threads of glittering gold woven through the silken strands. A delicate crown of stars rested atop her head like a halo, with thin, golden bands winding up her arms like climbing vines. Her skin, dark and smooth and utterly without flaw, gleamed beneath her dress—golden and brilliant, but simply designed, with a plunging neckline that revealed a small, golden hourglass resting from a thin chain around her neck.

"Whatever you may be planning," the Keeper said, startling Kai out of her unabashed staring. "Allow me to inform you that it will ultimately fail, and that you should abandon any ideas of trickery or betrayal now."

When her words were met with tense silence, both Kai and Thorne avoiding her expectant gaze, she extended her arm toward Kai, her brows lifting as she turned to Thorne. "Then let us get on with it, and not continue to waste precious time." Indeed, the minuscule grains of sand in the upper half of the tiny hourglass necklace seemed to be dwindling, and Kai realized with a start that it must be the time that she had put on Kai's life—the thirty-six hours that she had given Thorne to reap Kai's soul.

Slowly, Thorne shut the door and turned to approach Kai, his footsteps precise and measured, and the blood in Kai's veins went frigid at the blank, detached look in his eyes. Her brain scrambled to remember his words—*"Trust me"*—to remember his promises to keep her safe, his vow to not let anything touch her, but she couldn't stop herself from stumbling quickly away as he continued his steady approach.

Her back hit the wall, and her hands searched in vain for something to hold onto as Thorne finally came to a stop in front of her. She saw nothing of the man she had come to know in his expression, and the terror began to creep in, the fear that, somehow, this had all been some elaborate hoax to keep her calm while he saved his own skin, that he truly intended to reap her soul, after all.

"Thorne," she whispered, trying to fight off the petrified tears pressing against the backs of her eyes. "Thorne, *please.*" She wasn't going to plead for her life—she had already resigned herself to the fact that she was most likely going to die. But she didn't want to die at the hands of a stranger wearing a familiar face; she wanted it to be with someone she—someone she cared for. She *cared* for him, so deeply. "Thorne," she whispered again, but still he said nothing, simply staring down at her with that expression that lacked all recognition.

Her heart began to beat louder and louder with every passing second, quickening as the small black box from the mantle appeared in Thorne's open palm. He removed the lid, and plucked from the box a tiny, golden scythe. Kai's brows pushed together in confusion, and then her eyes widened, a sharp gasp escaping her as, with a blinding glow, the scythe suddenly grew to its true size, the length of it taller even than Thorne. The blade alone was larger than Kai's head and looked sharp enough to slice her open with the lightest touch, the gentle curve of it glinting brightly in the sunlight that had begun to filter through the blinds.

Kai felt true, unadulterated terror stop her heart, and she shrank into the wall, unable to mask her fear any longer as a tear made a slow descent down her cheek.

She flinched as Thorne raised his hand to wipe it away with his thumb, his knuckles brushing her cheek tenderly; if she wasn't so absolutely paralyzed with fear, she might have leaned into his touch. His gaze lowered briefly to her lips, something like regret pooling in the depths of his eyes.

The Keeper sighed impatiently from where she stood by the door, as if she couldn't wait to escape this small, drab apartment, which looked shabbier than ever in comparison to her almost blinding splendor.

"I have the utmost respect for tradition, Thorne, but cease your stalling. Reap her soul and be done with it, before I take her life myself." Kai saw Thorne's jaw clench slightly, and his expression shuttered once more as he took a step back. His features seemed to tear at the seams as he raised the scythe, his lips trembling as he bared his teeth, bringing the scythe down in a smooth, swift arc.

Kai drew in a sharp breath as she braced herself for the impact, unable to close her eyes or flinch away, her gaze frozen on Thorne's face. She could feel death coming for her, and she sent up a fleeting prayer that this would be painless. *I'm coming,* she thought, images of her family rising to the forefront of her mind. *Wait for me.*

She was ready, standing like a deer in headlights as she waited for death to claim her, unable to tear her eyes from Thorne's broken expression as time seemed to move in slow motion, the golden blade glittering as it came down upon her, and then—

Thorne vanished, reappearing in the blink of an eye in front of the Keeper, the scythe slicing cleanly through the air down toward her. There was an enraged shout and the clang of metal on metal as the golden blade was blocked by a gigantic silver sword wielded by Alastair, who had reacted faster than Kai could blink. He pushed his blade forward as he stood in front of the Keeper, resolutely protecting his Lady.

The scythe was knocked aside, and Alastair raised his booted foot to kick Thorne squarely in the chest, sending him crashing to the floor, flames leaping in the Reaper's eyes as he rolled swiftly back to his feet with a vicious, animalistic snarl.

Thorne held out his hand, and the scythe, which had skittered noisily across the room when Thorne had fallen, reappeared in his waiting palm, his fingers snapping shut around the staff as he raised it to meet Alastair's oncoming blow. The Keeper merely watched on in passive boredom, only a faint interest piquing her expression; she hardly seemed surprised at all, looking as though she were simply waiting for the battle to end.

Thorne and Alastair seemed to be relatively matched in strength, but as Alastair pushed forward, the scythe slipped, and time seemed once again to move in slow motion as Alastair's blade sliced through the air toward Thorne.

Before it could make contact, Thorne rolled out of the way, darkness rising from the floor to knock Alastair's blade aside as easily as if it had been a children's toy. The Guardian growled in frustration as Thorne regained his footing, shifting his weapon from one hand to the other and spinning it in a graceful figure eight by his side, waiting.

Swathed in shadow, Thorne was as smooth and effortless as a practiced warrior as he met Alastair's every attack, vanishing into and materializing out of thin air over and over again as he launched strategic strikes of his own, the ringing of metal clashing and grinding against metal echoing loudly through the apartment, hurting Kai's ears so that she had to clamp her hands over them.

Thorne reeled back with a grunt of pain as the hilt of Alastair's sword caught him in the face, thick, crimson blood dripping down his jaw as, freshly enraged, he spun to launch another assault. Just as his blade was about to connect once more with Alastair's, he vanished, only to reappear immediately behind Alastair, the blade of the scythe slicing diagonally across his back.

With a roar of pain, Alastair fell to his knees, his sword skittering across the floor as his palms slammed against the hardwood, muscular arms that gleamed with sweat trembling as he tried to push himself back to his feet. Standing above him, Thorne twisted the handle of the scythe in his hands and, as a sharp blade struck out from the bottom, he drove it forcefully through Alastair's back just between his shoulder blades, the horrible splintering of bone splitting through the room with a *crack!* as Alastair cried out in agony.

Chest and shoulders heaving, Thorne turned to look at Kai, his eyes widening as his lips parted to shout a warning.

H e was too late.

Time seemed to stand still as he saw the Keeper materialize behind Kai, who, sometime during the fight, had moved away from the wall, leaving her back unguarded and unprotected. There was no time to do anything but watch as the Keeper plunged her hand into Kai's back with a sickening *crunch* that seemed to echo through the apartment more loudly than any part of Thorne's fight with Alastair.

The Keeper's expression was twisted into one of unbridled rage as her eyes met Thorne's, and before he could drop to his knees or beg for mercy, she twisted her hand and ripped out Kai's heart.

Kai's lips were parted in shock, her eyes wide as they connected with Thorne's in the second before the life left them, knees buckling beneath her as she crumpled to the ground.

The world seemed to stop spinning, time grinding to a halt.

The floor underneath them began to tremble, and Thorne felt something deep and ancient and full of horrific rage light in his veins, burning him from the inside out, setting his skin aflame with grief-stricken fury. He could think of nothing else—could see nothing, could *feel* nothing, as an ocean roared to life in his ears, and his fingers closed around the handle of his scythe.

Thunder cracked as darkness suddenly blanketed the room and, as a bolt of lightning briefly lit it back up, Thorne appeared in front of the Keeper outlined in the glow, sinking the long, razor-sharp blade of his scythe deeply into her chest before she had time to react. Dimly, he could hear Alastair raging, screaming curses and threats as the Keeper, blood beginning to pool at the corners of her mouth, fell to the floor. Thorne turned to the Guardian, his face impassive.

"If you wish to remain intact enough to tend to your mistress, you will leave this place now and not return." His voice was detached, unrecognizable to his own ears, and Alastair must have realized that he was not in any way bluffing or incapable of following through on his words, because with a glare of hatred, he struggled to his feet, lifting the motionless Keeper tenderly into his arms and vanishing instantly.

The darkness dissipated as suddenly as it had appeared, and Thorne was instantly at Kai's side, pulling her broken, lifeless body into his arms. *Please,* he thought desperately, impossibly, as he shook her by the shoulders, knowing already that it was useless—he was too late. He had been too late.

"Please," he whispered, his voice breaking. Kai was perfectly still, all the life and color drained completely from her expressionless face. Her brown eyes that had been so vibrant and beautiful stared dully up at him, and as tears spilled from his own, Thorne gently brushed her eyelids shut. He curled inward to rest his forehead against hers, letting his tears mingle with the blood that had begun to dry on her lips. "I'm sorry," he whispered, feeling his heart shatter, completely and irreparably, in his chest as he pressed his trembling lips to her forehead. "I'm sorry," he said again, repeating it like a mantra, a spell that could bring her back. "I'm sorry. I love—I love you. I'm sorry." But she could not hear the words he had been too afraid to say while she was alive, and *sorry* could not bring her back.

So at last, after all that they had done to avoid this exact outcome, he reaped her soul, cradling it gently in his arms as he vanished from the apartment.

Chapter Forty-Three
AFTER

KAI

There was a blinding light, and then there was nothing.

Epilogue

They stared in shaken silence at the mirror before them, unable to tear their eyes away even as the image faded into foggy nothingness. None of them could find the words to break the silence for several moments, until finally, Cyrus took a deep, though not entirely steady, breath.

"Well," he said, running his palms down the front of his cloak, smoothing wrinkles that did not exist. Aristides couldn't help but notice the way his brother's fingers trembled slightly. "I suppose…it is finished, then. Good. This is good." He cleared his throat and nodded once, firmly, as though it were himself he was trying to convince. "Now we can move on from this mess, *at last.*"

"I must admit, I find myself at a loss for words," Aristides stated, still struggling to wrap his mind around the events that they had just witnessed. He clarified. "At the lengths that Thorne was willing to go to to protect the girl. I knew that he cared for her, but never in my wildest imaginings did I think that…I never…" he shook his head, and Cyrus nodded gravely.

"It would seem that we all underestimated the boy," he agreed. "But," he continued with a light sigh, "At least it is finally over, one way or another."

"Yes," Aristides said, albeit a little mournfully, thinking of the indescribable pain that he knew Thorne must be currently feeling. "I suppose we can all...go back to normal, now." Cyrus nodded once more, and Aristides turned to go, stopping short as he noticed the faint smile playing on the stitched lips of their third brother. "Linus, what can you *possibly* find amusing about this situation?" Linus shook his head, and Aristides rolled his eyes, moving to brush impatiently past him.

Fate works in mysterious ways, my brothers, said Linus' voice inside Aristides' head, and a shared glance with Cyrus told Aristides that he had heard their brother's words, as well.

What he meant, they knew not, for Linus did not elaborate further, merely shaking his head as his smile grew infinitesimally, as though sharing an inside joke with himself before leaving the room.

In a grand, bright palace worlds away, a small girl awoke in her bed—a large, goose-down mattress piled high with dozens of throw pillows and blankets softer than velvet, and supported by four dark, wooden posts that stretched nearly to the high, domed ceiling above. Leafy green vines wound their way about the frame, from which long, sheer curtains fell to envelope the luxurious sleeping space.

On the small, circular bedside table sat a glass of water, a small pitcher of fresh flowers, a leather-bound journal, and a quill.

The girl, clad simply in a loose nightgown of white silk, slipped from the bed, her bare feet sinking into a plush rug as she made her way across the room to a large, floor-length mirror framed in gold. She did not recognize the person that she saw within, nor did she find any memory of who she was in the dark, blank recesses of her mind. She had not the slightest idea of who she had been, or what she was supposed to be, only the vague feeling that she was someone important, and that this was not her first time in this bedroom, nor in this universe. She brushed childlike fingers to her round, faintly rosy cheek and examined her features, which she sensed were new.

Soft brown skin the shade of desert sand in the evening, golden and warm and lovely; a small, heart-shaped face with round brown eyes framed by short, dark eyelashes and a tiny, delicate button nose; she was short and thin, with hair so brown that it was nearly black falling in a straight, silky curtain to her waist. She had bangs. There was a familiarity, fleeting.

Her dark brows pushed together as a flash of something, quick as lightning, so faint that she couldn't quite grasp it, flickered in the back of her mind. Pulling down one strappy shoulder of her nightgown, her lips curved into a small frown as she found a long, white scar marring the perfect skin, jagged and deep, just over where she somehow knew her heart to be.

She sensed the abrupt arrival of another presence in the room and, shifting her nightgown back into place, she turned slowly to find a tall, broad-shouldered man with dark hair and a serious expression standing in the doorway. He placed a hand over his heart and bowed low, his back as straight as an iron rod.

"My lady," he greeted, his voice deep and steady. "It is good to have you back."

"It is good to be back," responded the girl, sensing, somehow, that she knew this man, and that it was the right thing to say. She crossed the floor to take his extended arm, allowing him to lead her from the room. "Tell me everything."

Acknowledgements

While I'm not sure how many people actually read these (I must admit that I, myself, only began acknowledging the acknowledgments in recent years), I would still like to take a moment to thank all the wonderful, amazing people who helped to make this book and its publication possible.

When I was 14 years old, I joined a writing website. A *fanfiction*-writing website. It was on here that I met some of my closest friends: Stephanie, who read literally every single draft from a barely-conceptualized draft zero to the polished final product, and has never failed to encourage my dreams of stardom and to give me inspiration when I am lacking. Olivia, who diligently filled out every single prompt on the beta reader questionnaire, and made me giggle every time that she thirsted over 'Daddy Thorne.' Torri, whose excited, encouraging comments on my TikToks can only be described as utterly feral and unhinged in their enthusiastic delivery. Aiden, Mother of Rats, who has always been inhumanely quick to comment kind words of encouragement and excitement on my writing updates. Abbey, my best friend and platonic soulmate, who has been a patient sounding board and patron of praise these years—nearly a decade, at the time I am writing this. Please also thank your parents for me. They know what for.

Thank you to my sister (you know which one you are, and to the other, I love you, but in this moment I remind you of when your response to me telling you you could be in these acknowledgments if you read my book someday was to laugh and say, *I don't care (that I can't be in them), I don't read.* I guess you're still in these acknowledgments after all though, I say with sisterly love). You have been the most relentless encourager in my final stretch to get this book done, and I hope that someday I can help your writing dreams come true, too.

Thank you to my brothers—I have four, but only three of them know about this book at the time that I am writing this. W, thank you for letting me use you for your medical expertise. R, thank you for letting me tell you all about my book when I know you'd far rather be gaming, and for checking in to check on my progress from time to time. And H, thank you for drawing my lovely Thorne and Kai; the sketch still hangs over my desk, and has been a source of inspiration and encouragement, a promise of what this book could someday be.

Though I don't know whether they will read this book, I would like to thank two of my grandmothers: first, my Mema, who has shared and encouraged my passion for writing since I was a child, and whose editing expertise helped shape the way that I write. And my Glamma, who let me borrow her laptop the year that I began to write this book in earnest while I was visiting her in Idaho. She may not have known what I was doing on the laptop—I have always been rather secretive of my writing, excepting with my closest friends—but I truly could not have finally busted out my first ever completed draft of an original story if it weren't for that borrowed laptop.

Thank you to my parents, whose decision to homeschool meant that I had the time and energy to hone my craft after rushing through my schoolwork so that I could get back to writing. Thank you for all the laptops that I somehow ran through like notebook paper. I love you both.

Thank you to the authors of YouTube and TikTok (*especially* Tik-tok!), whose expertise and willingness to share it I could not have done this without.

Thank *you,* the person reading this right now. Without your support, without the faith (that I pray was not misplaced) that you had in my writing ability when you spent your hard-earned money on this book, I would not have been able to realize this wonderful dream.

Thank you to my beautiful, wonderful ARC readers, who took a chance on my book and without whom I might not have had the confidence to press *publish.*

I would also like to give thanks to God, who gave me both the gift and ability to write, and also the motivation to see it through.

And finally, thank you to my utterly amazing husband, Elijah, whose response when my laptop broke shortly after we began dating was to give me his, so that I could pursue my dream without the interruption of saving for a new device. Thank you for trusting that I would someday make this dream come true, for never doubting and for always encouraging. Thank you for listening all those times I info-dumped about plotting and drafting and the various paths to publication. Thank you for lifting me up when I felt discouraged, and bringing me back to reality when I was getting too ahead of myself, reminding me that in order to have a published book, I actually had to *write* the darn thing. My love, my boy, my puzzle piece, I appreciate and love you with every line of prose written in the fiber of my being.

A born lover of the written word, Berkley Wamsley has dreamed of being an author since childhood, when she wrote a short story about a neglected pencil who eventually found the love it deserved in the company of a little girl with a big heart. When she's not cuddled up rewatching her favorite shows and movies with her husband, Elijah, and their veritable menagerie of pets (including their three canine sons: Foster, Jasper, and Joon, more affectionately known as Joonbug), the autistic Tennessean enjoys reading (of course!), solo Broadway karaoke in the living room, and playing videogames. The Cursed Heir is her debut novel. You can find her on social media under the handle @penpaperandbees, or keep an eye out for future projects at www.berkleywamsley.com.

Feminism is intersectional, Trans Rights are Human Rights and Black Lives Matter.